THE LISTENING SKY

DOROTHY GARLOCK

A Time Warner Company

WARNER BOOKS EDITION

Cover design by Elaine Groh
Cover illustration by Michael Racz

Warner Vision is a registered trademark of Warner Books, Inc.

Warner Books, Inc.
1271 Avenue of the Americas
New York, NY 10020

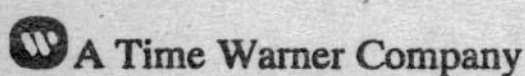
A Time Warner Company

Printed in the United States of America

First Printing: April, 1996

10 9 8 7 6 5 4 3 2 1

This book is dedicated with love
and appreciation to—

FREDDA ISAACSON

for her valuable contribution
to the twenty-two books we have
worked on together.
—And for being the editor all writers
dream of having.

LULLABY

No one knows my secret but the listening sky.
I won't tell the birds nor that floating butterfly.
The sky's high above and it's far away,
And that is where I'd like for my secret to stay.

It's nice to tell a secret if the secret's good.
But if the secret's bad, you never should.
You may speak your heart to the listening sky,
But be sure to look about you lest a man walk by.

Hush little baby, don't you cry.
Tears are not the answer, and I'll tell you why.
If you just grow strong and are unafraid,
You can win against the trouble that the secret's made.

—F. S. I.

THE LISTENING SKY

Wyoming Territory, 1882

Chapter 1

JANE Love's groping fingers found the pocket on her skirt and shoved the scrap of paper inside.

i know who yu are.

Hiding the crudely written words, however, did not erase them from her mind. Her heart hammered so hard that it was difficult to breathe. Without moving her head, she searched the crowd to see if anyone was watching her.

Standing in the dusty street of a run-down town with the group of women who had climbed down from the wagons after the thirty-mile trip from the stage station, Jane refused to allow any outward sign of the nervousness that was making her stomach churn.

Three families stood beside their wagons. Two of the mothers held babes in their arms, while older children clung to their skirts. A half-dozen men, bundles of their belongings at their feet, stood to one side waiting to be told where to go.

Jane's eyes were caught by those of a husky, dark-skinned man wearing a leather vest and a battered felt hat. He had been at the stage station when she arrived with the others from the train stop and had immediately singled her out for his attention.

He smiled and winked.

She tilted her chin and glared.

Last night in the dining hall of the station, she had hung her hat on a peg while she ate her supper. Later she had found the first note tucked in the crown.

yu cant hide.

She knew what the hateful message referred to—there was no doubt of that. The scribbled note had so unnerved her that she had hardly slept a wink all night.

The latest note had been pressed under one of the straps of the leather valise that held the sum total of her belongings. Had it been placed there by someone at the stage station, or after the baggage had been loaded and she had climbed into one of the lumbering wagons that had brought her and the other adventurous souls to this former ghost town in the northwest section of Wyoming Territory? Had the note-writer gone on with the train to some other destination? Or was he one of the people who had come here with her?

"Welcome to Timbertown. I'm T.C. Kilkenny." The man who spoke had stepped onto a bench so that he could see the faces of everyone in the crowd.

When Jane turned and looked up, she saw a big, wide-shouldered man with a lean, strong-boned face. A black flat-crowned hat sat squarely on his dark head in a no-nonsense fashion. Wide galluses held up duck britches, the legs of which were tucked into calf-high boots.

"Men, those of you who have families, get them settled in the cabins provided and then come to the store building and sign up. Your women and children are tired from the trip, so bring them to the cookhouse tonight for supper. Jeb Hobart is the building foreman." He gestured toward a stocky man who wore a billed cap and was smoking a pipe. "He will show you the way to the cabins. Each of them is furnished with a bed and a stove for heating and cooking. Our store is fully stocked, and you will be invited to run a tab which will be deducted from your pay by the Rowe Lumber Company, if you so wish."

Kilkenny waited while the families climbed back into wagons that were piled high with their possessions. The men started the tired teams moving down the dirt-packed road toward their new homes. Most of the lumbermen had requested a cabin on an acre or two of cleared ground. Wash hung from the lines behind a few of the town houses, and children playing on the doorsteps waved as the wagons passed.

After the crowd had moved away, Kilkenny spoke to the men who remained.

"I have a few things to say to those of you who are going to work on the town building, also the mill workers. Take your plunder to the space beyond the blacksmith and stake out a place to camp for tonight. Temporary quarters for the women are in the building next to the cookhouse. Ladies, I'll take you there presently.

"The population of our town is nearly a hundred people and there are that many others who live around it. At least thirty more will be here tomorrow, not counting the children. They will be the last addition to our town until spring, unless some folks happen to wander in and want to stay. So that we can live in a civilized manner, there must be rules. I am the town manager and part-owner of the land it sits on. Therefore, for the time being, I make the rules and enforce them.

"Drinking during a work shift will result in instant dismissal. No handguns are to be worn on the job nor in the saloon. I expect that you will have the normal number of disagreements among yourselves. If you want to fight, go out into the street and have at it in a civilized manner. A man who deliberately cripples his opponent will be fired on the spot. I will not tolerate biting, eye-gouging nor stomping. Other than that, I'll not interfere." These remarks were directed to the group of men.

Fight in a *civilized* manner? Jane suppressed the urge to roll her eyes to the heavens.

"Social functions will be provided so that the single men and women may become acquainted if they wish to," he added quickly. "Any man who fails to conduct himself in a gentlemanly manner toward the ladies will find himself in a peck of trouble. I intend to have a civilized, law-abiding community here.

"We have a well-stocked mercantile store. I expect a train of freight wagons soon. Prices will be fair. Each man who signs on to work for Rowe Lumber Company can run a tab. We have a blacksmith, a harness-maker, a wheelwright, and, of course, a livery. We'll soon have the hotel and rooming house usable. A bakery and an eatery will open to give us some relief from Bill's cooking."

A gray-haired man with a dingy white cloth wrapped around his waist lounged against the building with a screened door. At the remark about his cooking his toothless mouth spread in a broad smile.

"I expect a preacher soon, and we'll build a church. I'm hoping to engage one of you as schoolmaster. If our town continues to grow, a year from now we will elect a mayor, a city council, and a peace officer. You will notice that I do not call this place a lumber camp. We have two cutting camps. One to the north, one to the west. The sawmill is a mile upriver.

"We will rebuild this town. It will have all a well-run town has to offer. In a few years Wyoming Territory will become a state, and our town will have a chance to become a county seat. We are in the midst of one of the richest pine regions in the territory. With careful management of these resources, there will be jobs here for many years and this town will naturally grow and prosper.

"When the river freezes and work at the mill slows down, some of you will find work here in town as we continue to build. You will have credit to build or to fix up one of the more than a dozen abandoned cabins scattered around. Some are in not too bad a shape considering they've been vacant so long."

While the man was talking, Jane studied him. He seemed confident and well educated. He had shown compassion for the women holding their babes and the tired, crying children clinging to their skirts. He looked to be capable of backing up his intention to deal with anyone who broke the town laws. He was taller than average, with broad shoulders and a wide chest that tapered down to narrow hips and long, powerful legs. His hair was so black that it glinted blue. His high cheekbones and a wide, thin-lipped mouth told Jane that he was part-Indian even though Kilkenny was an Irish name and his eyes were a steel gray.

Oh, Lord! Had she made a mistake coming here?

Jane had been searching for just such a chance as this place offered. Maybe here she would be able to start a new life where her secret could stay hidden forever.

Being entirely on her own for the first time in her life and in Timbertown was the result of her having read a handbill tacked to the wall of a store back in Denver. The advertisement, dated July 30, 1882, had been printed a week earlier.

Wanted: People to populate the town of
Timbertown, a settlement in the northwest
section of Wyoming Territory.
Jobs available for hardworking timbermen.
Housing provided for families, rooms for
single men and women.
Single women wanted for cooking, sewing,
laundry and nursing.
Male or female schoolteacher needed with knowledge
of bookkeeping.
Backing available for qualified merchants.
Apply Carlson Hotel on Friday.

Buoyed by hope, Jane had applied. The solicitor, a stuffy man with a stiff high collar and small wire-rimmed spectacles, first asked if she were single, then asked about her health—because, he had said, Timbertown was in an isolated area. He looked closely at her after she spoke about her qualifications as a teacher and a bookkeeper. She told him that she could sew and knit and had had considerable experience nursing the sick.

Jane did not feel it necessary to explain that she had lived all her life in a Methodist Church home and that while there she had done everything from scrubbing the floors to keeping the books and writing to various organizations asking for donations. She did not mention that she had been expected to stay there and work for her board for the rest of her life, or that when she left the headmistress had slammed the door behind her after having called her an ungrateful chit and having predicted that she'd come crawling back within six months.

That had been six weeks ago.

The ride in the lumber wagon from the train stop, which was no more than a shack and a water tank, to the stage station, where they had spent the night sitting or lying on pallets, had already exhausted the women. And today the driver of the wagon had seemed to care not a whit for the comfort of his passengers during the thirty-mile drive from the station to Timbertown. His aim was to deliver this group and head back to the station to drink and play cards.

When the call came to load up, the driver had lifted her up into the last of a string of five wagons. She had taken a seat on the end of one of the planks that served as a bench. The slamming of the tailgate seemed to signify the end of one life and the beginning of another. For thirty miles she'd had to endure the stare of the man in the felt hat who rode alongside the wagon.

The excitement of finally being here in Timbertown was diminished not only by her fatigue but by the knowledge that some unknown person, who undoubtedly wished to make her life miserable, had been nearby, at least until she had climbed aboard the wagon. The hateful message left on her valise worried her. It meant that someone knew who she was and hated her for it.

She had not escaped from her shame; it had traveled with her.

Jane straightened her straw hat and with the palms of her hands tried to smooth some of the wrinkles out of her skirt. Her shoes were covered with dust, so her face must be too. She licked her lips and felt the grit. She cherished cleanliness and longed for a wet cloth to wipe her face and hands.

When a hand pressed her arm, Jane turned to see the drawn face of the young girl standing beside her. No more than sixteen, weary and frightened, she was very close to tears.

"What's the matter, Polly?"

"I'm so tired. And my back—"

"Sit down here on my valise. Honey, are you sick?" Jane asked when tears began to fill the girl's eyes.

"No. Just . . . tired."

Polly Wright had been with the group when Jane arrived in Laramie after having come up from Denver on the stage. They had shared a room at the hotel before they boarded the train for the middle leg of the journey. Polly had been very careful to slip the big loose nightdress over her head before she removed her petticoats. Her listlessness and upset stomach made Jane suspect the girl might be pregnant.

Jane knelt down and tucked her handkerchief into Polly's hand.

"Wipe your eyes," she whispered. "We don't want him to think you're sickly."

Polly sniffed back the tears and dabbed at her eyes. "I can't help . . . it. Will he send me back?"

"I don't know."

"I wish . . . I was . . . dead."

"No you don't. Nothing is that bad."

Jane patted the girl's shoulder and was about to stand when two big dusty boots planted themselves in the ground beside her skirt. Her eyes traveled up the long legs to the checked shirt and to the lean, sun-browned face with its piercing gray eyes. The memory of such eyes caused Jane to shiver again.

"What's the matter with her?"

"She's tired."

"Why is she tired? She hasn't done anything but ride for three days."

Jane stood. The top of her head came to the man's chin. Nevertheless, she looked up unflinchingly into, the eyes narrowed beneath heavy black brows.

"It was not a ride on a featherbed, mister."

"It was the best I could provide."

"I'm not disputing that. She'll be all right with a bath and a decent night's sleep."

"That I *can* provide."

"Thank God!" Jane murmured under her breath.

"What was that?" he asked, his lips twitching at the corners.

Jane felt her cheeks redden, but she refused to cower beneath his intense stare. Not for the world would she bow her head with this overbearing man and the entire group staring at her.

"I said, thank God."

"I thought that was what you said." He turned and walked away.

"Then why did you ask me?" Jane mouthed at his back.

Her eyes swept the group and caught the look on the face of one of the women who had held herself apart from the others since she had joined them at the stage station. She had arrived with a Mexican man, who had left immediately. Because the two had conversed in Spanish, Jane presumed her to be Mexican even though she seemed tall for a Mexican woman. She was large-boned and stood ramrod straight. Black straight hair hung down her back to her waist. The woman's gaze lingered on Jane's face for several seconds before she turned and watched Kilkenny as he made his way to the front of the crowd.

"Ladies, this way."

Twelve women followed T.C. Kilkenny. A tall, red-haired woman with green eyes hurried to walk beside him.

Then a quiet, dark-haired woman picked up her valise and trailed along, as did another gripping the hand of a small boy. A slender, obviously pregnant mother holding the hand of a girl hardly out of diapers and a woman with a shy young daughter were joined by several young, strong women in their teens. Jane and Polly brought up the rear.

Jane insisted on carrying Polly's carpetbag as well as her own heavy valise. After going a short distance, she stopped to shift the heavy load to her other hand. Kilkenny was beside her as she straightened, and he took the valise from her hand, leaving the lighter bag for her to carry. He walked away without a word, causing Jane to wonder if the man had eyes in the back of his head.

His action was noted by the Mexican woman and the one with dyed-red hair.

Kilkenny led them to a low log building. The moment Jane entered the newly built building she knew that it was not meant to be permanent quarters. So many women could not live in harmony for long in such close proximity.

Along the windowless wall was a field bed. It extended the length of the building. Narrow grass-filled mattresses lay along the wooden slab. Neatly folded blankets had been placed along the foot of the communal bed. On the wall at the far end of the room was a shelf with several basins and pitchers. A square glass mirror hung above them. Sitting in the middle of the room was a large Acme heater with a shiny tin chimney going up through the roof. The heat radiating from it was a welcome antidote to the chill of the late afternoon breeze that came down from the mountains.

A bench stretched along the foot of the long bed. Upon this Kilkenny placed Jane's valise. Then he went to the far corner of the room to pull back a curtain and reveal a tin bathtub and two large tin water buckets.

"We have no shortage of water. It comes from a spring and is piped to a reservoir behind the cookhouse. The cook will bring you the first bucket of hot water, and later you can heat your own on the laundry stove." He gestured toward a small two-burner stove with another shiny tin chimney going out the side of the building.

"How nice," Jane said, again under her breath.

"The privy out back is strictly for ladies only."

"Where do we eat?" The question came from a girl with a mass of unruly blond hair, a slender wiry build and a constant smile. She was young and healthy and seemed to take everything in stride. She had said to Jane, "Call me Sunday. My mama had a young'un for every day in the week. I'm glad I wasn't born on Saturday."

"You'll eat in the cookhouse. The men will eat first, then cook will send his helper for you. Tomorrow I'll interview each of you. There is plenty of work to keep you busy while you're waiting for the job you were hired to do."

"Like what?" Jane asked.

Kilkenny's eyes honed in on Jane's face and stayed there for a few seconds before he answered. Her heart pounded, but her expression did not change. A facade of haughty dignity was far more effective, she had learned, than cringing uncertainty.

"Washing, cooking, sewing—"

"—How long do we stay . . . here?" Jane interrupted. Then before he answered, "Do you not have a rooming house or a hotel?"

"The hotel and rooming house are being repaired. Have you run a hotel?"

"No. But—"

"—But?"

"But it wouldn't be too difficult."

"I can't very well put you up in a hotel or rooming house with a hole in the roof, can I?" He raised dark brows and his eyes raked over her coolly. Someone tittered. "Any more questions?"

"Not tonight." Her tone was frosty.

"Very well. I'll leave you to get settled in."

He walked the length of the building with quick, purposeful steps. He paused in front of the Mexican woman and tipped his hat.

"Señora Cabeza."

"*Hola*, T.C."

He continued toward the door. The flame-haired, green-eyed woman stepped out in front of him.

"Mr. Kilkenny . . ." The name rolled off her tongue like a caress. "I don't wish to stay here. I'll buy one of the completed cabins."

His stare would have intimidated most women. This one appeared to enjoy it. She tilted her head and flung a mass of loose red hair over her shoulder. She was not a young innocent and did not pretend to be.

"We'll discuss it tomorrow when you have your interview."

He stepped around her and continued on, but as his eyes met Jane's his steps slowed. Jane's eyes looked into his, straight and clean, not boldly, but with assurance and a little amusement. He regarded her with an icy stare, but his expression in no way detracted from the splendor of his face. He was as handsome a man as Jane had ever seen. No wonder the red-haired woman was panting after him.

T.C. walked past Jane, taking with him a flashing memory of rich, dark reddish-brown hair framing a fine-boned face, stormy smoke-blue eyes shot with silver, and a tilted pointed chin.

She was . . . proud as a peacock. And a lady to boot. Why in hell would such a woman come here? He had not had the time to study the applications sent by his solicitor, but you could bet your boots he would as soon as he got back to his house.

And . . . what the hell was Patrice Guzman Cabeza doing here? Was his solicitor out of his mind? Patrice's husband must still be alive. No word to the contrary had reached the town. If she figured to be coddled and waited on here, she was in for a surprise. Everyone carried his own weight in this town. It would be a sight to see Señor Ramon Cabeza's wife bent over a washtub. And the redhead—if she had money to buy her own house, why was she here? Hell, at times T.C. wondered at the craziness of sending for the women.

With a few exceptions Kilkenny was pleased with the newcomers. He had hoped for more big, strong ranch or farm women. He calculated that even after the arrivals tomorrow, there would still be two single men to every single woman in town. And when the men came in from the cutting camps, the ratio would be more like four to one. He had hoped to reduce the number of single men; he didn't want to resort to bringing in "ladies of the night."

Men without women for long stretches of time, especially during the winter months, became quarrelsome. Unhappy, restless men were unproductive workers. Families built towns, families with children, churches, schools and law and order.

Kilkenny had deliberately furnished the women's barracks with only the bare necessities. He was counting on their nesting instincts to take over. After a week crowded in with other women, a place of one's own and a man to do for would become very appealing.

He had caught disappointment in the faces of some. The town did look like a flash-mining town, which it had been ten years earlier. Tents and make-do shelters stood along the street among the weatherbeaten empty buildings. But in a month or two all of that would be changed.

Kilkenny had no scruples about his matchmaking. After all, God took a rib from Adam and made Eve. Women were created to mate with men to ensure the continuance of the human race. As the weaker of the sexes, women sought to be provided for and protected. And what better way to accomplish that than as wives and mothers?

He approached the group of new men waiting to speak to the foreman.

"Hey, boss man," one called. "That's a fine-lookin' herd a mares ya brought in."

"And I'm a rarin' to mount me one," said another.

T.C. tamped down the anger that boiled up in him. He looked at the face of each man before he spoke. It had long been a habit of his to look a man in the eyes and study him. He knew immediately that what he had here were two men showing off for a dozen others.

He folded his arms across his chest, spread his booted feet, rocked back on his heels and suppressed the desire to plant his fist in the man's face. He waited so long to speak that the men grew restless.

"You're going to get away with those remarks this time because there may be something wrong with your hearing and you didn't hear me the first time around. So I'm telling you again that if I hear of any of you referring to a woman in this town as a *mare* and being anxious to *mount* her, that man will spend the rest of his life eating without teeth, and he will ride out of here with his ass kicked up between his shoulders. Do I make myself clear?"

The last man to speak hung his head. "Ah . . . Milo said they was here for . . . that."

The man called Milo Callahan grinned inanely, showing a wide space between his two front teeth, one of which had been broken in half. He had a broad face and a cockiness that immediately rubbed Kilkenny the wrong way. He appeared to Kilkenny to be a braggart and a bully, tough in body and weak in mind. T.C. wondered vaguely if he were related to the Callahans who had a lumber business over in the Bitterroot Range.

"The ladies answered the advertisement the same as you did. I will provide jobs for them if they do not choose to marry. They are not whores."

"If'n they ain't, why'd they come?" Milo asked. "Ain't no *decent* woman comin' way out here thinkin' to find work 'cepts on her back."

"Their reasons are no business of yours. Three of them are widow ladies. One has a babe on the way. They will be treated with respect or you'll answer to me."

"I knowed right off what ya meant when I saw the bill nailed to the wall. What was we to think? *Single* women for cookin', washin'. Hell, men cook and wash. *Single* women mean jist one thin' to *single* men."

"Who gets first chance to court 'em?" The question came from a heavy-shouldered lumberjack with a scarred face. "It ain't fair fer the fellers already here to get first go at 'em."

Kilkenny's eyes honed in on the man with no betrayal of the disgust swirling through him. But there was a stillness about him that suggested a cougar poised to leap on prey.

"The ladies will do the choosing. If your attention is unwelcome, that's all there is to it. If you act in any way disrespectful toward any of them, you'll answer to me. Understand?" He looked at each of the men, then added, "You've been warned. After we get these buildings ready for winter we'll have some kind of shindig. There'll be games and a dance. You can pay your respects to the women then; but, like I said, if your attention is not wanted, back off."

In the answering stillness Kilkenny heard his name called. He looked toward his own house; the two-storied structure was the last building on the street and sat across from the cookhouse and the new building put up for the women. A man stood on the porch beckoning.

Kilkenny turned back to the group of new men. "Have you talked to the foreman?"

"We're waitin' fer him."

"Go on over to the cookhouse and eat. You can talk to him after supper."

He could feel the eyes of the men on his back as he crossed the street and went up the steps to his porch. Of the dozen new men, the two he'd needed to warn could very well be troublemakers. Another, the one with the felt hat and leather vest, had watched the exchange with a smirk on his face. Kilkenny mentally went over the list of the men and came up with the name Bob Fresno. He was smarter than the others. He had let Milo do the talking for him. Kilkenny could read a man just as he could read a good stand of timber. This one and Milo were the ones to watch.

The young man who met him on the porch and followed him into the house was as tall as Kilkenny but heavier. His hair was light, baby-fine, and hung over his ears. He had a thin sprinkling of light fuzz on his face. He wore a belt and a gun that lay snugly against his thigh.

"It's Doc again."

"Drunk?"

"As a skunk."

"Where did he get the whiskey?"

"Stole it from the saloon while Parker was in the back room, I reckon. He knows better than to give him any."

"Is he out cold?"

"As cold as a well-digger's ass."

"Let him sleep it off."

"Yeah? Well, a peeler from the north camp came in with a carbuncle boil under his arm."

"Bad one?"

"Big as a teacup."

"Can you lance it?"

"Hellfire, T.C., ya know I ain't got no stomach for doctorin'."

Kilkenny shook his head. "Guess I'll have to do it. Where's the man?"

"Sittin' back there, holdin' his arm over his head and cussin' Doc."

"Doc still spitting up blood?"

"Saw a spattering in the spittoon."

"Damn fool is killing himself. Let's take care of the peeler, Herb. Hell of a job to do before supper."

Herb made a gagging sound. "Why'd ya have to go and say that for?"

Kilkenny hung his hat on a peg and went down the center hallway to the room that served as the surgery.

Chapter 2

"PUT out the lamp and go to bed!"

Raw irritation edged the voice that came from the far end of the communal bed. Jane continued washing her arms and shoulders. The bathtub had been in constant use. Some of the women had taken as long as half an hour to bathe, then had left the water to be emptied by the next person who wished to use clean water. Knowing it would be midnight before they could use the tub, Jane had built a fire in the laundry stove and had heated a bucket of water for herself and Polly. They had washed in one of the large tin washbasins. The young girl now lay at the end of the bed, her face to the wall.

Jane set the basin on the floor and slipped her tired, aching feet into the warm water. It felt so good. She vowed to take a full bath and wash her hair at the first opportunity.

"Go to bed!"

"Hush yore mouth. Ya make more noise than she does." Jane recognized the cheerful voice of Sunday.

"She can pretty herself up in the mornin'."

"She'd not have to wash this late if you'd not hogged the tub," Sunday replied.

"Hogged the tub? Who the hell is talkin'?"

"If she's got her eye on the boss man, it'll do her no good." This voice had the slurry accent of the South.

"Who ain't got a eye on him? Lordy mercy. He's the best-lookin' thin' I've seen in all my born days. And the cook says he ain't got no wife."

"Bet he's wild as a turpentined cat in bed."

This brought a gaggle of giggles.

"He's gonna *interview* us tomorrow. What's that mean? Whatever it is, I'm glad I brought my rose toilet water."

"Did ya bring pads for yore bosom?"

"I ain't needin' 'em. I'd put my tits up against yores anyday."

"Not against mine, you won't!"

This brought a gale of laughter.

Jane opened the back door and threw out her wash water. After blowing out the lamp she undressed in the dark, slipped her nightdress over her head and lay down beside Polly.

Something wasn't right here. She had known it the minute the wagon arrived in Timbertown. This wasn't even a town . . . yet. No more than ten buildings lined the main street.

Jane was puzzled as to where the women were going to live and work. The hotel and what could be the rooming house were badly in need of repair. She had seen nothing that could be called a bake shop, laundry or eating place. Kilkenny had built a saloon, but not a church or school, even though she had seen a goodly number of children.

The solicitor had mentioned a need for women to make shirts and other clothing. Was the great Mr. Kilkenny going to put *all* of them to work sewing? Or was he of a mind to use them as saloon girls?

Anger quickened her heartbeat.

The building where they had eaten their supper was a new one. Bill Wassall, the cook, a man of about sixty years with a limp and a crooked arm, had told her the building would be a restaurant when the hotel was opened.

Jane and Polly, the last to go for supper, had lingered after the others had gone back to the barracks. Jane offered to help with the cleanup. Bill had declined the offer, saying he had a "bull cook" who would clean during the night and have a fire ready for the breakfast mess. He was fond of talking and was delighted to have found an interested listener. He explained that in a lumber camp the cook was "king bee" and his helper was "bull cook" or "cookie."

The cutting camps, several miles from town, would soon be going full blast. Most of the men in the camps worked by the season. Work would slack off at the mill when the river froze. Some of the men would spend the winter here in town repairing stores and other business places along Main Street. Sites for a tonsorial parlor, a laundry, a jail, a school and a church had been picked out. Another saloon would go up if someone came to run it.

Bill Wassall was enthusiastic about the town, and evidently considered T.C. Kilkenny a gift from heaven. He included the man's name in almost every sentence he uttered.

According to Bill, T.C. Kilkenny was a smart, fair-minded man. She learned that he was a cattleman, but that he was also the best all-around lumberjack in the territory. He was the top high-climber, river pig, peeler, topper, trimmer and all-around "bull of the woods." Bill explained that was another term for camp foreman. According to the cook, Kilkenny was also an outstanding bare-knuckle fighter and would take on all challengers once the work slackened.

By the time Bill finished singing Kilkenny's praises, Jane wanted to gag. She wondered why God had allowed such a perfect man to descend to earth.

"Known T.C. since he was a pup. Knowed Colin too. Colin'll be in in a day or two."

"Is he one of the owners?" Jane asked.

"Naw. Colin's a cattleman. His pa is John Tallman; guess ya heard a him."

Jane had not heard of the man, but gave no indication. She listened to the cook tell about how he first met Colin Tallman. He was cook for John Tallman's freight outfit crossing Indian Territory.

"Smart as a whip an' soaked up ever'thin' John taught him. Turned out to be 'bout as good a scout as his pa and grandpa, Rain Tallman.

"Lumber company's owned by a feller named Rowe over at Trinity. Colin and T.C.'s got a interest. T.C.'s logged most a his life but he'd rather ranch. Gonna do it soon's he gets the town goin' again."

Now, as she lay in the dark listening to the snores, it became clear in her mind. After mulling over the events of the day she came to the conclusion that Kilkenny would not immediately, perhaps would never, have full employment for *all* the women he had brought here.

The conniving jackass!

He had brought them here as prospective wives for the single men. That was the reason why the street back of the town had been marked off, and building sites prepared. A dozen cabins had already been built, cabins that with additions could house large families.

To advertise for brides was not unusual. Notices were routinely placed in public places. The women who answered the advertisements went into the arrangement with their eyes wide open. Not so here! *The honorable Mister Kilkenny had brought them here on the pretext of giving them jobs.* The jobs were waiting on and servicing some of his dirty, foul-mouthed lumberjacks.

Well, she had news for him!

She would give him an earful and demand to be sent back to Denver at once. She would rather be in Denver with hundreds of people who hated her than be here in this small place with one who was determined to make her life miserable, that is if he allowed her to keep it.

Thank God she had carefully hung onto the pitifully small hoard of money her Aunt Alice had left her five years earlier. The poke and the painting of her mother were securely locked in her valise.

Jane would never forget the day her curiosity had prodded her to remove the wooden back of the picture frame; she had hoped to find a date on the back of the canvas that would tell her mother's age at the time of the painting. What she had found hidden between the canvas and the back of the frame had changed her life forever.

At age ten it had been hard to understand all Mrs. Gillis had told her on that summer day long ago. From that day on, she had not been allowed to forget who she was, why she was there, and why more than any of the others she must study and work to redeem herself.

During the years that followed, Jane had lived in constant fear of discovery. Then gradually, her common sense had taken over and she had come to realize she was a person in her own right, and not responsible for the deeds of another.

Long ago Jane's orphanage records had mysteriously disappeared from the file. Jane had seen to that. Now someone had discovered her secret and held her responsible. Mrs. Gillis must have been the source. As she had grown older the woman had begun to guard her position as headmistress of the school with a zeal that bordered on desperation. Jane suspected she was secretly glad to see the last of one who had the qualifications to assume her job.

Jane's mind continued to mull over her immediate problem until gradually the demands of her exhausted body took over and she dropped into a deep sleep. She dreamed of being chased through the woods by an Indian warrior, tomahawk lifted for the kill. She awoke to the sound of a rooster announcing the start of another day.

Kilkenny dreaded the task ahead and wished that Colin were back in town. Colin didn't know much about the lumber business, but he knew a hell of a lot more about women than Kilkenny did. His friend of many years would not be at all happy to find Patrice here in Timbertown. T.C. wasn't happy about it either, but there was nothing to do now but talk to her, find out why she had come, and offer to send her back to the stage station.

He looked out the front window to see the woman leaving the cookshack. Herb would have told her to come here. T.C. sat down behind a square table he used as a desk. It was cluttered with papers and ledgers. He was not only unskilled in handling women, he was in desperate need of someone to put all this paperwork in order. Garrick Rowe, the mill owner, had promised to send a bookkeeper down from Trinity. If the man didn't arrive soon his job would become impossible.

Kilkenny's house was square, two-storied, with porches on the front and back. The four rooms on the ground floor were divided by a central hall running from the front door straight through to the back. The front two rooms were T.C.'s office and his bedroom. The back two were the kitchen and the surgery where Dr. Foote reigned—when he was sober. The kitchen was seldom used since it was easier to walk across the street to the cookhouse. The three upstairs bedrooms were occupied by the doctor, Herb and Colin, when he was there.

Kilkenny heard the sound of heels on the porch, then the opening of the door. He stood as Herb ushered Patrice Cabeza into the office.

"Good morning, Señora Cabeza."

"Good morning, T.C." Her voice was soft and had the flavor of her Spanish ancestors. "I prefer to be called Patrice Guzman."

"Sit down, Señora Guzman."

"We've known each other a long time, *T.C.* Too long to be so formal."

Large dark eyes studied the man behind the desk. As Patrice arranged her colorful shawl about her shoulders, the large silver rings in her ears moved against the olive skin of her neck. Hair as black as midnight hung straight and shiny to her waist. She was well aware of her beauty.

"Why have you come here?" T.C. asked bluntly, then added, "I think I know—"

"—Of course, you do."

"Colin isn't here."

"He will be sooner or later. He usually shows up where you are and vice versa."

"How is your husband?"

She shrugged. "Same."

"Does he know you're here?"

"I hope not. Look at your papers, T.C. You'll find Bertha Kotch's application."

He snorted. "Bertha Kotch? My, my what an imagination you have."

Not a flicker of amusement showed in Patrice's dark eyes.

"I have left Ramon."

"It doesn't take a law degree to figure that out. Why? He gave you everything you wanted. You couldn't see Colin for dirt after meeting Ramon."

"—What is between me and Colin is none of your business."

"This town is my business. I want you to leave. If you stay, you'll be nothing but trouble."

"You need cooks, seamstresses, laundresses"—a faint smile touched her lips—"women for your loggers."

"I can't see you doing any of those things."

"Why not? I'll work until Colin gets here."

"And then?"

"We'll see."

"If I remember right, Señora, you are quite useless at anything other than what will benefit Patrice Guzman Cabeza."

"I have a strong sense of self-preservation . . . as you have." She lifted her brows and spoke softly. "Can you fault me for that?"

"Have you ever *not* gotten what you wanted?" His voice was hard and impatient.

"A few times."

"I'll send you back to the stage station. Get your things—"

"I'm not going. If you try to make me, I'll raise such a stink half the *single* women you brought in will go with me. And men, real men, don't like to see a *lady* abused. You employed me to come here and work. What possible reason can you give for sending me away?"

"I don't need to *give* a reason, but if I did it would be that you're unsuitable. Anyone with half an eye can see you've not done a day's work in your life. You know damn good and well that Ramon will be here as soon as he finds out you're here. I want no trouble between him and Colin."

"Colin can take care of himself."

"Damn it to hell! You'll not use Colin to kill Ramon." T.C. slammed his fist down on his desk. "I can't make you leave, but if you stay, you'll work for your keep . . . as a laundress."

"I can pay for my keep."

"No. You'll work and be paid four cents a shirt, six cents for pants, plus your board."

"If I don't work, I don't eat. Is that it?"

"That's it. Until we set up a boarding house or the hotel is ready for guests."

"When do you expect Colin?"

Kilkenny shrugged. "Herb," he called. "Take the señora to the laundry and give her a pile of dirty clothes."

"Thank you, T.C." Patrice said sweetly, and smiled at the big, blond man who opened the door for her.

"T.C. . . . ?" Herb had a puzzled look on his face.

"Take her," Kilkenny almost shouted. "Get her out of here."

"Come on, Herb," Patrice said. "Your boss has a burr under his blanket this morning. You know, what this town needs is a good whorehouse. Don't you agree?" Her eyes flicked to T.C.'s angry face and then back to Herb's red one. She laughed and grasped his arm with both hands. "My, my, what do you know? A big, bad gunman who can still blush."

Kilkenny forked his long fingers through his thick, black hair, raking it back from his forehead. It was a gesture of frustration.

When Herb brought in the woman with the small boy, Kilkenny looked at the application on his desk. Mrs. Silas Winters was a widow from Fort Collins.

"Mornin', ma'am. Have a seat. Hello, son. What's your name?"

"Buddy. I'm five."

"Then you're about ready for school." T.C. sat down and leaned his elbows on the table.

"No!"

"No?"

"Pa said school was for sissies." The small freckle-faced boy rested his chin on the table and glared at T.C.

"Hummm . . . well, your ma will have to straighten you out on that. Mrs. Winters, it says here that you have worked in a bakery."

"Yes, sir. I worked in one after . . . after . . ."

"—After Pa killed hisself."

"Buddy!"

"Pa was a soldier. He killed lots a Indians."

"Hush up!"

T.C. looked more closely at the woman and judged her to be well past forty. There were streaks of gray in her dark hair and her face showed lines of age. Her hands were work-worn. A couple of generations back one of her Sioux or Cheyenne ancestors had roamed this land.

"What would you need in order to open a bakeshop besides the building to put it in?"

On hearing the words, the woman's mouth dropped and worked, but no words came out. When they did come, they were so hesitant that he could barely hear them.

"You mean . . . I could?"

"Why not? Every town needs a bakeshop. We've got a lot of working men to feed. If you're willing and have the know-how to run one, the company will back you."

"I'd like a chance at it."

"After you pay the company back for setting you up in

business, the profits are yours." T.C. gave her a sheet of paper. "List what kind of stove you need and anything else and I'll see that you get it in a week or two. In the meanwhile, we'll start fixing up the building between the mercantile and the harnesss shop. There's living space in the back for you and your boy. You can help Bill Wassall at the cookhouse while we're getting it ready. He would like to shift some of the cooking chores over to someone else. He's getting old and cranky," he added with a grin.

"Ma makes bear claws an' jelly cake." Buddy fingered the half-full inkwell on T.C.'s desk.

"Nothing I like better than bear claws." T.C. reached for the inkwell, covering the opening with his palm.

"Thank you." Mrs. Winters stood and took her son's hand. "Come on, Buddy."

"Is he a stinkin' Indian, Ma?"

"Oh . . . oh, my goodness! Buddy!" Mrs. Winters jerked on her son's arm, pulling him toward the door. "You shouldn't say such a thing."

T.C. came around the table and opened the door.

"Don't let it worry you, Mrs. Winters." He put his hand on Buddy's head. "I'm a quarter Blackfoot, Buddy. And all humans stink at one time or the other."

"Do you put paint on your face and scalp babies?"

T.C. laughed. "Not lately. I painted my face once and my mother made me wash it off. She was Blackfoot. Her father was an Englishman who came from across the water and married into the tribe. He was proud of his half-breed children."

"Did your pa come from cross the water?"

"He came from Ireland. Kilkenny is an Irish name."

"Is Winters a Irish name? My pa was—"

"Hush. You talk too much."

"He needs to be in school." T.C. glanced at Mrs. Winters' disapproving face. "We'll have one as soon as we can get a place for it and I can find a teacher."

"I'm sorry—"

"You've no cause to be sorry. And welcome to Timbertown. Both of you."

When Sunday Polinski left the office, T.C. was smiling. He wished for a couple of dozen like her. She had told him she came from a family of eight girls. With no sons, her pa had taught his girls to do most things a man could do. She had left home, she said, because her sisters were better looking than she was and she didn't stand a chance of getting a man of her choice.

T.C. doubted that. Sunday Polinski was a fine, healthy-looking woman with a happy disposition.

"My shortcomin's is I ain't much for geegaws and ribbons." Sunday continued with a wide grin. "I ain't carin 'bout quiltin' and tattin', but I can make ya some of the best dad-gum cedar shingles ya ever laid yore eyes on." She batted her eyes at T.C. "I'm goin' to find me a good man, get me my own homeplace an' raise me a batch a young'uns. *You* been asked for, Mr. Kilkenny?"

T.C. smiled. He liked the girl. She was open and honest.

"You'll have plenty to choose from, Miss Polinski. I just don't want you to start a war among the men."

"Oh, shoot, T.C. Call me Sunday. Now about the work I'm to do while I'm lookin' for a man—"

"We need someone to make soap and someone to make candles to sell at the mercantile."

"Flitter! I can make enough soap in two days to last the winter, that is if ya have the grease an' lye. Then what'll I do?"

"I figure you'll have a man by then, and I'll be out a soapmaker."

Sunday tilted her blond head, and her blue eyes sparkled with good humor.

"I ain't takin' the first one what asks me. I *sure* ain't takin' any what came in with us. I a'ready had a set-to with one of 'em."

"Which one?" T.C. asked quietly.

"The bushy-haired galoot with enough room 'tween his

front teeth to drive a wagon. They called him Milo. He pinched my bottom and I slapped his jaws."

"It won't happen again."

"That's sure as shootin'. I know jist where to put this"—she raised a clenched fist—"where it'd hurt him real bad."

T.C. grinned again. "You say your pa taught you to fight dirty?"

"My pa raised us girls to take care of ourselves. I've had to lay one on a time or two . . . or three. Takes the starch outta a struttin' rooster ever' time."

When Sunday left the office, T.C. watched her cross the street with Herb. She skipped along beside him taking two steps to his one, laughing up at him and talking a blue streak. Sunday Polinski was the kind of woman his friend, Colin Tallman, needed. She was not a great beauty like Patrice; she was full of laughter and well able to carry her own weight. She would be a loyal helpmate. A man should choose his life's companion very carefully.

Come to think of it, when the time came for him to take a wife, she would be the kind of woman he would look for. He certainly didn't want to go through life, grow old, and die without knowing that some part of himself was left behind. But there was plenty of time to think about choosing a mother for the children he planned to raise in the high country. He had to get this town on its feet. It was a commitment he had made to Garrick Rowe. No way in hell was he going to break his promise to the man.

T.C. stood at the window until he saw Herb start back across the street with another woman for him to interview. Why in hell had he volunteered for this job! Hell—he knew why. Money. Money to pay for something he had wanted all his life.

Polly Wright was a small girl with large dark eyes, a soft mouth and a dimple in each cheek. She wore her light brown hair parted in the middle and braided. Each braid was coiled and pinned neatly over her ears. The gray wool shawl was draped around her shoulders and crossed in front. She came into the room with quick nervous steps and sank down into the chair in front of the table.

"Polly Wright?"

"Yes, sir."

Sensing that his scrutiny was making the already nervous girl more nervous, T.C. looked down at the paper, although he already knew what it said.

"Were your folks willing for you to leave home at age sixteen?"

"I don't have any folks, sir." She kept her eyes on the floor and spoke scarcely above a whisper.

"It says here that you worked in a rooming house."

"Yes, sir. I worked for my board and I worked for a seamstress too."

T.C. noticed that she had balled a handkerchief in her hands and was plucking at the lace edge.

"We have plenty of work for a seamstress. There's a storeroom full of material for shirts, pants and underclothing. We've brought in four of Isaac Singer's sewing machines. Have you ever used one?"

"No, sir. Mrs. Bartley, the lady I worked for, wouldn't let me touch hers. I did the hand work. I can tat," she added, and looked up hopefully.

"Tat? What's that?"

"Lace. Real . . . nice lace."

"Lace? Oh, well . . . they tell me it's no trick to operate a sewing machine." His silver-colored eyes searched her face. Polly looked intently at the hands locked in her lap. "We have a large number of single men here, Miss Wright. Have you thought of getting married?"

She looked up quickly. "Why do you say that?"

He shrugged. "Most women want to marry . . . sometime. Don't you?"

"I guess so." Her voice was so low he barely heard her.

She placed the back of her hand to her forehead.

"Are you sick?"

"Just . . . a little bit. Can I trouble you for . . . a drink of water?"

"Herb!"

The bellow was so loud that Polly jumped, then burst into tears the instant Herb flung open the door.

"Jesus Christ, T.C.! What'd ya do to her?"

T.C. came around the table. "I didn't do anything. She wants water."

"I'll get it."

Herb returned seconds later with a dipper brimming full. In his haste water dripped on the floor. He knelt down beside the chair and offered it to Polly. She took a few sips, keeping her eyes down, not seeing the look of concern in the blue eyes almost level with her own or the man's light blond hair that touched the broad shoulders.

"Are you all right now?" Herb asked gently.

"I . . . think soooo—" Polly's words trailed as she fell sideways from the chair.

"Holy hell!" Herb dropped the dipper so he could catch her before she crashed to the floor.

Chapter 3

"WHAT the hell's the matter with her?"

"She's swooned."

"I can see that. Get Doc."

Herb snorted. "He ain't in no shape to see nobody, much less a young lady. I ain't seen him this bad in a long time. He looks an' smells somethin' awful. He'd scare the waddin' outta her."

"Then get that woman."

"What woman?"

"The one who helped her last night. She's about this high and not a bit bashful about speaking out." T.C. held his hand even with his chin. "She's got a head full of reddish-brown hair and holds her nose up so high you'd think she was the queen. Name's Love, I think."

"Love? Hell! What kind a name is that?"

"Just get her."

"You goin' to leave this'n layin' here?" Herb was supporting Polly's head and shoulders to keep them off the floor.

"Is the surgery clean?"

"Except for the puke on the floor and a bottle of spilled Indian whiskey. Doc knocked it off the table before he passed out."

T.C. murmured a few obscenities, then bent and lifted Polly in his arms. He was surprised by how light she was. Hell and high water! Up close she didn't look to be much more than a child.

"I'll put her on my bed. Get that woman. The girl could be dying for all we know."

"Dyin'? Ah, shit!" Herb bounded out the door like an awkward puppy and ran across the street to where the women were waiting.

* * *

Jane went back to the bench and sat down after walking with Polly to the door. After breakfast the poor child had gone behind the curtain and laced herself in a corset. It was so tight that she could hardly breathe. Being nervous about her meeting with Mr. Kilkenny had robbed her of her appetite and she'd eaten hardly anything. When her name was called for the interview she looked as if she would burst into tears. All signs pointed to the fact she was in the family way. When she returned, Jane was determined to ask her. If so, she was killing herself wearing a tight corset.

Jane was tired of hearing T.C. Kilkenny's praises sung by Mrs. Winters and Sunday Polinski. They couldn't say enough nice things about him. *Nice, my hind leg*! The conniving jackass had brought them here pretending to have jobs when what he really wanted was women for his loggers so they would stay and work.

Jane studied the faces of the women in the room. Three of them had children. Mrs. Brackey's little girl was about the same age as Buddy Winters. She was a sweet, shy child. Jane had seen children like her come to the orphanage; children who were afraid and confused. Mrs. Bries had a small girl and was expecting another child.

Jane dismissed the possibility that one of the women had written her the threatening notes, but it might be one of the seven men who had come in on the train from Laramie or one of the four who had been waiting at the stage station.

A cold clammy fear came over her. Had someone followed her here? Why? What had happened had been so long ago and was certainly no fault of hers, but evidently someone thought to punish her for being closely tied to it.

When Patrice had returned from her meeting with Kilkenny, she had gone to the end of the room, ignoring the questioning glances of the women who waited. It was as clear to Jane as it was to the others that the woman considered herself above them. Mrs. Winters hadn't been able to wait to tell everyone that she was going to open a bakery, and Sunday had repeated every word that had passed between her and the boss, as she called him, and had laughingly told them she was going to make soap while she searched for a husband.

"Can ya get ready for that? I can make enough soap in one day to last this town a month. I'd rather be out with a good axe makin' shingles. Never did care much for woman's work."

Jane's thoughts raced, and her anger at Kilkenny for his deceptive tactics kept pace. You could bet your boots she'd let him know what she thought of his bringing her here under false pretenses. Her valise was packed. She'd tell him what he could do with his *job*, then insist on being taken back to the stage station.

Her main reason for coming here was to escape her past; but if someone here knew who she was, it was just a matter of time until everyone in town would be looking down their noses at her. If she was going to be blabbed about, it might as well be in Denver or Laramie as here.

The door was suddenly flung open. The big blond man they called Herb stood there. He looked more like an overgrown boy than a man.

"Love," he shouted.

The women lounging on the bench and the bed broke out into a gale of laughter.

"You callin' me, honey?" the flame-haired woman asked.

"Now why'd he do that?"

"It's plain to see it's me he's callin'."

"Yore old enough to be his mama!"

"Oh, fiddle!" Sunday's voice boomed out over the others. "Hush up all of you. Stop teasing the poor man."

"*Miss* . . . Love!" Herb's face was brick red. "That young girl, ah . . . Polly Wright . . . swooned."

Jane was on her feet in an instant and headed for the door.

"I'm Miss Love. What did he do to her for heaven's sake? What did that scheming man do?" She pushed past him and onto the porch.

"He didn't do nothin'. She was sittin' in the chair and just keeled over."

"He probably told her she had to take one of his timber beasts for a man, and it scared her to death." Jane rushed down the steps. She had to trot to keep up with Herb's long stride as they crossed the rutted road. "The bully," she muttered under her breath.

Herb took the three steps to the porch in one giant stride, opened the door and stood aside for Jane to enter a wide hall. The open doorway on the left was filled with Kilkenny's broad shoulders. She didn't recognize him at first without his hat. His thick hair was blue-black, but not Indian straight as she had thought. It fell down over his ears in deep waves. He was pushing his forked fingers through the top to rake it from his forehead.

"In here," he said curtly.

Jane brushed past him to reach the small, pale girl lying on the bed. Her first thought was that Polly had been laid out as if she were dead. The shawl was still about her shoulders and crossed over her chest, her skirt pulled down to the top of her high-laced shoes; the soles of each had a large round hole.

"Good heavens!" Jane sputtered.

"What's the matter with her?"

"How do I know? I just got here." She frowned up at Kilkenny as if he were a small child asking dumb questions, then, with a toss of her head, dismissed him. She turned to look for Herb.

"I need a wet cloth."

Even as she spoke, Herb placed a washbowl on the table beside the bed. Jane wet a cloth and bathed Polly's face. The girl's breath was shallow. Jane threw off the shawl and felt along her ribs and waist. The corset she wore was heavily boned and much too long for a girl her size. It came up under her small breasts and squeezed her chest like an iron band. She began to open Polly's shirtwaist and then realized the two men were still standing beside the bed.

"I'm going to take off her corset. Do you plan to stand here and watch?"

T.C. turned without a word and walked out of the room. Herb started to follow, then turned back.

"I could get the smelling salts."

"You have some?"

"In the surgery. Doc usually has some around."

"There's a doctor here! Why didn't you say so?"

"Well . . . yes and no. Doc's got a tiger on his back. He's drunk most of the time."

"Drunk! What a waste." Jane followed him to the door. "I might not need the salts, I'll let you know." She closed the door behind him and hurried back to the bed.

Working swiftly, she unbuttoned Polly's dress, pulled it down over her shoulders and worked at the drawstring of her chemise. The corset beneath was laced so tightly that Jane couldn't get her fingers under the laces. When she finally found the ends of the strings, they were tucked underneath and tied in a hard knot.

"Drats!"

She looked around the room for something to cut the strings. On the washstand beside a shaving cup and a comb she found a straight-edged razor in a leather case. As she was removing the blade there was a knock on the door and then it was opened.

"Is she all right? What—? What the hell are you doing with my razor?" Kilkenny came into the room holding out his hand.

"I'm not going to cut her throat if that's what you're thinking." Jane paused at the foot of the bed. "I've got to cut the strings on her corset."

"Not with my razor you won't." He took the razor from

her hand, bent and pulled a thin-bladed knife from a pocket on his boot. "What do you need cut?"

"I can do it."

"What do you need cut?" he repeated.

"If Polly wakes and finds you bending over her with that knife, she'll swoon again."

By the time the words were out of Jane's mouth, Kilkenny was at the bedside. With a few deft strokes of the knife, the laces were cut, the corset spread open. Thank goodness Polly wore another chemise beneath it.

Kilkenny stared in dismay.

"Haven't you ever seen a corset?" Jane asked crossly.

"Why in the name of Satan would a woman put herself in such a contraption?"

"You wouldn't understand if I told you." Jane put herself between him and the bed to block his view. She retied the chemise and pulled Polly's dress back up over her arms and shoulders. After wetting the cloth again, she rubbed it gently over the pale face.

"Is she all right?" Herb asked from the doorway.

"I think so. She's breathing deeply now." As Jane spoke, Polly stirred. "Polly? Are you awake?"

"Oh . . . oh—" Polly's eyes flew open as did her mouth and she sucked in large gulps of air.

"You're all right," Jane said firmly. "Lie still and rest."

"What . . . happened?"

"You swooned is all."

Polly's eyes looked frantically up at Kilkenny, then filled with tears. She tugged at Jane's arm to pull her close.

"Will he . . . will he send me back?" she whispered.

"Let's ask him." Jane stood and looked T.C. in the eye. "Are you sending her back?"

He seemed to be taken aback by the question. He narrowed his eyes and studied the face turned up to his. He should have known that she'd come right to the point.

"'Cause she's dumb enough to lace herself in that . . .

that thing?"

"That may not be all."

"What else could there be?"

Jane held tightly to Polly's hand. "I . . . think she's . . . expecting."

"Expecting . . . what?"

"Good Lord! You're the dumb one. What do you *think* she'd expect?"

"You mean she's breeding?"

"That's a . . . crude way of saying it." Jane took a deep breath, refusing to look away from the silver-gray eyes that held hers. "If you don't wish to employ her, I'll take her with me when I leave . . . today, tomorrow or whenever I can get a ride back to the train stop." She heard a whimper from Polly, turned and bent over her, wiping her face with the wet cloth.

"I . . . don't have any money—"

"I've got enough to get us back to Laramie."

"I'm not sending you back to Denver. Isn't that where you came from?"

"What . . . did you say?"

"I said I'm not sending you back. You signed on to work here. Both of you."

"You can't keep us here if we want to leave."

"No, I can't. But I paid your way from Denver and put you up in a hotel in Laramie. You can pay me back and walk out of here anytime you feel like it."

A flood of anger washed over Jane. It was reflected in the sparkle of her eyes and the color in her cheeks.

"T.C.—" Herb's voice came from the doorway.

"Stay out of this, Herb." Kilkenny's eyes never left Jane's face. "I have money invested in the two of you. You'll stay and work it off."

"You . . . you . . . horse's ass—"

"I've been called worse."

"I'm not finished, *sir*! You're a conniving, sneaky, stony-hearted, slimy toad!"

"Well . . . that's different. I really didn't mind being called a horse's ass."

Jane was too angry to see the glint of amusement in his eyes or the twitching at the corners of his mouth. Between the fringe of heavy dark lashes her smoke-blue eyes glowered at him like those of a small spitting cat.

"You may have the rest of these women fooled, Mister Conniver, but not me! You don't have jobs for us. You cooked up this scheme to get us here for the sole purpose of servicing your timber beasts so they'd be content to stay here and work in your damned old lumber mill."

T.C. folded his arms over his chest and rocked back on his heels.

"Miss Lovey—"

"Love. My name is L-O-V-E."

"Miss Love, if and when I hire whores to service my men they will be good-looking, full-bodied women." His eyes flicked over her slim figure. She wanted to hit him.

You'd know about that . . . I'm sure." The sarcasm in Jane's voice seemed to irritate him.

"You're damn right I would. The women over there"—he jerked his head toward the barracks building—"with the exception of a couple of them, look about as much like whores as I do a preacher."

"Oh, I'm certain you'll have one of those handy too. You'll tidy it all up with weddings. Count me out! Polly, too! I'll not marry one of your bully boys in order to have a roof over my head."

"You'll not be *forced* to marry anyone," he said angrily.

"I realize we'll not be *forced*. We'll just twiddle our thumbs doing mundane work until we get so bored and sick of that barracks that we take one of the men to get out of it."

She had come so close to the truth that T.C. felt a flash of momentary guilt. It made him say something he instantly regretted.

"I don't think you need worry the men will beat a path to your door, Miss . . . Pickle."

Standing in the doorway, Herb took a deep breath and shook his head with dismay. What in holy hell had gotten into T.C.? He could hardly believe what he was hearing. In all the years he had known the man he had never heard him be rude to a woman. In fact he was overly shy around them.

"That will suit me just fine, Mr. Kilkenny. When I marry it will be to a man whose intelligence equals mine. I'm quite sure that I would not be overwhelmed with choices here in your precious town."

T.C. had a difficult time keeping the grin off his face.

"Face the facts. You're stuck here, Miss Pickle."

"You are an obnoxious man, Mr. Kilkenny," Jane said bitterly with lips so tight they barely moved.

There was no way he could hold back the grin that spread around his wide mouth and crinkled the corners of his eyes.

"Miss Love, I'll try to forget you said that. I suggest that you make the best of things . . . for now."

Jane was so angry that she could hardly tamp down the urge to fling the wet cloth she clutched in her hands as she watched him walk to the door. Before he closed it behind him, he turned.

"I'll speak to you later."

Polly was crying softly. Jane pulled up a chair and sat down beside her.

"What'll I do, Miss Love?"

Jane pushed her own personal anguish to the back of her mind and tried to give her attention to the young girl.

"Call me Jane, Polly. You'll be all right. I don't have enough money to pay him for both our fares and then pay our way back to Denver."

"How did you know . . . about me?"

"I guessed. You can't wear that corset, Polly. It will kill you . . . and the baby."

"I don't care. I don't know how I can take care of it anyway."

"There's always a way. Did the father not want to marry you?"

"You know I'm not married?"

"I guessed that too."

"I'm . . . so ashamed—"

"We all do things we regret. Some mistakes have more devastating effects than others."

"I was so scared. I had to let him—"

Polly's story came out in bits and pieces. Her mother had died when she was ten. At age twelve she was left by her father at a rooming house in Laramie; he never returned. The landlord and his wife had been kind to her. She stayed with them for three years and worked for her keep. She earned a few dollars each month working for a seamstress. When the landlord died, his wife sold the rooming house and went to live with her daughter.

The new owner was not as selective with his boarders as her former employers had been. One night she awoke to find one of the men in her room, a teamster who hauled freight out to the fort. He told her that if she refused his advances, he'd spread it all over town that she was a whore, then set her up in a shack and bring in soldiers, scouts and wagoneers for her to service. Frightened half out of her mind, Polly endured the painful experience twice a week until her monthy flow failed to arrive.

She waited a few weeks, then, desperate to get away before it was discovered she was pregnant and unwed, she took the few dollars she had saved from her meager earnings and hid away in another rooming house. She had only sixteen cents to her name when she boarded the train to come to Timbertown.

Jane held onto the girl's hand. Once she had started, Polly couldn't seem to stop talking.

"What'll happen to the poor little mite? 'Twasn't his

fault." Tears from Polly's eyes wet the pillow she lay on.

"It wasn't yours either, Polly. You're young and pretty. Someday you may meet a man who will want you and your child."

"No! No! I ain't never goin' to marry an' have to do *that* again. Never!"

While listening to Polly's story, Jane had been aware of voices coming from the room across the hall. Theda Cruise, the woman with the flaming red hair, musical laughter, and soft seductive voice, was leaving. It was too much of a temptation not to listen.

"I just knew we'd get along like a house afire, T.C."

So did I, Jane thought. *You're just his type*.

"We've got to work on the hotel before we can work on the other saloon. But you'll be in business before the snow flies."

He's pleased now. He's getting his whorehouse.

"Everything I need is down at Rock Springs, including sixteen barrels of the best whiskey in the territory."

Whorehouse and saloon. That should bring families to town!

"Freighters will be here today or tomorrow. You can talk to them. They should be glad for the work."

"I run a good place. If I bring women in it will be to sing and dance, wait tables and socialize with the customers. Whores are nothing but trouble in a saloon." Theda's laugh rang out. "If you want a brothel, build me a house. Every town needs a bit o' bawdy," she said with a heavy Irish accent. "We could go partners, T.C."

"No, thanks. I've got enough to do. I'll speak to Parker at the Pleasure Palace about your helping out until you can get your own place. He's got a couple of rooms upstairs. You can use one of them."

"I'm glad of that. I don't think I can stand another day in that bunkhouse with those boring women."

You're not the only one who's glad. Jane's lower lip was firmly caught between her teeth.

"Why did you come here pretending to be looking for work, Theda?"

"I wanted to look the place over first. You, too, T.C. If I hitch my wagon to a star I have to know where it's going."

"Welcome to Timbertown."

Chapter 4

"I feel much better now."

Jane helped Polly stand and remove her corset.

"It isn't anyone's business that you've not been married, Polly. The less said about it the better."

"But . . . what'll I say if someone asks me?"

"Say the baby's father was a soldier and let them draw their own conclusions."

"But he . . . wasn't."

"He might have been at one time."

"I hadn't thought of that."

"I wager that half the people who came here have things in their pasts that they would like to bury. You can start a new life here. When your baby comes, you'll have someone of your very own to care for."

"But . . . it'll be a . . . bastard. Folks'll look down on it and . . . me."

Oh, Lord! This conversation was bringing back a flood of memories. Jane saw herself, a ten-year-old girl, sitting on a blanket under a tree. Both she and her Aunt Alice were crying.

"Not if they don't know it." Jane gathered herself and shoved the memories aside. "Bastard is just a word. The parents of many great men in history were not legally wed."

"Really? Who?"

"Alexander Hamilton's parents were not married when he was born. His mother was married to someone else."

"Who's he?"

A knock sounded and saved Jane the trouble of explaining to the young girl, who more than likely had never read a history book. The door opened before Jane could get to her feet.

"Your turn, Miss Love," Kilkenny said crisply.

Herb stepped around T.C. and took a hesitant step into the room.

"Miss Polly, ya need a fresh drink of water or . . . somethin'?" Herb had a concerned look on his boyish face.

Polly's face turned a rosy pink when she realized he was speaking to her. Looking down at the hands in her lap, she shook her head.

"This won't take long." Jane placed her hand on Polly's shoulder as she passed her. On the way to the door she poked at the pins holding the coil of hair at the nape of her neck, more out of habit than necessity.

T.C. stood aside and allowed Jane to walk ahead of him into the room. She was slim to the point of fragility; but the set of her shoulders, the candor in her eyes, and the way she carried herself all showed strength. She was trim and neat and held herself as straight as a tree trunk.

He moved around behind his table and openly studied her face. For the first time he noticed a few freckles on her nose. Her huge wide-spaced, smoke-blue eyes refused to look away from his. This was no empty-headed woman, but a strong-willed, determined one.

He swallowed the chuckles that rumbled in his chest. He'd had to think fast when she demanded to be taken back to catch the train to Denver, and he was quite sure he had persuaded her she had to stay.

"Sit down, Miss Love."

"I'll stand. What I have to say won't take long—"

T.C. walked over and closed the door. "Sit down," he said again. "I was taught not to sit while a lady was standing."

"Very well." Jane perched on the edge of the chair. "As I said before, I've changed my mind about staying and working in Timbertown. I'll pay you for the train fare from Denver and my fare back to the stage station. From there I should be able to get a ride to the train stop."

T.C. leaned back in his chair and gave her a thin smile that was very close to a sneer.

Damn! He had congratulated himself too soon.

"No guts for the rough life, huh?"

Jane ignored the sarcasm. "I want to leave as soon as possible."

"Are you taking *Miss* Wright with you?"

"No. *Mrs.* Wright is a seamstress. She's perfectly capable of sewing shirts for your store right up to the time she gives birth, then shortly after. She'll earn her keep."

"And when her time comes?" He lifted his dark brows.

"In a town this size any number of women must have helped birth a baby. You may as well know now that she isn't interested in marrying one of your loggers." Jane felt compelled for Polly's sake to set him straight on that.

"I'd think that would be her main interest . . . at the moment."

"Well, it isn't. Her *experience* with a man was far from pleasant."

As the import of her words sank into his mind, his face hardened.

"Son of a bitch!"

"My sentiments exactly."

"Did you know her before?"

"I met her in Laramie. We roomed together at the hotel before boarding the train."

"—And you took her under your wing?"

"Do you find fault with that?"

"Not at all. The strong should help the weak."

"You said the wagons from the stage station would be here today," Jane said, changing the subject. "I'd like to go back with them."

"They won't be going back."

"Can I hire a buggy?"

"You're in an awful yank to leave here."

"Yes. This . . . Timbertown is not what I expected."

"What was that?"

"A town where I could work, earn my living, make

friends and have a decent place to live."

"All of that is here. What did you expect of a frontier town?" She made no reply and T.C. looked down at the paper before him. "Have you been married?"

"No! Do you think I lied on my application?"

"What have you got against the . . . state of wedlock?"

"My personal feelings are not your concern." Jane stood.

"Sit down, Miss Love. Within a month a schoolhouse with rooms in the back for a teacher will be completed. There are fifteen children in town under the age of twelve — "

"No."

"No? It says here you've taught classes one through six."

"I have. But that doesn't mean I want to teach here." Jane's hand sought her pocket. Her fingers closed around the note: *yu can't hide*. How long would she last as a teacher if she were exposed? The humiliation would be more than she could bear. Her heart pounded with fear, but her expression did not change.

T.C. got to his feet. "You won't change your mind?"

"No." She stood ramrod straight, chin tilted so that she could look up at him. Her eyes locked with his.

"Well, it's best to find out right off that you're too soft to live here. I'll get you back to the stage station in a day or two."

"Thank you."

After she closed the door behind her, T.C. sat down and picked up the report written by his solicitor. *Jane Love, age 23, unmarried, no close kin*. Twenty-three? Why hadn't she married? A woman at that age was usually married, unless she was ugly as sin. That wasn't the case with this one. She must have had numerous opportunities. He quickly scanned the summary of her abilities, then reviewed the personal remarks made by the interviewer.

"Miss Love is an educated, refined lady. She informed me that she has lived and worked all her adult life in a church-owned orphanage. She refused to give the name and the location. Her penmanship is excellent and she proved to be knowledgeable when I presented her with a few bookkeeping problems. It is my opinion that she would be suitable in that capacity if not willing to be a teacher. I was also informed by Miss Love that she has had considerable experience in nursing the sick. She appeared to be very eager to be accepted and seemed undaunted by the fact that Timbertown is a raw frontier town."

T.C. turned in his chair and looked out the window toward the cookshack. *What changed your mind, Miss Love?* He had the feeling that it was more than the sleeping quarters or her suspicion that he had recruited the women to mate up with the single men that was sending her scurrying away. He put his palms on the table and pushed himself to his feet. Hell! If she didn't want to stay she could go, but not until the end of the week when he sent a man to the station to collect the mail.

Just before sundown a caravan of covered wagons arrived. Jane stood with Polly and Sunday to watch the newcomers get stiffly down out of the wagons. As he had done before, T.C. led the single women, one with a young girl, to the barracks building. The five women stood together in the middle of the room, their belongings on the floor at their feet, and listened to T.C. saying essentially the same things he had the night before. When he had finished he looked over their heads and his eyes caught Jane's.

"Miss Love, would you be kind enough to help the ladies get settled and take them to supper?"

All eyes turned to Jane. She wanted to say no. She wanted to tell him to do it himself or ask Miss Flame-hair. Most of all she wanted to kick him. He knew, and she knew, that she'd be making a fool of herself if she refused. So she nodded.

On his way to the door he stopped in front of her, and his silver eyes held hers. Something flickered there and then was gone. He could make her angry and he knew it, but he'd not shake her from her purpose.

"Herb will bring over several canvas cots that can be set up along the wall. If you need anything tell him."

"Just a min—" Jane began, but he was out the door. The sneaky polecat! He had put her in an untenable position. The tired, hungry, uncertain women would look to her to tell them what to do. How in the world could she refuse?

"How come *Miss Love's* in charge?" a whiny voice asked from the communal bed. It came from a pretty girl who wallowed in self-pity.

"I reckon she made the most of her time while she was over there," another woman speculated. Low husky laughter followed the remark.

"Didn't take her long to get in tight with him," still another muttered.

"Still waters run deep—"

"Did ya get real close to him, Miss *Love*? Ya was gone long enough."

"Ya ornery bitches! I'll give ya all somethin'—my fist in yore mouth if ya don't hush it up." Sunday, her hands on her hips, spoke in a loud firm voice. The eyes of the newcomers went wide with shock. "Yo're a bunch a cats is what ya are. I thought my sisters was mean and mouthy, but y'all take the cake. Go on, Jane, get these women settled. They're plumb wore out, just like we was last night. If one of these *ladies* opens her mouth, she'll get her tail twisted."

Jane lifted her chin. Her eyes surveyed the faces of the woman. Most of them were embarrassed by the spiteful remarks of a few and turned away. Jane sent Sunday an amused but grateful look and wished fervently that Kilkenny had put her in charge.

The women appreciated Jane's help. They accepted the crowded quarters without complaint. Maude Henderson insisted that she and her small daughter could sleep on one canvas cot. The girl, her eyes on the floor, clung to her mother's arm. She was a thin child and terribly bashful.

"There's an extra cot. She can have one of her own," Jane explained.

"She's afraid—" Mrs. Henderson spoke hesitantly. The woman appeared calm, but her hands trembled and at times her voice quivered.

Jane placed her hand on the girl's head and gently stroked her hair. She had seen the same frightened, lost look on the faces of children that had been brought to the orphanage.

"What's your name?"

The girl turned her face into her mother's arm and refused to answer.

"Stella. Her name is Stella."

Jane looked into the woman's face. She returned Jane's glance cautiously and then turned away. A red scar ran from the corner of her mouth down over her jawbone; her nose was humped and slightly off center; but she had obviously once been a pretty woman.

"I'm sure you're eager to wash off some of that road dust. Use the warm water from the pot on the laundry stove. After you get settled, I'll take you to get something to eat."

The cook's helper rapped three times on the back door to call the women to supper. They all trooped out leaving the room empty except for Jane, Polly and the new arrivals, who were washing and stowing their belongings beneath their cots.

"Yo're not goin' to stay, are ya?" Polly asked as soon as she and Jane sat down on the end of the bench.

"No. I think it best to move on."

"Where will you go?"

"I'm not sure, but maybe California."

"I wish I could go with ya."

"I wish you could too, but we both know it's impossible."

"The baby won't come for five months," Polly said hopefully.

"You'll be better off here. I'll speak to Sunday. I think you can count on her after I'm gone. That terrible man won't find you; but if he does, I'm sure Mr. Kilkenny wouldn't stand by and let him take you away from here if you didn't want to go."

"Ya don't like him, do ya?"

"I don't care for his sneaky tactics. He brought us here hoping we'd marry his workers and build his town. He doesn't really have work for all of us."

"A lot of the women want to find a man here and marry. Sunday is tickled pink to have so many to choose from."

"That's fine if it's what she wants. It isn't what I want."

"Don't you want to marry, have a family?"

"Sure, someday, but not to a man who'd want me only for cooking his meals and washing his dirty clothes."

"Before Mamma died we were a family . . . of sorts. Papa never wanted to settle down in one place. We moved a lot. Mamma made us a home wherever we happened to be."

As most young girls do, Jane had dreamed of meeting a man who would love her and not care who she was. He would be tall and handsome and very kind. He would take her away to a mountaintop where they would raise beautiful children and be gloriously happy. By her twentieth birthday she had realized that her dream was silly and unrealistic. No prince was coming to sweep her away to heavenly bliss. She had to take charge of her own future, be the master of her own destiny.

Jane's shoulders slumped wearily. She had pinned her hopes on a job here in Timbertown. Now that wasn't to be. It seems that someone had discovered who she was and planned to make her life miserable, maybe to hurt or kill her. Some people were fanatic in their hatred. And why shouldn't they be? Hundreds of innocent people had been killed because of one dastardly act . . .

T.C. crossed the street to his house. He didn't know why he took such pleasure in needling Miss Jane Love. He felt a restless stirring inside him as he admitted to himself that she had been a bright spot in his day. The lady wouldn't back up for anyone. Her gaze had been as direct as a saber thrust and her voice cold as steel when he had passed by her after asking her to take charge of the newcomers. He'd boxed her into a corner without a way to wiggle out and save face.

Aware she had plenty of argument left in her, he had made a fast retreat. T.C. chuckled as he bounded up onto the porch.

Herb was coming down the hall when he opened the door.

"Doc's goin' plumb outta his head. He's talkin' 'bout snakes crawlin' outta them soldier boys he whittled on durin' the war. Wants me to kill 'em. He's sick. Real sick."

"Where is he?"

"In the kitchen. I locked the door to the surgery. 'Fraid he'll get in there and smash things up."

Crash! Herb spun on his heel and hurried back down the hall.

T.C. followed and dodged the end of the broom as he stepped into the kitchen.

"Get that s-son . . . son'abitch! He'ish a hangin' there from the ceilin'. Watch out! He'ish a big 'un."

A small man, his sparse gray hair in wild disorder, swung a broom at the lamp. T.C. grabbed the broom. His swift reflexes saved the lamp from crashing to the floor. He pulled the broom from the doctor's hand and leaned it against the wall.

"Calm down, Doc. I'll take care of them."

"B-bastids is-sh crawlin' all over." He lurched toward the table. "Get them devils off there. I gotta take that boy's leg off."

Herb bent and put a shoulder in the small man's midsection. When he stood, Doc was jackknifed over his shoulder.

"Don't ya puke on me, Doc."

"Boom! Boom! Ya hear it? Get them . . . spiders off—" Doc yelled and began to buck. His feeble attempts were nothing against Herb's strength. He held Doc's legs and ignored his flailing arms.

T.C. followed Herb and his burden up the stairs.

"I hate to do it, T.C., but I'll have to tie him to the bed. This is the worst I've seen him."

"I'll help you. It's for his own good."

In a small room at the back of the upper hallway, they stripped the doctor and tied his hands and feet to the bedstead. Doc cursed them. He fought them and the demons that tormented him. His body was so wasted that his strength was not much more than that of a child.

"Lord! I hate to do this," Herb moaned. "Look at 'im. He's scared outta his mind."

"Let's give him some laudanum. Just enough to make him sleep."

"I hid that from him. He almost tore up the surgery lookin' for it."

T.C. placed his hand on Herb's shoulder. He knew how fond of Doc the young man was.

"I wonder if he knows all you do for him."

"It don't matter." Herb turned to look at the man on the bed. "I'd be dead if not for him. Little runt stood over me and dared them fellers to shoot me again. Said if they did, he'd not doctor the one I shot. When I needed him, he stood by. Now he needs me. I ain't goin' to let him die, even if he wants to."

"I'll stay with him while you get the laudanum."

After the doctor went to sleep, Herb covered him with a

blanket, and the two men went back down to the kitchen.

"Do I smell coffee?"

"Yeah. I tried to get Doc to drink some. He'd take a swaller and spew it out."

T.C. sipped coffee while Herb put the kitchen in order. Doc had turned over chairs and knocked pans from the shelves. He'd cleared the table, thinking in his drunken stupor that he was going to operate.

At the sound of boot heels on the plank floor, both men turned. Out of the corner of his eyes, T.C. saw Herb tense, shift and bend his knees slightly. His hand hovered over the gun strapped to his thigh. It was a natural reflex for the young man, who was reported to have one of the fastest draws in the West. Until he had come to Timbertown with Doc, Herb had often been sought out by those who wished to win a reputation by out-drawing him. Some challengers had lived, but some had died when Herb failed to put the bullet where he had intended. Always he and Doc had moved on.

In the doorway a man stood on long spread legs, his hands on his hips.

"Colin!" T.C. set his cup down and was across the room in two strides, his hand extended. "You old sidewinder. I didn't think you'd get here for another week."

The two men shook hands; then, testing their strength, they danced around each other like a couple of young bear cubs.

After the horseplay, Colin extended his hand to a grinning Herb.

"Thought it time I got back to keep you two out of trouble. How'er ya, Herb?"

"Glad to see ya, Colin."

"Got anything to eat? My belly button's been ridin' on my backbone for the last twenty miles."

"Not here. We're still eating at the cookshack. Bill's a better cook than Herb."

Colin grinned. "That'd not take much," he teased. "How's the old belly-robber?"

"Good . . . now." T.C. laughed. "Haven't heard a thing about his achin' bones for a day or more."

"We had a bunch of women come in," Herb added. "And he's shinin' up to 'em."

"That sounds like the old goat."

Colin was a big man with sandy hair and steady blue eyes. A life of constant riding and hard work had given him a lean trimness and a vast supply of vitality. He wore a buckskin shirt belted about the waist with its tail outside the fringed leather pants that molded to his long legs like an outer layer of skin. Moccasins encased his legs to the knees.

"Before we go eat you'd better know that you've got a surprise waiting for you."

"Surprise? What are you talkin' about?" Colin's eyes went from T.C. to Herb, who suddenly busied himself sweeping up ashes from the cookstove.

"Patrice is here."

Colin looked stunned. "Patrice Guzman Cabeza?"

"Patrice Guzman Cabeza."

"What the hell is she doin' here?"

"Said she came to see you."

"But . . . Ramon. Good Lord! Has something happened to Ramon?"

"Not that I know of. She says she's left him."

"Why come here? What was between us was over a long time ago."

"Not according to Patrice."

"Dammit to hell, T.C., I was over Patrice *before* she married Ramon. I'll admit that I was hot for her for a while. But it didn't last."

"As soon as Ramon finds out where she is he'll come for her."

"What's that to do with me?"

"You know what, Colin. He's got hot Spanish blood. If he thinks there's anything between you and Patrice, he'll kill you."

"If he can," Colin replied quietly.

"He won't face you. He's not *that* honorable. He'll hire someone to shoot you in the back."

"Then what I've got to do is get rid of her before he gets here." Colin spoke lightly, but his brows puckered in a frown.

"That'll be easier said than done." T.C. took his hat off the peg in the hall and slapped it on his head. "My guess is that she left Ramon for some reason other than that she couldn't live without you."

"You really know how to take a man down a peg or two."

"You know what I mean. Patrice is a mercenary bitch, but she's no fool. She knows that Ramon will follow her here. Maybe she thinks you will kill him and leave her a widow. She'll have all that money and be rid of Ramon."

Colin laughed and clapped his friend on the shoulder. "You know something, friend? I had the same thought."

"Let's go see Bill. I heard thunder. Is it raining?"

"Not yet, but there's thunder clouds and heat lightning all around." Colin slapped his hat down on his head. "Damn! Women are more trouble than they're worth."

A grin danced around the corners of T.C.'s mouth.

"I wouldn't go that far."

Chapter 5

BILL Wassall, known as Sweet William because of his fondness for sweets, hated the cold weather and vowed to hibernate like a bear in his cookhouse until spring. He had spent most of his life cooking for freight haulers in Texas, Oklahoma and New Mexico and had come north with his friend Colin Tallman thinking to stay only a month or two. That was a year ago.

Sweet William also had a liking for women . . . all of them, young and old, pretty or not. He liked talking to them, doing for them, teasing them. His head was bald except for a fringe of gray hair, his teeth were almost gone, and he suffered from stiff joints. Yet Bill had a twinkle in his eyes, a quick wit and a glib tongue. His friend Colin said that if there were no humans or animals around for him to talk to, Bill would talk to a stump.

"I got a treat for a pretty little gal." Bill placed a piece of brittle brown candy on the edge of Stella's plate. The girl looked at him with frightened eyes and bent her head so low her chin rested on her thin chest.

"Thank the nice man, Stella," Mrs. Henderson urged.

"That's a'right, ma'am," Bill said cheerfully. "This place takes some gettin' used to. Have a bear claw. Mrs. Winters makes a fine bear claw. Almost as good as mine." He sent the woman a teasing grin and forked a golden-brown fried cake out of a dishpan, dropped it in a bowl of sugar and rolled it around. "Fellers that came in to supper wiped out this whole pan. Said if they didn't eat 'em, they'd use 'em fer sinkers. That's when they thought I'd made 'em," Bill said aside to the women. His laugh made his stomach jiggle. "Ya should'a seen the red faces when I said the woman here made 'em."

"Buddy!" Mrs. Winters, her face flushed from the heat of the cookstove, turned from the boiling kettle of grease where she was frying the dough. "You've had two pieces of candy. That's enough."

"Ah . . . shoot, Ma!"

"No backtalk, young man."

As soon as Mrs. Winters turned back to the stove, Bill winked at the boy and slipped him a small piece of the brittle brown sugar. Buddy scooted around the tables, then darted out of the way when the door opened and two men came in, bringing with them the cool smell of wet cedar trees. They gawked at the women, then hung their wet coats and hats on the pegs in the wall. The one who tried to slick his hair down with his palms was a tall, thin man with a receding chin and weak watery eyes. The other one was the man who had tried to make Jane's acquaintance at the stage station.

At the sound of the rough male voices and the scraping of boots on the plank floor, Stella dropped her spoon and turned her face into her mother's arm. Mrs. Henderson's shoulders went rigid, but she didn't turn and look at the men.

"Somethin' smells larrapin'! I'm hungry enough ta eat the ass-end outta a skunk."

"Hush yore mouth!" Bill said sharply. "Watch yore manners. Ladies is here."

"Beg pardon, ladies." The one who spoke had a growth of dark whiskers shadowing his cheeks.

"You been up to the north camp?"

"Yeah. Could get a storm. Clouds looks like a sonofa—" The word cut off abruptly. The man stepped over the bench and sat down.

"Rain?" Bill began dishing beans and deer meat onto a large tin plate. "Once it starts a-rainin' in this blasted cold country, it takes a week or more for it to stop. That'll put the kibosh on the buildin' T.C.'s plannin' on havin'."

"We heared somethin' about a fair. When's it goin' to be?"

"After the buildin'. Between now an' snow."

"Boss man said he'd give us all a day off fer it. Hell! I ain't seen no dancin' since the hogs ate my little brother."

The dark-whiskered lumberjack laughed uproariously at his own joke. He looked toward the back of the room where Jane sat, and his hot eyes moved slowly over her in an attitude of open appraisal. The disrespectful way he stared first at her and then at Polly, who was next to her, raised Jane's hackles. It was as if he were choosing a whore.

For a minute rage clouded her mind. Then reason returned. The men had been told the women were here to be courted and wed. In all honesty she couldn't blame the lumberjack for staring at them. It was Kilkenny's fault for bringing her and the rest of the women here under false pretenses.

As the man's eyes roamed curiously over Jane, she met his look with frosty composure. Then, to her dismay, the rogue winked. Indignation registered in every line of her slender body, but he seemed immune to her obvious rejection. He got up from the table, walked over to her and made a courtly bow.

"Ma'am, my name is Bob Fresno and I'm puttin' my bid in fer the first dance on fair day."

Jane met his eyes unflinchingly. He was a handsome man in a devilish sort of way. Black eyes, black curly hair falling down over his forehead, even white teeth. He was confident of his charm and probably had had a good deal of success with the ladies.

"I'll not be here on fair day. You'll have to put your bid in someplace else."

"I'm plumb sorry to hear it. Ya got a man waitin' for ya?" He glanced down at her ringless hand.

"That's none of your business, sir."

"I ain't so sure, ma'am. Bob Fresno ain't one to backpedal when he sees somethin' he wants."

Bill came around the table and shoved a pan of biscuits

in the man's hands, taking with him the cloth he'd used to protect his hands from the hot pan.

"Gawddamn!" Bob Fresno dropped the pan on the table. "You old . . . bas . . . old— That's hot!"

"Sure it is." Bill turned and winked at Jane. "Sit down and eat 'em before they cool off. And keep—"

Bill would have said more, but Kilkenny stuck his head in, looked around and then came in followed by another man as tall as himself who wore a broad-brimmed hat and a frontier-type shirt.

"Some no-good, shiftless son of a gun left the gate open. This hungry lobo came wandering in outta the woods." T.C.'s usually somber face was smiling.

"Colin! Gal-dam!" Bill made his way between the tables to shake the man's hand. "You doin' a'right, lad?" The two banged on each other in obviously real affection.

"Good, Bill. You? T.C. treatin' you all right?"

"He's as ornery a scutter as ever cut a trail." Bill was excited, his laugh was loud. "How's your ma and John? Give me the lowdown, son."

"Grandpa Rain died—"

"Ah . . . law!" Bill exclaimed sorrowfully. "I'm just as sorry as I can be to hear it." He placed a comforting hand on Colin's shoulder.

"It was a blessing in a way. He'd grieved somethin' awful over losing Grandma Amy and was goin' downhill fast. I think he was ready to go. It was hard on Pa and the rest of the family." Colin Tallman hung his hat beside the door and slipped off the wet poncho.

"How's yore sister and Dillon?"

"Jane Ann had another young'un. Makes three now. And Dillon joined the Texas Rangers. Ma says he's out sowing his wild oats but someday he'll come home and run the ranch."

"She's probably right." Bill laughed and his belly moved up and down beneath the apron. "You young'uns had 'bout as much chance a puttin' one over on yore ma as ya had puttin' socks on a rooster."

"I won't argue that. Dish me up some grub, Bill. I could eat a bear."

"I'll get right at it, boy. If I'd a knowed ya was comin' I'd a made up a peach cobbler. Remember how ya'd lap 'em up on that trip across the Indian Nations?"

"Sure do, Sweet William." Colin pinched Bill's cheek between his thumb and forefinger. The cook jerked away and scooted back behind the serving table.

"Ah . . . now. Cut it out—"

Jane had watched and listened to the exchange, as had the others in the cookhouse. Colin Tallman was a ruggedly handsome man. His voice was softer than Kilkenny's and had a faint flavor of the South. Their presence filled the cookhouse, making Jane anxious to leave.

She finished her meal and carried her plate and Polly's to the pan of water that sat on the long table in the back of the kitchen. On the way to get her cloak she was stopped by T.C., who stepped from around a table into her path. He was so close that Jane had to tilt her head back to glare at him.

"Did the women get settled in?"

"Of course," she retorted in a low voice. "And without a clue as to what you have planned for them."

"Want to bet?"

His devilish grin irritated yet fascinated Jane because it changed his whole persona. Through the tangle of his black lashes, she could see the gleam in his silver eyes.

He enjoyed baiting her!

"Excuse me." Jane went to the door. T.C. followed.

"Hold on. Miss Jane Pickle," he murmured for her ears and the man's standing beside him. "Meet my good friend, Colin Tallman."

Jane heard the note of laughter in T.C.'s voice and was determined not to furnish him with more entertainment. She smiled up at Colin and held out her hand.

"Colin, this is Miss Pickle."

"It's a pleasure to meet you, Miss Pickle." Colin clasped her hand briefly.

"Thank you," Jane said sweetly with a frozen smile. "Now if you'll excuse me I'll take Mr. Kilkenny's latest *victims* back to the *hotel*."

"Victims . . .?" Colin's brows furrowed and he shot a glance at Kilkenny.

T.C.'s eyes were still on Jane's face. "The lady and I have a difference of opinion."

Colin gave his friend a puzzled look and held the door open for the women who followed Jane out onto the porch. In the near darkness he and T.C. stood beneath the shelter and watched them hurry from the cookhouse to the building next door. Then Colin turned back to T.C.

"What's that all about?"

"She doesn't like it here."

"What's so strange about that? I don't much like it here myself."

"She wants me to send her back to the station."

"That shouldn't be a problem. Send her."

"No."

Colin looked sharply at his friend following the blunt answer. There was a sudden wall of silence between them. After a moment, Colin opened the door and stepped back into the cookhouse.

Jane was tired all over. She had spent most of the day lounging around waiting to be summoned by Mr. T.C. Kilkenny. She would much rather have been doing hard labor. And now, longing for a moment of privacy, she could feel herself the center of attention. The women's quarters were abuzz with the news that she was not going to be a permanent resident of Timbertown.

"Why'er ya not wantin' to stay?" Sunday asked, then hurried on. "It's excitin' to build a town. You got booklearnin'. You could be the teacher—"

"I don't want to be a teacher." Jane walked to the end of the room. Sunday followed.

"Mr. Kilkenny brought us here as prospective wives on the pretext of having jobs for all of us. I'm not interested in taking one of his loggers for my life's mate. And it doesn't take half an eye to see that he doesn't have enough work for all of us." Jane's fingers found the folded notes in her pocket; she hoped her explanation seemed plausible. She didn't dare tell Sunday the *real* reason she had to leave.

"Most of us come here to get away from somethin', Jane. My pa wanted me to take a namby-pamby, pot-bellied man 'cause he owned five hundred acres free and clear. My sisters got to choose 'cause they was prettier than me."

"I can't believe that."

"It's true. Shoot fire, Jane. We ain't so dumb that we didn't figure it out a mill and lumber camp would have single men. How do ya know ya won't fall for one of 'em? Yo're 'bout the prettiest one here. I seen one of 'em givin' ya the eye—that black-haired one wearin' the felt hat. 'Course, I'd not have him if ever' tooth in his head was a gold nugget."

"Sunday," Jane turned her back on the chattering women in the room and lowered her voice. "I'm leaving as soon as the all-powerful Mr. Kilkenny allows me transportation back to the station. I've a favor to ask. After I'm gone will you keep an eye on Polly?"

"Yo're really goin'?"

"Will you look out for Polly?" Jane asked again.

"She's havin' a young'un, ain't she?"

"Yes, and she's scared."

"She a widder?"

"No. A teamster raped her in a rooming house back in Laramie."

"The dirty, stinkin' pissant! She ain't much more'n a young'un herself."

"Barely sixteen."

"Poor kid," Sunday said sorrowfully. Then she brightened. "Polly's pretty. It won't be no trouble a'tall for her to find a husband . . . even if she is expectin'."

"She doesn't want a husband."

"Don't be worryin', Jane. T.C. won't make her take a man she don't want."

"T.C.?"

"Why don't ya like him?"

"There's not time to go into that. It'd take all night." Sunday's wide-spaced eyes reflected her thoughts. She was puzzled. Then, abruptly, her expression changed.

"You like him! My sister, Tuesday, was like that. She claimed to *hate* Arnold Moody until he started lookin' at our other sister. After that she fell all over herself being nice to him. Butter wouldn't melt in her mouth when she was 'round him. They married. Now she gets a kid ever' ten months. I told her he was randy as a billy goat but she wouldn't listen."

In spite of her irritation, Jane had to smile.

"About Polly, Sunday. Will you look after her?"

"'Course, I will. But I wish ya'd change yore mind. Some of them biddies out there ain't got the sense they was born with. This town needs the likes of you, Jane. Ya know, I've been thinkin' I'm not so sure anymore that I want a man. Not any I've seen here anyway. I might open a business."

"What kind of business?"

"It won't be sewin' shirts and makin' hats, I'll tell ya that. Anyhow . . . well, looky at Miss Snooty-puss! She's all decked out like she was goin' to a ball."

Patrice Guzman Cabeza emerged from behind the curtain that was stretched across the corner of the room and sailed past them, her nose in the air, looking neither left nor right, the aroma of expensive perfume wafting in her wake. Around her shoulders was a white fringed shawl, elaborately embroidered in silk thread, a perfect background for her dark hair and olive skin. Large gold hoops hung from her earlobes. The two-inch heels of her shoes made tapping sounds on the board floor. She went out the door and shut it firmly behind her.

T.C. sat at a table with Colin and Bill. The cookhouse was empty except for the three of them and the bull cook, who was washing pots and dishes and scrubbing the work tables.

"We got buildings to fit up. Crew is coming in tomorrow, Bill. That'll mean a half-hundred more men to feed."

"I got a steer cookin' in the pit. Texas style."

"Meat holdin' out?"

"Colin can fetch us in a couple a deer." Bill grinned. "Ya ain't lost yore touch have ya, boy?"

"I saw a herd on the way in. I could get you one by noon tomorrow if I had to."

"If it rains it'll slow things down. I wanted to raise up a building and repair three more in the next couple of weeks."

"It'll take more than that to make this place a town. I hope one of them buildin's is a tonsorial parlor." Colin ran his fingers through his overly long hair.

"One is." T.C. grinned.

"Ya got a barber?"

"Yeah."

"I could sure use a bath and a haircut."

"We got a washtub over at the house. You can ask the lady to cut your hair out on the porch."

"Lady?" Colin asked.

"Holy hell!" Bill exclaimed. "A lady barber. I ain't never heard of a such."

"You have now and you'll see one—as soon as we get the building up. We've got a barber chair, shaving mugs and a tin bathtub coming in on the freight wagons."

"Is . . . she here a'ready?"

"Yeah."

"Jumpin' Jehoshaphat! Which one?"

"You'd never guess." T.C. was enjoying the game he was playing with Bill.

"Ah . . . don't tell me it's that sweet little Miss Love!"

"Miss Love? Sweet?"

"Yeah, sweet. Well, now, ain't that somethin'? A lady barber. She looks like she ort to be a schoolteacher or a preacher's wife. I wonder if she could make me one of them pointed beards." Bill fingered the straggly hair hanging from his chin. "I've seen 'em on tobaccy cans."

"Ask her." T.C. passed his hand over his face to hide his grin.

All three men turned when the door opened. Patrice stood in the doorway, her eyes on Colin. She paused for a moment before crossing the room with her hands outstretched.

"Colin! One of the women said a tall, handsome man was here with T.C. I knew it had to be you!" Ignoring both T.C. and Bill, she went straight to Colin.

He got to his feet. T.C. pushed the bench back from the table and stood politely. Bill remained seated and scowled down at his coffee mug.

"Hello, Patrice. T.C. told me you were here." Colin took one of her hands and held it briefly.

"It's good to see you, Colin."

"Why are you here?" he asked bluntly.

"Can we talk, Colin? I've so much to tell you." Her dark eyes seemed to devour his face.

"Sure. Sit down."

Patrice glanced at T.C. and Bill, then back to Colin.

"Not here. Can't we . . . go someplace?"

"Where do you want to go? The saloon, the women's quarters or the store. I don't imagine you want to go to the men's barracks."

"Let's go over to T.C.'s."

"I don't think that's such a good idea."

"Why not?"

"Patrice, you're a married lady," Colin said patiently. "It's not fittin'."

"I just want to talk to you. We're old friends . . . aren't we?"

"Sure. Sit down and tell me what's on your mind."

"Hell and be dammed!" Patrice swore, her temper taking over. "I don't care what these yokels think! I just want a private conversation, not go to bed with you."

"Well, talk."

"At least come out on the porch." She lifted her chin and her dark eyes flashed angrily. "You can leave the door open and yell for T.C. if you're afraid I'll rape you."

"Oh, well, in that case . . ." Colin winked at T.C., causing Patrice to stamp her foot.

"This is no damn joke, Colin. Ramon tried to kill me!" She turned on her heel and went out onto the porch. Colin reluctantly followed.

"She's hell-bent on gettin' her claws in 'im," Bill said, as soon as Colin passed through the doorway.

"'Fraid so."

"I ain't doubtin' Ramon tried to kill 'er. She's enough ta make a preacher cuss."

"She wanted his fancy house and someone to wait on her, the clothes and the importance of being the wife of one of the richest men in New Mexico. He gave her everything she wanted. She owes the man."

"Ya think he tried to kill 'er?"

"He's got pride. It would depend on what she did to rile him. If she embarrassed him in front of his family or his friends, he might have."

"What ya reckon happened?"

"Patrice's got a roving eye. Ramon is hot-blooded and jealous. I can about imagine what happened."

"Do ya think he'll come here?"

"There's no think about it. He'll be here as soon as he finds out where she is."

Out on the porch, Colin was telling Patrice the same thing.

"Ramon will not sit and wait for you to come back. He'll be here as soon as he finds out where you are."

"He tried to kill me, Colin."

"Now, Patrice. Ramon wouldn't destroy his beautiful possession. What would people think?"

"You're not taking this seriously."

"Ramon is a puffed-up, cocky little rooster. He likes to strut and he likes to show off his beautiful wife. Why would he want to kill his pride and joy?"

"He choked me almost to death!"

"You must have really riled him. Good Lord, Patrice, you're as big as he is. Taller, in fact. What were you doing all that time?"

"I was in bed."

"Alone?"

"You're insulting. You've spent so much time with T.C. Kilkenny you're getting to be as crude as he is."

"Don't start that again. I've known T.C. a hell of a lot longer than I've known you." Anger was evident in Colin's voice. "He may not have Ramon's fancy manners, but he's as loyal and decent as any man I've met so far."

"He's living in the only decent house in town. He could have given me a room, but he's never liked me. Both of us know that."

"T.C. didn't invite you here. Why should he inconvenience himself by giving up his room?"

"It would have been the gentlemanly thing to do." She lowered her voice to a seductive whisper. "You don't know how awful it is to be in with so many . . . sleep with them—"

"You should have thought of that before you came here. T.C. said he gave you a job, the same as he did the others."

"He was insulting! But that was to be expected from one of his background."

"What, may I ask, is wrong with T.C.'s background?" Colin's voice was angry, and he backed away from her.

"I'm sorry." Patrice moved close to him and put her hand on his arm. "I'm scared, Colin."

"Why did you come here?" he asked bluntly.

"Because I knew that sooner or later you'd be here."

"It's over, Patrice. I admit I fell hard for you . . . once. But I soon realized we aren't suited and I got over it. You're the wife of a man who used to be my friend."

"Your ma and John Tallman had a hand in turning you against me, didn't they?" she asked bitterly.

"I'm a grown man. My parents had nothing to do with it. Why are you dragging this up?"

"I want to stay here," she said, ignoring the question. "Ask T.C. to let me have one of the cabins."

"There is nothing in them—"

"Freighters are coming in. I can buy what I need. I've got money, plenty of it."

"This is crazy. Are you going to build your own fires, carry water, cook? How long has it been since you've cooked a meal? Winters are long and cold here," he continued, without giving her a chance to answer.

"Please, Colin. Please. Just ask him. I can't stand being cooped up with those women another day. They're crude and vulgar—"

"You don't fit in here, Patrice."

"You loved me once. Please help me—" Her voice broke. She leaned against his arm and dabbed at her eyes with a lace-trimmed scrap of fine lawn cloth.

"I think you'd better go on back."

"I . . . still love you, Colin. I've been so miserable. I'd never have married Ramon if not for Papa—"

"That's all in the past. Go to bed."

"All right, Colin. I'm so glad you're here. I feel so much . . . safer."

Her lips touched his cheek briefly before she stepped off the porch.

Colin watched her until she entered the building. He had been a callow youth when he had first met Patrice. Grandpa Rain had put up with his moping around until one day he had said:

"You're itchin' to get burnt, son. So trot on after that hot little filly and get it out of your system."

He did. She gave him a merry chase. She lifted him to heaven and dropped him to hell. It took a year for him finally to come to his senses. And when he did, he was utterly ashamed of having been such a fool.

Chapter 6

THE night dragged by slowly, and dawn found Jane wide awake. She was glad to see the darkness end. She was a day person, a lark rather than an owl. She recalled the long dark nights when she had huddled on her cot at the orphanage, her imaginative mind living once again the frightening experience of being awakened in the night and carried from her bed by a big, black-bearded man with cold gray eyes. Time had erased that fear from her mind, but it had only recently been replaced by another fear.

Jane slipped from her pallet on the long plank shelf, gathered her clothes and moved behind the curtain to dress in the dark. She needed to go to the privy. Last night's rain had discouraged her from making a before-bedtime trip and her bladder was painfully full. After dressing, she sat down on the bench to put on her stockings and shoes.

When she slid her foot into her shoe she felt paper where there should be none. Immediately she knew that it was another note from her unknown enemy. A prickle of uneasiness ran down her spine. She drew in a deep shuddering breath, reached down and drew out a square of folded paper and hurriedly shoved it into her pocket. For a long moment she sat in the darkness no more confusing than her thoughts and tried to think through the fear that clouded her mind. She swallowed repeatedly and fought the fear. Breathing as if she had run for miles, she deliberately took her time putting on her shoes, laced them and tied the strings about her ankles.

Even though she could hear the snores of a dozen women, Jane felt as if every eye was on her as she flung her shawl over her shoulders and tiptoed to the back door. She had no fear of stepping out into the semi-dark morning because she was leaving behind the one who hated her—an enemy who had been sleeping on the same communal bed. Until now she had not been sure the note writer was still among those who had come to town, and she had not even considered that her harrasser might be one of the women who had ridden on the train with her, or whom she had met at the station. She had been sure her adversary was a man.

In the small dark cubicle of the privy Jane reviewed in her mind the face of each of the women. Polly was ruled out as the one who sent her the notes, as were Sunday and Mrs. Guzman Cabeza. She dismissed as possibilities the women with children. The red-haired woman had already moved to a room above the saloon. Her enemy, she reasoned, was one of the five women left.

Was it that whiner, Paralee Jenkins? She was envious enough. According to her, the mattress she slept on was not as thick as that of the other women and her blanket was thinner. She was sure that everyone was against her and continually complained about the food, the privy, the weather, the preferential treatment given the other women. But the first note had come before Paralee had reason for envy.

Minnie Perkins, a short, big-breasted girl, had boarded the train at the first stop after Laramie. She liked to talk and seemed to think it was an accomplishment that since she was tall enough to reach a washtub, she had been a laundress in a mining camp. Jane doubted that she could ever read, let alone write a note.

Bessie Miller was as young as Polly but not as pretty. She seemed too interested in how she looked to the male population of the town to be so determined a hater. A practiced flirt, she was constantly dabbing toilet water behind her ears and pinching her cheeks to make them rosy.

Bertha Phillips was the oldest of the group. She had a stern, sour expression and kept to herself. She spoke seldom, offering each word as if it was were a gold nugget she was reluctant to part with. She resented being addressed by her first name and insisted on being called Mrs. Phillips. She was distant but never nasty.

Could it be Grace Schwab? She was a large woman with broad shoulders and a loud voice, quick to express her opinion on any subject. She had been one of those most vocal when Kilkenny asked Jane to see to it that the new arrivals settled in. She seemed too open to harbor a secret hate, though.

Still after thinking it over carefully, Jane came to the conclusion it might be Bessie or Grace. But why would they be so vindictive after all these years and why would either of them want to hurt her? *Damn!* Why couldn't people live and let live?

Morning was approaching when Jane came out of the privy, but there still was not sufficient light to read the note. In the east, spikes of pale, opalescent pink, the first glow of dawn's radiant face, filled the sky. The rooster in Sweet William's chicken yard was announcing not only the day but his superiority over the lazy fat hens in his harem.

A light shone briefly when someone opened the back door of the cookhouse and came out. Swinging a bucket, the man made for the barn where the milch cows were kept. A gate squeaked, and then all was quiet except for the chirping of birds preparing to leave their roosting places in the branches of the tall pines that towered above the privy.

Standing beside the small building, Jane had not felt so alone since she was a child. It was hard to accept that it was one of the women who wanted to hurt her. She would not go back to the women's quarters until daylight, of that she was sure. After a moment she walked back up the path, skirted alongside the building, then crossed over to the cookshack and stepped up on the porch.

She stood quietly. If things has been different she would have enjoyed staying here and being a part of this new venture. She had to admire Kilkenny for taking on the task of making a spot of civilization in the depth of this vast forest.

Tents and makeshift shelters along the street were dots in the early-morning light. The deserted buildings under repair loomed like dark shadows. Across the street a glow came from the upstairs window of Kilkenny's house. A campfire lit up a small area beside the cookhouse and over it coffee was being made in a large oblong boiler.

The inside of the cookhouse was brightly lighted. The aroma of coffee and the smell of frying meat greeted Jane when she opened the door. Bill was at the iron grill turning strips of meat with a long-handled fork.

"Need some help?" she asked cheerfully.

"Mornin', Miss Love. Ain't ya up mighty early?"

"Couldn't sleep. Thought I'd lend a hand."

"I'd be plumb outta my mind to turn down help from a pretty woman."

"Now I know why they call you Sweet William." Jane forced a smile. "I must wash. I didn't want to wake everyone—" she finished lamely and went to the bench. After washing her face and hands, she dried them on the towel that hung on a nail above the basin. She felt the note in her pocket and was tempted to take it out and read it but didn't want to arouse Bill's curiosity.

"What can I do?"

"Take over here. I'll get the griddle ready for the flapjacks. Bull cook's gone to milk. I swear he ain't got the brains of a bull *frog*." Bill handed her the fork.

A dishpan of sliced meat sat on the reservoir end of the stove.

"Do you need all this?"

"Yeah, an' I ain't sure it's enough. Might have to slice more. T.C. said a big crew was comin' in this mornin'. Most of 'em will have et, though." Bill pulled a white cloth from a box under the table. "Wrap up in this here flour sack so's not to get that pretty dress all grease-splattered."

"Thank you. I'd just as soon not get it soiled."

Trying to keep her mind off the paper in her pocket, Jane worked at the grill. When the strips were brown on both sides, she put them in a shallow pan and set it aside to keep warm. Pans of biscuits were ready for the oven. Bill dipped a brush in the meat drippings and whisked it across the tops of the biscuits. He whipped eggs in a large pan and added buttermilk, flour, soda and salt. When he finished he added a large handful of sugar to the mixture, then set the first pan of biscuits in the oven.

Jane marveled at how effortlessly he went about the work, and how organized he was. He was pouring batter onto the griddle from a large pitcher when she heard him greet Kilkenny.

"Mornin', T.C."

"Morning. I see you have a new helper."

"Yup."

As much as Jane would have liked to ignore him, politeness was a part of her nature. She nodded a greeting, then turned back to the grill.

"That gal-danged Cookie got drunk again," Bill complained. "He's out milkin'. Hope to hell he knows a teat from a tail."

Jane busied herself turning the meat. She was aware when Kilkenny came behind the work counter and poured coffee from the pot on the stove.

"Cookie tending the boiler outside? Men from the cutting camp will be here soon yellin' for coffee."

"Supposed to be. He ort to be able to handle it. I was glad Miss Love popped in. Ain't had no chance yet to ask 'er to fix me up with one of them pointed whisker thin's when she sets up shop. Goin' to though. Think I'd look real stylish in one. Women'll be swarmin' all over me."

When it dawned on Jane that Bill was talking about her, she turned from the stove and gave him a puzzled look.

"Are you talking about me, Mr. Wassall?"

Bill laughed. "Ain't nobody else I'd trust my whiskers with."

"But . . . I'm not setting up a shop. I'm leaving here as soon as I can find a way back to the station."

"Leavin'?" Bill flipped flapjacks on the iron griddle with a long-handled turner. "Ya jist got here. What ya want to be leavin' for? T.C. said he was buildin' ya a parlor."

"Parlor?"

"Tonsorial parlor. Yo're a barber, ain't ya?"

"I'm *not* a barber. Where in the world did you get such a crazy idea?"

"Now, Bill, I never said that Miss Pickle—"

"Pickle? Who's that? Ain't yore name Miss Love?"

"It is," Jane said angrily. "That's *his* idea of being funny because I don't fall in with his . . . hare-brained schemes. I'm not staying in Timbertown. I'm leaving here today . . . if I have to walk." Anger turned to despair, and she was terribly afraid she would cry.

"I'll be dang-bustit. I thought sure—Well, never mind. How many flapjacks ya want, T.C.?" Bill spoke sharply, his annoyance at T.C. for causing him to make a fool of himself reflected in his tone. He firmly intended to give his boss good raking over the coals when he had the time.

"Start with four."

Jane had taken biscuits from the oven and was placing the pan on the serving counter when Mrs. Winters came in. She had just opened her mouth to greet the woman when Mrs. Winters turned to Kilkenny.

"You give her my job?" she asked.

"No!" Jane said hastily before Kilkenny could answer. "I came in for coffee and was helping until you got here." She whipped off the flour sack and handed it to Mrs. Winters.

"You said five o'clock," Mrs. Winters said accusingly to Bill and wrapped the sack around her middle.

"I meant four o'clock," he said crossly. "Sit and eat, Miss Love. Three flapjacks or four?"

"One, please." Jane wanted to run out the door, but was determined not to retreat. She took the plate Bill handed her and went to the far end of the table. T.C. picked up his plate and moved down the table to sit beside her.

"Coffee?"

"I'll get it."

"Sit still."

Burning with resentment, her stomach in such turmoil she was afraid it would reject the food, Jane remained seated. Kilkenny filled the coffeepot from the large boiler on the stove and carried it and two mugs to the table.

"Thank you," Jane murmured without looking at him.

"Don't mention it. Bill, shove that platter of biscuits over here. Have a biscuit, Miss Pickle."

Jane slammed her fork down on the table. Anger overcame reason and the tears that had been dangerously close. When she looked at him, her eyes spit blue flame. She wanted to slam her fist in his eye with every ounce of her strength. The thought sobered her. What were this place and this man doing to her? She couldn't remember ever wanting to strike anyone before. Her practical side argued that if not for the threatening notes she might have been able to take the teasing.

"This has gone on long enough!" Jane choked back her temper and, in spite of her anger, her voice was not loud. "I'm tired of your making fun of my name. It was not a name I chose, but one that was given to me at birth. You are a small-minded, vindictive man, Mr. Kilkenny. The sooner I leave your town the better I'll like it."

For a moment her eyes, like daggers, fiercely met the gaze of eyes as silver as a shiny new sword. A black brow quirked upward as T.C. responded.

"You're right, Miss Love. I apologize for having fun at your expense. But you should learn not to rise to the bait." His lips curved in a semblance of a smile. "Last night you deprived me of my fun."

"It was childish of you to bait me in front of your friend." She spoke coolly, refusing to look away as his eyes raked her face.

He squinted at her but didn't speak, giving himself a moment to assemble his thoughts. Anger had added a rosy tint to the otherwise clear skin of her perfectly oval face. Her mouth was full and soft, her eyes that deep, deep, smoky blue. There was something different about them this morning. They were shining with something more than anger. Was it tears? She didn't appear to be one of those women who cried when things didn't suit her.

"I agree. Now eat. I have a favor to ask."

A look of astonishment came over her face. "You have the nerve to ask me a favor after your despicable behavior?"

"It's not for me." He looked away from her. "Bill, dish up some breakfast for Doc. Miss Love has agreed to help me get him to eat it."

"I never agreed to any such thing!"

"That's just the ticket," Bill said happily. "Herb said Doc ain't et enough lately to keep a bird alive. He'll not last the week if he don't eat. Doc's got a soft spot for a pretty woman. Sweet-talk him into eatin', Miss Love."

"See there? Do you want to be responsible for a man's death?" T.C. murmured for her ears alone.

His voice held a trace of amusement and her eyes darted to him. From the laughter in his eyes she knew he was teasing, and she was in no mood for it.

"You're a . . . wretched man!" she declared, and bristled even more when she heard his low chuckle.

Jeb Hobart stuck his head in the door.

"Wagons comin'. Men and supplies."

"I hope they've et," Bill shouted from the back of the kitchen.

"They have, but send Cookie out with a bag of cups."

"He's outside. Here." Bill carried a large sack of tin cups

to the foreman. "Keep 'em out till I get the men in the bunkhouse fed, then the women."

"Speak to you for a moment, T.C.?"

"Sure." T.C. drained his coffee cup, got to his feet and looked down at Jane: "Don't go away, Miss Love." He followed the foreman outside.

Alone at the end of the table, Jane put her hand in her pocket and felt the square of folded paper. Both Mrs. Winters and Bill were in the back of the kitchen. She pulled the paper from her pocket and unfolded it. Glancing down, she read the printed words quickly.

leave here
yu be sorry.

She refolded the note and shoved it back into her pocket. What did it mean? Was it a threat to frighten her into staying so her enemy could continue to torment her?

Her hands were shaking and fear had dried up her throat. She forced herself to take a few sips of the hot coffee, then found that she could drain the cup.

"Here's some grub for Doc." Bill placed a tin plate in front of her. "Herb's got coffee made by now. Kid can't cook for sh—Kid can't cook a'tall."

Jane looked down at the stack of flapjacks swimming in thick dark syrup and the strips of greasy meat. Not the meal she would feed a sick man.

"Shouldn't he have a glass of milk?"

"Milk?" Bill laughed as he wrapped a plate of biscuits in a cloth. "Doc'd puke at the sight of a glass a milk."

"Nevertheless, if he's sick he needs it."

"Bet ya two bits against a cow chip he won't drink it." Bill lifted the lid from a crock and scooped up milk in a tin cup.

"If I had two bits to spare I'd take you up on that."

"Ready, Miss Love?" T.C. came past the rows of tables

and stood waiting. "I'll take you over, then I've got a hundred things to do."

The porch was crowded with men waiting for Bill to ring the bell for breakfast.

"Mornin' ma'am" The man who spoke was Bob Fresno, the one who had approached her the previous night. He stood amid the men with his cap in his hand.

"Morning," Jane said, after glancing to see who had spoken.

"You bringin' me my breakfast?" Bob asked, trying to keep the conversation going.

Jane ignored the question. Kilkenny's hand on her elbow urged her through the crowd and off the porch.

It was hardly daylight, but light enough for Jane to see that the town had come to life. A string of supply wagons lined the street. Dozens of men were unloading sawed lumber and kegs. Jeb Hobart was very much in evidence directing placement of the building supplies. Jane and T.C. crossed the road just as more wagons rattled into town.

"Will Mr. Wassall have to feed all these men?"

"He's prepared. He pit-cooked a steer yesterday and he's got gallons of beans. They'll be fed."

Colin Tallman was standing on the porch with a cup of coffee in his hand when they came up the steps.

"Mornin', ma'am. You had breakfast already, T.C.?"

"'Course. I'm not used to lazin' in bed like some I know."

"You didn't ride fifty miles yesterday either. Who's this for? Me or Herb?"

"Doc. I heard him cussin' Herb this morning, so I know he's awake."

Colin opened the door and waited for them to enter, then followed them into the house. A light fanned out into the hallway from a room at the back of the house.

"Herb's in there tryin' to fix up somethin'. He's worried about Doc."

"I thought maybe he'd eat something for Miss Love. Herb says he hasn't eaten much for a week."

"Miss Love?" Colin said. "You said her name was—"

"—I was mistaken," T.C. said hastily. "Her name is Love."

Jane looked up at the tall, fair-haired man. He was grinning.

"I'd be happy to hit him for you, Miss Love."

"Thank you, Mr. Tallman, but I'm reserving that pleasure for myself."

Jane and Colin followed T.C. to the kitchen, where he placed the plate of food on the table and hung his hat on the knob of a kitchen chair.

Herb was vigorously stirring something in an iron pot.

"What's that?"

Herb ignored the question, looked over his shoulder and spoke to Jane.

"Mornin', ma'am."

"Morning." Jane stood beside the table still holding the cup of milk and the plate of biscuits.

"You cooking mush?" T.C. peered into the iron pot.

"What's it look like?" Herb growled.

"Whatever it is, it's burning."

"Horse-hockey!" Herb muttered as he grabbed a rag, wrapped it around the bail on the pot and lifted it. Flames shot up out of the round hole on the iron surface of the stove. T.C. moved quickly to cover the hole with a round iron lid.

"You fixin' to plaster the walls with that mess, Herb?" Colin, a grin on his wide mouth, eyed the spoon stuck in the thick mush.

"I wasn't plannin' on it." Herb spoke irritably. His eyes were bloodshot as if he'd gone for days without sleep. "That for Doc?" He jerked his head toward the plate piled high with flapjacks and fried meat.

"Yeah. I thought Miss Love might have better luck getting him to eat."

"I don't know." Herb shook his shaggy blond head and rubbed the stubble of whiskers on his chin. "He had a hell of a night and he ain't in a very good mood."

"He's got to eat, Herb. If you wait for Doc to be in a good mood—"

"—You'll wait forever," Colin added.

"If he don't eat, he'll die. How long's it been since he had a solid meal?" T.C. asked.

"Long time." The bottom of the iron pot rasped against the range top as Herb pushed it farther back on the stove.

"May I say something?" Like a musical note, Jane's voice broke into the male chatter.

As if suddenly remembering she was there, the three men turned to look at her. It was T.C. who finally spoke.

"You've not been bashful about speaking up before. Why now?"

Refusing to rise to the bait, Jane took her time and placed the milk and the plate of biscuits on the table.

"If the doctor hasn't eaten solid food for a week, his stomach certainly will not welcome this." She moved the plate of flapjacks and meat they had brought from the cookhouse across the table toward Herb. "You eat it, Mr. . . . ah, Herb, and I'll make the mush to go with this milk."

"Herb, ma'am. Ya don't need to be addin' a mister to it." He took a step closer to the table. "That milk for Doc? He'll puke!"

"I doubt it. From what you say there's nothing in him to come up."

"I'd be obliged, ma'am, if ya made the mush. What I got here is a thick, lumpy mess. But I'll tell ya right now, Doc ain't goin' to drink that milk."

"Want to bet?"

Chapter 7

"NOW that that's settled, I've things to do." T.C. snatched his hat off the chair post. "Coming, Colin?" At the door he turned. "We've not had a chance to fully discuss your employment, Miss Love. Work here today. We'll discuss the pay later. God knows there's plenty to do. This house hasn't been cleaned since we moved in."

"You're either ignoring or have forgotten what I've told you repeatedly. I'm not—"

"I haven't forgotten. I just don't have time to deal with it right now. I've got fifty men out there waiting to be told what to do." By the time he had finished speaking he was in the hallway.

Colin lifted his shoulders, grinned at Jane and left the kitchen.

In the quiet that followed, Herb spoke softly and sincerely.

"I'm purdee sorry ya ain't stayin'."

"I expected the town to be more . . . settled."

"It'll be more lawful than most towns. T.C.'ll see to it."

"That's a big job for one man." Jane took the spoon from the mush in the pot and decided that what was there could not be salvaged.

"He can do it," Herb said confidently. "Once he sets his mind, he won't back down."

"I've noticed that."

"He made a deal with Garrick Rowe to get the town going so that men who work for his lumber company can bring their families here and have a place to live."

"Who's Garrick Rowe?" Jane had scraped the thick mush from the pot and now was washing it.

"He owns the lumber mills over at Trinity. Ya see, T.C. and Colin had filed on the land here that included the town, but they want to ranch the part east a here. T.C. don't want any part of the lumber business even if he has been lumberjackin' most a his life. They sold the timber to Rowe. In the bargain T.C. agreed to stay a year and get the town goin' again."

Jane poured water into the pot from the teakettle and set it over the hole in the top of the range.

"Where's the meal?"

Herb lifted a cloth sack up on the counter.

"I opened it this mornin'," he said when Jane dipped some of it out into a bowl and looked carefully for weevils.

"It should be in a tin with a tight lid."

"Miss Jane, will Miss Polly be goin' with ya?"

"No."

"She's in the family way, ain't she?"

"Yes."

"Where's her man?"

"She doesn't have one." Jane turned and looked at the boyish face of the big man. "She was . . . forced."

Herb's mouth opened in surprise, then snapped shut.

"Gawdamighty!" The word exploded from him. "A man who'd do that to a young girl ain't fit to live."

"I agree." Jane took the salt box to the stove and sprinkled salt in the boiling water. "Mr. Kilkenny and Sunday Polinski and now you know Polly's situation. I'm telling you this because Polly will need friends, understanding friends, in the months ahead."

"Ya can count on it, Miss Jane. I'll see to it nobody hurts her."

Jane's gaze flicked up to the youth's face. It was cold and void of expression, but the skin at the corners of his eyes tightened ever so slightly, narrowing his gaze. It occurred to her that this man, scarcely old enough to grow a beard, had a deep-seated sense of moral obligation, but a hard life and strong survival instincts had left their mark. *He could be deadly if crossed.*

"It eases my mind to know that you'll be around if she . . . if something should come up."

"I'll be here." Herb shook his head. "It's a shame . . . ya ain't stayin', Miss Jane."

"We can't always do what we want to do. You've probably discovered that."

"Ya mean ya don't want to go?"

"No. No, I didn't mean that," Jane said quickly, and while stirring with a wooden spoon, began to sprinkle the cornmeal into the boiling water. She'd let her mouth run away with her and it was best to drop the subject.

When the gruel had thickened to her satisfaction, Jane removed it from the stove. On a shelf above a work bench were several bowls. Choosing the one with the fewest chips, she wiped it with a cloth, and poured some of the gruel into it.

"Ain't it a wonder what a little know-how will do? I put a cup a meal in all at once."

"I've made mush hundreds, maybe thousands, of times. It's thin now, but in a few minutes it will set up." Jane spooned onto the gruel some of the syrup from the flapjacks they had brought from the cookhouse. "You better eat these before they get any colder I'll take this up to the doctor."

"Ya best let me take it, Miss Jane. Doc's not been in his right mind lately."

"I've dealt with sick children—"

"—He ain't no young'un, ma'am. He's got a nasty mouth when he's feelin' poorly."

"At least he won't ignore me."

"But, Miss Jane—"

"I promise I won't be offended no matter what he says. Show me the way, Herb, then come back down here and eat. Before we go, set the biscuits in the oven to keep warm."

"Won't they burn?"

"Not if you leave the oven door down."

Jane looked around for something to serve as a tray, but could find nothing. The kitchen was in need not only of a good cleaning, but of decent dishes as well as cooking pots. She placed the bowl on a tin plate, handed the milk to Herb and followed him out of the kitchen.

In the upper hall Herb stopped and spoke to Jane.

"Ma'am, I wish ya wouldn't go in. I ain't wantin' ya to see Doc like this. He's a good man. He just can't forget 'bout all them arms and legs he took off during the war and all them that died 'cause he didn't have time to help 'em. He ain't never been like this before. He's sick, too. And scared."

"Drink has ruined many good men."

"But . . . it stinks in there."

"No worse than what I've smelled before."

Herb's shoulders slumped in resignation and he opened the door.

Jane noticed the odor first. Her next impression was that the room was sparsely furnished: a narrow bed, a chair and a washstand. The morning light coming in the curtainless window revealed a startling sight. A man, who appeared to be not much larger than a child and who was spidery thin, lay on his back. A cloth rope bound his skinny ankles to the end of the wrought-iron bedstead and a wide cloth, reaching from his knees to his chest, was stretched tightly and tucked beneath the mattress on each side of the bed.

"What in the world!"

"I had to, ma'am. He'd get up an' hurt hisself."

"You sonofabitch!" The feverish sunken eyes glared up at Herb. "I despise the day I kept that outlaw from killing you."

"Doc . . . it's for yore own good—"

"If you had a ounce a gratitude for what I've done for you, you'd not have taken my whiskey." The weak, raspy voice rose to a screech. "What's this slut doin' here? I don't need a whore. Get her outta here! And get me my whiskey!"

"Hush up that kind a talk, Doc." Herb said sharply.

"Miss Jane's brought ya some breakfast."

"My guts are on fire and you bring me a prissy-ass woman with . . . *breakfast*! You stupid, backwoods bastard! Get my bottle or, by holy hell, I'll cut off your damned pecker when I get up from here!"

Herb winced. The doctor's cruel words hurt. Jane set the bowl of gruel on the washstand and took the cup of milk from Herb's hand.

"Go on downstairs," she said, ignoring the man on the bed, then added when she turned to look down at him, "I'll see to it that he eats."

"You'll do nothing, you pig-ugly old spinster!"

"Doc! For God's sake! Ma'am, he don't mean it."

"I know. He's lashing out like a spoiled little boy. Go eat your breakfast."

"Get . . . her out . . . of here." The doctor coughed, leaned over the edge of the bed and spit on the floor. He made no attempt to use the can beside the bed. Jane saw flicks of blood in the spittle and on his lips.

She shoved Herb gently out the door, but left it open. Then she went to the window, raised it and propped it up with a stick that lay on the sill.

"Herb!" The doctor tried to shout but his voice was weak. "Get back in here, you sorry piece a horseshit!"

"Phew!" Jane waved her hand before her nose. "It smells like a privy in here."

"It is a privy, you stupid whore! Touch me and I'll piss all over you."

At that Jane turned on him.

"Keep a civil tongue in your head or I'll slap you so hard your teeth will rattle." Her face was rigid with impatience and anger.

"You do and I'll spit in your face."

"You're a poor excuse for a human being, lying there wallowing in self-pity. Look at yourself; a whiskey-soaked sot wasting the brains and talent God gave you."

"I don't need a nasty-nice little heifer telling me what I am. If you're so much why'd you have to come to this god-forsaken place to get a man? I know why T.C. sent out that bill wanting women to *work*."

"So do I . . . now. But bear this in mind, Doctor, I'm on my feet and you're not. However, that's got nothing to do with the pitiful condition you're in now." Jane spoke as if to an unruly child. "Let's get something straight right now. I'll not suffer your insults in silence. I do not feel sorry for you; therefore, I will give you back as good as you give."

"The thieving son of a bitch stole my whiskey."

"Your brain is so pickled you don't realize what that young man is doing for you. You don't deserve such loyalty."

"Loyalty, my ass! He stole my whiskey!"

"Shut up whining!" Jane was surprised by her own words. She poured water from the pitcher on the washstand into a bowl and wet the end of a towel.

"Wash your face and hands. Heaven knows they need it."

"Loose the damn sheet. I can't move."

Jane pulled on one side of the sheet, giving it some slack, but left it stretched over him. While he rubbed the wet towel over his face and hands, Jane studied him. His breathing was labored. The skin on his face and neck was like yellow parchment. His eyes were deep-set in their sockets and his whiskered cheeks sunken. The thin hands that lay on his bony chest were long and slender.

He wiped his hands with the wet cloth, then laid it over his face for a moment as if enjoying the cool dampness. He removed the cloth and left it to lie on his chest.

"Don't spit on the floor again. It was a childish act of defiance."

"Untie my feet."

"No."

"I'll do it myself." He leaned forward on one elbow, his shaking hand reaching for his ankles. Unable to reach past the calf of his leg, he sank back down on the pillows. Weak tears filled his eyes.

"You'll feel better after you eat," Jane said. "I've made cornmeal mush. It's easy on the stomach."

"You a doctor?" he asked sarcastically.

"Heavens, no. But I've taken care of many sick children and carried out the orders the doctors gave me. After you've eaten you'll drink the milk. It'll coat the lining of your stomach and keep it from burning."

"Milk! Christ almighty. I'm not drinking any dad-blasted milk!"

"Yes, you are."

"I won't."

"You'll eat and you'll drink the milk, or I'll pour this pitcher of water on you, shut the door and leave you alone all day."

"Herb will come."

"Not if I tell him you've gone to sleep."

"I'll yell."

"Not with a gag in your mouth," Jane said calmly. "Now open it. And, I'm warning you—spit it out and I'll smear the whole bowlful on your face and walk out."

"You're a . . . bitch!"

"And you're a . . . miserable old sot." Jane held the spoonful of mush close to his lips and waited.

"I can feed myself," he sputtered, and then his thin lips parted.

"I don't trust you." She thrust the spoonful of mush inside.

He held the food in his mouth while his eyes battled hers, then with a grimace he swallowed. His feverish eyes stayed on her face while she fed him. When he had eaten half of the mush, Jane could see that he was having a difficult time swallowing. She set the bowl on the washstand and picked up the cup.

"Drink a little milk," she said and put her arm under his

thin shoulders to raise him up. Without making a fuss, he took several swallows.

"Aren't you going to pat me on the head and tell me I was a good boy?"

"Sure. Good boy." Jane laughed as she patted the top of his head, then dropped her eyelid in a wink.

"What's your name?"

"Jane. What's yours?"

After a pause he said, "Nathan Foote. It's been a long time since I said it."

"Nathan. After Nathan Hale?"

"I'm no hero."

"Maybe you're the villain. Every town should have one."

Jane began working at the knots in the cloth holding his feet to the bedstead. When they were free, she swung his thin legs over the side of the bed.

"Sit up and I'll get a pan of water so you can wash yourself."

"Aren't you scared I'll run off?"

"Not one bit." She made a fist and shook it under his nose. "I've had to deal with unruly boys bigger than you. I learned where to hit so it will hurt."

A gleam of admiration lit his eyes. "Where were you twenty years ago?"

"Oh, I was probably a moonbeam or a snowflake or the song of a lark."

"More than likely the croak of a frog," he growled.

"You haven't lost your sense of humor. Do you have a clean nightshirt?"

"I don't *own* a nightshirt."

"Or clean sheets?"

"Or clean sheets."

"Wait right here. I'll be back."

She left the doctor sitting on the side of the bed and went downstairs. She found Herb standing on the porch with Colin Tallman. The street was filled with men, horses, wagons. Shouts and good-natured banter rang out over the ring of the hammer and saw, the stamping of dray mules and the slapping sound of lumber being unloaded.

"Doc all right?" Herb asked the minute she came out the door.

"He ate a little and drank a little milk. Where can I get a nightshirt for him and some clean sheets?"

Herb frowned and tilted his head. "He don't have a nightshirt. Don't reckon he'd wear it if he did. About sheets—We got plenty a blankets."

"They must have sheets at the mercantile."

"Ah . . . yes. I believe they do."

"Would you please get four sheets and a nightshirt. If they don't have a regular nightshirt, get a big soft shirt."

"Ma'am, is he . . . calmed down some?"

"Docile as a lamb. He's very sick, you know."

"I've knowed it a while."

"I'll make potato soup for his dinner if you'll get me a few potatoes and some more milk from the cookhouse."

On the way back upstairs to the doctor's room Jane realized that she hadn't thought about the note in her pocket for an hour or more. Being busy was what she needed to keep her fear at bay until she could leave this place.

Before noon the room was clean, the chamber pot had been emptied and the doctor lay in a clean shirt on clean sheets. As she worked, she told him about the activity out on the street, the sounds of which came in the open window.

"They're putting up two buildings. One on the other side of the store and one by the blacksmith. One looks like it will be two-story. They got two cookfires going along the side of the cookhouse and you can smell meat cooking."

"Which one of the men have you got your eye on?"

"You," Jane said with a quirked brow. She was rinsing the cloth she had been using to wipe the windowpane. "I thought you knew that."

"Bullfoot," he snorted.

"You look like a good prospect to me."

"Is that what you're looking for? A man with one foot in the grave?"

"Sure. That way, I'm boss."

"Herb'd make you a good man."

"He's too young. Besides, I'm a pig-ugly old spinster. Remember?"

"There'll be a dozen trying to court you . . . even if you are."

"I'm not staying to be courted."

"Where're you going?"

"I've not decided yet."

"When?"

"As soon as Mr. Kilkenny finds someone to take me to catch the train."

"Why?"

"You should have been a lawyer instead of a doctor."

The doctor remained quiet, but his eyes followed Jane as she rolled the soiled bedclothes and placed them outside the door.

"I'm . . . dying." He spoke as Jane came back into the room.

"I know."

"It won't be long now."

"It could be a while—"

"No. It's been a while coming on."

"Rest and good food will make things easier."

"I want it to be over."

"If you were trying to kill yourself with whiskey, it made it hard for those who care about you."

"No one cares."

"Herb cares. The things you said hurt him."

"Herb tied himself to me because he had no one else."

"You underestimate yourself and Herb."

The doctor turned his face away and was silent for a long

while. Jane was tucking stray wisps of dark auburn curls back up under the coiled hair on the top of her head when she felt his eyes on her.

"I've not had a pretty woman doing for me in more years than I care to think about."

"Pretty? Me? What changed your mind?"

"Will you stay . . . till . . . the end?"

"I thought you didn't like me."

"I didn't think I did. Only a fool doesn't change his mind once every forty years."

"I'm an old maid . . . and bossy," she said, trying to tease him out of his serious mood. It didn't work.

He closed his eyes. "I hate asking, but will you stay? I . . . don't want to be alone."

"You won't be."

"I never had a family. I was too busy. There were my studies . . . then the war—"

Jane sat down in the chair beside the bed, reached over and took one of his hands in hers.

"You won't be alone, Doctor Foote."

"Thank you." His fingers tightened on her hand. "Call me Nathan. Doesn't make me feel so damned old."

In the minutes that followed, Jane tried to think of a way to explain that *someone* would be with him when the end came, but not she. Any number of the women would come to tend him if Mr. Kilkenny asked them. No words came to mind and she sat in stony silence.

She was relieved when she heard Herb calling her name from the bottom of the stairs. She released Doc's hand and stood.

"I'll be back. Sleep if you can. This afternoon I'll read to you if you like."

"There's a Bible down in the surgery."

Herb was waiting at the foot of the stairs.

"Miss Jane, there's a woman in the surgery with a sick

young'un. I shut the door so Doc wouldn't hear the little 'an cryin'."

"I'm not a doctor. I'm not even a trained nurse."

"Talk to the woman anyhow." Herb led the way to the surgery. "Ma'am, this is Miss Jane."

The woman was walking the floor with a small wailing child in her arms. She looked at Jane, then accusingly at Herb.

"Where's the doctor?"

"He's very sick," Jane said.

"Can't he look at her? She's been like this since last night. Her stomach hurts real bad, and she don't want to straighten out her legs."

"Put her down on the table and let me look at her, then I'll go up and ask the doctor what to to."

The little girl shrieked as cramps knotted her stomach. In spite of the child's clinging arms the mother laid her down. She turned on her side and drew her knees up to her chest. Jane felt her forehead, then discovered that her little stomach was bloated and hard. She knew immediately the little girl was constipated. She felt a stab of fear. Children died from locked bowels.

"When was her last bowel movement?"

"I ain't sure. Few days ago maybe."

"Stay here and rub her stomach. I'll go up and talk to the doctor."

Jane hurried back up the stairs. The doctor's eyes were on the door when she entered.

"I heard a young'un crying."

"The child's about two years old. Her stomach is hard as a rock. She insists on keeping her knees drawn up. The mother isn't sure when she had a bowel movement."

"Constipated."

"It's what I thought. What do I do?"

"Take the corner of a towel and twist it into a cone shape. Coat it heavily with petroleum jelly and work it like a corkscrew up into the rectum. While you do that hold your hand tight over her lower abdomen. If that doesn't work put several spoonfuls of warm olive oil up in there with the bulb syringe. It's been cleaned. After you use it, pour boiling water over and through the tube."

"If that doesn't work, shall I give an enema?"

"That's right. Give her an enema using warm water with a spoonful of soda."

"Is the soda in the surgery?"

"In a jar on the top shelf. It's labeled. Wash your hands before and after with the bar of castile soap on the washstand. Check the stool for worms. If she's got 'em tell the mother to bring her back tomorrow."

"I'm not a doctor."

"I know that. You said you took care of sick kids."

"Yes. But—"

"No buts. Go do it." He turned his head and closed his eyes.

Responsibility for the sick child weighed heavily on Jane for the next hour. She first used the petroleum jelly, then the warm olive oil. When nothing passed, she prepared the enema. Finally, with the mother holding the screaming child, Jane was able, after the third attempt, to get enough water in the lower bowel to dislodge the blockage. The defecation came in the form of hard round balls. The exhausted child stopped crying and drooped against her mother.

Jane checked the stool and found no signs of worms.

"Don't let her eat a lot of bread for a while. She should have apples or raisins."

By the time they were ready to leave the surgery, the child was sleeping peacefully on the mother's shoulder.

"Thank you, Miss Jane. When one of my young'uns is sick, I'm scared plumb silly."

"I can understand that."

"My man will be around to pay."

"There's no charge. I'm not a doctor."

"Ya ort to be. Ya got a knack for it."

Jane carried the teakettle from the kichen and scalded the syringe, the bedpan and anything she had used in connection with the child's visit. She had learned to do that from a young doctor who donated two days' service a month to the orphanage. Jane had been attracted to him until he refused to come and tend a sick child because he had plans to attend a ball given by one of Denver's leading citizens.

While she cleaned the surgery, Jane chided herself for feeling so good about what she had done. She washed her hands again with the castile soap, then took the Bible she found tucked among Doc's medical books and left the room.

Chapter 8

POLLY was worried. Jane had not been beside her when she awoke, nor had she been in the cookhouse when Polly had gone there for breakfast. The valise that held all of Janes's belongings was still sitting at the foot of the portion of the bed where they slept. Jane would not have left Timbertown without it.

Where was she?

When Polly asked Sunday, she shrugged off Jane's absence by saying she must be around somewhere and that Polly shouldn't worry. Sunday had been so excited about the activity in town that she had paid scant attention to Polly's concern. The bubbly, energetic girl had eaten a hasty breakfast and then disappeared after announcing to one and all that she was as good as any man with a saw and a hammer and better than some, especially a lumberjack with two left hands and the space between his ears filled with nothing but hot air.

Another huge wagon pulled by two teams of mules and loaded with lumber came into town. Polly stood on the porch of the women's barracks and watched the mule skinner send his whip out over the backs of the dray animals.

"Gee, Buster! Wo-ah, Dewey! Move on over thar, Big Boy!"

The orders were punctuated with cracks of the whip. The wicked lash could take a strip of hide from the animals, but as long as the sound was sufficient to make them obey, the mule skinner was careful not to strike the beasts.

Polly cringed against the wall. The wheels of the huge wagon were higher than her head. But it wasn't the wagon that frightened her, it was the voice of the mule skinner. It sounded like that of the man who had violated her. The driver was not the same man, of course. She realized that at first glance because she'd never, as long as she lived, forget the whiskered, ferret-like face and cruel hands of Dank Forestal.

"Hello, little lady."

Polly jumped and let out a cry of fright. The voice had come close to her ear. She hadn't even been aware that the man had come up the side of the building and stepped onto the porch. Her attention had been on the freight wagon.

Polly moved sideways along the wall.

"Scare ya, did I?"

A confident grin showed a large space between the man's two front teeth, one of which had been broken off. His nose was flat and pushed slightly to the side. He had thick black brows and hair. A heavy mustache covered his upper lip.

"Yo're the prettiest woman here. Me an' you's goin' to get acquainted. Name's Milo. Milo Callahan. Ya ever heard of Callahan Lumber Company over in the Bitterroot?"

Polly shook her head.

"I own it. Half anyway. Ya see, I ain't just no ordinary lumberjack. I could buy and sell these fellers here twice over if I had a mind to," he bragged. "If yo're lookin' for a man ta set ya up in one a them cabins, take care of ya real good, I'm the man."

Polly shook her head vigorously. "No."

"Ya don't mean that, honey. Ya want a good man 'tween your legs. It's why ya come here, ain't it?"

"No! I came to work."

He chuckled. His hot dark eyes moved to her breasts and lingered.

"Ya come to get a man. Girl like you can't get along in this country without one. Ya got to have somebody to feed ya, look after ya."

"I'll work and take care of myself," she blurted.

"If it's work ya want, sweet thin', I can give ya plenty a work right on yore pretty little backside, doin' what women was made to be doin'. Ya'd not have to do a lick a work outdoors, little doll. All ya'd have to do is wait fer me to come pleasure ya."

"Go away!"

"Ya don't mean that, honey," he said again.

"I said . . . go away!" Polly began to tremble. She looked around for help. The big dray wagon had stopped in the street in front of the building and was blocking the view. She glanced toward the door. She would not be able to get around him to reach it.

"Name's Polly, ain't it? Pretty name for a pretty gal. I'm puttin' in for ya, Polly. I want ya for my woman. I like 'em young an' soft and squealin'—" He reached out a finger to touch her cheek and she jerked away. "Don't shy away. I'll be real good to ya. Ya ain't had no man, have ya?" His hand came out and clasped her wrist.

"Get away! Let go of me!" Polly tried to pull away, but her strength was nothing against his.

"Don't fight it, honeybunch. Ya'll come to like what a real man does to ya. I've done set my sights on ya and I usually gets—"

"Ya rotten sonofabitch!"

Herb grasped Milo by the back of the neck with a powerful hand. He jerked him off his feet, off the porch, and threw him to the ground. Agile as a cat, Milo rolled to his feet with a fist drawn back.

"Why'd ya do that for? Ya dealin' in, kid?" he snarled before he looked closely at the hard face of the man who stood ready to draw his gun. Sudden fear sent a shiver racing over his skin.

Hellfire! The bastard was set to kill him!

"I made the first move. What's yores?"

Milo's eyes flicked down to the hand hovering over the six-gun strapped to a thigh the size of a tree trunk. Christamighty! This big overgrown kid was coiled like a rattler ready to strike.

"I ain't armed."

"Ya got fists, same as me."

Milo looked at the size of the man challenging him. Hell, he was outweighed by fifty pounds.

"Make up yore mind, if ya got one." Herb's sarcastic tone added to the insult.

Milo knew when to stand and when to back down. He grinned and winked.

"I was just talkin' to her. Shit, friend, that's what she's here for, ain't it?"

Herb snorted an obscenity and suppressed the urge to pound the man to a bloody pulp.

"No, that ain't what she's here for. And I ain't yore friend. I don't have addle-brained, shit-eatin' buzzards for friends."

"Touchy, ain't ya? Why'd they brin' the women in fer if they warn't to be used?"

"They wasn't brought here to be *used*. My job's to keep scum like you away from 'em. Especially this'n."

"Ya puttin' a claim on this baggage?"

"She's not *baggage* to be *claimed*." Herb's face froze into lines of anger.

Milo shrugged. "She ain't the only woman here lookin' for a man." He eyed. Polly with smiling interest. "But she's the youngest and I do like 'em young. I'll give her a day or two. She'll come 'round to my way a thinkin'."

Milo turned away and forced himself to walk slowly and confidently. *Ya snot-nosed sonofabitch! Ya'll get yore whacker cut off or my name ain't Milo Callahan.*

Herb watched until Milo joined the crew digging the foundation for another building before he stepped back up onto the porch.

"He hurt ya, Miss Polly?"

She shook her head, but she rubbed the spot on her arm where Milo had grabbed her. When she finally looked up at Herb, she was blinking tears from her soft dark eyes.

"Thank you." Her quivering voice came out in a whisper.

"Shoot, Miss Polly. I should'a come over here soon as I couldn't see ya for the wagon."

"I . . . I can't find Jane." Tears overflowed and ran down Polly's cheeks. The vision of the months ahead filled with fear and uncertainties almost overwhelmed her.

"Here, now. It's nothin' to cry 'bout. Miss Jane's over to the house lookin' after Doc. Here, now—" Herb moved so that his broad shoulders would shield her from the road when he heard the freight wagon moving. "Lordy mercy! Have ya been standin' over here a 'frettin' 'bout that? I should'a come and eased yore mind."

Polly took a cloth from the string purse looped over her arm and dabbed at her eyes.

"I was afraid she'd gone."

"Doc's mighty sick. Miss Jane made mush and got him to eat some of it. I ain't knowin' how she did it. Doc can be stubborn as a army mule when he sets his mind." Herb's face was furrowed with concern. "Ya all right now? I'm sorry I didn't get here sooner, Miss Polly. I saw ya standin' here, and was kind'a keepin' my eye on ya when that dray wagon moved in. I never even saw that mangy polecat come over here."

"He came along the building. I didn't see him or I'd a gone back in."

"Ya shouldn't ought to have to be worryin'. T.C. wants womenfolk to feel safe in this town."

He looked down on her soft, shiny light-brown hair. It was parted in the middle with loose braids coiled over each of her ears. She was as sweet and as helpless as a kitten. She had been sorely used by a lowlife passing himself off as a man. Herb made a silent vow that if he ever set eyes on the varmint, he would gun him down the same as he would a rabid dog.

He didn't know why he'd had the sudden urge to cross the road. Something had drawn him to come to Polly when she needed him. He was so glad he had. The poor little thing was trembling like a little scared rabbit.

"If ya want, I'll take ya over to the house where Miss Jane is." He spoke softly so as not to frighten her.

"Mr. Kilkenny wouldn't care?" She raised large dark eyes to search his face.

"Naw. He'd not stand for anybody botherin' ya."

"I don't want to cause trouble."

"Miss Polly, that feller just might of been tryin' to court ya, in a rough way, that is. I can't blame him for wantin' to, 'cause yo're awful pretty." Herb was trying to put *her* at ease. "I don't want ya to be feelin' scared."

"I . . . can't help it. He's so sure." She shuddered and looked away from him.

"Sure a what?"

"Ah . . . sure I can't take care of myself, that I got to take a—" Her voice faded when she found she couldn't utter the distasteful word.

"—Ya don't have to take anybody. Ya don't have to do nothin' ya don't want to."

"I think it's why Jane wants to leave. She says Mr. Kilkenny brought us here to marry with his lumberjacks and mill workers."

"T.C.'s job is to build this town. He needs womenfolk to do women's work. If a woman wants to wed, she can. If she don't want to, she'll have work here. He made that plain right off."

"Jane don't like him."

"T.C.'s all right. Him and Colin is straight-shootin' as they come."

"She don't trust him."

"Maybe we can change her mind."

"Oh, I wish we could."

The smile Polly gave him was one of girlish sweetness, warm with the glow of complete trust.

"We'll work on it."

When they stepped off the porch to cross the road, his

hand beneath Polly's elbow, Herb was walking about two feet off the ground and his heart was like a runaway horse in his chest.

The tall, slim woman shook the mass of unruly blond hair from her forehead, lifted the end of a plank and playfully jabbed it at the man on the other end. They were transporting the sawed lumber from the wagon to the site where men were erecting the frame of the hotel. She moved freely in her dark split skirt, but the faded red shirt tucked tightly into the waistband clung to her, emphasizing her small waist and full breasts. Her sleeves were rolled to the elbows and she wore a pair of leather gloves.

Colin had been watching her for some time and listening as her merry laughter rang out. There was nothing coy or pretentious about her. She was enjoying the physical labor and the companionship of her fellow workers.

Colin was smiling when T.C. stepped up onto the porch.

"She's quite a woman." T.C.'s eyes followed Colin's.

"She keeps the fellers unloading that wagon movin'," Colin said with a chuckle. "They don't dare slow up and let her outdo them."

"Her name is Sunday Polinski. She told me she was damn good at making cedar shingles."

"I don't doubt it. I saw her swing an axe."

"Have the men treated her right?"

"Not a one's laid a hand on her yet."

"She's a woman who can take care of herself. I don't know as I'd want to tangle with her if she had an edge. She could hurt a man real bad."

Both men noticed Patrice picking her way daintily across the rough road. Her shiny black hair was piled high on her shapely head and secured with a fancy comb. Large silver loops hung from her ears. Even though it was a warm day she wore an elaborately decorated shawl over her shoulders.

"I think I'll go check up on Doc." T.C. headed for the door.

"Some friend you are," Colin muttered.

Patrice came up the steps to the porch. "Morning, Colin."

"Mornin'."

"The goings-on here are enough to make a person's head swim. I swear to goodness. Does T.C. really think he can build up this old town?"

"I guess he does or he wouldn't have started it."

"How long are you staying here, Colin?"

"I haven't decided."

"I can't imagine you liking this place. When are you going back to your ranch?"

"Sometime."

"Go now and take me." Patrice was undaunted by Colin's short answers. "Please, Colin. I'll be a help to you. I swear it."

Colin looked at her and shook his head in amazement.

"I've not completely lost my mind. You're married, Patrice. And if you weren't, I'd still not take you. Christ on a horse! You'd be about as much help on a ranch as a newborn babe."

"I can learn—"

"No.

"I heard that you and T.C. brought a big herd of longhorns up from Texas."

"We did." Colin didn't feel it necessary to tell her that by building this town T.C. was helping to pay for them.

"I hope they're there when you get back. Rustlers stole half a herd from Ramon."

"They'll be there."

"How can you be sure? Who is watching the herd? Who is watching the men watching the herd?"

"That is none of your business. Is there anything else you want to know?"

"Well, my goodness. I was just trying to make conversation. You're getting to be as rude as T.C." After a pause, she placed her hand on his arm. "I'm sorry, Colin. I want to talk to you, be with you, and you . . . just won't cooperate."

"We have nothing to talk about, Señora Cabeza. I told you that last night. You shouldn't have come here. You should be at home with your husband."

"You're still bitter about that."

"Think what you want."

"Ramon threatened to kill me."

"Ramon is too tight with a buck to destroy his valuable property. And to Ramon you are like a beautiful piece of furniture to show off and prove how well-off he is. It's a life you chose."

"But he said he'd kill me."

"He may give you a beating, but he won't leave permanent scars."

"How can you be so callous after all we've been to each other?"

"To each other? If I remember right the feeling was all on one side. I'll admit that I owe Ramon a debt of gratitude. He married you and brought me to my senses before I made the biggest mistake of my life."

"Colin! You're being . . . unkind." Her large dark eyes filled with tears.

"I'm being truthful."

Patrice sniffed and dabbed at her eyes with a lacy handkerchief. After a moment or two she looked up to see that Colin was unmoved by her tears. He was watching the activity down the street.

"Did you ask T.C. to find me another place to stay?"

"No. Look around you, Patrice. They're workin' to fix up the hotel and the other buildings. You can bed down in the funerary. I don't think you'd be alone for very long." Colin gestured toward a narrow building with a sagging roof.

"You're poking fun at me now."

"I'm tellin' it as it is."

"This is a big house. Surely there's one little room I can use. You don't know how awful it is to be in the room with those dreadful low-class women. Look at that blond hussy out there unloading lumber like a man." Patrice pointed a finger toward Sunday. "She's not got one ladylike quality. She's loud and crude and—"

"—Carrying her own weight; not sitting on her keister expecting to be waited on."

"Colin! I can't believe that you'd approve of a woman working alongside those rough men. Look at her! She loves it. What would your mother say?"

"My mother was that kind of woman." Colin's voice was hard and impatient. "During the war she raised sheep, spun the wool into thread, and knitted socks and caps so she could feed three little kids and a young girl. She did more than that, she gave up the farm where she'd lived all her life to take us away when she thought we'd be taken from her."

Colin settled his hat more firmly on his head and crossed his arms over his chest. He was angry at himself for even talking about his mother to this selfish creature.

"Colin," Patrice began again in a wheedling voice. "Please ask T.C. to let me stay here."

"Ask him yourself," he said as T.C. came out onto the porch and headed down the steps.

"T.C., I need to speak to you for a minute."

"Then make it snappy. I've got to get some papers over to Jeb."

"It seems you have time for everyone but me."

"This may come as a surprise to you, but I'm too busy to jump when you holler. What do you want?" He spoke with exaggerated patience.

"Well . . . I'd really appreciate it, T.C., if you'd make room for me here. I'll take any little space. I promise not to be in the way—"

"There's not a spare bed in the house, Patrice."

"I'll sleep on the floor."

"No, señora. You're not moving in here. When the hotel is opened you're welcome to rent a room there for as long as you can pay for it."

"It'll take weeks for that run-down thing to be fixed."

"Then you've got something to look forward to. Don't you have washing to do?"

"Don't be funny!" she snapped. "Why do you give that big lummox . . . Herb, or what ever his name is, a room here and you won't give me one?"

"I don't have to explain my actions to you. But I'll tell you this—I wouldn't want you in my house even if I had the room. When your husband gets here, he's goin' to be as mad as a hornet. I've got enough on my mind without having to defend myself against a cocky little rooster who thinks I've compromised his wife."

Patrice sucked in a deep breath. Anger made her eyes hard and her nostrils flare.

"Ramon knows me well enough to know that I'd never consider having an affair with *you*!"

"That takes a load off my mind. I guess then he's Colin's worry 'cause he'll be sure you're sleepin' with someone." T.C. turned his back to her and spoke to Colin. "Bill said to cut out a young steer and get it ready for the pit. Jeb struck a bargain with the mill boss and the timber bull to keep the crew here for three days."

"I'll get right to it." Colin tipped his hat politely to Patrice, stepped off the porch and crossed the street.

"Hold on, Colin," Patrice called and hurried after him. "I'll walk with you."

Herb helped Doc use the chamber pot. When he came down to the kitchen his brow was wrinkled with concern.

"He's passin' blood, Miss Jane. Lots of it."

"Oh, dear. Is he in pain?"

"He's begging for laudanum."

"He knows laudanum is addictive, and he also knows the end is near. I think we should give it to him."

"I was hopin' ya'd think that."

Jane gave the doctor one drop of laudanum and sat with him until he fell asleep.

When she returned to the kitchen, she put the potatoes on for the soup she was making for him, then rolled her sleeves up past her elbows and wrapped one of Herb's dirty shirts about her waist, tying the sleeves in the back. In a large pan of warm soapy water, she washed every dish and utensil in the kitchen, then scrubbed the table and the counters. She found a broom that looked as if it had never been used, dampened it in the water to hold down the dust and thoroughly swept the room.

Such a nice room, she thought as she worked, but so bare. Just a few extras would make a world of difference; curtains at the window, a cloth on the table, a lamp with a shiny chimney, the smell of bread baking. The larder was empty except for cornmeal, potatoes, salt and coffee. Herb had brought over a pail of milk and a pan of biscuits. She had eaten a couple with milk for her noonday meal.

Jane was enjoying the fresh smell of scrubbed wood when she heard T.C.'s voice in the hall. A minute later he appeared in the doorway.

"How's Doc?"

"Sleeping."

His eyes roamed the kitchen, then honed in on her for a long moment before he spoke.

"Looks good. Get what you need to stock the larder from the mercantile and put it on my tab. Herb can get meat from the smokehouse."

"No."

"No?"

"I'll not stock your larder, and I'll not cook your meals."

"Why not? You'd cook for Doc and Herb and Colin, if he's here."

"I'm not working here on a permanent basis, Mr. Kilkenny. I'll be here but a day or two, or until I can find transport back to the station."

"You'd run out on Doc? Herb says you're the only one that can do anything with him. He also said you've a knack in the surgery. We need you here."

"I've made up my mind, Mr. Kilkenny. No amount of persuasion from you will change it."

He shrugged in a way she had come to recognize as not giving up the argument, but postponing it.

"Then make out a list of the things needed to stock the kitchen and give it to Herb. Meanwhile you've got a patient waiting in the surgery."

"*I've* got a patient?"

"One of the loggers let an adze slip and cut a hole in his leg. Unless you're willing to let him bleed to death, you'd better get in there."

"Well for goodness sake! Why didn't you say so instead of standing there yammering?"

Chapter 9

JANE removed her makeshift apron and hung it on the back of a chair. She smoothed her hair back with her palms and hurried across the hall to the surgery. Much to her discomfort, Kilkenny stayed close behind her.

The injured man sat on a chair holding a blood-soaked rag to his thigh.

"Murphy, this is Miss Love. She'll fix you up."

"Where's the doc?"

"He's very sick. Don't worry, Miss Love knows what she's doing."

Jane nodded a greeting and went immediately to the washbowl to wash her hands with Doc's castile soap. On hearing Kilkenny's words that she knew what she was doing, she rolled her eyes toward the ceiling. The man was an accomplished liar. She dried her hands and turned to look at the heavily bearded patient. He was middle-aged and built like an oak tree.

"Help him up onto the table, Mr. Kilkenny, so I can see the wound."

"I ain't needin' no help." The timberman, embarrassed to be showing weakness in front of a woman, hopped to the table and perched on the edge.

"Lie down. Mr. Kilkenny, please remove that dirty rag and split the leg of his britches with your knife."

"Now, hold on. These be the only britches I got."

"Would you rather take them off?" Jane asked, with a haughty lift of her brows.

"Consarn it!" He looked at T.C. for help.

"You can get another pair at the mercantile."

T.C. unwrapped the rag from around the massive thigh, then split the man's britches, exposing a deep cut several inches long above his knee. Jane did her best not to shudder when she saw the gaping hole. She went to Doc's medicine cabinet and plucked a wad of clean lint from a container. She returned to the table with the lint and a bottle marked ANTISEPTIC. She glanced up to see T.C. watching her with eyes so narrow that she could just barely see the silver glint. She looked back at him with more composure than she possessed.

"While I clean the wound, wash your hands. You'll have to hold the flesh together while I stitch it."

"Stitch it?" The man's head and shoulders came up off the table. "Jist put some salve on it and tie it up."

"No. That won't do at all. Germs that cause lockjaw and putrid flesh can get in the wound. I can either sew it or put a hot iron to it. Which do you prefer?"

"Sew it."

Jane's shoulders slumped with relief. What in the world would she have done if he had chosen the hot iron?

Murphy dropped his head back down and rolled it from side to side, lifted it again and looked at her.

"Ma'am, have ya done this before?"

"Many times," Jane's brows went up as she lied convincingly. "I'm just a few weeks from my Medical Certificate."

"It's glad I am to know it, ma'am. I just ain't never seen no woman doctor."

"This is the eighties, Mr. Murphy. There are some mighty good women doctors practicing in the West. Dr. Mary Walker was a surgeon in the U.S. Army during the war. They said she did a fine job." While she was cleaning the wound Jane spoke of Mary Walker's struggle to make a place for herself in her chosen profession. The story was to keep her mind as well as Murphy's off what she was doing.

"Wal, don't that jist take the cake? I ain't never heard 'bout a woman doin' all that."

Jane went back to Doc's supply cabinet and for the count of a dozen heartbeats closed her eyes; she wondered if she would be able to do what had to be done. She had helped the doctor stitch wounds at the orphanage, and had one time closed the wound of a plowman when the headmistress refused to send for the doctor. If she didn't act now, she told herself firmly, the man could get lockjaw and die.

After threading the needle with linen thread from a spool in the cabinet, she doused it in the bottle marked CARBOLIC ACID. By the time she had returned to the table, she had her features well under control.

The hardest part was piercing the flesh with the needle the first time. After that she worked swiftly and efficiently. It helped that the logger never flinched while she closed the gaping hole in his thigh. T.C. proved to be helpful, too. He held the flesh together and she worked around his strong clean fingers. After Jane smeared the wound with salve, T.C. wrapped the man's thigh with a length of clean cloth and Jane was free to wash her bloody hands.

"Thanks, Doc." Murphy sat up on the edge of the table.

"I'm not a doctor," Jane said over her shoulder. "You'd better come back in a few days and let someone here take a look. You'll need the bandage changed and after a while the thread will have to be plucked out."

"Someone? Ain't ya goin' to be here, Doc?"

"I'm not a—"

"She'll be here, Murphy. Do you need help getting to your tent?"

"Naw. I can manage." He hobbled to the door. "Much obliged, Doc."

T.C. walked with the man to the door and saw him off the porch before he returned to the surgery to lounge in the door and watch her.

"Did you mean it about the certificate?"

"You know I didn't. The man needed reassurance."

"You're about as good a liar as you are a doctor."

"Would you rather I told him that the sight of that hole in his leg almost caused me to throw up all over him? And that I wasn't sure I would be able to poke him with the needle?"

"That bad, huh? You're not only a good liar, you're gutsy. I thought you were enjoying yourself." T.C.'s silver eyes glinted mischievously from between heavy black lashes and a chuckle rumbled from his chest.

Jane returned the supplies to the cabinet, her body stiff with indignation. She hated being the source of his amusement.

"Am I to take that as a compliment?"

"That's the way I meant it." His eyes ranged up and down her length.

"A backhanded compliment if I ever heard one."

She had not felt as angry with any single person in a long while as she was now. This man who was keeping her here when she so desperately wanted to leave made her furious. Since there was no possible way of releasing her anger without humiliating herself, she remained quiet while she finished putting the surgery in order.

"You've got blood on your dress." T.C.'s eyes flicked down over her breasts and on to the spots on her skirt. "Use one of Doc's aprons next time."

"There wouldn't be a next time if you'd help me get back to the station."

"Doc would be pleased at the job you did on Murphy," T.C. said, ignoring her remark. Pinpoints of light glittered in his silver eyes.

"I doubt that. Excuse me." Jane went to the door and tried to pass him. "I'll soak the stain in cold water before it sets." She spoke quietly, but nervousness and anger had made her wet under the arms.

She knew that on no account must she let this infuriating man suspect how much his very presence played on her emotions. He was arrogant, insufferably so, and yet, she instinctively knew that he took his responsibilities seriously and that he left no stone unturned in order to complete whatever task he set out to do. What really disturbed her the most was knowing that he would despise her more than anyone else when her secret was revealed.

T.C. moved just enough for her to squeeze by. Her shoulder rubbed against his chest, wisps of dark-red hair caught in the whiskers on his chin. She smelled like soap and . . . sunshine. She was both fascinating and irritating. He was determined that she would not leave Timbertown until he satisfied his curiosity about her reasons for leaving. She was afraid of something here. He was sure of that.

After Jane disappeared into the kitchen, T.C. went back down the hallway to the porch. Herb and Polly were coming up the steps. He tipped his hat to Polly and paused to speak to Herb.

"Miss Love will make out a list of supplies needed to stock the larder. Get her what she wants and put it on my tab. It's time we had meals here at the house now that there's a decent cook around." He gave Herb a good-natured swat on the shoulder.

"I ain't no great shakes as a cook, I admit it. I'll get to the mercantile as soon as I take Miss Polly in to stay with Miss Jane."

T.C. had not missed the possessive hand on the girl's elbow. The thought occurred to him that without Doc, Herb would have nothing to tie to. The boy, man now, had spent the past few years taking care of his old friend. Perhaps it was good that he had met someone else who needed his protection.

"Miss Wright, I'd be pleased if you'd help Miss Love. She has her hands full with Doc and the patients that come to the surgery. You'll need to take over the cleaning as well as helping with meals. Ask Miss Love what needs to be done. You'll be paid a wage along with your bed and board."

"Yes, sir! Oh, I'd be pleased to."

"Herb, do you think you could find a place to throw down a bedroll so the ladies could have your room? It's right across from Doc's and he's going to have to have someone sit with him nights. Colin can come in with me. For propriety's sake the ladies should have the upstairs to themselves—except for Doc, of course."

"Sure thing, T.C. I'll throw my blankets there in the office or on the porch. See there, Miss Polly. I told you things'd work out." Herb's boyish face was split with a huge grin. "You'll be right here where we can keep a eye out for that feller. He ain't goin' to come messin' around here."

"What feller?" T.C. was quick to pick up on Herb's words and the look he gave the young girl.

"One of the loggers was pesterin' her."

"If he bothers you again, let me know." T.C. stepped off the porch and then turned. "You'd better bring their things over. And, Herb, take two of the cots from over there. A couple of the women can have their places on the bed. You can take one, Colin the other."

T.C. went away whistling, pleased with himself that he had blocked any move Jane could make against staying and working in his house.

"Jane, I was so scared you'd gone." Polly left Herb in the doorway and went to put her arms around Jane's waist and hug her. "Mr. Kilkenny said I can stay here and help you. Ain't that grand?"

"Yes, grand," Jane said halfheartedly. "I wouldn't have gone away without telling you. Besides, my things are still there, aren't they?"

Jane's eyes went from Polly's flushed happy face to Herb's. He was grinning like a schoolboy with a frog in his pocket.

"What's that on your dress?" Polly was looking at the large wet spot just below the waist.

"I fixed a cut on a man's leg and got blood on it. I soaked it with cold water."

"Miss Jane's real good at doctorin'." Herb's eyes were filled with admiration. "I ain't no good a'tall. Even lancin' a boil makes me sick." He failed to see Jane grimace and hurried on. "Doc likes you, Miss Jane. He don't like many folks."

Jane had to smile. "Doc's got you buffaloed. He only browbeats those who let him."

"T.C. said yo're makin' out a list for me to get at the mercantile. He said we'd have meals here now that thar's somebody beside me to cook 'em."

"I haven't started the list." Jane poured the water off the potatoes, added milk and set the pan on the back of the stove. "I'm making potato soup for Doc when he wakes up. You make out the list, Polly. Herb can show you what's here and what's not. I'm goin' up to look in on the doctor."

Jane made her departure before they saw the tears of frustration in her eyes. T.C. Kilkenny was weaving her into a web. He was doing his best to make it impossible for her to leave. First he had her caring for the doctor, and now taking over in the surgery. And somehow he sought to lay a blanket of guilt on her if she deserted Polly.

Doc was awake, his eyes on the doorway. "I was getting all set to yell."

"Why in the world would you do that?"

"You said you'd be here."

"I can't stay here every single minute." Her voice came out on a lower note. "Don't give me any sass, Dr. Foote. I just sewed up a deep cut in a man's leg, and my stomach is not in very stable condition."

"Call me Nathan. I like hearing you say it. Sewed up a cut, did you? Find what you needed? Tell me what you did."

Jane sat on the chair beside the bed and told him, step by step, what she had done from the first time she washed her hands to the last.

"Needle sharp enough?"

Jane nodded.

"I give them a few strokes on the whetstone after I use them."

"He wanted only some salve and a bandage, but I was afraid he'd get lockjaw or putrid flesh and his leg might have to come off."

"You did the right thing." Doc turned from her and looked out the window. "I've filled a wagon with arms and legs. Fifteen minutes was all the time I could give each of the poor bastards. Many's the time I wished I'd been a lawyer, a merchant, or even a politician."

Jane reached for his hand and held it in hers.

"Think of how many men would have died if you'd become a lawyer, a merchant or a politician. Count the wins, Nathan, not the losses."

"Where did you learn these words of wisdom you're always spouting, girl?" His bony fingers squeezed hers. "Tell me about your folks."

Jane felt suddenly weak. She looked at the man on the bed. He had honest eyes, light brown and surrounded by tiny wrinkles. They looked frankly into hers. Instinct told her that he was not prying, he was genuinely interested.

"My mother died when I was very young. She was beautiful and talented. She played the piano and the organ. My life was never the same after that. All I had was Aunt Alice, and she was not a relative but a dear friend of my mother's."

"Your papa?"

"I only saw him one time. He came to the house after Mamma died. It was nighttime. He wrapped me in a blanket and carried me out of Aunt Alice's house to a carriage and took me to an orphanage. I stayed there until a few months ago working for my bed and board. So you see there is nothing mysterious or unusual about me."

"I think there is. You're smart and perceptive. Why did you come here?"

"I didn't want to work at that orphanage for the rest of my life taking care of someone else's children. I wanted to see and feel and experience life outside that place. I read the notice about the jobs for women here in Timbertown. I was too naive to realize Mr. Kilkenny had other plans for the single women." She said the last bitterly with a toss of her hair.

The doctor chuckled, then coughed. Jane hurriedly lifted the can beside the bed for him to spit in. Afterward he lay back exhausted.

"T.C.'s got a job to do. He meant no harm. I'm sure that most of the women knew what they were getting into."

"I certainly didn't. Do you think you could eat a spoonful or two of potato soup? You slept through the noon meal."

"Ah, girl." The doctor made a face. "I ate that mush you were poking down me. Isn't that enough for one day?"

Jane tilted her head and wrinkled her brow as if she were studying the matter.

"If I were lying *there* and you were sitting *here*, how would you answer that question?"

There was a twinkle in the eyes that turned to her.

"You're a pistol, Jane. I'd say, 'Hush your damn complaining and eat the soup.' "

"Well?"

"Get the damn soup," he said with resignation.

Jane heard Herb and Polly in the hall seconds before they appeared in the doorway.

"Are ya awake, Doc?"

"I got my eyes open, haven't I?"

"I want ya to meet someone. This is Miss Polly Wright. She's goin' to be stayin' here with Miss Jane. They'll be sleepin' in my room just across—"

"—Wait a minute," Jane interrupted quickly. "I've not heard anything about this. What do you mean we'll sleep in your room?"

"Good idea," Doc said, ignoring Jane's protest. "How do you do, Miss Wright?" He was watching Herb, who had eyes only for the young girl and the sudden frightened expression that crossed her face when Jane spoke.

"Jane?" Polly asked hesitantly. "Mr. Kilkenny was kind enough to say I could help you here."

"Mr. Kilkenny takes much for granted where I'm concerned, Polly."

"Ya mean ya don't want me?"

"Lord o'mercy, Polly. You know I didn't mean that at all."

"Don't ya like workin' here? Has Mr. Kilkenny been mean to ya?"

"No. He hasn't been exactly mean. He just arranges things to suit himself without regard to what others want to do. We can talk about this later." She tried to shoo Polly toward the door. "The doctor doesn't want to hear about . . . our . . . my differences with Mr. Kilkenny."

"Yes, he does." Doc's voice coming from the bed was

strong. "The doctor wants to hear about everything going on here. Just because I'm flat on my back doesn't mean my brain isn't working. And I want my soup, Jane. Herb and Miss Wright will keep me company while you get it."

Jane turned on him. "You've gotten all-fired bossy of a sudden."

"It's not sudden. I've always been bossy. Ask Herb."

Jane gave them all a fulminating look and left the room. She paused on the stairway before she reached the bottom and leaned against the wall. Her hand sought the notes in her pocket. They were real. She brought out the latest one and reread it. *leave here yu be sorry*. Was it only this morning that she had found this last warning?

"Polly, did you find Jane?"

Sunday called and came over to speak to Polly and Herb as they passed on their way to the mercantile.

She was not the only one who noticed the couple. Milo Callahan stopped work to watch them make their way to the porch of the store, and his dark eyes seethed with anger.

"She's over at Mr. Kilkenny's. We're goin' to stay there. Jane's takin' care of the doctor and I'm goin' to help her."

"You two sure took the prize." Sunday laughed and winked at Herb. "That'll make the biddies back there at the henhouse crazy."

"Oh, Sunday!"

"Go along, I'm just teasin' ya—" She turned to watch a rider who was approaching on a big gray speckled horse. It was the ugliest-colored horse she'd ever seen, but magnificently built.

Herb called out to him. "T.C. was lookin' for ya a while ago."

The rider reined in, tipped his hat to the ladies and swung from the saddle.

"I'll go see as soon as I stable my horse." He looked first at Polly, then at Sunday and waited for Herb to make the introductions.

"Me and Miss Polly is goin' to the store."

Herb was not well-versed in etiquette. Sunday, on the other hand, had not a bashful bone in her body. She yanked off her glove and held out her hand.

"Howdy. I'm Miss Sunday Polinski and this is Miss Polly Wright."

"Colin Tallman."

He took her strong hand in his and looked into the most startlingly direct blue eyes he'd ever seen. They played up and down his length and over the gray stallion like live things, missing nothing. She returned her gaze to his face without the slightest hint of coyness. She was a tall, fine-looking woman with clear golden skin and a great mass of golden-blond curly hair.

Sunday Polinski was not a classic beauty: her mouth was wide, her eyes were large and far apart, and her brown brows were straight and heavy. The curls looked as if they had never been tamed with a hairbrush. Damp with sweat, her tight ringlets framed her face. A pouch-like cloth around her waist was weighed down with nails. From her gloved hand hung a hammer.

"Glad to meet ya, Colin Tallman." Sunday gripped his hand and pumped it up and down. "That's a damn good horse you got there."

"The best. We've been together a long time." Colin stroked the big gray's nose.

Sunday put her hand on the horse's rump and dipped her head to peer beneath his belly.

"I knowed it right off. He's still a stallion. I hate it when a good horse is cut. What's his name?"

"Del Norte."

"You name him?"

"My grandpa did." Colin thumbed back his hat. "He came down with a wild herd from the north. Grandpa caught him. I coaxed him to accept me."

Sunday loosed a hearty laugh. She walked around admiring the horse.

"I like that. Ya didn't *break* him, ya coaxed him to take to ya." She hung the hammer on the cloth belt about her waist and cupped the big gray's face with her palms. Except for the inquiring flick of its ears, the stallion stood rooted in his tracks.

"He's been known to bite," Colin said quickly.

Sunday glanced at Colin. The warning registered in the barest widening of her vivid blue eyes; then the heavy lashes shuttered her gaze and she turned back to the horse.

"Ya ain't goin' to bite me are ya, big fella? Yo're a lucky son of a gun to have a master who coaxed ya and didn't break yore spirit, ya know that?" Her quick laugh broke with a throaty vibrance when the stallion stamped and switched his tail at the pesky flies. "Yo're sayin' ya know what I'm tellin' ya."

"As a rule he doesn't like ladies."

"I'm female, but I can't say I'm a *lady*." She laughed again. "Nothin' I like better than a good horse. Nice meetin' ya, Del Norte. You, too, Colin Tallman."

"Nice meetin' you, Miss Polinski."

"Call me Sunday . . . Monday and Tuesday, too, if ya want to." Musical laughter came from her lips; her eyes looked frankly into his.

Colin smiled and inclined his head in a mock salute. "I'll give it some thought."

"Be seein' ya, Polly." Sunday began to move away. "I can't wait to get back to the henhouse and tell Miss Snooty-puss you and Jane are stayin' at Kilkenny's. She's goin' to have a conniption fit!"

Polly and Herb went into the mercantile and Colin led his horse to the livery. He had never met a woman who was as free-speaking or who appeared to be as happy as Sunday Polinski. He had the impression that she would be able to see herself through any situation. And this puzzled him for the simple reason that she was so obviously feminine.

Colin began to smile as an indescribable feeling of elation came over him.

Chapter 10

JANE lay beside Polly, gazing at the soft glow coming through the doorway of Doc's room. She had given him a few drops of the laudanum, hoping he would get a few hours of sleep, and had left a lamp burning low. For the first time since morning she had a little time for herself.

It was a relief, she grudgingly admitted, to be away from the place Sunday called the henhouse—and from her unknown enemy. Now that she had narrowed the list down to a few of the women, she doubted that she would have closed her eyes all night had she been there. When she had opened her valise here and spread out the contents, she had had no fear that someone would prowl through them.

Her most valuable possession, the framed oil painting of her mother, leaned against the wall; two of her dresses—she had only three besides her good black skirt and white shirtwaist—had been shaken out and hung on a peg beside the door. Not wanting it to appear that she was settling in permanently, she had left the rest of her things in the case.

So much had happened during this one day. Had she really sewn up a cut in a man's leg and given an enema to a sick child? She had tamed the doctor much as she'd had to tame many an unruly child during her years at the orphanage. The poor man was dying and he was afraid, but the last thing he needed now was sympathy. That would take away his dignity and she didn't think the doctor could endure that. Could she leave him if the opportunity came to get back to the station? Of course she could. Any number of the women in the henhouse would be happy to come in to tend to him if they were asked.

Polly had been asleep when Jane tiptoed into their darkened room, undressed, washed and put on her nightdress. For a long while she stood beside the uncurtained window brushing her hair, scraping her scalp with the stiff bristles of the brush and looking down on the street.

Even at this late hour men were moving about among the buildings. Some sat around campfires; some lounged on the porch of the cookhouse, which was well lit as was the saloon. Jane thought briefly of Theda, the flame-haired woman, and imagined her there serving drinks to the men.

She had not thought it possible that so much progress on the buildings could be made in one day. Several roofs had shiny new tin over the rotted shingles, porches were shored up, windows and floors replaced. Framework for the new buildings was in place—and, according to Kilkenny, the crew from the mill and the cutting camps would be here two more days.

Jane felt a momentary pang of sadness at the thought of leaving the town while it was being brought back to life. She would have liked to have been here to see the school filled with children and the church full on Sunday morning. Someday a courthouse would be there in the town square. Maybe even a library . . .

It was soothing to brush her hair. In her opinion, it was her one claim to beauty. When let down, it came to her waist. She'd often wondered what it would be like to have a man standing behind her running the brush lovingly through her hair. It had happened to the heroine in a book she had read, and long after she had finished the last page, the scene stayed in her mind.

Jane was totally unaware that she was a very pretty young woman. She felt old and was convinced that she was plain. A woman was considered in her prime between fifteen and twenty. She would be twenty-four in a day or two. Many women had four or five children by the time they reached her age. She had cared for the children who came and went from the home and had strived not to become too attached to any of them. She had been lonely all her life, longing for someone of her own, a brother or a sister, or a man who would love her despite who she was.

Fanciful notions, she thought with a pang of regret and

scolded herself. She must concentrate on getting away from here and finding a place where she could live without the threat of exposure always hanging over her head. She put away the brush and shivered a little. Nights were as cool here as they were in Denver.

Lying still so as not to disturb Polly, Jane thought about what a difference this day had made in the life of the young girl. Polly had put away the supplies she and Herb had brought from the mercantile and had prepared supper efficiently and cheerfully. Jane was sure that Herb had something to do with that cheer. He had made himself available to help her every possible minute. When it came time to sit down to eat the meal of meat, brown gravy, potatoes and biscuits, Jane had managed to be upstairs in the doctor's room. She went down and ate her supper after T.C. and Colin had left the house.

Jane feared that she was becoming too fond of the testy little doctor, which she had not allowed herself to do with the children because partings were too painful. She sensed that Doc had been lonely too. In another time and another place, she would have been eager to work with him and to learn from him. She was touched when he asked her to call him Nathan.

"For too long I've been just the doc, the sawbones who patched up gunshot holes and fixed broken bones and then was forgotten until needed again. For the little time I have left, I want to be a man called Nathan."

"I can understand that."

"You know, I drank all that whiskey thinking it would speed this thing along and make me forget about it until I was too far gone to care. Didn't help. All it did was make me puke and brought back all the misery and suffering I've seen in my forty-four years. How old are you, Jane?" he asked abruptly.

"How old is an old maid?"

"You'll not let me forget that, will you?"

"No. You jarred me a little with that one—especially the pig-ugly part. I had thought of myself as a raving beauty."

Doc didn't even smile at her joke. He was in pain. It was evident in the way he grimaced from time to time and gripped the bedclothes with his strong, slender surgeon's hands. Visiting with her was a way to put off as long as possible the need for the sleep-inducing drug.

They talked of many things. She told him about each of the women who had come to Timbertown, and about the old buildings being repaired and the new ones going up. Running short of something to talk about, she told him about Bill Wassall thinking she was the lady barber.

Finally, she related Polly Wright's story.

"She was afraid Mr. Kilkenny would send her back when he discovered she was going to have a baby. Before she came over here, she laced herself so tight in a corset that she swooned."

"She's showing that much?"

"She's small and thin. Yes, it shows."

"Foolish, foolish," Doc sputtered.

"She's just sixteen. Yet she had the courage to get away from the man who violated her and who had planned to make money by letting other men violate her."

"A man who'd do such a thing to a young girl should be castrated."

"He's a teamster. Wagons come in here every day. I hope he's not on one of them. I think Polly would go all to pieces if she saw him again."

"Herb's taken a shine to her. I've not seen him stuck on a girl before. If he knows what happened and that teamster shows his face around here, he won't stand a chance."

"He'd kill him?"

"He'd not be singing 'Rock of Ages' after Herb got through with him,"

"Is Herb a gunman?"

"He is if pushed, but he's not a hired gun. Herb's not a

bad kid. Fact is, I'm surprised he's as decent as he is. He's been footloose since he knew hockey from cornbread. When I came on to him, he was a skinny, scared kid in a man's body and had already killed two men. He couldn't be blamed for that. They were trying to kill him. He got handy with a gun to protect himself, and hard life put a chip on his shoulder. We kind of took to each other. He saved my bacon more than once."

"I expect you did the same for him."

"He's smart and could've made something of himself if he'd had the chance."

"How did you happen to come here?"

"Herb and I met Garrick Rowe up at Trinity. He owns the sawmill there and the one here and wanted to get this town going again so the mill workers would bring in their families and stay. A town needs a doctor, and Trinity already had one."

"The surgery is as up to date as the one or two that I saw in Denver."

"That's all mine down there. T.C. just furnished me a place to put it."

"They got a bargain."

"I know now that I shouldn't have taken the job. I knew even then I wasn't going to last long, but I figured I had time to get things started and someone else could take over. A man can't just sit around and wait to die. This thing just came on faster than I thought it would. Maybe the whiskey helped after all. Should'a drunk more of it."

"Do you want the laudanum now?" She had been watching his fingers pluck at the covers.

"Yeah, give it to me. You need some rest, girl. Your eyes look like two burnt holes in a blanket."

"If you want me in the night, call out. I'm a light sleeper."

With her palms together, her hands beneath her cheek, Jane lay listening to the sounds and recalling the conversation. She heard a chair scrape downstairs, and then low masculine voices. Without being quite aware of it, she felt safer here than she'd felt since leaving her tiny room at the Methodist Home. She drifted off into a dreamless sleep.

Jane rolled over on the bed and sat up. She had been deeply asleep and the next instant, she was wide awake. A sound had awakened her, and she hurried across the hall to the doctor's room, her feet bare, her nightdress swirling about her calves. Doc was leaning over the side of the bed gagging and spitting in the chamber pot. What had awakened her was the clatter of the lid dropping to the floor.

She wet a cloth in the tin basin and waited for him to finish. Finally, exhausted, he lay back on the pillow.

"You didn't need to get up, girl."

"I told you I was a light sleeper." She bent over him and gently wiped his face. When her hair fell down over his hand, he combed his fingers through the silky strands.

"Been a long time since I touched hair like this."

When Jane saw Doc's eyes go to the doorway, she turned. T.C. was standing there, shirtless and barefoot.

"I heard something—" The sight of Jane in the modest white gown buttoned to the neck and cuffed at the wrists, her ankles and feet bare, and that magnificent dark-red hair flowing over her shoulders and down her back, sent a rush of blood into his groin.

"What . . . what . . ." she sputtered and backed away from the bed, her arms crossed over her breasts. "I'm . . . not dressed!"

"Hellfire!" he snorted "Doesn't seem to bother you that Doc's seeing you in your nightclothes. Besides, nothing's showing but your bare feet. I've seen plenty of them." Despite the suffocating heat that flashed through him, depriving him of breath, T.C. managed to speak normally.

"I had to puke and dropped the damn pot lid." Doc's voice broke the embarrassed silence.

T.C. pulled his eyes from a vision that would haunt his nights for weeks to come, walked into the room and looked down at the man on the bed.

"You all right, Doc?"

"That's a hell of a question to ask a dying man." Doc scowled up at T.C. "Just my luck to have the prettiest woman in the territory come to my room in her nightdress and I be on my last legs."

Flushing to the roots of her hair, Jane stared first at one man and then the other, knowing there was no way to get out of the mortifying situation except to flee, and she'd not give Kilkenny the satisfaction of *that*.

T.C. went back to the door, passing near enough to Jane to reach out and touch her—near enough to take in the faint, definable woman smell of her. The emotion rioting through him was wholly concealed behind the noncommittal expression that settled over his face when he spoke.

"Is there anything I can do?"

"Yeah," Doc said. "Bring up the bottle of laudanum—and leave it."

T.C. looked at Jane. Her eyes met his, then moved down across his chest and fell to the floor between his bare feet. She stepped back and came up against the chair.

"Anything else, Jane?" he asked.

Jane forced herself to look into his dark face. "Water." She took the pitcher from the washstand, handed it to him and was relieved when he was gone. She moved back to the bed and found Doc smiling.

"What's tickled your funny-bone all of a sudden?"

"Nothing," he lied. "Put on that shirt over there if you think T.C. is seeing something he shouldn't. Lord knows that thing you've got on would hide a bucket a spuds if you had one under there."

"It's the . . . idea that he just pops in when and where he wants to," she fumed, and snatched the shirt from the peg and quickly put it on.

"It's his house. I think you threw old T.C. a side loop." Doc chuckled. "His eyes almost popped out of his head when he saw you in that gown and your hair hanging down. T.C. don't get bumfuzzled very often."

"He should have knocked—" Jane said, refusing to acknowledge that the door was already open.

"Doggit!" Doc made an attempt to look disappointed. "I'm going to miss the excitement."

"What excitement?"

"You and T.C." His sunken eyes appeared brighter.

"What are you talking about?" Jane asked impatiently.

"I'll be six feet under by the time he gets down to doin' some serious courting."

"That is the stupidest thing you've said yet," Jane sputtered. She stood with her hands on her hips, her bare feet spread, her body stiff with indignation. "I swear to goodness, if I didn't know better, I'd think you didn't have an ounce of brains in your head."

"On the other hand, I think I'll hold on so I can see the fireworks."

"Nathan, you're the limit. For a doctor you're certainly lacking in gumption."

"Horse-hockey," he snorted. "I got gumption I've not used yet. And you ought to have more respect than to insult a man who's flat on his back breathing his last."

"That's another thing. Stop playing on my sympathy."

"It's working, isn't it? All I got to do is puke and you come running."

"Well, I won't the next time. You can puke your fool head off for all I care."

Jane backed away from the bed and the washstand when T.C. came in. Thank heavens he had put on a shirt and she no longer had to look at his wide naked shoulders and furry chest.

"Fresh water. Herb got it just before he went to bed." T.C. put the pitcher on the washstand and handed Jane the bottle of laudanum.

"Been wanting a word with you, T.C., if you've got the time." T.C. nodded, and Doc continued. "I'd be obliged if you'd get a leather packet out of the top drawer in my desk, a paper and pen and something to write on."

T.C. went back out into the darkened hallway.

He roamed around in the dark as silent and as sneaky as a cat, Jane observed to herself. She looked down at Doc and found him watching her as she measured drops of the drug into a glass of water.

"T.C. can give me that later. I don't want to sleep before I've said what I got to say."

"I'll go back to bed and leave you to it." She picked up the bottle of laudanum and headed for the door, anxious to leave before T.C. returned.

"Leave that."

"No," she said firmly. "If you want it, call me."

"Dammit, Jane. I said leave it. I'm the doctor!"

"Dammit, Nathan. *You're* the patient. *I'm* the doctor."

"Hell and damnation! You're a know-it-all, irritating, bossy—"

"—Pig-ugly old maid?"

"I didn't say that."

"You were thinking it."

"Good gawdamighty! How in tarnation do you know what I'm thinking?"

"You shouldn't take the Lord's name in vain. You'll be meeting him soon, and he won't like it."

"Chrissake! Where did you come from? A convent?"

"An orphanage. And it wouldn't matter if I came from a manger in Bethlehem, I'm not leaving this bottle, and that's that!"

"You'd not be so smart-alecky if I was on my feet."

"If you were on your feet you'd not want it."

"I paid good money for that damn bottle of laudanum. I'll drink every drop if I want to."

"Not as long as I'm here, you won't."

"Well, I can fix that!"

"Go ahead. It would suit me just fine. Find me a way back to the station, and I'll leave at dawn."

"You think you know every damn thing to be known!"

"I may not be the smartest person in the world, but I know enough not to leave this bottle of laudanum here with a crazy old man who might take too much of it. Not that I care! But I won't have your death on my conscience."

"You don't have one!"

From the doorway, Jane looked back over her shoulder ready to fire another angry retort. She came up against a hard, warm body and backed away from it as if it were a hot stove. T.C. had come silently to the doorway. To cover her confusion she directed her anger at him.

"Don't you ever make any noise?"

"Sometimes."

"Ha!"

"What are you two fussin' about? I could hear you all the way downstairs."

"There are three drops of laudanum in that glass of water," she said, ignoring his question and nodding toward the washstand. "Give it to the old coot when he's ready for it. I'm going to bed."

With her arms crossed tightly over the bottle, she brushed past T.C. and hurried to the room across the hall. She didn't see the puzzled look that followed her, or the grin on Doc's face, or the wink he gave T.C.

Four men sat around a small fire swapping yarns—or lies, depending on who was talking.

"She was the fattest woman I ever did see. Bouncin' on her was like bouncin' on a featherbed. Never did know if I got it in the right place. Haw! Haw! Haw! Didn't matter none. I went off good anyhow."

"Are women all ya ever talk about?" Bob Fresno asked

the question in an offhand way, but inwardly he was disgusted. He was tired of listening to Milo bragging about the women he'd had and about the lumber company he'd owned with his brother. It was lies, all lies, or he'd not be here working his butt off for two bits a day and board.

"Ain't nothin' better to talk about. Ain't that right?" Milo grinned, and looked at the other men for confirmation. "I a'ready got me one picked out here. Young and juicy. Ain't nothin' better."

Bob had been watching the faintly lighted window in the upstairs room at Kilkenny's house. Jane had gone there early in the morning with Kilkenny, and Bob had not seen her again all day. He'd heard talk that the doctor was sick and that she was tending him. After that someone said *she* had sewn up a cut on a man's leg. He wanted to know what the hell was going on. He didn't like it one bit that she was over there with Kilkenny and the scout who had come in last night.

Bob listened with half an ear to Milo's going on about the young girl.

"I like 'em untried and scared. 'Course it's all a put-on. Oncet they get a taste fer it, they like it. Everybody knows that. Gives a man a mighty powerful feelin'."

"Are ya talkin' 'bout the little 'un ya was pesterin' when that big kid come over and knocked ya on yore arse?" The man who spoke leaned over to expel a played-out chaw of tobacco from his jaw.

"I wasn't pesterin' her. We was jist talkin'," Milo flared. "And that kid won't stand in my way. I'll tell ya that right off. He caught me off guard, is what he done."

"That kid ain't no slouch with a gun."

"That ass-hole kid's goin' to be took for a elk or a deer one of these days and get his stupid head blowed off."

"Is that how ya do yore fightin'? Shoot a man in the back?"

"Why not, if he's needin' killin'? You one a them *honor-*

able fellers that give a bastard a go at ya?" Milo was completely unaware of the dangerous ground he was on.

"I face a man if I plan to kill him."

"With that pig-sticker?"

"Don't have to worry 'bout running outta bullets." The soft slurry voice had an edge to it.

"Haw! Haw! Haw! One chance is all ya got. Shi . . . it. I ain't dumb enough ta go huntin' with one bullet in my gun."

"It's been enough so far."

Bob suddenly took notice of the quiet voice and was instantly on guard. Forest Tennihill was whiplash thin. He had a long, narrow, weathered face, a mustache that drooped down on each side of his mouth, and a slow way of speaking. He also had a long thin knife in a sheath on his thigh. Bob suspected that he had another one in his boot. Tennihill was a man of a few words and obviously was not to be fooled with.

"You turnin' in, Milo?" Bob stood and stretched.

"Ain't ya goin' back to the saloon? That red-headed woman's kinda pretty. She's old and ain't very friendly, but she's got big tits."

"No. I'm hittin' the hay," Bob replied, his eyes on the upstairs window again. *I wonder if Jane's in there.*

"Guess I'll go along with ya. Sonofabitchin' breed says no credit at the saloon," Milo said.

"What you need credit for?" Bob asked as they left the campfire. "Thought ya owned a company over in the Bitterroot."

"I do, gawddammit. I own half a it. Get my money anytime I go back fer it."

"Hell. If I had money someplace I'd have my butt in the saddle and be headin' for it."

"I got my reasons."

I bet you have, you lying son of a bitch.

They walked down the street toward a shack where they

were bunking with several other men.

"I ain't stayin' here if the breed don't give me a decent job. Hell, I know everythin' there is to know 'bout a donkey engine, and I'm as good a sawyer as ever sawed a plank. I can do it all."

"I'd not be so free with callin' Kilkenny a breed, if I was you. He ain't the one hirin' mill hands anyway. And I'd not be messin' with Tennihill unless yo're anxious to see what yore gizzard looks like. That sucker'll cut ya up bad."

Milo immediately went on the defensive. "Wal, ya ain't me, and I ain't backin' up fer nobody, breed or pig-sticker."

"Suit yourself."

"Ya think he's got his eye on my gal?"

"Who? Kilkenny?"

"Shit no! Tennihill."

"How the hell would I know?"

"I picked her right off. I jist missed gettin' me one last year. I ain't missin' out on this'n."

They kept walking and Milo kept mumbling his threats against Tennihill, against Kilkenny. Bob didn't give a damn if Milo got his throat cut or his head blown off as long as he didn't set his sights on Jane Love.

She was his.

Chapter 11

EARLY morning light filtered into the room as Jane made ready to face the new day. She shook the wrinkles out of her serviceable brown dress, put it on, and tied a blue and white print apron about her waist. With the three threatening notes safe in her apron pocket, she did up her hair, then sat down on the edge of the bed to put on her shoes and stockings.

Polly awoke and sat up knuckling her eyes with her fists. "Is it time to get up already?"

"I'm afraid so."

"It's so good to be sleepin' in a real honest-to-goodness bed. Did you have to get up with the doctor?"

"A couple of times."

"A herd of buffalo could've passed and I'd not a heard. I was awful tired."

"You've cooked and scrubbed here for three straight days. It's no wonder you're tired."

"I'm tickled to be here with ya. I got to earn my keep."

"I don't want to see you lifting anymore big buckets of scrub water." Jane went to the door. "I looked in on Doc a little while ago too. He's still sleeping. I'm going to speak to Mr. Kilkenny today about washing his towels and sheets and bringing someone else in to care for him."

"Yo're still goin'?"

"I've not changed my mind. Get dressed. I'll go ahead and fire the cookstove."

"Will ya wait and go to the privy with me?"

"If you hurry."

When Jane reached the kitchen, a lighted lamp sat on the table and the coffeepot was sending up the aroma of freshly ground beans. There was no sign that a meal had been prepared. Down the hallway a light shone from the doorway of Kilkenny's office. While she was pondering whether or not to start breakfast, Polly arrived; and the two women went out onto the back porch and down the path to the outhouse.

The air was cool. The slight breeze was fresh with the clean, sweet smell of pine. The mill crews had left the day before, but a sizeable number of men remained to finish the hotel. It was unbelievable that so much had been accomplished in three days. Even now men were lined up at the cookfires for coffee and waiting to get into the cookhouse. Another busy day was about to begin.

While standing outside the privy waiting for Polly, Jane planned ahead. Sometime today she hoped to have the opportunity to speak to Colin Tallman and ask him to take her to the stage station or to arrange for a ride on one of the freight wagons. Polly would be all right here in Kilkenny's house. Herb would not let any harm come to her. Nathan could linger for days. Others could take care of him. She could not afford to stay any longer and run the risk of being humiliated and scorned should her enemy speak out.

With that thought entrenched firmly in her mind, she went with Polly back to the house.

"Ask Mr. Kilkenny if he wants breakfast, Polly."

Jane carried the teakettle from the stove, warmed the water in the basin and washed her face and hands. The towel she used to dry her face was damp and smelled of soap. One of the men had shaved here this morning.

"He ate already. He wants to see you," Polly said from the doorway.

"Did you ask him if Herb and Mr. Tallman wanted breakfast?"

"They've gone off somewhere."

"Guess it's just the two of us and Nathan. I'll make some mush."

"I'll make it while you talk to Mr. Kilkenny."

Jane looked longingly at the coffeepot. She would have preferred to have been fortified with at least one cup before facing the lion in his den. Since it was not to be, she braced herself and headed down the hall to the front of the house.

At the door to Kilkenny's office she paused and watched him. His head was bent over the table he used as a desk. A pen was grasped firmly in his big hand. His neatly combed blue-black hair glistened in the lamplight. It was wet. He had bathed already. But where?

"Come in, Jane," he said without taking his eyes from the paper he was working on. Jane wondered how he knew she was there because she had made no sound.

She entered and stood before the table, waiting for him to look up. He didn't.

"Sit down. If you don't, I'll have to stand. And if I turn loose of this damn pen, I might never pick it up again."

Jane sat on the edge of the chair and watched him dip his pen into the ink well and write a few words before, he looked up.

"How do you spell request?"

"R-E-Q-U-E-S-T."

"No wonder it didn't look right. I had a G instead of a Q." He inked the pen again and scratched out the word. In the process a huge drop of ink fell on the letter. "Damn!" He dropped a blotter on the paper and hit it with the side of his hand. When he lifted the blotter, the blob had spread and blotted out the word. He muttered another cuss word.

"What did you want to talk to me about, Mr. Kilkenny?"

"Have you had breakfast?"

"Not even coffee."

He must have caught the trace of irritation in her voice. A smile deepened the brackets on each side of his mouth, and small lines fanned out from the corners of his eyes.

"Need your coffee, huh?"

"I'm a blithering idiot without it."

"Blithering? I've not heard that word in a long time. My pa used to say it." He looked down at the ink blots on the paper and frowned. "After you've had breakfast, will you copy this letter for me? I need to send it off to our solicitor in Laramie."

"I'll be glad to if you let me go with whoever is going to take it to the train stop."

The hands shuffling the papers stilled. "Eat your breakfast and we'll talk about it."

After Jane left the room, T.C. sat back in his chair and twirled the pen around and around in his ink-stained fingers.

She was still determined to leave.

He had thought about it a lot. The only conclusion he could come to was that something had happened since she arrived in Timbertown that had changed her mind about staying here. She had some reasons other than her suspicion that he had brought the single women here with the hope they would wed and settle permanently. T.C. did not like a mystery, and he suddenly felt that he was knee-deep in the one that surrounded Jane.

A year and a half earlier he and Colin had discovered the town on land they had bought with money T.C. had inherited from his father and money lent to Colin by John Tallman. They had ridden up over a hill, and there they had seen it, nestled in a valley surrounded by pines and fir. Ten ramshackle buildings lined a weed-infested road. Five years had taken a toll on the town that had been deserted when a silver vein petered out.

Garrick Rowe of Trinity was aware of the vast resources that surrounded the town adjoining his land and offered to buy it if T.C. would stay and help bring the town back to life as Rowe had done for Trinity. The money would not only help pay off the loan at the bank, it would also pay for the longhorns he and Colin were bringing up from Texas.

T.C. was satisfied with the rebuilding so far, satisfied with the people he had brought in—with the exception of a few. By this time next year the job should be completed and he and Colin, Bill Wassall, and possibly Herb would be out of here building their own place.

His mind shifted back to Jane. Thinking of her was occupying altogether too much of his time of late. He had thought she would feel obligated to stay here in Timbertown, if not for Polly's sake, then for Doc's.

Would she stay after he showed her the paper he had written out and Doc had signed? Somehow T.C. believed it would not make the slightest difference. In spite of the fact that she knew she was needed here, something was driving Jane from Timbertown, and T.C. was determined to find out what it was.

An hour later when she had not returned to the office, T.C. went looking for her. He found her in Doc's room. The two of them were verbally sparring as usual. T.C. admired the tactics she used on the sick man.

During the past twenty-four hours the doctor's skin had taken on a yellowish tinge, and he seemed to have withered away to bones covered with a thin layer of skin. He would not last long.

"I'm glad you're here." Doc gasped for breath as he spoke. "She's the most irritating woman I've ever met. She'd argue with a stump."

"Fiddle-faddle! You're no prize yourself." Jane picked up the towels she'd used to wash him.

"Is she giving you trouble, Doc?"

"You could say that. She just told me that if I died on her, she'd be as mad as a wet hen. Hell, I've got no say-so in the matter!"

"You two sure strike sparks off each other."

"I've been trying to get her out so I can use the pot."

"I'll go now that you've got help." T.C. glanced at Jane's red face as she marched from the room and closed the door behind her.

T.C. helped Doc sit up on the side of the bed and held the chamber pot so that he could urinate. Doc was so weak that by the time he finished and lay back down, he was trembling.

"Bullet in the head isn't a bad way to go, huh, T.C.?"

"Guess you're right, Doc."

"Herb was here this morning. He has no stomach for seeing me like this."

"It's hard on the boy. He thinks a great deal of you."

"He's sweet on that little gal that's staying here, isn't he?"

"It appears that way. At supper last night he looked like a sick calf and fell all over himself trying to help her."

"That's good. He needs somebody to care for and to care for him. I worry about him."

"Don't. We'd like for him to come to the ranch and work for us for a while. If we run as many cattle as we plan, we'll need good men." It was true. T.C. had discussed it with Colin only that morning.

"He isn't going to know how to handle things."

"I know. He'll have help from Garrick Rowe as well as me and Colin."

"I'm glad we came here. It's a good place to die, as long as you've got to do it."

"I'm glad you came too, Doc. You're quite a man."

"Shit! Tell that to the boys behind the barn. A man passes through life only one time. He does what he has to do."

"You've done more than most."

"I can't figure out why Jane's so set on leaving. How are you planning to keep her here?"

"I don't know yet."

"You like her, don't you? I mean more than *like*."

"I do. But if she stays, it'll be for you."

"I told her I didn't want one of them feather-headed women watchin' me die. She said she'd tell them to shut their eyes." A wheezing chuckle came from him. "She's a pistol."

"I'll see that she stays . . . to the end, Doc. You've got my word on that."

"Find out what's eating at her, boy." Doc closed his eyes wearily. "Marry her. You couldn't do better."

"Do you want her to come in now?"

Doc didn't answer and T.C. went to the door. He found Jane standing at the end of the hall wiping her eyes on the end of her apron. She dropped it and lifted her head when she saw him. T.C. came close to her before he spoke.

"He's much worse, isn't he?"

"He couldn't swallow the mush. I don't know what to do."

"If there was anything to be done, he would know it. He's a good doctor." T.C. placed his hand on her upper arm and rubbed it gently.

"I feel so . . . bad." The lashes that surrounded her eyes were spiked with tears.

"He's worried you'll leave . . . before the end."

She moved away and his hand fell from her back. "I've got . . . I want to."

"Will a few days make a difference?"

"I . . . don't know."

"It would mean a lot to Doc. He likes you."

"It's"—Jane sniffed back a fresh batch of tears—"because I sass him."

"Fussing with you takes his mind off things for a while."

"Somebody else can do it. It . . . hurts! Can't you understand that?" Her eyes mirrored her distress.

"I understand. It's hard to see someone you're fond of die. I watched my father die, my mother and my brother. Each time it hurt in a different way."

Jane straightened her shoulders, tilted her head and stepped farther away from him.

"You're trying to make me feel guilty for leaving him."

"It's only for a few days."

"When it's over . . . you'll let me go?"

"When it's over, I'll take you to the station myself if you still want to go."

"How do I know you'll keep your word?"

"Ask Colin or Doc if my word is good."

"I guess . . . I've no choice."

"Why don't you trust me?"

She stood under his steady gaze. The frown of disapproval she gave him did nothing but intensify his stare.

"Because you've . . . got shifty eyes." Jane didn't know why she had said such a stupid thing. Her only excuse for the absurdity was that she would not let him think she would knuckle under completely.

"Shall we shake on it?" A smile lengthened his lips as he held out his hand and waited. His silver eyes held hers and she couldn't look away.

"All right, I'll stay . . . until the end." She placed her hand in his. Their palms met and he squeezed her fingers lightly.

"I know you have reasons for wanting to leave here other than the one you told me about, reasons you didn't have until you came here. It makes me think that someone is threatening you. If that is so, I'm here to help you."

She jerked her hand from his. He had come so close to the truth that it caused her to tremble. She hid her anxiety with sarcasm.

"Thank you very much, sir, but I don't need a hero riding to my rescue. It appears to me that you know very little about women, if you're unaware that one can change her mind once in a while."

T.C. dipped his head in a curt nod. Her words required no reply on his part. He looked at her face as if to fix it in his mind. The faint color that appeared in her cheeks told him that she was not as unruffled as she pretended to be. She was scared and doing her best not to show it. No harm would come to her as long as she was here in his house. He wanted to tell her, but she was in no mood to accept assurances from him. He had a week, maybe, to find out what was scaring her and to do something about it.

"I'll hire one of the women to come over. She can do the wash and help Polly with the other work. There hasn't been any washing done in a while."

"Send it to the washhouse."

"Have you been there lately? They're swamped with washing for the men. I want it done here. Polly's in no condition to be doing hard work. You'll have your hands full with Doc and helping me. There's a string of freight wagons coming in today. Colin went out early this morning to meet them."

"I'm not the only one in town who can write," she blurted. "You may have to do more doctoring." His eyes bored into Jane's, a hint of suppressed laughter behind them. When he grinned, the corner of his mouth lifted. "Murphy is out there singin' your praises to the men. I'd not be surprised if we had a sickness break out just so they can visit the pretty doctor."

"I'm not . . . either of those things! It's not right that I be passed off as such."

"Without Doc, you're the best we've got. Which one of the women do you want to come over?"

"The choice is not mine."

"Which one is most suitable?" he insisted. "You talked to them. I didn't."

"Mrs. Henderson. Her girl can help Polly."

"I'll go and ask her to come over. After you get Doc settled, come write my letters. I want them on the evening train."

By the end of the day, Jane knew she'd not been wrong about Maude Henderson. The woman not only was a willing worker, she was careful not to make Polly feel she was in any way trying to take her place here. Stella was never far from her mother's side; but because Polly was young, she was easy in her company. By noon clothes were drying on the line. The sheets and towels Jane had used for Doc were boiling in a black iron pot, and a noon meal of beef and rice was on the table.

Polly had told Maude about the doctor not being able to

swallow the mush. She suggested they make a broth he could drink. Polly sent Herb to get a cut of beef from the cookhouse. After it had simmered on the stove for a couple of hours, the broth was poured off and seasoned with bay leaves and sage. Doc drank half a cup, then lay back exhausted.

The morning passed quickly for Jane. She had not only copied T.C.'s letter to his solicitor but she had also written three more and entered a staggering stack of bills in a ledger. It was work she liked to do. In between, she had run up the stairs to check on the doctor, bandaged a smashed finger, talked to a mother about a colicky baby and suggested a sugar-tit with a drop of camphor oil. Later she had refused to pull a logger's wisdom tooth and called T.C. in to do it.

Since noon T.C. had been in and out of the house. After he checked in the freight from each of the wagons that lined the street, he brought the invoices to Jane.

"I've got to be sure we're getting every stove, every tool and every barrel we pay for. Freighters are famous for dropping off a little freight here and there. They go back for it later, take it to some out-of-the-way place, and sell it to someone who is well aware it's stolen goods."

He leaned over Jane's shoulder to show her where to list the inventory. Her hair brushed his cheek. He only had to turn his head and his nose would burrow into the fragrant mass. He had an almost uncontrollable desire to touch her, but didn't. Instead he stood behind her for a minute longer than necessary and looked down on her bent head, at the soft curls at the nape of her slender neck, at her finely etched profile. An unexplained feeling of longing shot through him. The feeling was so strong that he lifted a hand to stroke her hair, then let it drop back to his side and went quickly out the door.

Jane left the office at sundown and spent the rest of the daylight hours sitting beside Doc's bed. She told him all that had occurred during the day. He laughed when she told him about her remedy for the colicky baby.

"Couldn't a done better myself."

"I gave her some sugar with a few drops of camphor oil in it to take home."

"Are you getting pay?"

"No! I couldn't take pay. I'm no doctor."

"Harrumpt! Folks don't value anything they don't pay for even if it's a nickel."

"These are poor folk, Nathan."

"I've treated plenty of poor folk and have come away with a half-dozen eggs, a sack of beans or a fried pie"

"What do you think of Maude Henderson and her little girl?" "Don't like 'em."

"That's unkind. She's a nice woman and I think she's had a peck of trouble in her life. Why didn't you like her?"

"She was all right, but she wasn't you."

"Nathan! You're the limit!"

He lifted his hand and let it drop back to the bed.

"I wish I had life to live over again."

"You certainly haven't wasted your life, Nathan. Not many men can say that during their lifetime they saved hundreds of lives."

"If I'd met a woman like you, I'd have married her and had sons and daughters to grieve for me."

"You've got Herb . . . and you've got me and Mr. Kilkenny. Children don't get to choose their parents, but we've all chosen you. I'll miss you, Nathan." In spite of her resolve not to cry, tears flooded her eyes.

"Now . . . now—I'm torn between telling you to dry up and to keep on bawling. My mother was the last woman to cry over me."

"When was that?"

"I must have been eight or ten." He gasped and clutched at the bedclothes. "Give me the laudanum—"

Jane diluted the drug with a small amount of water and

held his head and shoulders up off the pillow while he drank it.

"If I'm lucky, I'll not wake up." He closed his eyes.

Jane sat down, took his hand in hers and let the tears run unchecked.

Chapter 12

JANE sat beside the doctor until he was deep in sleep, free of his pain for a while, then went down the stairs to the kitchen. She paused in the doorway when she saw Polly and Herb sitting at the table, their heads close in conversation. Not wanting to intrude, she backed away and went down the hall to the front door and out onto the porch.

The late evening air was sharp and cool. She hugged herself with her arms, turned her face to the mountains and took a deep breath. She never tired of looking at the snow-capped mountains with their endless belts of green. How desperate the Sioux, the Blackfoot, the Arapaho, the Cheyenne and all the other tribes must be knowing that the white man had destroyed the huge buffalo herds and now with axes and steam engines were gutting the forest.

Jane shook her head in silent denial at the thought of the obliteration of villages and of the women and children so relentlessly cut down. No! No! No! She could not, would not, think of *that*!

Lights shone from the cookhouse door and from the buildings up the street. Horses were tied to the hitching rails in front of the store, the saloon and a few other buildings. Men lounged on the porches, and even at this late hour she heard the ring of the blacksmith's hammer. Buddy Winters rolled a hoop down the dusty street, and somewhere behind the town where the rows of cabins stood, a dog barked. In the homesteads that ringed the town it was suppertime.

The setting was peaceful, but Jane felt no peace.

Late one evening T.C. heard Jane's footsteps going down the hall toward the door. It seemed strange having a woman about and stranger still having one to *think* about. There comes a time when a man starts to think of the years ahead and finds a vacant spot in his life. He had always known that someday . . .

He fingered his clean-shaven chin, then chuckled as he rubbed his fingertips over the smooth planes of his cheek. Had that someday finally arrived? He had shaved twice since she had been here. Even Colin had remarked on it.

His mother and father had been devoted to each other. He valued love, attention, and the nearness of someone. Still, he had not considered himself a lonely man—until now.

T.C. suddenly realized that something very important had happened to him that he did not completely understand. Somehow he shared a tie with this slim, capable, troubled woman, more of a tie than he'd ever shared with another human being. The knowledge of this warmed him, yet made him feel strange.

He went quietly to the door and looked out. She stood at the end of the porch, her face turned away from the town. He remembered the sunlight shining on the rich strands of her hair. He saw the slim figure beneath the worn, faded dress and wondered where her strength came from. There was something fine about her, something that spoke of pride and quality.

When he stepped out onto the porch, she turned as quickly as a doe sensing danger.

"It's only me." He hastened to reassure her. When she said nothing, he ventured, "Nice evening."

"Winter comes early here, doesn't it?"

"Yes. We can expect snow in another six weeks."

"The evergreens are pretty against the white background." She turned back to face the mountains, still hugging herself with her arms.

When T.C. came up behind her, he saw her shoulders straighten and her head come up as if she were preparing to defend herself against his touch.

"You've hardly been out of the house for the past week.

Would you like to take a walk up the street and see—"

"No! But . . . thank you—"

"The hotel will be ready for guests soon, and a few of the ladies have already moved into the rooming house. Mrs. Fowler is going to run it. We're keeping it strictly for ladies for a while."

"Until they marry and leave?"

"You'll be surprised to know that some are already keeping company."

"It's what you wanted."

"Jane—It's what *they* want. Have you never been lonely?"

"I've been too busy to be lonely."

Because of the edge in her voice, T.C. decided not to pursue the subject.

"Are you sure you wouldn't like to see what progress we've made?"

"Some other time. I'm not . . . dressed to be out in public."

"You look fine to me. Get a shawl and come walk with me."

"No. I couldn't—"

"What are you afraid of? No harm will come to you while you're with me. I swear it."

"I'm not afraid!" she protested.

"Well then . . .?"

"Oh, all right. I'll get my shawl."

In the room she shared with Polly, she whipped off the apron, then transferred the notes to her dress pocket for fear someone would find them and picked up her shawl. She looked into the doctor's room and, finding him as she had left him, went down to where T.C. waited. He had put on a sleeveless vest to ward off the evening chill.

To Jane's annoyance, T.C. held her firmly to his side with his hand beneath her elbow. She had made an attempt to draw away; but he refused to release her, and she walked along beside him, stiff and resentful. They passed the saloon where male voices, the scraping of boot heels on the plank floor, and drunken laughter came through the wide entrance with its twin swinging doors.

"This will be the tonsorial parlor." T.C. stopped before a narrow building next to the saloon. "It will have two chairs and baths in the back. One of the ladies is a barber. Did you know that?"

"How can I forget? You let Mr. Wassall think it was me."

T.C. chuckled, and she could feel the movement against the arm he held to his side.

"He raked me over good after you left."

"You deserved it. Which one of the women is the barber?"

"Guess." He turned her toward him and smiled down at her.

"Bertha Phillips."

T.C.'s grin widened. "The men would be afraid she'd cut their throats."

"Theda Cruise."

"She's going to open another saloon."

"You'd have two saloons before you build a school?"

"That's another matter. We're talking about the barber." He took her arm and they walked on down the street toward the store. "The owner and operator of the new barber shop will be Mrs. Brackey."

"Mrs. Brackey!" Jane stopped, turned and looked up at him. "I don't believe it. She's got a little girl."

"Believe it. Her husband was a barber and taught her the trade before he became so sick that he could no long carry on. She ran the shop for four years and supported the family. When he died, she no longer wanted to be in the place where he had suffered. She sold out and came here."

"She doesn't seem . . . the type."

"No, she doesn't. She'll do all right. I doubt there'll be any cussing or spitting on the floor in her place. The men will be so bumfuzzled over a woman barber that they'll behave."

The sagging porch of the next building had been removed and the one large window replaced.

"This is the bakery. There are rooms in the back where Mrs. Winters and her boy will live. They've already moved in, and she is waiting for her stove to arrive. She's doing the baking over at Bill's now. I've got to get her out of there. The two don't get along. She's too moody and bossy for our Sweet William."

By the time they stepped up onto the porch at the store, Jane had loosened up and was actually enjoying the walk and T.C.'s company. Before they went inside the store, he turned her to face the street.

"We've planned for the church to be built over there in that grove of aspens."

"And the school?"

"On the road just beyond."

"When?"

He grinned down at her. "Next week."

"And the church?"

"Next year. By then someone else will take over. Colin and I will be working on our own place east of here."

"Oh." This brought questions to Jane's mind that she refused to utter.

"Shall we go into the store? Is there anything you want?"

"Nothing, but I'd like to look."

Jane had not expected the store to be chock full of all manner of supplies essential to life in an isolated town. The scent of spices mixed with wool blankets, leather goods, new wood, and oiled tools was pleasant. T.C. and Jane had to maneuver around barrels, wagon seats and plows to reach the wooden churns, crocks, iron kettles, dishpans and washtubs that lined the aisles. Drums of lamp oil were kept in the back, but the smell reached into the store. Boxes of candles were displayed on the same table as crockery and tinwear.

Food items were lined along one wall. Canned goods sat on the shelves, and barrels of crackers, raisins, dried fruit and salted meat stood in front of the long counter. Sacks of flour and cornmeal, as well as barrels of sugar, were stacked at the end.

Even at this late hour, the merchant and two women were still unpacking merchandise and arranging it on the shelves. Jane paused beside a table piled high with bolts of dress and shirt material and boxes of buttons and lace trimmings, with a spool cabinet of thread at the end. She fingered the soft material used for undergarments and baby clothing, forgetting about T.C. until she looked up and caught him watching her.

Jane moved away from him, and around a pile of men's hats. She came face to face with Paralee Jenkins.

"Goodness gracious! If it ain't Miss Love—the know-it-all Miss Love. Ya moved in and got ya a soft spot, didn't ya? How come ya ain't been over to lord it over the rest of us? We been expectin' ya."

"Hello, Paralee." Jane turned sideways to go around the girl. Paralee blocked her path, her face red with anger.

"We all know ya mealy-mouthed yore way in with Mr. Kilkenny and took that little bawl-baby with ya."

"Paralee! Say one more word and I'll put my fist in yore mouth!" Sunday was suddenly beside Jane. She stood on spread feet, her hands on her hips, glaring down at the startled girl. "Yo're lyin'. Nobody'd say anythin' but you and yore cronies. None of ya'd say a good word for a body if yore mouths was full a hockey and that was the only way to get it out."

"Well . . . well—

"That's too deep a subject for ya to talk about, featherhead. Now go weep and moan on Bessie's shoulder so I can visit with Jane."

Paralee stuck out her tongue in a childish gesture of defiance before she wheeled around the end of the counter and left them. Sunday let loose a free burst of laughter and threw her arm across Jane's shoulder.

"It's good to see ya. I hear the doctor's bad off."

Paralee didn't see T.C. until she ran up against him. She backed off and looked up with a smile. It quickly faded when she saw the disapproving look on his face. Darting around him, she headed for the door.

Seeing that Jane was in conversation with Sunday, T.C. went back up the aisle. She would be embarrassed to know that he had overheard the jealous little twit's comments.

"I'll be there a little while longer, Sunday. Why don't you come over?"

"It's all over town that you're doin' the doctorin' now."

"I'm not a doctor! All I do is some of the things I learned from the . . . school where I worked. I ask Nathan . . . Dr. Foote to tell me what to do if he's awake. Tell folks I'm not a doctor, not even a trained nurse."

"Nobody's complainin'. They're tickled pink yo're here. Murphy's tellin' everybody ya can take his leg off any time ya want to."

"Oh, that man! All I did was put some stitches in a cut in his leg and a new bandage every day or so."

"I think he's sweet on ya."

"Oh, pooh. Enough about me. What are you doing?"

"Little bit of ever'thin'. I had a face-off with Miss Snooty-puss. The high-brow Mexican señora," Sunday added when she read the question on Jane's face. "She saw me talking to Colin Tallman and told me in no uncertain terms that he belonged to her, and if I was smart, I'd stay clear of him." Sunday's hearty laughter bubbled up again. "Can you beat that?"

"Goodness sake! What a thing to say. She's married, isn't she?"

"'Pears that she is. I heard Colin tell Sweet William her husband could have her."

"What in the world did you say to her?"

"I said, Señora, tellin' me to not do somethin' is like wavin' a red flag in front of a bull. And she said that I reminded her of one. The hussy!" Sunday's eyes sparkled with amusement.

"I suppose you told her you'd stay away from him."

"I told her I'd wrestle or bare-knuckle fight her for him. I thought she was goin' to faint and fall in it."

Jane's laughter joined Sunday's. She really is pretty, Jane thought. Pretty and good-natured and confident. *If I could only be like her!* The man that gets her will be lucky. She will make his home a place of joy, stand by his side through thick and thin—laughing all the while. The thought crossed Jane's mind that Sunday would be perfect for Colin Tallman or . . . T.C. Kilkenny.

Jane heard someone speak to Kilkenny and then saw Mrs. Winters coming down the aisle.

"You still here? I thought ya was leavin'," she confronted Jane without as much as a greeting.

"Hello, Mrs. Winters. I'll be going in a day or two."

The woman's eyes flicked over Jane's face, then rested on Sunday's before she turned away.

"I'm lookin' for Buddy."

"He was in the street rollin' a hoop a while ago. Little bugger's probably in the saloon by now," Sunday called after her.

Jane smiled. It was always a pleasure to be with Sunday Polinski. They walked along the crowded aisles to where Kilkenny stood at the counter talking to the proprietor. He pulled back his vest and put something in his shirt pocket.

"Howdy, Miss Sunday."

"Howdy yoreself, Mister T.C. Kilkenny. By the way, what does T.C. stand for?"

"If I told you, you'd not believe me." He smiled down at her. It was clear to Jane that he enjoyed Sunday's company too.

"Guess I'll just have to make up my own. T.C. Could it

be Tom Cat?" Sunday's laughter was loud and merry.

Kilkenny's laughter joined hers. "How about Tall Cowboy?" He took Jane's arm and urged her toward the door.

"Somehow I don't believe that. Hey! Are you two walkin' out together?" Sunday called from behind them.

"Could be."

Jane was so mortified that she wanted the ground to open up and swallow her. At that moment she wished she'd never come and vowed not to speak to Sunday again. She fumed at T.C. too. He could have put a stop to the rumors that were sure to spread now. On the porch she yanked her elbow from his grasp.

"Why did you say that?"

"She wouldn't have believed me if I'd said no. Would it be so bad to let folks think you walked out with me?"

"No. It's just that . . . it's not true."

He took her elbow again. "I want to walk you down past the hotel."

As they went down the steps, a man came out of the darkness and bumped as if by accident into Jane on the side away from T.C. His hand was hard on her arm for a few seconds, then gently squeezed it.

"Evenin', Miss Love. Beg pardon."

Jane looked into the face of Bob Fresno and knew that he had touched her deliberately. His face had been so close to hers that she could feel the warmth of his breath. It all happened so quickly, she had no time to say anything before he vanished in the dark.

Kilkenny also suspected it was no chance meeting that had brought the man up against Jane, but he chose not to speak of it at the moment and risk spoiling the short time he had with her.

The darkness away from the lighted store was complete. Jane was almost grateful for the hand on her elbow as they walked down the rutted street toward the big building that loomed in the darkness. They did not go up the steps to the porch, but rather stood in the street and looked at what soon would be quite a fancy hotel.

New glass filled the windowpanes; new wood fronted the building. Inside a lamp burned and Jane could see a man fitting a railing on a stairway going to the upper floor. Across the front stretched a long porch with steps leading down each side, its roof serving as a porch for the upper story.

"The rooms already have beds and washstands. The women have been working on the rooms and getting the kitchen ready. The dining area is small, but there's room to enlarge it later on."

"When will it be ready?"

"By the end of the week."

"Who will stay in it?"

"Travelers from the stage."

"From the stage?" She knew that he was looking at her, enjoying her surprise. "You've known all along that the stage was coming," she said accusingly.

"I didn't know exactly when."

"Then I needn't depend on you to take me to the train."

"Not if you wait a few weeks."

"I can't wait that long."

"Señora Cabeza's husband will be coming soon. He'll be a good customer for the hotel," he said, not wanting her to dwell on the subject of her leaving. His voice came out of the darkness from someplace above her head. "Now he's a sight to see." They began to walk back down the street.

"What do you mean?"

"Ramon Cabeza is a strutting little peacock. He'll arrive in a fine carriage with servants and a dozen or so body-guards that he calls estate troops. He puts on quite a show. I plan for his hotel bill to pay for restoring the hotel."

"Is he very rich?"

"His family is an old Spanish family. Their land, they

say, was a grant from the King of Spain way back in the early 1600s. I'm not sure how they got it, but they've a lot of it."

"That's no reason to dislike him."

"I don't like or dislike him. At times he's laughable. But a fool with more pride than brains can also be dangerous."

"She must have had a reason for leaving him."

"Patrice has a reason for everything she does, and it usually has a dollar sign in front of it."

As they reached the house and walked up the steps to the porch, T.C. was reluctant to part with her.

"I need a sign painter. With all the people here there's not one that can paint a sign." He spoke more to prolong the time spent with her than anything else.

"I can paint signs," she said, and could have bitten her tongue.

"You can? That's a load off my mind. We need—"

"Don't count on me staying to paint your signs. Someone else will come along to do it."

T.C.'s mind worked fast. Now was not the time to argue the point. He changed the subject.

"What do you think of the town now?"

"A lot has been done—"

"We won't make as much progress now. The hands at the mill and the men at the cutting camps have their own work. Coming from Denver, it probably doesn't seem like much of a town to you."

"I didn't live *in* Denver. The place where I grew up was way out of town. But when I left, the town was spreading out to it."

"You're not a town girl?" he said in a teasing tone of voice.

"If I could live any place I wanted to live, I'd pick the top of a faraway mountain where there was only the whispering forest, the singing birds and the listening sky."

"You think the sky listens?"

"Of course it does. It hears the cry of the hawk high above the earth and the sun snarling when a cloud passes in front of it."

T.C. was speechless for a moment. "You're a poet! I never thought of the sun snarling."

"I'm not a poet. I just think . . . things." Jane was pleased that he hadn't laughed at her fanciful notions. But it was possible that he was just being polite.

"Do you want a man to live with you on your mountain? Give you children? Grow old with you?"

"I . . . I've not thought about it. I'd better go see about Nathan."

"Jane—" His hand had found the curve of her waist. "I like talking to you. Shall we do this again?"

"I don't think it's wise. The whole town will be talking as it is. You're an important man here, and they watch every move you make. Besides that, you'll miss your chance with Sunday or Theda Cruise or some of the others."

"I don't want to miss my chance with you."

He didn't know how it happened. He certainly hadn't planned to kiss her. His arm snaked around her waist and pulled her to him. She looked up in surprise and his mouth swooped down on hers. The kiss was gentle, yet persistent. He didn't give her the chance to turn her face away. Her lips were soft, her breath warm and sweet. He moved his mouth gently against hers for what seemed to him only seconds. Her slender body fit perfectly against his. For that short time there were only the two of them in a vast cocoon of darkness. If it had suddenly become daylight, he would not have noticed.

As if detached from the physical world, he held her tightly against him, his head bowed, his cheek against hers.

"Jane . . . Jane—" His voice was husky, his breathing rapid.

When he lifted his head, she stood shaking and numb, too confused to know what she should do about this awful sheer physical desire she felt for him. She was shaking all over, the most peculiar sensation. She stood still, forcing herself to conquer this ridiculous fluttering weakness. Finally, when able to speak, she hid her feeling with sarcasm.

"I didn't know you . . . expected payment for escorting me."

"I didn't know . . . I was going to kiss you. But I'm glad I did."

"Why?" His arms were still around her and would not allow her to move away.

"Because you're . . . because—Hell! I wanted to."

"And you take what you want because you have superior strength."

"That's not true, and I think you know it."

"Then to compare?"

"With what? I—"

"—Never mind." She pulled away and he let her go. "I must go see about Nathan." She opened the door and disappeared inside.

T.C. stood on the porch after she left him. He reached into his pocket for a cigar and found the stick candy he had bought at the store and had forgotten to give to her. *Damn*!

He could probably count on one hand the number of women he had kissed. He could not even remember their faces. None of them had prepared him for kissing Jane Love. The miracle was—she had not rebuffed him. Had she been as stunned by the kiss as he had been? Other thoughts came on the tail of that one. Had he scared her off? Would she be reluctant to be alone with him now?

Sitting down on the edge of the porch, he put the cigar in his mouth, struck a match and, protecting the flame with his cupped hands, lit it.

He sure as hell wished he knew more about women.

In the deep shadows across the street, Bob Fresno stood with his shoulder hunched against the wall. He had seen Jane leave the house with Kilkenny, followed them up the street and waited while they were in the store. To his knowledge, it was the first time in four or five days she had been out of the house except to go to the privy.

She was in the upstairs room now. The lamp had been turned up. Kilkenny was on the porch. He could see the glow of whatever he was smoking. If he had his rifle he could kill him now and no one would be the wiser. He didn't want to do it if he didn't have to. He had seen him friendly with the redhead at the saloon and a couple of other women. But how in hell could he *not* be interested in the best-looking woman in town, one living right there in his own house?

Bob was unhappy with the situation here in Timbertown. If Jane were not here, he would move on. Milo Callahan was not a man he wanted to trail with, and he was letting it be known that they had only met at the stage station and were not trailing partners.

He didn't understand a man like Milo. He had been wild for Polly, but the past few days he had stopped talking about Polly and now talked about Bessie, who was not so standoffish. Milo was taking bets that he'd have the girl on her back in a week. Some of the men thought him a joke and egged him on.

Bob didn't care if Milo raped every woman in town as long as Jane wasn't one of them.

Chapter 13

A day passed, then another and another, each one more quickly than the last. Jane had seen T.C. only briefly since the evening he kissed her and always in the company of Colin, Herb or Jeb Hobart, the carpenter in charge of repairing the buildings. She suspected that he was avoiding her company because he was ashamed of what had happened between them and was afraid that she might take it for more than it was.

When she was not in the doctor's room, she was in the surgery treating a variety of minor ailments that could have been tended to by anyone. She put a poultice on a boil to bring it to a head, and wrapped a sprained wrist. She told a mother to rub the gums of her teething child with a silver spoon handle to help the teeth come through. For a hacking cough, she suggested spoonfuls of equal parts of whiskey, honey and vinegar. Thank heavens, there had been no serious injuries for her to handle.

Nathan had begun sleeping for longer and longer periods of time, and she wondered how many more days his wasted body would cling to life. He was not eating at all now and only occasionally drank water or tea unless it had the pain-numbing drug in it.

Jane awoke at dawn, stood and stretched every part of her body. She was stiff, her muscles aching from sitting long hours beside Nathan. Sometime after midnight she had dozed and then been awakened by Herb's touch on her shoulder.

"Go to bed," he had said quietly. "I'll call ya if there's a change."

Jane dressed hurriedly now, used the chamber pot and shoved it back under the bed, being careful not to awaken Polly. Across the hall in Doc's room she found Herb still sitting beside the bed. His elbows rested on his spread thighs, his chin in the palm of his hand. She thought he might be asleep until the floor creaked and he turned to look at her with bloodshot eyes. The lamp on the table cast a soft glow over the man on the bed. His mouth was open, his breathing shallow.

"How is he?"

"He woke up once. Never asked for the laudanum, just went back to sleep."

Jane placed her hand on his shoulder. "He may be beyond the pain."

"Don't know why it has to be him when there's a heap of no-goods that *needs* killin'."

"Life isn't always fair."

"He's the smartest man I ever knowed," Herb said, then added, his voice barely above a whisper, "and the best."

"Yes. He gave a lot to the world while he was here."

"He told me this mornin' not to waste my life rammin' around. He said he didn't want me to end up like him. Said to settle down and get me a wife and kids."

"I think he wishes he had done that."

"If I get to talk to him again, I'm goin' to tell him that I'm goin' to marry Polly if she'll have me. Her young'un'll be mine, and we'll have more."

"Have you talked to Polly about it?"

"Not yet. Do ya think she'll have me?"

"She would be foolish not to. You're a good man, Herb. Do you want me to sit with him for a while?"

"If ya want. I'll go fire up the stove and make coffee." He got stiffly to his feet, stretched, and went to the door.

"Ah . . . Herb." Jane followed. "Throw out the coffee grounds. They've been used for four days now. Surely Mr. Kilkenny can afford fresh grounds."

"Yes, ma'am. Me and T.C. just add a dab more grounds each time 'cause it's faster. I'll throw 'em all out."

Jane had carried her hairbrush with her to Doc's room. After Herb went downstairs, she stood beside Nathan's bed and loosened her hair from the braid she had put it in as she did each night before she went to bed. How had it happened that she had become so attached to this cranky old man? He really wasn't old, she realized. Life's experiences had aged him.

She went to the window, looked down on the street and began to brush her hair. The street looked nothing like it had when she first saw it. So much had been accomplished in the short while she had been here. She brushed the hair back from her face, then gathered it and brought it forward to brush the ends.

Some unseen force pulled her around to see T.C. watching her from the doorway. She threw the long flow of hair back over her shoulder. His eyes caught hers and they looked at each other for a long moment. Jane's heart began palpitating. Days ago she had come to realize that she had feelings for this man. Did he know? How could he possibly know that she had lived and relived the kiss they had shared and that now he was the principal reason she must leave as soon as her promise to Nathan was fulfilled.

T.C. nodded and moved into the room to stand beside the bed.

"How is he?"

"He's sleeping without the laudanum."

"Is that good?"

"It's both good and bad. He isn't suffering. He may be in an unconscious sleep. It's called a coma."

"I came up last night. Herb was here. I would have spelled him a while, but he wanted to stay."

"Herb's taking this hard."

He was gazing at her so intently with his silver eyes that she feared he could read her every thought. Those eyes, fixed upon hers, were looking into her very soul.

They knew. They were waiting.

Jane stepped back and turned to the window.

"Herb's grinding beans to make coffee. I'll bring you a cup."

"I'll come get it."

It had been a mistake to turn her back on him. She knew the instant he was there behind her even though he had made no sound. She knew before she felt his hand on her hair.

"You've got beautiful hair."

"It needs washing," she blurted mindlessly.

"You've had no time to do anything for yourself, have you?"

"I will . . . soon."

"Jane—" She felt him lift the hair from the back of her neck. "You've avoided me for days. Did you hate my kiss so much?"

She laughed. She meant for it to be lighthearted, but it came out a nervous titter. She was mortified.

"Flitter! That? I thought nothing of it."

"I did. I've thought about it a lot." There was a note of impatience in his tone. "Someday soon I want to do it again."

"Theda will oblige. Or Bessie. Don't try it with Sunday or she'll—"

"Hush! You know good and well what I'm talking about." His hands, hard on her shoulders, swung her around to face him. For a moment he stood studying her, a deep furrow between his brows. Then a slow smile altered the stern cast of his face. "Every minute I'm with you makes me more and more sure that you're the one."

Fear knifed through her. "The one for . . . what?"

He pulled her to him. She had no chance to resist. They were so close her breasts were against his chest. She looked up into his down-turned face in total confusion.

"Something has happened between us—something that makes me want to be with you every minute of the day. I think . . . I hope you feel that way too."

"I . . . I—"

"Are you trying to think of a way to deny it?" His face was grave, but she could see that his eyes had changed. Was it tenderness she saw there?

His gaze dropped to her mouth and her heart seemed to stall before it settled into a pounding rhythm. It was then that he placed a quick, hard kiss on her lips.

"You know it's true, my sweet Miss Pickle," he whispered, and wheeled out the door on his silent bootless feet.

Jane pressed the back of her hand to her lips. Then she turned back to the window and held the sides of her pounding head with her two hands as if to squeeze him from her mind.

Just before noon another headache arrived in the form of Bob Fresno. Jane was in the surgery cleaning up after treating a burn on a man's forearm. A knock sounded on the door. She opened it and there Bob stood behind Polly. Jane could feel his hot dark eyes fastened on her face.

"He says he's sick," Polly said.

"I'm not a doctor."

"Ya'd refuse a dyin' man?" Fresno moved around in front of Polly, forcing her to back away.

"You don't look sick to me." She turned away, dismissing him. He pushed at the door when she tried to close it, came into the surgery, closed the door and leaned against it.

"I had to say I was sick to see ya. Don't ya ever come outta this place?"

"Open the door, Mr. Fresno."

"Not until you say you'll come out tonight and walk with me like you did Kilkenny."

"Open the door."

"I just want to talk to ya, get to know ya."

"Open the door."

"Hell, ya'd think I had cholera or the pox. I'm not a bad sort."

"I'm very busy—"

"Ya wasn't too busy to go strollin' with Kilkenny."

"That is none of your business."

"He ain't courtin' ya. I know that fer a fact."

"What you know or don't know is of no importance to me. Now, please leave."

"He walks out with a different one ever' night. Goes down behind the livery to that pile a cut grass. All the fellers hee-haw about it."

"What Mr. Kilkenny does is none of my business or yours." Pain swirled around her heart. Was he telling the truth?

"I was just tellin' ya 'cause I don't want ya to get yore hopes up. Oh, I know he's the big dog 'round here. That's jist it. He can have any woman he wants."

"Open the door and get out!"

"Ya been on my mind since I first saw ya."

She looked squarely at him. He had been at the station when she got the first threatening note and had eyed her then but in a more flirtatious way than he was doing now. He was serious and unsmiling. Could he be behind the notes left for her? Was he going to blackmail her into . . . being with him?

Into the silence a heavy fist pounded hard on the door.

"Jane! Hurry!" Herb's voice sounded frantic.

"Get out of my way," Jane snarled, and the startled man moved. She flung open the door. Herb was bounding up the stairs. Polly stood at the bottom wringing her hands. "Get that man out," Jane said harshly. "If he won't go, go out into the street and scream your head off."

She didn't wait to see if her orders were obeyed. She lifted her skirts and ran up the stairs to Doc's room. Herb was on his knees beside the bed. Jane went to stand behind him. Doc's eyes were open. He looked up at her.

"This . . . is it, girl." His voice was barely audible.

"No, Doc!" Herb's big shoulders shook. Jane pressed

close to his side and put her hand on his shoulder.

She had to swallow the lump in her throat before she could speak calmly.

"I know, Nathan. We've been expecting it, haven't we? I'm glad we have a chance to say good-bye."

"You're a pistol—"

"And you've got more guts than any ten men I've ever met."

His lids floated down, then up. Faded eyes focused on Herb.

"You've been as good a son . . . as I could a wished for."

"Doc—I never thanked ya—" Tears flowed freely down freshly shaven cheeks. He placed Doc's hand in his open palm. The strong holding the weak, the young holding the old.

"Didn't have to, boy."

"I never told ya how . . . much I thought of ya, either."

"I . . . knew. T.C. 'll keep a eye on you. Kinda go along with what he says." Doc's fingers moved against Herb's. "Never thought I'd die in bed. Thought sure somebody'd shoot me."

Jane had to strain to hear his words. His eyes closed, then opened again.

"Is it night?"

"Almost," Jane said softly.

"Thought I'd be scared, but I'm not." His eyes closed again, and Jane knew somehow they would never open.

She went to the other side of the bed, sat down and picked up his hand. This fragile man had used this hand to save lives—many, many lives. She held it tightly and, because he would not see them, she let the tears flow freely down her cheeks.

An hour later, maybe two, because there was no measure of the time Jane and Herb sat beside him, Doc breathed his last. T.C. came in before the end and stood like a tall, silent sentinel beside the window.

Dr. Nathan Foote did not die alone and unloved.

Maude proved to be a blessing. While Stella stayed with Polly, she and Jane washed the doctor and dressed him in a black suit, a white shirt and high celluloid collar. T.C. and Colin brought the burial box and set it up on two sawhorses in T.C.'s office. Herb carried Doc's body down the stairs and placed him in it after Jane had lined it with the blanket Herb had brought from the store.

Jane and Herb looked in the surgery for a memento of his life's work to place beside him. T.C. came in, unlocked a drawer in Doc's desk and took out a box. In it was a medal inscribed: Nathan Foote, Doctor of Medicine, for bravery on the battlefield. It had been presented by President Ulysses S. Grant. Also in the box were newspaper clippings extolling the young doctor who had braved the fire from his own Confederate soldiers to treat men on the Union side. He was described as a true American hero, who tended the Blue, the Gray, and the fighting freed slaves with the same devotion whenever the need arose.

"He was quite a man," T.C. said softly and handed the medal to Herb to pin on the doctor's dark suit.

Word spread quickly of the doctor's death, and all afternoon women came to the back door with covered dishes, their faces solemn in respect for the dead. By sundown the table was laden with a variety of food including pies, canned beets and pickles, loaves of bread and even pickled eggs. The merchant at the store sent down a block of cheese and, not to be outdone, Sweet William made his famous peach cobbler.

"What will we do with all this?" Polly asked in bewilderment.

Jane looked at Maude. "What do you suggest?"

"You might ask Mr. Kilkenny if, after the burial tomorrow, we can put tables out on the porch and folks could come by and eat."

"Doc didn't know many people here. Maybe no one will come to the burying."

"The whole town will turn out," Maude said with a small smile. "I see you've not lived in a town this small. In such a little place weddings and burials are sort of a social event."

"Social event," Jane echoed the words and thought of the burials at the school orphanage. An hour was set aside for a brief service in the church and burial in the church cemetery with only the clergy and one or two of the teachers attending.

"People will come who have never set eyes on the doctor," Maude said. "We must prepare for them."

Maude Henderson had changed from the cowed woman she had been when she arrived three weeks earlier. Stella had changed too. She still clung close to her mother, but was no longer her shadow. Maude never talked about herself or where she and Stella had lived before coming to Timbertown. Jane knew no more about the pair than she had learned that first day, but she liked Maude very much. It was evident that the woman had had a painful past and was trying to put it behind her to make a better life for herself and her daughter.

"Will you speak to Mr. Kilkenny?" Jane asked. "I think I'll go up and lie down. I've got a splitting headache."

"It ain't no wonder. Why'd that logger that come here shut the door? Did he say somethin' nasty to ya?" Polly turned a worried face to Jane. "He was mad as a hornet when he left. He just stomped out."

Jane waved her hand as if to dismiss the matter. She had been too busy to think about Bob Fresno, but now it all came back. Had she been wrong about its being one of the women who sent the notes? If he was the one, how could he have gotten into the women's bunkhouse to put the paper in her shoe? Maybe he was using one of the women as his messenger.

These thoughts raced through her head as she went up to the room she shared with Polly. After taking her precious few hairpins out of her hair and placing them on the top of her valise, she took off her shoes and lay down on the bed. She was tired in body, but more so in her mind. Tears slid down her cheeks, but she was too weary to wipe them away.

T.C., when he knew that the end was near for Doc, had asked Jeb to have one of his best carpenters build a burial box. It brought to T.C.'s mind the need to have the funerary repaired. With a population of more than a hundred people in town alone and a hundred more in the surrounding area, there were bound to be more deaths before long.

Work would stop until noon the next day to allow time for those who wished to to pay their respects to Doc. The saloon and most of the businesses would close, as was the custom when a prominent person such as the town doctor passed away.

It was the golden time of the evening. In the mountains the time between sundown and dark was short. Lights were flickering on all over town. T.C. stood on the porch with Colin.

"I haven't seen Jane for a while."

"Mrs. Henderson said she went upstairs." T.C. was still mulling over what Polly had told him about the man who had gone into the surgery with Jane and shut the door. She said that Jane had been angry when she came out. It could mean something or it could mean nothing. He didn't think any of the men were foolish enough to insult Jane here in his house. If that were the case, the man, whoever he was, was in for a sound thrashing.

Sunday came from across the street. Her cloud of blond hair was in disarray as usual.

"Howdy. Sorry about the doc."

"Howdy, Sunday. Come on up and sit." Colin indicated the bench next to the wall.

"I come to ask Jane if there was anythin' I could do."

"Jane's worn out. I think she's sleeping. Polly and Herb are sitting with Doc. Go in if you want to." T.C. watched Colin's interchange with the girl, who still had not come up onto the porch.

"I don't want to bother her. Tell her I called."

When she turned away, Colin stepped down off the porch.

"Have ya got anythin' more important to do than walk with me to the livery? I'm goin' to take a look-see at Del Norte."

A smile flicked across Sunday's face, but she didn't laugh.

"I reckon the queen can wait while I walk with you," she said with mock haughtiness.

Colin's chuckle was low and warm. They walked away with their shoulders almost touching, Colin's head slightly bent toward her.

T.C. stood on the porch and finished smoking his cigarette. Then he stepped down and carefully ground the butt into the dirt with the toe of his boot. A lifetime of being in the woods and seeing whole sections of forests go up in flames had left him with a healthy respect for fire.

Inside the house, he paused in the doorway of his office. Beside Doc's casket in the candlelit room, Polly and Herb sat on straight-backed chairs brought from the kitchen. It was a godsend that Polly was here and that Herb had taken to her. She hold onto his hand, giving silent comfort to the grieving boy. Doc had been like a father to him, and he was feeling the loss deeply.

In the kitchen Mrs. Henderson was busy picking the pinfeathers from a fowl.

"I hope that's Bill's rooster that's been waking me every morning."

"It isn't." She gave him a pleasant smile. "Mr. Tallman brought in six pheasants—all shot in the head. It's a pleasure to clean one that isn't shot to pieces."

"That's Colin. He's good with a knife, too. I've seen him hit a fly speck on the wall. When you're ready to go back to the bunkhouse, I'll carry Stella for you." He glanced at the young girl asleep on a pallet.

"No! But thank you. It would scare her to death to wake up bein' carr—" Maude's voice trailed to a halt. A shadow of fright darkened her eyes, and she drew her lower lip between her teeth.

Another time T.C. would have noticed, but his mind was on Jane.

"Has Jane come down for something to eat?"

"I haven't seen her. Poor girl's frazzled to the bone. I didn't want to bother her, so I went ahead and brought down all the bedding and . . . things from the doctor's room."

T.C. nodded his approval and left the kitchen. He stood at the foot of the stairs for a long minute. The house was quiet except for the occasional rattle of tin on the roof as a gust of wind rippled over it. Someday he would buy Jane a mantel clock. She would like the pleasant sound of ticking in a quiet house. The thought brought him up short. *Kilkenny, you don't know any such thing.*

As if drawn by invisible strings, T.C. went slowly up the stairs. Halfway up he paused. It had been a long while since anyone had seen Jane. She might have picked up her things and left the house. She had promised to stay only until Doc was gone. Fear clouded his reasoning, and he took the remainder of the steps two at a time.

At the door to her room, he paused again to listen, then shoved open the door and went in. His fear drained away, and relief washed over him like a warm summer rain.

In the dim light he could see Jane lying on the bed. She was asleep.

T.C. took a deep breath. He was so relieved that he was shaking. Moving quietly, he struck a match and lit the lamp on the washstand. He heard a whimper and turned, thinking he had awakened her. Jane lay on her side, her palms tucked beneath her cheek. Thick waves of dark-red hair spread out over the pillow. Lashes, long and tear-spiked, lay on her cheeks.

On the floor beside the bed, one of her shoes stood upright; the other had fallen over, the laces trailing. T.C. bent down and picked up the shoes. He held them in his hand. They were small and narrow, the sole on one of them was worn almost through and the back seam had been repaired with heavy black thread. He held them for a minute or two before he returned them to the floor.

He stood beside her. He had never before observed a woman sleep. As he watched, she sucked in her lower lip and a frown brought her brows together. A whimper sighed from her parted lips. It tore at T.C.'s heart.

He squatted down beside the bed and smoothed the hair back from her face with a trembling hand.

"Shhh—Don't cry," he whispered. "You're all right. You're just worn out."

"It's not . . . fair—" she murmured.

"What's not fair, Jane? You don't have to do anything you don't want to do." His arm curved up around her head and his lips pressed a kiss on her forehead. His touch awakened her.

"Oh! Oh—" Her eyes flew open. "T.C., ah . . . Mr. Kilkenny." She looked as if she would burst into tears again.

He smoothed the hair back from her face and wiped her wet cheeks with the ball of his thumb. Their faces were close. He put his hand into her hair, feeling the soft, silky tresses.

"I've . . . got to get up." She moved and made another soft little whimpering sound.

"You were crying in your sleep."

"No. I seldom cry."

He lowered his lips to her cheek. "Then what's this on

your cheeks? You needn't be ashamed of crying."

"I'm not—"

"Jane, love,"—he paused between the two words—"someday you'll tell me why you're always on the defensive."

"I've got to get up," she said again. "There's a lot to do."

"It's being done. Have you eaten since morning?"

"I don't remember."

He moved back, and she sat up on the bed. She reached for her shoes, but he had them in his hand. With a firm grip on her ankles, he guided her feet, first into one shoe and then the other. Jane looked down on his dark head as he tied the laces. She would give almost anything to slide her fingers through that shiny dark hair, but she didn't dare.

Jane stood, trembling and feeling like an utter fool.

Not knowing what else to do, she began to braid her hair.

"Do you have to put it up? Can't you tie it back with a string?"

"No. I've got to put it up. I can't go traipsing downstairs like this. What'll people think?"

With his hands on her shoulders, he shook her gently. "I don't care what folks think."

"Folks think badly enough of me as it is."

"Why?"

"Because . . . I'm here, and—"

"I don't see how we could have managed without you." He stroked her hair back from her temples. Reluctantly he dropped his hand and went to the door. "Go ahead and do up your hair. Now that I think about it, I'd rather no man but me ever see it like that."

"Would you mind going on ahead? I don't want Mrs. Henderson to think that I . . . you . . . were doing something improper."

"I'll wait in the kitchen, then we'll sit on the porch awhile. Bring your shawl." He left before she had a chance to refuse.

Jane stood for a moment reliving the wonder of his stroking her hair, kissing her wet cheeks and putting on her shoes. She had had practically no experience with men, but she knew that he was an unusual one, hard as a rock one moment and so gentle the next. She was glad she had come here, otherwise she might never have known the joy of being held close in a man's arms nor have felt the tender touch of his lips.

It would be heaven to be free to love him and have him love her in return. If he were hers to love, she would put all her toil, her thoughts and her affection into making a home for him and their children.

Fate had dealt her a cruel blow. Her dreams would never come true, but she would now have some sweet memories to hold in her heart.

Chapter 14

IT was a spectacle, Jane thought. Never had she seen such a sight.

Shortly after the open casket had been carried to the porch and sprays of freshly cut evergreens and bunches of wildflowers, which she later learned had been gathered by Sunday and Colin, had been placed around it, people began arriving to pay their respects.

The men came with freshly shaven faces and slicked-down hair, wearing clean shirts. They paused beside the casket with their hats in their hands. Families came. Women carried babies in their arms. Older children led their young siblings by the hand. After they had viewed the body, they stood along the street and talked in hushed tones. Some of the mothers, trying to visit with friends, scolded the excited children, shushing them.

Jane wore her good black skirt and white shirtwaist. She had a short black cape she would wear to the burial ground. At dawn Herb and T.C. had gone to the knoll outside of town that had been designated as the cemetery during the town's heyday. It was already occupied by more than a dozen souls who had come to Timbertown during the silver strike and had never left. After choosing Doc's final resting place, T.C. and Herb had cleared the area of brush and weeds and had dug the grave.

Standing at the end of the porch with Maude, Jane noticed a tall, whiplash-thin man as he approached the casket. His long-handled mustache curved down on each side of his mouth. Thin sandy hair that reached almost to his shoulders was stirred by the morning breeze. He was neatly dressed in a clean shirt, with a black string tie, and duck pants. He carried a wide-brimmed Texas-style hat.

What drew Jane's attention was that he lingered so long, gazing down at Doc's body. When he looked up, sharp blue eyes met hers. He moved around to the end of the porch, his hat beneath his arm.

"Mornin', ma'am. I wish I'd knowed he was here." He spoke in a slow drawl.

"Did you know him?"

"Yes, ma'am. I could'a picked him out of a million. Forest Tennihill's my name, but mostly I'm just called Tennihill."

"How do you do, Mr. Tennihill. I'm Miss Jane Love and this is Mrs. Henderson."

"Glad to make yore acquaintances." He dipped his head to each of them, then looked back down into the casket. "We called him Little Doc. He warn't much bigger and not much older than a bugle boy, but he had enough grit fer ten men."

"Were you in the War? Is that where you met him?"

"Yes, ma'am. It was durin' the battle of Middle Creek in eastern Kentucky when I first met him. Wasn't no big battle as battles go, but the enemy had us pinned down in a dry creek bed. For hours we'd been hearin' this blue-belly cryin' an' callin' for help. Night come, and he started callin' for his maw. It was pure pitiful.

"I was layin' on my belly and felt somethin' crawlin' over me. It was Little Doc. He was goin' to help that boy. I tried to hold him back, an' he let loose with a streak of cuss words that'd burn the ears off a mule."

Jane smiled for the first time that morning. It was enough encouragement for Tennihill to continue with his story.

"Couldn't let the little feller go by hisself. He'd be sure to get his head shot off. 'Sides, I figured I might be needin' his help myself. After tellin' him how many different kinds of a fool he was, which he didn't pay no heed to a'tall, we wiggled on down that creek bed and up through the Northern lines, Little Doc hangin' tight to my heels.

"We had a couple tight squeezes before we found the boy. His foot was smashed all to pieces. Little Doc gagged him so he'd make no noise and told me to carry him back through the lines to his hospital tent. I almost swallered my tongue when he said that. Never thought we'd make it, but we did. That was in '62. I'd a give ya odds then that Little Doc'd wouldn't a outlasted the War."

"He got a medal from President Grant, you know," Jane said.

"I ain't a bit surprised at it. Tales 'bout Little Doc spread from Chickamauga to Pea Ridge. Wish I'd a knowed he was here."

"How long have you been here, Mr. Tennihill?"

"Week. Little more, maybe."

"Doc took to his bed several weeks ago."

"I heared there was a woman doin' the doctorin'."

"The woman you heard about was probably me, but I'm no more a doctor than this porch post. I bandage a few cuts and that's all."

T.C. stepped up onto the porch. He came directly to Jane and in a possessive manner cupped her elbow with his palm.

"Howdy, Tennihill."

"Kilkenny. I been tellin' the ladies I met the doctor durin' the war."

"You've never mentioned knowing Doc Foote."

"Never heard him called anythin' but Little Doc. I knew him right off." The tall man's eyes went from Jane to Maude Henderson. He backed away. "Nice meetin' ya, ladies. Thanky for listenin' to my tales."

"It was our pleasure, Mr. Tennihill. Thank you for sharing them."

"Tennihill, I'd be obliged if you'd step in and help carry Doc to his final resting place. Not many here knew him."

"I'd be plumb proud to, T.C. The kind a man Little Doc was don't come by but oncet in a coon's age."

Jane watched the tall, lanky man walk away. She tried to disengage her elbow from T.C.'s hand, but he refused to let it go. Holding tightly, he spoke to Maude.

"Where's Herb and Polly?"

"They walked up to the store. Polly decided Herb needed a tie. Stella went with them."

"Stella went with them?" Jane echoed. "Maude, she usually won't let you out of her sight."

"She likes Polly." Maude smiled broadly. "It's been good for her to be around Herb too. He's such a gentle boy."

"I need Jane for a while, Mrs. Henderson. If you need anything Colin will be here in a minute."

T.C. ushered Jane into the house and into his office.

"Polly said you've packed your bag," he said the instant he had closed the door. A note of impatience tinged his words. He went to his desk, sat on the edge and folded his arms over his chest.

"Of course I have. You must know I can't stay here now. And . . . you've no business picking Polly about my affairs."

"Why is now any different from yesterday or the day before?"

"You are dense, Mr. Kilkenny, if you don't know the answer to that. Polly and I can't stay in this house with three single men just to be staying here. We had a reason while I was nursing Doc. Polly was here to help me. That was acceptable. Doc is no longer here for me to nurse."

"You're leaving because Doc's gone?" Silver eyes battled with blue ones.

"You promised to take me . . . or send me to the stage station if I stayed with him to the end."

"Things have come up that change that."

"You're going back on your word! I should have known you have no honor," Jane said coolly.

"Don't get in a snit, love. As I said, things have come up. You and Polly will stay right here. I'll have Mrs.

Henderson move in if it'll make you feel better."

"Don't you care that my reputation is already in shreds? Minnie Perkins and Grace Schwab are having the time of their lives talking about the *fallen* woman in your house. Paralee fans the flames as much as she can. The only friends I have in town are Sunday and Polly."

"Mrs. Henderson?"

"Of course. Maude has more brains that the lot of them put together."

"Then I don't understand why you care what they say."

"I won't care when I'm gone. They can say what they want then, and they'll say plenty."

"Jane—love," he paused between her name and the endearment so she'd not mistake his intent. "Stay here. I'll have Mrs. Henderson and Stella move into Doc's room. We'll talk more about this in a day or so."

"You . . . promised."

He hardened his heart and refused to acknowledge the whispered words or the strained, worried look on her face.

"A preacher came in last night. He's coming over as soon as he gets spruced up. He'll conduct a service for Doc."

"You knew he was coming?"

"No. Garrick Rowe said he'd see what he could do about a preacher coming to start a church, but I didn't know he'd be here this soon."

"What is he?" Jane asked tightly.

"What do you mean?"

"Is he a Catholic? Baptist? Methodist? Mormon?" A vision of a black-bearded man flashed before her eyes.

"I didn't ask him what he was. Does it matter?"

"I guess not." Her shoulders slumped wearily.

T.C. stood, walked over to her and put his hands on her upper arms. He wanted to hold her, protect her. In such a short time she had crept into his heart and wrapped herself firmly around it. His father, the wisest man he had ever known, had told him that love and hate were the two strongest ties in the world. He hadn't really understood then, but he did now. It was agony to think of her leaving, of never seeing her again.

"Jane, let me help you. Tell me why you feel you must leave here."

"Because I don't like a backwoods town. I'm used to the city."

"That's not true. What about your mountains and your listening sky? They know your secrets. Won't you share them with me?" He put his arms around her and for just an instant Jane closed her eyes, leaned against him, savored his warmth and his protecting strength.

A knock sounded on the door. T.C. reluctantly dropped his arms from around Jane and went to open it. Maude stood back to allow a man wearing a dark suit and small round spectacles to enter. He was young, slightly built and about T.C.'s age. His ruddy cheeks were clean-shaven.

"Come in, Reverend Davis. I want you to meet Miss Jane Love."

Jane held out her hand. "How do you do?"

The preacher shifted the Bible from his right hand to his left and took Jane's hand in a firm clasp. His eyes flicked from her to Kilkenny. The hand on the woman's back said clearly that she belonged to this tall black-haired man who had more than a trace of Indian blood.

"Pleased to meet you."

T.C. picked up a paper from his desk. "I've written out a few things about Dr. Foote. You may want to read them over."

"Is either of you related to Dr. Foote?"

"No. The doctor has no blood relatives that I know of."

"Herb," Jane prompted.

"Herb Banks is his foster son, so to speak."

"Do you know if the doctor was baptized? And if so, what church?"

"I don't know."

The preacher looked over what T.C. had written, folded the paper and put it in his Bible.

"What time did you want to start the service?"

T.C. looked at Jane. She lifted her brows in a question. T.C. held her eyes with his as he answered.

"Any time now."

Fifty or more people followed Doc's body to the cemetery. The young preacher walked directly behind the wagon, followed by Herb holding Polly's hand as if the small girl were his anchor during this sorrowful time. Jane walked between T.C. and Colin and was the envy of more than one female in the crowd. When the wagon stopped at the foot of the knoll, Herb, T.C., Colin, and the man called Tennihill gently lifted the coffin to their shoulders and carried it up the grassy hill.

The place where Doc would spend eternity was a quiet, beautiful spot shaded by tall pines with a clear view of the mountains to the west. Jane thought it symbolic that the clear melodious sound of a mourning dove came from faraway as the box was lowered to the ground beside the gaping hole. As the mourners gathered around, T.C. reached for Jane's hand and pulled her up beside him.

The service was short. The preacher read the eulogy T.C. had written. Nathan Foote had been born in Virginia, had gone to medical school there and had served in the Confederate Army.The preacher read of his deeds on the battlefield and told of his commendation by the president of the United States.

After reading a short passage from his Bible, the preacher began to sing "The Lord's Prayer" in the most beautiful voice Jane had ever heard. His voice was rich and vibrant. It reached to Jane's listening sky. The mourners were awed into silence. Jane felt the spell of a strange enchantment settle over her. Her eyes were drawn to those of the tall man beside her. He gazed down at her and squeezed her hand, and for a short while she felt as if she really belonged to him.

"Join me in singing 'Shall We Gather at the River.' "

The mourners at first were hesitant. The preacher sang as if all had joined in, and soon most of them had. Jane was surprised not only to hear T.C. sing, but that he knew all the words. Raised in the church school, she believed she knew every word of every hymn ever written.

Standing at a distance where he had an unrestricted view, Bob Fresno saw the look exchanged between Jane and Kilkenny. The look was one of . . . intimacy. A feeling of frustration and anger knifed through him. Hell! She was damn lucky he'd noticed her. What was Kilkenny, but a . . . breed?

Jane lifted her eyes and saw Bob Fresno gazing at her. During the few seconds when their eyes met, Bob lowered his eyelid. When Jane realized what he had done, her face flamed. She had not been so isolated at the school that she had not learned about the flirtatious wink of an eye when a man wanted a woman to know that he desired her. She didn't dare look around to see if anyone else had noticed.

T.C. let go of Jane's hand to join with the others when it was time to hold the ropes and lower the box into the ground. It was then that Jane's eyes flooded with tears. She remembered standing beside Aunt Alice, when her mother was buried. At that young age she had not realized the finality of death. Out of time immemorial Nathan Foote had spent a mere fifty years on this earth and now he was no more than—

"Ashes to ashes," the preacher said, "Dust to dust."

Nature had provided a beautiful late summer day for Nathan Foote's burial and the gathering that followed in front of the house where he had lived his last days.

The tables brought over from the cookhouse were lined up in front of the porch. Maude, Polly, Sunday and Jane carried the food from the kitchen. Families had gone home, changed out of their Sunday best and returned with more food to add to the meal.

The day before, on hearing that Dr. Foote had passed away, Sweet William had had a steer butchered. In the pit lined with adobe bricks, the steer was placed over a fire of hickory wood. A tin lid, fashioned to hold the smoke, covered the pit. All morning, before and after the service, men lounged around the pit, giving advice and swapping yarns about pit-smoked meat.

The roasted steer was pulled from the pit with a chain and a pulley and swung over a table where Sweet William had an array of knives and cleavers. He sliced the meat and placed it in large pans to be carried to the table.

Theda Cruise came, her flaming red hair tied back with a ribbon. She wore a dark blue satin dress with a bustle on the back. Her waist was tightly cinched, the corset pushing her breasts up to show a slight cleavage at the neckline. Her dress was modest and stylish according to Denver standards.

Her contribution to the affair was a sack of stick candy she had purchased at the store as a treat for the children. Jane was more than mildly surprised by the saloon woman's gesture.

Noticeably absent was Patrice Guzman Cabeza, who had moved to the hotel. When asked about Patrice, Maude said she had been told that the woman complained of not feeling well and wanted to be left alone.

Sunday and Colin were spending more time together. Perhaps Patrice Guzman Cabeza was not ill but unhappy over the fact that she had been unable to bring Colin Tallman to heel.

The picnic atmosphere of the gathering was baffling to Jane . . . such a gala event arising from a death. All those attending seemed to be enjoying themselves. Buddy Winters, for one, was reveling in unusual freedom. He ran and played with the other children while their mothers visited with their neighbors. To Jane it all seemed rather . . . disrespectful to Doc.

She was in the kitchen with Maude and Polly when T.C. came in. He still wore his white shirt and string tie. His blue-black hair was still neatly combed. Jane was drying cups as Maude washed them. He came up close behind her, so close his lips touched her ear.

"Honey, folks are getting impatient to eat."

Jane looked quickly to see if Maude had heard, then sent a jabbing blow to his abdomen with her elbow. He grunted but didn't move.

"Then let the feast begin! This whole thing is barbaric."

Maude turned in surprise, her hands dripping dishwater.

"Jane, no! Folks in small towns always get together after a burial. They're celebrating the doctor's life, not his death."

"I've never seen the like. People are acting as if . . . as if they were at a fair."

"They've not forgotten Doc. They are remembering him, honey." T.C. emphasized the endearment. He turned her around to face him. "Every story that was ever told about Doc is being told and retold. Herb is out there bragging about how Doc stood up to a bunch of outlaws and dared them to shoot him again. Tennihill is telling all he knows or heard about Doc during the War. By the end of the day folks will swear he was a saint."

"None of them will ever accomplish in their lives what he did in his." Tears flooded Jane's eyes, and she had to look away from him.

"Aren't you about through here, Mrs. Henderson?" T.C. exchanged a knowing look with Maude. "As soon as you are, will you and Polly come on out on the porch?"

T.C. untied the strings on Jane's apron and hung it on the back of a chair. With his hand in the small of her back, he propelled her out into the hall and toward the door. Before they reached it, she dug in her heels and refused to take another step.

"Just a minute. I look a mess." She began poking the loose strands of hair into the knot on the back of her neck.

"Honey, even if you looked a mess, which you don't, you'd still be the prettiest woman in town."

"Stop calling me that and . . . stop lying. You know it isn't true. You're just buttering me up thinking you'll not have to honor your promise to take me to the railroad, and you'll have one more female in town."

"You don't want me to call you honey?" His silver eyes glinted with amusement. Doc was right about her. She's a pistol!

"No. It's nothing but senseless twaddle." She stepped back and raked him with unkind eyes.

"Humm—And you don't want me to say you're pretty, either. Is that it?"

"More twaddle. It isn't true and you know it."

"You really believe that, don't you?"

"I may have been stupid for coming here, Mr. Kilkenny. But I'm not blind."

"Mr. Kilkenny? We've kissed—several times. You know me well enough to call me T.C."

"I don't even know what T.C. means."

"I'll whisper it if you promise not to tell anyone." He put his lips to her ear, nipped the lobe gently with his teeth, then kissed it. "Thunder Cloud," he whispered.

She jerked away. Her face was set. She refused to look at him when he tilted her chin to look into her face.

"Someday we're going to have to talk."

T.C. heard Maude and Polly come out of the kitchen and urged Jane ahead of him out the door.

The preacher stood on the porch. At T.C.'s nod, he raised his hand and a hush fell over the waiting crowd. He began to pray in his beautiful vibrant voice.

"Our Heavenly Father, we are gathered here to remember our brother, Nathan Foote, who has by now been welcomed into Your Kingdom and into Your warm embrace where he will have eternal life. While on earth he was a man among men, often risking his own precious life to help others. Bless this food provided by his friends. Bless those gathered here to honor his memory. Keep them safe. Help them by their hard work to prosper. I ask this in Your name. Amen."

The preacher stepped back.

T.C., holding tightly to Jane's arm so she could not move away, stepped forward. *Drat him!* He was deliberately making it appear that they were an engaged couple. A pair. Mates or mates-to-be.

All Jane could do was stand there and fume silently. She endured being made a spectacle of by thinking of all the things she would like to do to him, including hitting him squarely in that beautiful, smiling, lying mouth!

"Reverend Davis will be holding church services on Sunday. I've not yet figured out a place. As long as the weather holds I reckon we can hold the services outdoors."

"How long will ya be here, Parson?" A man from the back shouted. "I'm plannin' to get married."

"I intend to make this my home. I hope to bring my family here in a few weeks. Mr. Kilkenny tells me that he will furnish building materials for a church. I'm not a bad carpenter. Not good, but not bad."

"I'm the best dang carpenter in the territory. Ain't no sense havin' a church house that'll cave in at the first snowfall."

"I'm better'n him, Parson."

"And I'm better'n him." This brought hee-haws from the crowd.

"Yo, Pastor"

"I'll do the mason work."

"Ya gotta roof, preacher."

"Bullfoot! Ya couldn't hit a nail on the head with a sledge. Count me in."

On and on it went. The preacher seemed to have won over his future congregation.

Chapter 15

BOB Fresno watched Jane.

He had heard something today that had given him hope that all was not well between Jane and Kilkenny. The talk was that she planned to leave Timbertown. A scatter-brained twit named Bessie was spreading it around that Kilkenny had promised to take Jane to the train if she would stay and nurse the doctor to the end.

Bob could hardly believe his luck.

He went through the motions of filling his plate, talking to the men who sat on the ground to eat, but his mind was busy. He was trying to think of a way he could get close to Jane. The opportunity came when she brought something from the house and walked down the row of tables to find a vacant place to set it.

Bob put his plate on the ground and hurried to the table on the pretext of getting more bread. He reached around her and, not knowing he was there, she backed up against him.

"Pardon." She glanced over her shoulder.

"Jane," Bob said quickly, his hand clasping her upper arm. "I hear ya want to leave. I'll take ya to the train, now, tonight. Just let me know when ya want to go."

"Thank you, but I've made arrangements."

"No, ya ain't."

"Let go of me."

"I'd not hurt ya for the world, Jane. Kilkenny ain't goin' to let ya go. He wants ya in his bed."

"You are rude and crude." She jerked her arm from his grasp and hurried into the house.

It wasn't what Bob had hoped for, but it was something. He would watch. If Kilkenny took her, he'd follow. You could bet your life on that.

Tennihill watched Bob Fresno watch Jane. He sat on the porch of the cookhouse and whittled on a stick. From that vantage point he could see not only across to Kilkenny's house, but down the street toward the saloon that had opened up after the burial and was doing a thriving business.

The men, having eaten before the women and children, were gathered in bunches, enjoying the free day.

Tennihill had noticed Fresno at the graveyard, standing off to the side staring at Kilkenny and Miss Love. At first he had thought it was Kilkenny who was the center of Fresno's attention; then his sharp eyes discovered the man was in a state of discomfort due to the bulge that he soon covered with his hat.

If Tennihill had read the cards right, Miss Love was Kilkenny's woman. He had known T.C. and Colin Tallman for a few years, having first met them at Trinity through Garrick Rowe. T.C. Kilkenny was not a man to fool with when it came to something that belonged to T.C. Kilkenny. If Fresno didn't know that, he would soon find out.

This little by-play was amusing, a diversion from the reason Tennihill was here. He folded his pocketknife and put it in his pocket. It was time to mosey on up to the saloon and see what Milo Callahan was up to.

Jane thought it grossly unfair and terribly rude when the men came to the tables first. The women and children stood back and waited. The preacher seemed to think nothing of it. He was the first to fill his plate. Mrs. Gillis, the matron at the school, had been strict about proper etiquette and had insisted the children be taught manners. Jane tried to think of an excuse for this behavior and nothing came to mind except that, because the men were the providers, they had first choice. In Jane's view, it was a very primitive custom.

The women from the henhouse were none too friendly with Jane. Not so the women from the cabins and homesteads. Word had spread about the sick children Jane had helped, and now all were anxious to know if she was staying until a new doctor arrived. The news had spread fast that she would be leaving. She supposed that anything vaguely connected to Kilkenny was of great interest. She could imagine what would happen if her secret were revealed. It would travel through the town like a wildfire, and T.C. would lose no time getting her to the train. She had no doubt that he would be decent enough to do that.

Jane tried to keep her eye on Paralee, Bessie and Minnie Perkins. They stuck together except when one of them had a chance to walk off with a man. Jane now believed none of the three knew her secret because they seemed to be unable to hold their tongues about any bit of gossip. That left Bertha Phillips and Grace Schwab as suspects.

Jane's head began to ache with the nervous strain of keeping up appearances and not showing her worry. There were plenty of willing hands helping to clear the tables. Assuming she wouldn't be missed, Jane went upstairs to the room she had shared with Polly.

She opened her valise and took stock of the contents. The blue dress she had worn when she arrived had been washed and ironed. She would save it for traveling. The drab brown dress would do for this evening. She changed clothes and, after carefully folding her good skirt and her shirtwaist, repacked her valise.

Standing beside the window, she looked down on the street and thought about Polly. She would be all right now. Herb would marry her. He was not much more than a boy, but with help from Colin and T.C. they would make out.

Polly had been disappointed that she and Jane could no longer stay here in T.C.'s house at night. Maude had invited the girl to live with her and Stella. Jane was hoping to spend the night with Sunday, who was staying at the boarding house. She had not yet asked her, but if that were not possible, she would go to the henhouse, even though the women she suspected of sending her the notes were there, and she'd not dare sleep.

Looking down the street, Jane saw T.C. talking to the lanky Mr. Tennihill. It was pure pleasure to look at T.C. He stood with one foot resting on the edge of the cookhouse porch, his forearm on his thigh. As she watched, he lifted his hand and tilted back his hat. He had a large frame, but life had given him a lean trimness. Hard work had built a powerful body with a vast supply of vitality. He was self-assured and confident. T.C. Kilkenny was comfortable with who he was: one-quarter English, one-quarter Blackfoot and one-half Irish. Had he been teasing her when he said T.C. stood for Thunder Cloud?

Jane's eyes fastened on his face. If things had been different, she would have enjoyed the attention of such a man, even knowing his intentions were not serious. Jane believed herself to be level-headed. T.C.'s interest in her was not romantic. He wanted her to stay because she was a teacher, a nurse of sorts, an adequate letter writer and a bookkeeper. She was merely an asset to his town, and he was using his charm to keep her here.

Next spring his job would be done, and he and Colin would go to their ranch. Right now, getting this town on its feet was what was uppermost in his mind.

Summer was winding down and the days were getting shorter. The time between sundown and dark was especially short here in the mountains. The room was in a deep gloom when Jane turned from the window on hearing Polly call.

"Jane, are ya up here?"

"Yes, I'm getting ready to come down. Is Sunday still down there?"

"She went off somewhere with Colin. Ya know, I think he likes her. They always got their heads together talkin'."

"I wanted to talk to her about my staying with her at the rooming house."

"There ain't no need for us to go now. Maude and Stella are comin' to stay in Doc's room so folks won't talk. Maude already changed the bed."

"When was this decided?"

"Maude said T.C. asked her 'cause you feared we'd be talked about."

"I'm glad for you, Polly. I know you wanted to stay."

"Maude and Stella are tickled. Stella is gettin' to where she ain't so bashful no more." Polly began fumbling in her pocket. "Maude found this on the table under a butter crock.

She says it's got your name on it." Polly giggled. "We think ya got a feller and he's bashful." As Jane accepted the folded paper, she had a sinking feeling in the pit of her stomach. "He'd better watch out for T.C.," Polly added. "Maude thinks T.C. likes ya. Really likes ya."

"Maude is as wrong as wrong can be." Jane shoved the note down in her pocket with a shaking hand. "I'll read this later."

"I'm goin' for a walk with Herb. I come to get my shawl. Ya'll be here when I get back?"

"I'll be here or over at the henhouse."

"Oh, Jane. Be here. Please be here."

"We'll see. Run along and have a good time with Herb."

"He is so . . . nice. I ain't never met nobody as kind as Herb. I just never thought anybody like *him* would like *me*."

"Why not? You're sweet and pretty—"

"But, you know . . . the other. Do you think he knows about *that*?"

"I'm sure he does. Some men would hold that against you, but not Herb."

"Oh I hope yo're right."

"I'm sure I am. Now run along."

Jane was afraid she'd burst into tears before Polly got out of the room. She hurried to the table and struck a match to light the lamp. In the flickering light she took the note from her pocket. This one was different. The paper had been folded. To keep it closed, two little tears had been made on three sides. The paper between the tears was folded down. Her name was on the outside fold. Jane held it in her hands, dreading to open it, and was tempted to hold it to the flame in the lamp and destroy it. Unaware that she was holding her breath, she separated the folds to read the message. The frightening words jumped out at her.

stay here
or I kill yu

Her eyes blurred as she read, She could almost feel the hatred directed toward her. As if destroying her peace of mind and threatening to humiliate her were not enough, her enemy was ready to kill.

Jane unfastened the safety pin on the pocket where she kept the notes and slipped the new one in alongside the others. She blew out the lamp, sank down on the edge of the bed and tried to think. This message put a whole new light on things. Neither of the women she suspected of sending the notes seemed capable of murdering anyone, though both had vicious tongues.

One of the men must be behind this. But which one?

Bob Fresno had offered to take her to the train. Had he plans to get her out of Timbertown, then to kill her? She'd never leave town with *him*. Besides, his willingness to take her away ran contrary to the words "stay here" in the note. The man called Milo could be the one. She had judged him to be a shallow, mean man, but would he make a plan and carry it out in secret. No, he would want credit for it.

She was not sure if one of the two Mexican men who had come to the station with Patrice Guzman Cabeza had traveled on to Timbertown. One had ridden away; she was sure of that. A Mexican would have no interest in her, she reasoned. Or would he? Her secret shame concerned a deed that had touched the lives of almost everyone in the Western territories.

Jane tried to remember the other men who had been at the stage station. Most of them had been looking for work. Some were family men, hoping to bring their families after they were settled. She hadn't paid enough attention to any of them even to remember who was there. And several men had arrived that day on horseback. She must not forget about them.

The hands she pressed to her cheeks were cold and clammy. One thought was clear. Someone *wanted* her to stay here to continue the tormenting until the appropriate time came to expose her and to enjoy her humiliation.

Dear God, she was tired of this black cloud hanging over her head.

The room was in darkness. Jane heard activity downstairs: the sound of the door closing followed by heavy footsteps on the porch. T.C. was leaving the house. Herb was with Polly and Colin with Sunday.

The sensible thing to do would be to stay here for the night. Tomorrow, if T.C. refused to honor his promise to take her to the stage station, she would ask Mr. Tennihill. If it came down to having to tell someone why she must go, she would rather confide in a stranger. She did not think . . . no she was sure that she would not be able to bear the look of contempt on T.C.'s face when he heard who she was.

Having made her decision, she decided the best way to avoid T.C. was to go to bed. But first she had to use the outhouse. She took her nightdress out of her valise and placed it on the foot of the bed and left the room.

A wall lamp lit the lower hallway. As Jane reached the bottom of the stairs, she heard footsteps on the porch, Stella giggling and then Maude's calm voice. The door opened before she could flee. Maude and Stella came in carrying bags and several heavy books.

"Set them down before you drop them," Maude told her daughter. Then she saw Jane. "Feeling better, Jane?"

"Not much. I'll be going to bed soon."

"Mr. Kilkenny gave Stella some map books to look at. Did you know he's been ever'where?"

"I know very little about Mr. Kilkenny."

"We didn't know we'd be here and Stella took them to the rooming house. She's excited and going to want to look at them tonight. We'll be quiet."

"Don't worry about bothering me," Jane said, thinking of the years she'd slept in the same room with ten or twelve girls.

When Maude and Stella began the struggle to get their belongings up the stairs, Jane escaped to the kitchen and on out the back door to the porch. The air was cool; the sky was alight with a million stars, some so bright it appeared that a person could almost reach out and touch them. Jane stood for a long moment, her face tilted to the sky, and hugged herself with her arms.

Doc, are you up there? I wish you could tell me what to do. Why didn't I ask you on one of those nights when it seemed that you and I were the only people in the whole world? I should have trusted you. If there was anyone who would have understood—it Was you.

A shout of laughter from the street brought back to mind her original intent to do the necessary and get back to the room. She stepped off the porch and hurried down the path to the privy.

When she reached the outhouse, she turned the small swivel board that kept the door closed. Inside she secured it by looping a leather strap with a slit in the end over a peg. The privy was a sturdy structure with a floor, a feature that some thought unnecessary. The wood on the seat was smooth and she had no trouble finding the opening in the dark.

Anxious to get back into the house and into bed before

T.C. returned, Jane completed what needed to be done. She would have a clearer head in the morning and would be more able to cope with his persuasive tactics, she reasoned as she adjusted her clothing and opened the door. She pushed it outward, stepped out into the starlit night and turned to close it.

The blow came without warning. An agony of pain shot through her head like a fiery bolt. Brightly colored stars flashed before her eyes and she felt herself pitch forward. Vaguely she knew she was falling toward the open door of the privy. Then blackness closed in.

Polly walked beside Herb to the knoll where only this morning they had buried Doc. They stood silently beside the fresh grave. Herb's arm moved around her waist and pulled her close to his side. It was quiet and dark. Polly snuggled close to him. The feeling of being cared for was so new, it made her almost giddy.

"Ya liked him a lot, didn't ya?"

"Yeah. Doc was all right."

"Did ya know what all he'd done in the war?"

"I knowed he was in it. Sometimes he had nightmares about what all he'd done. He didn't do a lot of drinkin' till lately. When he was real drunk, he lived it again."

"Jane said he knew he was goin' to die and was tryin' to get it over."

"It's what he'd do. I ain't knowin' where I'd be or what I'd be doin' if it warn't for Doc. Probably dead, or crippled up by some back-shooter."

"He thought a heap of ya, Herb. Ya could just tell it."

"I'm goin' to miss him. He wasn't always as cantankerous as he was at the last. Miss Jane knew how to handle him. He liked her 'cause she stood up to him. I . . . couldn't do it him bein' sick and all."

"At the last ya did. Jane said so. He'd a killed hisself if ya hadn't took care of him."

"Maybe I ought to a let him. He'd not a suffered so much." They moved on around to the other side of the grave.

"I'm goin' to get him one of them great big stones with his name on it. I'm goin' to have 'Little Doc' put on it too. Then I'll put a fence around here. Maybe an iron one like I saw in Denver."

"This whole hilltop should be cleaned off. This is a pretty place."

"I'll do that too. I ain't forgettin' Doc."

"Of course not. But after a while it won't hurt so much."

"How are ya knowin' that?"

"My maw died, then my paw. I thought I'd cry my eyes out at first. But a body's got to live on and make the best of it."

"Yo're awful smart. Polly."

"I ain't half as smart as ya are."

"Bullfoot! I can do one thing real good and that's all."

"That's not so—"

He turned her around with his hands on her shoulders and looked down into her face.

"The thing I'm best at doin' is pullin' my gun, shootin' and hittin' what I shoot at."

"That's a good thin' to be good at."

"I got me a gun. Stole it off a old drunk who'd kicked me outta the livery. I pert nigh froze to death that night. I told myself it'd not happen again and it didn't. I practiced and practiced. I just got tired of eatin' ever'body's dirt, gettin' called a stray, a woods-colt, a good-for-nothin' clabber-head. I was big, even as a kid. But I warn't a man yet." He said this in a rush, as if he were in a hurry to get it out.

"Ah, Herb. Ya've had it rougher'n me. How old was ya when ya decided all this?"

"I was about ten or twelve. I can't even swear how old I am if ya get right down to it. Nobody ever told me. When I first met Doc, he thought I was fourteen or fifteen. I took that to be my age. I'm twenty now."

"Ya've done good, Herb. Ya raised yoreself till ya met Doc."

"I couldn't write my name. Doc said I had to if I was goin' to trail with him. I did it. Did it damn quick. I didn't want to lose Doc."

She laughed. "I betcha ya can do anythin' ya set yore mind to."

"Polly? Doc told me to settle down, get a wife and a bunch a young 'uns. I told him I was goin' to ask ya . . . if ya'd have me."

She stood silently with bowed head.

"Polly?" He lifted her chin with shaking fingers. "Don't ya want to?"

Her big eyes filled with tears. She tried to speak and choked back a sob. Then tried again.

"Do . . . ya know?"

"About what was done to ya? Miss Jane told me 'cause she wanted me to look out for ya after she goes."

"Ya know I'm . . . I'm . . . goin' to have—?"

"I know it," he said quickly. "If I ever set eyes on who done it, I'll kill him."

"Oh, no . . . no. Please—"

Herb drew in a deep breath. "Ya like him?

"I despise him! He's mean. I'm afraid he'll hurt you." Herb's arms moved around her, and he hugged her to him.

"The only way he'd hurt me is to shoot me in the back." He chuckled.

"Don't ya dare laugh about such a thin'."

"Polly . . . little Polly. I been thinkin' 'bout ya since that first day. Yo're so pretty." He touched her temples with his fingertips. "Yore hair is soft. I like it when ya let the braid hang down yore back. Yore eyes are pretty, too. I just can't keep myself from lookin' at ya. Polly," he whispered, his palms on her cheeks holding her face up to his, "Do ya think ya could put up with me?"

"What about . . . it?"

"The babe? Don't ya think I'd make a good papa?"

"It wouldn't be . . . yores."

"Only if ya didn't want it to be mine. I wasn't Doc's but I felt like I was."

"I'd not want ya to . . . hate it. It wasn't *its* fault."

"Why'd I do that? The bastard just planted the seed. I'll raise it. It'll be mine. Don't ya want to wed me?"

"I want it more'n anythin' in the world."

"Can I kiss ya? I been wantin' to since that day ya swooned and I carried ya to the bed."

"I ain't sure I know how."

"Me neither." He chuckled. "I kissed a saloon gal once. Don't think she wanted me to, but I wanted to know why folks sneak around to do it."

"Did ya find out?"

"It wasn't what I thought it'd be. I never wanted to do it again till I saw you."

"I'd like ya to kiss me, Herb."

Polly closed her eyes when his fingers lifted her chin and his lips softly met hers. She felt her insides warm with pleasure and allowed herself the pure joy of feeling his nose against her cheek and the rough drag of the whiskers on his chin. His mouth was warm and careful with hers. She felt none of the panic she had felt before when the freighter had come to her room and grabbed her. This was different. A lovely feeling unfolded in her midsection and traveled slowly through her body.

She wanted it to last forever. His lips moved against hers ever so slightly. He held her gently as if she were something so fragile she would break. His mouth left hers and moved to her cheeks, her brows, and touched her closed eyelids. She leaned against him, her arms finding their way around him. A surge of pleasure rushed through her when his lips returned to hers and she heard the soft moan that came from her throat.

Herb lifted his head and looked down at her.

"Did ya like it?"

"Oh, yes. I didn't know it would be like this."

"I wasn't too rough? I'm so big. Yo're so little."

"Ya wasn't rough." She reached for his face with her hands and stroked his cheeks with her palms. "Yo're sweeter than I ever thought a man could be. I didn't want ya to stop."

"Ya mean that?"

"'Course, I do, silly."

"Ya liked it?"

"I liked it a lot."

"Polly, sweet Polly. I like ever'thing about ya." His arms tightened and he hugged her to him fiercely, then let her go. "I got to be careful not to hurt ya. I like to hold ya. It makes me feel like I could . . . whip ever' man in this town with a willow switch."

Her laugh was soft and just for him.

"Ya can!" she said staunchly. "Ya can do anythin' ya want."

"Polly—" He held her away from him and looked earnestly into her face. "I don't have much in the way a money. I'm plannin' on askin' T.C. and Colin to take me on to work at their place. I ain't a town man. I stayed in town with Doc, but I want a little place where I can run a few cows and maybe horses—"

"Whatever ya do is all right."

"Ya sure? There ain't much in the way of company on a ranch, but we could visit a town once in a while."

"I won't miss town. I'll have you, Herb."

"Ah, Polly, when I look at ya, my insides gets all shaky. I swear ta ya, I'll take care a ya the best I know how."

His arms held her gently. She nestled in the warm protection of his embrace and crooned to him.

"I'll take care of ya, too, my sweet man. Ya'll not be by yoreself ever again."

Chapter 16

JANE did not know if she was awake or asleep. She opened her eyes and saw nothing but darkness. Her head pounded with a pain that throbbed through every part of her body. She gradually became aware that she was sitting on the floor, her back and head leaning against something hard. Her legs, folded beneath her, began to cramp. She tried to straighten them and discovered she was in a small boxed-in place.

As her mind cleared the stench of the outhouse was strong and repugnant. She realized where she was. But what was she doing on the floor between the seat and the door? She tried to get up from her cramped position. Her head seemed to weigh a ton. Her hand reached out for something to pull on and found a rough board, but her strength was gone and her head felt as if it were being pounded on with a hammer.

She sank back down and put her hand to her face to pull away whatever it was that clung to her cheeks. Her fingers slid across her face and followed the thick substance into her hair.

When she realized what her fingers were trailing through, waves of shock, terror and nausea swept over her. The heavy cloud of horror that dropped around her came close to robbing her of her senses. She grabbed at her skirt to wipe away the bodily waste from the cesspit, only to discover that it was not only on her face, but on her hands, her arms, and her clothing.

Sobbing with terror and shame, Jane slid down onto the floor of the privy. She drew her knees up to her chest. Hysteria spread through her brain like a vicious serpent, engulfing her. It was more than she could endure. She slipped back into blessed darkness.

T.C. sat at Doc's desk in the surgery and listened for any sound of movement upstairs. Maude had been in the kitchen when he returned to the house and told him Jane had gone to bed. He had feared she would not be here.

The lamp shone down on his dark head as he bent over the papers he had taken from the leather folder Doc had entrusted to his care. He finally put them aside and leaned back in the chair. He couldn't concentrate on figures and legal documents when his mind was awash with thoughts of Jane and her odd behavior.

His father had insisted that he leave the Wyoming Territory and see some of the world before he settled down. He had visited the big cities in the east, had traveled across the ocean to London and Paris. While in that dazzling city, he had decided that there was no place he'd rather be than home.

T.C. had been a lumberjack, a drover, a teamster and a lawman and had spent some time at law school. He had met women of all types, from society matrons and their pretty but useless daughters to ranch and farm women who were as handy as their men with a gun. Not one of them had even come close to tying him in knots as Jane was doing. There was an indefinable something between him and the prim Miss Jane Love. He wanted to be with her every moment. At night he lay awake thinking about her.

He was reasonably sure she felt the same. She had melted against him when he kissed her. Her mouth had clung sweetly to his. A woman would not kiss a man as she had done if there were not some feeling involved.

T.C. had tried to tell himself that his fascination with her was due to the pleasure it gave him to tease her. She had a sassy way when she got her back up. He'd always gotten along with women, what few he'd had to deal with. As a rule they liked him well enough—all but Patrice, and he knew well the reason for that. At one time he had dealt a blow to her pride and she had turned her charms on Colin.

The door squeaked open and he heard Herb's voice, then Polly's. They came down the hall and soon were standing in the doorway, Herb behind Polly, his hands on her shoulders.

"Me and Polly's gettin' married." Herb blurted out the news. His face was wreathed in smiles, Polly's beet-red.

"Well, now. Congratulations." T.C. stood and held out his hand. Herb reached around Polly to grasp it eagerly. "When will this happy event take place?"

"As soon as I can talk to the preacher. I'm not wantin' folks to get the idea . . . that Polly's babe ain't mine," Herb explained in his blunt way. He glanced down when Polly's elbow dug into his stomach. "T.C. knows 'bout it, honey-girl."

Polly was staring at the floor. She looked as if she were about to burst into tears.

"No one knows but me and Jane and maybe Sunday. You're getting a good man, Polly. I've known Herb for more than three years. One bad thing about this fellow you'd better look out for. He's the worst dang-blasted cook that ever slapped a skillet over a fire."

Polly raised tear-bright eyes.

"I ain't got no doubt at all that he's a good man. He won't have to cook. I can cook as good a meal as ya ever et if I got the stuff to do it with."

Herb's big hands squeezed her arms. He laughed in her ear. He seemed not to mind at all that T.C. watched as he lovingly nuzzled his nose into her hair.

"Ya better run on up to bed, little love. We got plans to make tomorrow and I got a thin' to talk over with T.C."

Polly turned to leave, then turned back to ask, "Did Jane go to the other. . . place to sleep?"

"She's still here."

"I was scared she'd go."

"So was I," T.C. muttered the words as Herb walked with Polly to the foot of the stairs.

He sat back down in the chair. He had papers to sort out before he could put down figures. He wished Jane were here to help him; but as she was involved, it was best he do this first part alone. He folded the papers and placed them in a drawer of the desk and waited for Herb to come back in. He was reasonably sure he knew what Herb wanted to talk about.

Polly went up the stairs wondering if it was sinful to be so happy on the day they had buried Dr. Foote, the man Herb thought the world of. Even if Jane was asleep, she would wake her and tell her the news. She had to share this miracle or she would burst!

The room was as dark as the night when she entered. Moving slowly with her hands in front of her, she felt her way to the end of the bed. Her toe connected with something hard. She stumbled and caught herself on the iron bedstead. She paused to consider if she should light the lamp. She desperately needed to use the chamber pot and it was somewhere under the bed. Holding on to the bedstead, Polly moved back along it until she could reach out and touch the bureau that held the lamp.

A minute later, with the light from the lamp illuminating the room, she turned back to the bed to get the chamber pot.

Jane was not in the bed!

With a frown puckering her brow, she used the pot. It was a blessed relief to empty her full bladder. When she finished she replaced the lid and pushed the pot back under the bed. It was then that she noticed Jane's nightdress lying at the foot. All of her things except for her shawl were packed in the closed suitcase.

Polly began to worry. It was not like Jane to be away from the house, especially at night. Polly went into the hall and stood for a moment outside Doc's old room. A light shone under the door and she heard Maude's voice. She knocked softly. Maude opened the door.

"Is Jane in here?"

"No. She went to bed quite a while ago."

"She ain't there. Her nightdress is on the bed. If she'd gone to stay with Sunday, she'd a took it and her other things."

"Is she downstairs?"

"I don't think so."

"She may be in the kitchen—"

"No light was on."

Maude came out into the hall, crossed it and looked into the room.

"The last I saw of her was when Stella and I came. She said she was going to the outhouse and then to bed. She may be with Mr. Kilkenny."

"She ain't. She'd not go out at night and not tell nobody. She's scared to be out at night."

"She knew I was here. I think she would have told me if she was leaving."

"I'm goin' to ask Mr. Kilkenny. If she went to the hotel, or the rooming house, he'd know."

"I'll come with you. Stay here, Stella. I'll be right back."

Herb looked up as Polly appeared in the doorway of the surgery. The worried look on her face drew him to his feet.

"What's the matter, honey-girl?"

"Jane ain't up there.

"Is she with Sunday?" T.C. asked, rising to his feet.

"Her nightdress and suitcase are here. I'm worried."

T.C. strode to the doorway. Polly and Maude stepped aside. He looked over Polly's head and spoke to Maude.

"You said she'd gone to bed."

"She told me she was goin' to bed soon. I thought after she went to the . . . privy. That was an hour or so ago."

By the time she had finished speaking, T.C. was taking the stairs two at a time. The door to the room Jane shared with Polly was open. It was as Polly said. Her nightdress lay at the foot of the bed. Her valise was there. Only a shawl hung on the peg on the wall. T.C.'s heart began to slam against his chest.

"Herb," he shouted on his way downstairs. "Find Colin." His voice was unnecessarily loud and harsh.

"I'm here." Colin opened the door. "What'er you yellin' for? What's wrong?"

"Jane—" T.C. couldn't bring himself to say that she was gone. "Did she go to stay with Sunday?"

"I just come from there." A frown spread across Colin's face. "She wasn't there. Isn't she here?"

"No. Her things are her, but no one has seen her for an hour or more." T.C. made no attempt to hide his anxiety. "Somebody go see if she's at the henhouse." He unconsciously used Sunday's word for the women's bunkhouse.

"I'll do that," Maude said quickly. "If Polly will stay with Stella." Without waiting for an answer she was out the front door.

"Get a lantern." T.C. was strapping on his gun belt.

"You think you'll need that?" Colin asked.

"I will if somebody's got her someplace she don't want to be." Herb came from the kitchen with a lighted lantern. "Is that the only one we've got?"

"Bill's got a couple."

"Something's not right. I feel it. If we don't find her soon, I'll ring the fire bell. We'll turn out every man in town to search."

"Calm down, T.C." Colin took his own gun belt from the hall peg and strapped it on. "She may have gone to the hotel. They've got some beds ready."

"She wouldn't go without telling Maude. She'd not leave her things. She guards that suitcase as if it were full of gold nuggets. But go look. Herb, go to the livery and see if anyone has left town in the last hour or two. Do you know where that fellow Fresno stays?" he asked Colin.

"No, but Tennihill does."

"Go up and stay with Stella." Herb gently urged Polly toward the stairs.

The men were gone when Maude returned to the house with Sunday. When she didn't find Jane in the henhouse, she had gone to the boarding house and roused Sunday. First Colin, then Herb returned to the porch where Maude and Sunday waited. Minutes later, T.C. arrived with Tennihill.

"Has anyone seen her?" T.C. demanded.

"No," Colin replied. "I didn't ask anyone either. Let's don't rouse the town yet."

"Did anyone look in the outhouse?" Sunday asked. "Maude said that's where she was goin' when she saw her last."

"I did," T.C. said. "The door is shut, the swivel bar down. Let's spread out one more time, then we'll ring the bell. If you find her, whistle two sharp ones."

Maude had gone into the house to get a shawl. When she returned, Sunday was waiting on the porch with a lantern.

"Could somebody, maybe a Indian, a carried her off her when she went to the outhouse?" Maude asked.

"Colin said they hadn't had no Indian trouble here for a long while. If anybody carried her off it'd more'n likely be one a them horny lumberjacks."

"Ah . . . no! She's such a nice woman. I'd bet she's had a hard life. At times I see sadness in her eyes."

Maude cringed inwardly. She *knew* about a hard life. But she hoped that now it was behind her and Stella. She walked with Sunday around the house.

"It's spooky here in the dark."

"I got my pistol in my pocket," Sunday replied. "I don't go out at night without it. Ain't no tellin' what kind a varmint ya might meet up with. Could have four legs. Could have two."

The moon had come up. It shone brightly, clearly outlining the outhouse. The women went toward it, lifted the lantern and saw that the board was turned to keep the door closed. They parted; one went on one side, one the other. They looked in the underbrush behind it and, finding nothing, retraced their steps back to the outhouse.

As Sunday passed the privy, she paused. Maude went on a few steps, then stopped.

"What—?"

"Shhh . . ."

A low, soft, keening sound came from inside the privy.

"Did ya hear that?" Maude stood close to Sunday.

Sunday nodded. She handed Maude the lantern and took the pistol from her pocket. They moved to the privy door. Sunday placed her ear against it. The sound that she heard was like that of a wounded animal suffering intense pain.

"Somethin's in there. Stand back! It could be a mad coon or polecat."

Maude held the lantern high as Sunday opened the door a crack. She kept her shoulder against it should something try to spring out. When nothing happened, she opened it wider, then wider. Both women gasped in shock, then relief, when the light from the lantern shone down on a figure huddled in a corner, her face and head covered with the skirt of her dress and her petticoat. They knew it was Jane. Her knee-length drawers were all that covered her thighs. She was hugging herself with her arms, shaking, and rocking back and forth.

"Oh, my Gawd!" Maude exclaimed. "What's the matter with her?"

"Lord a'mercy!" The hand holding the gun fell to Sunday's side. She shoved the gun in her pocket and knelt down. "Jane—" She said the name several times. Jane didn't respond until Sunday tried to pull the dress away from her head. Then she lashed out with hands covered with filth. One glimpse at her face and the two women rocked back.

"Oh, Lord! Christ in heaven!" Bile rose up in Maude's throat and she gagged.

Sunday recovered first.

"Now ain't the time to get squishy!" she said sharply. "Go let 'em know we found her afore T.C. rings the bell."

Maude set the lantern on the ground and ran up the path toward the house. A swinging light came around from the side and she called out.

"We found her."

Two sharp blasts of a whistle sounded, and the man hurried down the path.

Sunday stood as Colin approached. "She's in here. I ain't never seen anything so . . . awful."

"Is she hurt bad?"

"There's blood on the side of her head, but it's more'n that. She's covered with—Hell!" Sunday shouted in anguish. "She's covered with shit from the privy and she might of lost her mind!"

Sunday's anguished words reached T.C. as he rounded the house. An instant later he was there, pushing her aside so he could see. What he saw stunned him. Jane lay curled up on the floor of the privy, her head covered with the tail of her dress. The keening sounds that came from her were of deep, horrendous grief.

"What's the matter with her?" he demanded, and bent to kneel down. Sunday grabbed his arm.

"It's plain to me," she retorted angrily and moved to shield Jane from the eyes of the two men. "Get away, both of ya. Can't ya see she dyin' a shame?"

"Who did this?" The emotional croaking question came from T.C.

"That ain't what's important now. We got to get this stuff off her. Somebody get that bathin' tub from the henhouse and get the cookstove fired up for water. And . . . don't ya let her catch ya lookin' at her." Sunday issued the orders, then waited for the men to move. "Well? Are yore feet stuck in mud?"

"There's blood on her . . . dress—"

"I'm thinkin' it's from the whack on the head, but I ain't sure. What I am sure of is . . . it'll kill her for ya to see her with shit smeared all over her face. Now go!"

T.C. masked his anguish with anger. "I'll kill the bastard

who did this. I'll strip ever inch of hide off his back first, then, by Gawd, he'll wish he was dead a hundred times before he is!"

"I'll take Polly to see if anybody's in the tub." Herb spoke calmly, his voice battling T.C.'s angry tirade. "If there ain't, I'll get it out the back door without them knowin' about it."

Colin took T.C.'s arm. "Come on. Let the women handle it for now."

"Why would anybody do . . . such a thing to her?" T.C. allowed Colin to pull him away.

"Maybe we can find out after the women clean her up a bit. Come on to the house, Tennihill," Colin said as they passed the man standing a distance away. "We got to get to the bottom of this."

The first thing Sunday did when she got Jane into the house was clean her face. Maude dipped towel after towel in warm water and handed them to Sunday. Jane stood as docilely as a whipped dog. Both Sunday and Maude realized that she was in deep shock. Her arms hung to her sides; her eyes were blank. When her face was clean, they found marks on her cheeks and forehead where the stick that had been dipped into the cesspit had scraped the skin.

Maude placed a cold, wet cloth on the side of her head where blood still oozed.

"They knocked her senseless before they did this." Maude clicked her tongue sorrowfully. "Why in the world?"

"They could'a killed her if'n they wanted to. I'm just bumfuzzled about it." Sunday unbuttoned the waist of Jane's dress and pulled it down to let it fall to the floor.

It wasn't until all her filthy clothes had been removed and Maude and Sunday were lowering her into the warm tub of water that she came out of her mindless state. She looked wildly about, screamed, struck out at Sunday, and tried to climb out of the tub.

Sunday's superior strength held her firmly.

"Jane! Jane! Yo're all right. It's me, Sunday. Ain't nobody goin' to hurt ya. Yo're here with me and Maude."

The door was flung open. T.C. came storming into the room.

"What'er you doing to her?" he demanded.

"Christ on a horse!" Sunday yelled. "Get out of here."

"Go, Mr. Kilkenny. It'd be awful for her if she saw ya lookin' at her." Maude pushed T.C. firmly out the door and shut it.

"Some men ain't got no more sense than a pissant," Sunday sputtered.

"He's worried." Maude handed her the castile soap from the surgery that T.C. had brought in when Herb had returned with the tub. She placed it on a chair, along with a stack of clean towels.

On her knees beside the tub, Sunday lathered Jane with soap, then worked it into her hair. Jane was now perfectly still. Great racking sobs tore from her throat. She cried openly, her hands in the water at her sides, her face turned up. Her bald-faced misery was one of the saddest sights Sunday had ever seen.

"I'm washin' it off ya, Jane. Ain't nobody goin' to see ya like this but me and Maude. Ya got a good bashin' up beside yore head. I got to wash yore hair, but I'll be careful."

T.C. paced up and down the hall. The Indian side of him tried to be calm; the Irish side wouldn't permit it. He uttered cuss words he hadn't used in years.

"I've heard of meanness, but nothing like this." Pacing like a caged cat, T.C. stopped in front of Colin, who sat on the stairs. "Have you ever heard of anybody doin' this?" He didn't wait for an answer. "Was it meant to shame her, like Sunday said? Why? What has she done to be shamed for?"

"No Indian did it." Tennihill, sitting on the floor, offered his opinion while he pared at his fingernails with his pocketknife.

"When I find out who did it, I'll roast his ass over a slow fire, Indian fashion."

"Don't figure he hit her with the stick he used to smear her. That stick was poked down in the hole."

T.C. glanced at Colin. "Could it have been the butt of a pistol?"

"More'n like a stick of stove wood to knock her out. She'd a put up a fight. I didn't see no sign a one."

"The dirty, low-down, cowardly sonofabitch!"

Maude came out of the kitchen and closed the door behind her.

"Is she all right?" T.C. asked quickly.

"She's got a awful bash on the head. We tried to be careful of it when we washed that . . . stuff out of her hair. Sunday's dryin' it now. I'm goin' to get her nightdress. I thought you ought to see these." She held out small pieces of folded paper. "I found them in the pocket of her dress. I emptied out the pocket when I went to soak the dress in a bucket of water."

T.C. took the papers from Maude and went into the surgery where a lamp was burning on the desk. Colin and Tennihill followed. He unfolded the notes and read them one after the other. He gave a low whistle of amazement and stepped back, leaving the notes on the desk for Colin and Tennihill to read.

"That explains why she didn't want to stay here. She probably got the first one the day she arrived. It was the next day that she was so determined to leave, and it wasn't because she thought I had brought the women here to marry them off. She used that as an excuse."

T.C. began to pace again. Tennihill arranged the notes in the order he figured they might have been received, the last one being the one that threatened to kill her.

"I heard talk today that Miss Love was not stayin' on.

Guess ever'body knowed about it."

"Why ya reckon he wanted her to stay?"

"Beats me."

T.C. looked at Tennihill. "You don't think it's Bob Fresno?"

"I'm thinkin' not. He's got a hard-on fer her. Be tickled to get her off to hisself. Like I told ya today."

"Maybe he met her outside. When she wouldn't go with him, he did this?"

"Doubt it. Ain't his style."

"You said he was sly as a fox."

"He is that."

"Dangerous, when he don't get his way?"

"As a cornered rattler."

"She's not getting out of my sight until we find out who sent her these threats and who waylaid her." T.C. marched out of the surgery and went to the door of the kitchen.

Colin lounged in the doorway. "That's goin' to be pretty hard to do, friend."

"Yeah? Well, you watch me." T.C. knocked on the door, then opened it. "Is she dressed?"

"Yes. Come in."

Jane was in the nightdress she had worn the night he went to Doc's room. Ignoring his presence, she stood quietly as Sunday rubbed the ends of her damp hair with a towel. Her eyes were red-rimmed and focused on a spot on the wall. Deep scratches marked her cheeks, her forehead and the backs of her hands.

"How is she?"

Sunday shook her head in a silent warning before she spoke.

"She's got a big lump on her head, but the cut's not deep. We've done 'bout all we can tonight. We'll take her up to bed. I'll stay tonight if ya want me too."

"That won't be necessary. I'll take care of her." T.C. crossed the room and swung Jane up into his arms. She made no protest and let her head drop to his shoulder. He strode across the hall to his room. Before he entered he said, "Find another place to sleep tonight, Colin." He went inside and kicked the door shut with his foot.

"Well, don't *that* beat all?" Sunday stood in the kitchen doorway with her hands on her hips. Her dress was wet down the front, her blond ringlets a tangled mess as usual.

Tennihill headed for the door.

"Our Mr. Kilkenny's got a bad case of heart trouble, I'm thinkin'. I better pull foot. It might be catchin'. 'Night, folks."

Chapter 17

THE room was dark.

Jane threw her arms around the neck of the warm body holding her and clung tightly.

"No . . . no . . . no. . .—"

"Don't be scared. You're all right, sweet girl. Just hold on tight—" T.C. murmured to her. "Nothing will hurt you."

When she felt herself being lowered to the bed and the arms pull away, she panicked and cried out.

"Don't go!"

"I'm going to light the lamp and get covers for you. You're shaking."

"Don't go!"

"All right. I won't leave you." T.C. sat down on the side of the bed with her on his lap.

An implacable hatred for the one who had done this to her caused droplets of sweat to break out on his forehead.

Her arms were locked around him as if he were an anchor and she were being swept to sea. She couldn't seem to get close enough to him. Her face burrowed in the curve of his neck and she shook violently. T.C. felt the heavy hand of fear as he realized she might be sinking deeper into that black mindless void.

He put his hand over her ear and pressed her head to his shoulder.

"Colin!" he bellowed.

The door opened almost instantly and a ribbon of light shone from the hallway. Colin, with Sunday behind him, came into the room.

"Light the lamp. She's scared to death."

"Don't look at me."

Quite suddenly she was soundlessly and helplessly crying. Her silent agony was something T.C. could hardly endure.

"I won't, love. Shhhh—Don't cry."

Colin lit the lamp and light flooded the room. He turned the wick down until there was no smoke going up the chimney, then with his hand on Sunday's back urged her to the door.

"I've got to cover you, honey." T.C. placed tender kisses on her forehead. "Your hands and feet are like ice."

"I'm so . . . bad—"

"Bad? You're not bad! You're good and sweet. The sweetest woman I ever knew."

"Bad . . . blood—"

"No. no—There's no such thing as bad blood."

"I'm . . . dirt . . . filth—"

"You're not" He felt her confusion, heard it in the unsteady murmur of her words. "Trust me, sweetheart. You're a smart, spunky, pretty girl and . . . and I love you—"

The words came out without T.C. planning to say them. Saying them aloud shocked him. But he knew, without doubt, that he was deeply, irreversibly in love with the woman he held in his arms. He had not known the feeling of being in love, had not known what to expect, but he knew that this was it.

She didn't speak after that. He didn't know if she had heard him. After a while he stood with her in his arms, turned, and lowered her to the bed. Her eyes, smoky blue and pleading, looked into his.

"Don't . . . leave me—"

"I'm not leaving. I'm getting a blanket."

He lifted the long flow of damp hair and spread it out on the pillow. Her eyes followed him as he crossed the room then returned to her. He covered her with the blanket, pulling it up to her chin. Her eyes never left his face. When he sat down on the side of the bed, her hand came out from under the blanket and reached for his. She was still in shock.

With eyes wide open, she no longer looked at his face, but at the hand that was holding hers carefully so as not to irritate the scratches on the back. After a while she stopped shivering. Her eyelids finally drooped and she fell asleep.

The skinned side of her face was exposed to the light. The marks from the stick would be there for days. With trembling fingers T.C. pushed the damp hair back from her neck. He had seen plenty of cruelty before, but God in heaven, this was a different kind. Whoever did this meant to humiliate her beyond her endurance, to shame her to the point where she would cower, hide and possibly lose her reasoning.

She had not been aware, he was sure, of what she had said to him. Those words had come from the depths of her despair. For days she had held up her head and gone about the task of taking care of Doc with the threats hanging over her. No wonder she had been so desperate to leave town.

T.C. leaned over her and kissed her cheek.

"It's over, sweetheart. You'll not be alone again, and I promise you, I'll find out who did this to you, and make them sorry they ever lived."

Looking back, T.C. could recognize the signs of her panic. She had not left the house once since she had arrived. Only at his insistent urging had she gone for the walk with him that one evening. She had received the final note today, he believed, sometime after the funeral, because she had talked and laughed with some of the people during and after the meal. She had taken a woman and her child into the surgery and had given the mother some ointment for ringworm. He had heard her telling a small group of women how to rid their children of head lice.

Tonight he didn't want to think about who had done this to her. Tomorrow was time enough for that. Tonight he was going to hold her in his arms all night long, and he didn't care if the whole damn town knew it. He wanted her to know that she was not alone and would never be alone again.

And tomorrow he was going to marry her. Her troubles

would be his troubles. He unbuckled his belt, removed his clothing except for his underdrawers, got into bed and took her into his arms. Her breasts were soft against his chest, her face fit in the curve of his neck. His hand caressed her buttock and pressed her to him. She moved, mumbled, put her arm around him and snuggled closer. Her legs were between his, her thigh tight against his sex.

The feeling he had for her now was of tenderness. He could wait for their physical mating. He wanted her to be well, to revel with him in the delight of warm bare flesh against warm bare flesh.

"Sleep, little love," he murmured with his lips against her hair.

"Guess ya'll have to find ya another place to sleep."

Using buckets, Sunday and Colin had emptied the bathtub and carried the water to the porch. Now Colin straddled a kitchen chair and watched as she tidied the kitchen.

"You offerin'?" His eyes smiled into hers.

"Ha! And have that Mexican wildcat on my back?"

"She's got no claim on me."

"She thinks she has."

"I *know* she don't."

Sunday hung the wet towels on a string that ran across the corner of the room. She turned, put her hands on her hips and looked him straight in the eye.

"About offerin' ya a place in my bed. No man gets in my bed, Mr. Tallman, till his name's tacked on the end of mine."

"Hummm . . . Good point." Colin tilted his head and appeared to be studying the matter. "I don't know if it'd be worth the price I'd have to pay."

A wet towel slammed into his face.

"I got a notion to pull my gun and shoot ya!" she spat out angrily, but when he looked at her, she was choking with laughter.

He got up off the chair. "You got a gun on ya?"

"Damn right. I don't go nowhere at night without one. I might meet up with a two-legged varmint wearin' a leather shirt and knee-high moccasins."

"Can you use it?" Colin began stalking her around the table.

"I can hit the eye outta a jackrabbit goin' full speed." She sidled on around to get behind a chair.

"I can do *that* with my eyes shut."

"I can do it goin' full speed standing on my head with my eyes shut." She moved quickly when he reached for her.

His eyes went past her toward the door.

"Mrs. Henderson—"

Sunday looked over her shoulder and Colin pounced. He put his arms around her and held her against him. She struggled, but not too much.

"Dang yore hide! That's cheatin'."

"Yeah. And it worked."

"What worked?"

"Caught ya, didn't I"

"Why'd ya want to do that for?"

"I think you know."

"'Course, I do." She was smiling at him.

"I want to kiss you. Been wantin' to for a long while."

"Ya've only known me a week or two . . . or three."

"Do you ever stop talkin'?"

"Not often. But there's a way to stop me." Her arms slid over his shoulders and around his neck.

His hand slipped up beneath her hair and stroked the nape of her neck. She was a tall woman. He had to bend his head only slightly until his lips touched hers. She was surprised that his lips were so soft, so gentle, surprised at the pleasant drag of his whiskers on her cheek. He held her head with his hand, working his fingers through her tangled curls while his lips made little caressing movements against hers.

With a swift motion he dropped his hand to her back, pulled her tightly to him and deepened the kiss. He gave her no chance to withdraw, and she wanted none. She gave herself up to his embrace, fitting her tall, slender body into every curve of his, and returned his kiss passionately. She wanted it to go on, and it did for a long while.

They parted. She let her breath out slowly. She hadn't wanted it to end. She looked into his eyes. He had not wanted it to end either. She could see it reflected in the tense lines of his face.

"What' a ya think now, Miss Sunday?"

"It was a . . . good kiss as kisses go . . . I guess." She had meant to sound flip, but the words came out a strangled whisper. "How'd it strike you?"

"I'll have to do it again before I can say for sure if it was up to snuff."

"I don't want ya to be . . . frettin' over it."

The first touch of his lips had awakened a bittersweet ache of passion in her. A lovely feeling unfolded in Sunday's midsection as she allowed herself the pure joy of pressing her body from her knees to her breast tightly against his unyielding hardness. There was the union of soft lips and tongues as their mouths parted and clung with wild sweetness that held still the moments of time.

When he drew back, his eyes slid hungrily over her face. She rose slightly on her toes and kissed him hard on the mouth.

"You liked it, huh?"

"I just wanted to give ya something back, Tallman."

Their breaths mingled for an instant before he covered her mouth with his again. He held her tightly, knowing she was not fragile and that she wanted the contact as much as he. This time he took his time with closed eyes and pounding heart. She gave willingly, their bodies meshed, close and warm and hard.

The kiss ended. Her head went to his shoulder and she leaned against him for a long moment.

"What ya think now?" she whispered.

"I think I'd better go find myself a place to sleep or I'll be bayin' at the moon."

He felt her laughter against his chest and the warm puffs of breath against his neck.

"Do ya think I'm a pretty good kisser?"

"Not any better than me."

She lifted her head to look at him. "You've had plenty of practice. The lips on that hot tamale over at the hotel's got a permanent pucker."

"I kissed her a few times. Who taught you?"

"One other man has kissed me and he married my sister. I lucked out. He turned out to be a pickled poot."

Colin laughed. She was the most wonderful, exciting woman he'd ever met. Open and honest. His mother would love her.

"He taught ya good."

"Bullfoot! He didn't teach me nothin'. You did."

"I'm a better teacher than I thought. I'd better give you another lesson."

"Ya kiss me like ya did the last time and I'll crawl right inside yore skin. We'd better put a damper on kissin' for a while and figure out where yo're goin' to sleep."

"I'll throw a bedroll down in T.C.'s office after I walk you back to the rooming house."

They left the kitchen and walked toward the door.

"Haven't heard a squeak outta T.C. and Jane," Sunday said as they passed T.C.'s door, went out the front door and stepped into the night. "Tongues'll wag if it gets out she spent the night in his bed."

"He won't care a whit about that."

"He was riled up, that's sure."

"He couldn't have fallen any harder if I'd hit him in the head with a hammer. I've not seen him in such a state before. He was as worked up as a dog passin' peach seeds."

Sunday's laugh floated on the still night. "Ya made a funny, Colin."

His laughter joined hers. "Wouldn't a been funny to the dog."

They strolled on down the street toward the rooming house, unaware that a pair of hate-filled eyes followed them.

Another pair of eyes stared at a dark ceiling. The head on the pillow shook in silent laughter. Finally the eyes closed in peaceful sleep. An unstable mind was satisfied with the night's work.

Jane was dreaming.

"You wicked, wicked girl!" Mrs. Gillis, in her high-necked black dress, stood over the small girl cowering in the corner. Her thin lips were pressed in the familiar line of disapproval. Her arms were folded across her flat chest. "You did not empty the chamber pot as you were told to do.

"Get up this instant. I've been trying to decide what to do with you. A switching seems to do no good." The long bony hand reached for the braid that hung over Jane's shoulder and she hauled her to her feet.

"Oh . . . oh—" Tears rolled down the small freckled cheeks. "I . . . forgot. I'm sorry—"

"It seems I've heard that before. There may be something wrong with your brain as well as your blood." The hand moved quickly from the braid to the earlobe. "I think it's time the good children of this school knew who is among them—eating the same food, sleeping in a good bed, just as if she were as good as they were. I've shielded you long enough, Miss Jane Bastard Love."

"I'm sorry, Mrs. Gillis. Please . . . don't—"

"Don't? Don't you think they have the right to know who is living among them? Answer me" She tugged viciously on the earlobe when the child remainded silent.

"Yes, ma'am."

"Haven't I been good to you here, in spite of who you are?"

"Yes, ma'am." Walking on her toes to take some of the pressure off her ear, Jane was propelled up the stairs to the classroom. "I'll be good! Please, Mrs. Gillis. I'll be good."

"Of course you will. Every child in this school will despise you. If you make one wrong move, I'll hear about it."

A hush fell over the room when Mrs. Gillis arrived, not so much because she had Jane in tow, but because each of them feared her as if she were the boogyman she often threatened to call forth to punish them.

"Children! Quiet," the headmistress instructed, although there wasn't a sound in the room. "It grieves me deeply to have to inform you that in our midst we have—"

"I'm sorry! I'm sorry!" Jane cried out, as she straightened her legs and flung her arms. "Please, ma'am, don't tell. I'll be . . . good—"

T.C. awoke. His hand caught one of her thrashing arms after she had hit him with her fist. He flung a leg over hers to hold them firmly, but gently. In the dim light from the lamp tears glistened on her cheeks.

"Wake up, honey." He bent over her. "Jane, Jane, you're dreaming."

Suddenly she was still. Her eyes, large and clear, opened and looked into his with full understanding.

"Nothing will hurt you. You're safe . . . with me—"

She didn't speak, just looked at him.

"Are you awake, sweetheart?" T.C. brushed the tangled deep-red curls back from her cheek with the tips of his fingers. His bare chest was pressed against her breast, his face just above hers.

"Why . . . am I here?"

"I brought you here. You were cold and scared. I wanted to keep you warm and safe."

"Why?"

"Because you mean a great deal to me."

She looked away from him. "I . . . shouldn't be here."

"You're exactly where you belong. I hope to sleep with you in my arms every night for the rest of my life. I love you, Jane."

Her eyes came back to his, but she made no response to his declaration.

"Who found me?"

"Sunday and Mrs. Henderson."

"Did you see me?" she asked quietly.

"No. Only Sunday and Maude saw you."

"But you *know*." It was not a question, but a statement of fact. She was calm and had not moved since she had awakened.

"I know that someone did a cruel thing to you. And I know someone is sending you threats. Maude found the notes in the pocket of your dress, and I read them."

She twitched and moved restlessly. Her eyes darted away and then back. She suddenly sighed and her head rolled to the side, so that he could see only her profile.

"It had to happen, I guess," she said with resignation.

"I intend to find out who sent them and who did that to you. When I do . . . God help them!"

"Let it be. I . . . can't bear any more. I wish they . . . they had finished it."

"Can't bear what, my love? Share it with me. Let me help you."

"There is nothing you can do. Nothing anyone can do. If I stay here, I might as well be dead. If I go, I will be. It will be easier if I go and let them do what they want to do."

"You're not leaving, Jane. Didn't you hear me when I said that I love you? I'm going to marry you, come hell or high water. I've looked for you all my life. I'll not let you go now."

Tears trickled from the corners of her eyes and rolled

down her temples and into her hair.

"Thank you for saying that. They're the most beautiful words I've ever heard. But understand, I cannot, will not accept your generous offer of a few days of happiness knowing what would lie ahead."

"Jane, Jane—" He lowered his head and kissed her lips gently and reverently. "Trust me. Marry me. There is nothing that can be so bad that would make me not want you. Together we'll face whatever comes."

"I can't. I can't bring shame to you." She rolled her head slowly in denial.

"Honey, I'm far from perfect. You'll have to accept my faults as I will accept yours."

"I . . . can't—"

"You have feelings for me, don't you, Jane? You were willing to come to me last night. You let me hold you. You felt safe with me."

She was silent, her eyes on his face as he lowered his head to kiss her.

To Jane each kiss, each sigh was unbearably sweet. His touch was exquisitely tender. His warm mouth glided over her cheek to her eyes. She heard him murmur soft words of love and incredible promises that she would hold in her heart until the day she died.

He watched the emotions flicker across her face in the lamplight. Utter, complete misery was etched there.

"Jane, sweetheart. Don't look at me like that. It tears me up."

"I'm . . . sorry. I'm . . . sorry." Her voice was a ragged whisper so sad that it tore at his heart. They were the same words she'd said as she was waking from her nightmare.

"Ah . . . honey—" He lay back and cuddled her in his arms, holding her firmly against him, kissing the top of her head.

She lay against him docile and unmoving, lifeless as a rag doll. She was no longer the spunky, sassy Jane he had met that first day, nor the one who had ripped into him when Polly had swooned in his office. She was no longer the Jane who had seen Doc through his last days or sewn up the cut in Murphy's leg.

The woman he held so lovingly against him was a mere shell of his Jane, and he was determined to get the whole of her back.

Chapter 18

MORNING came, and with it T.C.'s deep frustration returned. When he was reasonably sure Jane was sleeping, he eased away from her and out of the bed. He stood for a moment looking down at her. She murmured something, frowned, and wedged her palm beneath her cheek.

He didn't want to stop looking at her. Jane Love was all the woman he hoped he would find to share his life. He not only liked her because she had a quick, inquisitive mind, but he liked the way she looked . . . and smelled . . . and talked. Her dark auburn hair, tangled from the washing, curled about her face and stuck to cheeks that were slightly flushed. He especially liked her full expressive mouth, the way the corners tilted up when she smiled. He bent to leave her with a kiss, but straightened for fear of waking her.

After dressing quietly, T.C. blew out the lamp, which had burned all night and was beginning to flicker from lack of fuel. With his boots in his hand, he left the room and walked down the hall to the kitchen.

"Morning." He spoke to Maude, Polly and Herb, who were seated around the table eating flapjacks.

"Mornin'," they answered him in unison. Maude stood. "Sit down, Mr. Kilkenny. I'll fix your breakfast."

"Finish yours. I'll just have coffee for now."

T.C. went to the washstand, ladled water from the bucket into the basin, lathered his hands and scrubbed his face. He could feel his whiskers, but he decided he didn't have time to shave now. After he dried his face, he took the comb from the combcase attached to the wall above the washstand and ran it through his hair.

When he returned to the table, a mug of steaming coffee waited for him.

"She's sleeping," he said in answer to the inquiring eyes. "She had a bad dream in the night. She's worn out."

"Did she come . . . out of—" Maude searched for a word to describe Jane's mental state.

"She's over the shock. That is, she knows what she's saying and where she is." T.C. took a sip of the strong coffee. "I don't want a word of what happened here last night to leave this house. Where's Colin?"

"He ain't goin' to say nothin', T.C. He already told us not to." Herb's pleasant face was set in stern lines. "It ain't goin' down good fer whoever did that to Miss Jane."

"That's the God's truth. Where's Colin?" he asked again.

Maude answered. "He didn't wait for breakfast. He said he was going over to see Mr. Wassall. Well"—she smiled—" what he really said was that he was going over to see the moth-eaten, mouthy old goat."

T.C. swallowed his coffee and put on his boots.

"Mrs. Henderson, keep an eye on Jane. Don't let her leave the house, not that I think she'll try." He went to the door, then turned. "Would you put a chamber pot in the room?" The reason for the request was not necessary. They all knew it would be a while before Jane would want to go back out to the outhouse.

The morning was cool, sunless. T.C. looked at the sky as he stepped off the porch. The leaves on the trees were turning to gold and would soon be fluttering down. Iron-blue storm clouds rode the northern horizon pushing a chilly wind ahead of them, another sign that winter was approaching. In another few weeks the snow would fall, and the geese would be passing overhead on their yearly journey to the south.

Work here had gone well. T.C. had not thought he would enjoy the challenge of rebuilding the town, but he had. Now all he wanted to do was take Jane and get the hell out of it—but first his very blood demanded revenge on the one who had treated her so cruelly.

Men were leaving the cookhouse and gathering in groups to start the work day. Jeb had one crew working on the new saloon and was forming another crew to work on the schoolhouse. The day after T.C. and Jane had taken their evening stroll, Jeb and T.C. had marked off the building site.

The cookhouse was being converted into Timbertown's first restaurant. Actually it would be the second. At the end of the town's heyday, the only eatery in town had burned to the ground. Bill Wassall wanted no part of the operation other than consenting to the name of the establishment suggested by Colin: SWEET WILLIAM'S CAFE.

"I ain't doin' no fancy cookin' and that's that. I can barbecue ya a steer, cook ya up a gallon a beans, or make ya a barrel a sauerkraut, but I ain't cookin' no suck-e-tash and I ain't bakin' no jelly roll."

Having had his say, Bill considered the subject closed. Garrick Rowe was sending two women, who early in the spring had been widowed by an accident at the mill in Trinity, to operate the cafe. They would be arriving any day.

The dining area of the cookhouse was empty except for two men finishing their breakfast and Bill and Colin, who sat at one of the long tables near the front. Bill's helper was cleaning up the kitchen, trying to stay out of the way of Mrs. Winters, who was frying a batch of bear claws.

"Mornin'."

T.C. went to the table where the clean dishes were stacked and picked up a heavy china mug. He filled it with coffee from the pot on the stove and carried it back to the table where Bill and Colin were seated. He had no more than seated himself when a plate of hot bear claws generously sprinkled with sugar was set down in front of him. The aroma drifted up to him. He smiled up at the woman who stood expectantly waiting for praise.

"Thanks, Mrs. Winters. They look mighty good. Smell good too."

She turned her back to Bill, obviously giving him what

she considered a cold shoulder.

"Ain't nothin' too good fer ya, Mr. Kilkenny," she said and returned to the kitchen.

"Ain't nothin' too good fer ya, Mr. Kilkenny," Bill mocked as soon as she was out of earshot. "The sooner I see the last a her, the better it'll be."

"She likes you, Bill," Colin teased. "Don't you think it's time you settled down and raised a passel of young'uns to take care of you in your old age?"

Bill began to sputter. "I'd as soon tie up with a she-bear."

"She'll be out of here tomorrow. Jeb's got a man setting up her stove. We're starting her bakery off with a couple cords of stove wood and supplies from the store."

"Can't be soon enough to suit me. Bossy is what she is. Ya ort to do this. Ya ort to do that!" Bill mimicked in a high voice. "Moody, too. Can't never tell what'll raise her hackles."

Colin grinned, reached over and patted Bill's ample belly.

"Her complaining hasn't caused you to miss a meal."

T.C. waited until Bill left the table before he spoke about what was on his mind.

"Heard anything?"

Colin signaled silence by raising a couple of fingers.

Several minutes and several bear claws later, T.C. stood with the plate in his hand.

"How about a refill, Mrs. Winters?" He dropped a coin on the counter.

She brought a plate heaped with the heavily sugared fried dough. Her thin mouth was spread in a smile as she picked up the coin.

"It was a fancy send-off ya gave the doctor, Mr. Kilkenny."

"It was no more than he deserved."

"Is another doctor comin'?"

"I expect one soon." T.C. picked up the plate and headed

for the door. "Tell Buddy the new school building will be ready before the snow flies."

"I ain't better tell him that. He might run off to the mountains."

"Bill says that woman can hear a pin drop a dozen yards away. That's why I hushed you," Colin said, as they crossed the street.

"Women like to gossip."

"Bill's not used to sharin' his kitchen. He's not too happy nowadays."

"Can't say as I blame him. We'll get her out and in her own place today."

Both men knew they were dancing around the subject that was on their minds. Before they stepped up onto the porch of T.C.'s house they stopped.

"Did you hear anything?"

"Nothin'. I went early, mingled with the men. Her name wasn't mentioned or even hinted at."

"Did Tennihill come in?"

"Didn't see him."

"Did you tell Bill?"

"Didn't get a chance, but I will. He sees and hears a lot we don't. How's Jane?"

"She's worn out, but she came out of the shock. She was sleeping when I left. I'm going to marry her today."

The statement was dropped matter-of-factly into the conversation, and Colin's face reflected his surprise. He said nothing for several minutes.

"What does she say to that?"

"I haven't told her."

"Shhhh . . . eee—" Colin whistled softly between his teeth. "A decision like that ain't to be made lightly, T.C. Are ya sure she's up to it?"

"That's why I'm doing it today, this morning. I don't want to give her a chance to think about it. One way to help keep her safe in this town is to be with me, in my bed at night, by my side during the day."

"Rather a drastic way to keep her safe. We could get her out of here in the middle of the night, put her on a train and send her back east. It'd take a Pinkerton man to find her."

"I *want* her to be my wife, Colin. She wants it too but there's something in her past that's scaring the hell out of her."

"You might not like what you find out about her."

"I know she's a good, sweet woman—"

"She could already be married."

"The solicitor would have told me. He said she'd lived all her life at that orphans' school."

"Why don't you come right out and admit that you fell tail over teakettle for her."

"I love her." As he spoke, T.C. looked his friend straight in the eye.

Colin clapped him on the shoulder.

"This may surprise you, but I understand completely."

T.C. laughed in relief, then said, "Sunday?"

"She's a corker! She'd keep a man on his toes."

"Here comes that *corker*." T.C. looked past Colin and saw Sunday walking toward them.

"How's Jane?" she asked, without offering either man a greeting when she reached them.

"As of an hour ago she was sleeping."

Sunday plucked a bear claw off the plate T.C. was holding and bit into it.

"Still hot! Let's go have some decent coffee. That stuff at the rooming house is weak as baby pee." Her sparkling eyes caught Colin's. "Well . . . not *that* weak. Still, it's pretty damn weak," she concluded with a burst of laughter.

T.C. shot a look at Colin before he followed them into the house. He was grinning like an idiot.

Shortly after T.C. left the room, Jane awoke. Although her head felt as if a thousand drums were beating inside it, she was fully alert. She pressed her fingertips to her scalp and felt the lump and the broken skin. It was terribly sore to the touch. Her hair was spread out, tangled, and she could smell vinegar. Vinegar was almost as good an antiseptic on a cut as alcohol.

She lay quietly. Memories of Sunday bathing her in the tub and of being carried to this bed came back to her. For the first time she had slept in a man's arms. Not just any man's arms. T.C. Kilkenny's arms. She had felt warm and safe stretched out next to him, being sheltered, cosseted. Sometime during the night she had been aware of his heart beating beneath her cheek, and his lips on her forehead. Never had she had anyone hold her so lovingly. It was like a heavenly dream after being pulled up from the fires of hell.

What had she said to him during the time when all she wanted was to be held close in his warm embrace? Nothing had happened between them. She was sure. She would have remembered *that*. He had said that he would take care of her, that nothing would hurt her ever again. But what had *she* said? She closed her eyes and tried to remember, but nothing came to mind.

Jane began to panic. She couldn't be here in his bed when he came back. She scooted to the side, eased her way up, and put her feet on the cold floor. Her head throbbed viciously, and she waited for the dizziness to pass. When it did, she looked closely at the scratches on her hands.

The terror of being alone in the dark outhouse with the only air she could draw into her lungs fouled with the stench of excrement came roaring back. She put her hand to her mouth to stifle a sob.

"Stop it!" she whispered aloud to herself. "Get a hold on yourself. Hold up your head. You swore you'd never cower in a corner again. But, oh . . . it's so hard."

Jane stood and held onto the end of the bed until her head stopped swimming before she attempted to walk to the door. When she did, she opened it a crack and looked down the hall toward the kitchen. She had to risk passing the door to get to the stairway. Walking silently on her bare feet and as quickly as her aching head would permit, Jane went down the hall and up the stairs to the room she shared with Polly.

Had Jane looked into the kitchen she would have seen Maude look up when she finished pouring coffee for Herb. Maude set the coffeepot back on the stove and returned to the table.

"She went upstairs."

Polly moved her chair back and stood. "I'll go up."

"I think we should leave her be," Maude said kindly, and looked to Herb to back her words. He was already tugging on Polly's hand to urge her back down on the chair.

"Wait a bit, Pol. She can't leave without comin' back down stairs."

"I just never seen nothin' so pitiful." Maude clicked her tongue sadly and shook her head. "I swear I don't know what I'd a done if *that'd* been done to me. I'd a lost my mind, most likely."

"It's just so . . . nasty." Polly pulled Herb's hand over into her lap and held it between hers. "Hittin' her was bad, but smearin' her was . . . just awful."

"The person who did it is crazy mean, I'm thinkin'. And he's holdin' somethin' against her."

"If they'd wanted to kill her outright, a couple more whacks on the head with that piece of stove wood would'a done it," Herb said.

At daylight Colin had found the club with several long dark red hairs stuck in the bark and had shown it to Herb. It had been left on the back porch.

"Poor Jane. She'll want to leave sure 'nuff now. I was hopin' she'd stay."

Polly hadn't been told about the notes. Maude and Herb had agreed to that before she had come down for breakfast.

"It'd just worry her more," Herb had said. "Miss Jane said that she ain't to be carryin' a big load or worryin' overly much now."

Maude had looked into the face of the serious young man. At times during the last few years when she had begun to think that life wasn't worth living, she had almost forgotten that there were some good men left in the world.

"You know?" Maude had asked.

"I know she was sorely used. The man what done it won't be livin' two minutes after I set eyes on him."

Polly had come down then and Herb had-gone to the door to meet her.

A little later, when T.C., Colin and Sunday came in, T.C. handed the plate of bear claws to Sunday and paused at his bedroom door until she and Colin entered the kitchen. He opened the door and stood there for a full minute looking at the rumpled empty bed. His heart gave an odd little lurch. He had expected to see that beautiful dark-red hair spread out over his pillow. He closed the door and walked quickly to the kitchen.

"She's upstairs," Maude said as soon as their eyes met.

"Did she say anything?"

Maude shook her head. "Just hurried past the door and up the stairs."

When T.C. spoke to Herb, who was already on his second bear claw, a smile of real affection broke over his face. He put a heavy hand on his shoulder.

"Finish the plate, Herb. I got a job for you."

"He'll finish that plate of bear claws over my dead body." Sunday picked up a two-tine fork and held it over the plate.

"Better watch her, Herb," Colin cautioned and winked at T.C. "She's mean."

"And she can shoot a jackrabbit in the eye riding full speed, blindfolded, and standin' on her head," Sunday added seriously.

"Huh?" Herb looked puzzled.

Colin laughed, his eyes holding Sunday's.

If T.C. had not had so much on his mind, he would have noticed the special awareness between his friend and Sunday. Maude noticed and turned away with a smile.

"What you want me to do, T.C?" Herb got to his feet, wiped the sugar off his mouth with the back of his hand, then rubbed it on the seat of his pants.

"Go to the hotel and get Preacher Davis. He's in the first room on the left. Tell him to be here in fifteen minutes and to bring his Bible or whatever he uses when he marries folks."

Sunday recovered first. "Who's gettin' married?"

"Me," T.C. said, his eyes sweeping the group. "Me and Jane."

"Well, name of a cow!" Sunday exclaimed.

"Get goin', Herb." T.C. followed Herb to the hall, saw him leave the house, then turned and went up the stairs.

He was not nearly as confident as he pretended. His heart began to do crazy things—like racing, leaping and pounding. He had to act fast. If he gave Jane too much time to think she would reject the idea completely. He had already decided on a backup plan if one was necessary—that she had spent the night in his bed and that she was *duty-bound* to marry him.

The door was shut when he reached it. He rapped softly, waited a moment, then opened it to find Jane standing beside the window, her back to him. She was dressed in the blue dress she had worn the first time he had seen her. Her hair was coiled loosely at the nape of her neck. She looked so lonely, so forlorn, so small, so unprotected.

"It's me, Jane." T.C. stood looking at her for a moment before he went to stand close behind her. He put his hands on her upper arms and pulled her back against him. "Are you all right?"

"Yes, of course."

"How about some breakfast?"

"No . . . not yet."

"Only Sunday and Colin are here besides Maude and, of course, Herb and Polly."

"In a little while."

He turned her to face him and looked searchingly at her face. The scratches stood out boldly on her white skin. He had to tamp down his anger at the unknown person who had done this to her, lest she be frightened by it.

"Honey, word of what happened here last night will never leave this house. No one but those of us that were here knows about it. I take that back," he said quickly. "I called in Tennihill to help when we couldn't find you. But you needn't worry about him."

"I know and you know," she said slowly.

"I know what happened, but not why. And I'm mad as hell! I'm like my Irish pa. When someone does something to my loved one, it'll go worse for them than if it were done to me."

She looked steadily into his eyes without the slightest change in her expression. How close he had come to the basis of her troubles.

"Then you can see why I must leave?"

"I can't see. I read the notes, Jane. All of them. Someone wants you here to torment you. If you leave now, you'll be dogged by that person for the rest of your life. You must stay here, with me, as my wife. Together we'll find out who is doing this to you."

She looked at him in total silence. Then tears began to trickle down her cheeks. She stood with her head up, her hands at her sides, and made no attempt to wipe them away.

"Honey, don't cry." His hands moved behind her back and pressed her to him.

"I thank you for the offer." Jane pulled back until she no

longer was touching him. "I couldn't possibly accept."

"Why not? It's the perfect solution—"

"I'd ruin your life."

"It will be ruined if you *don't* marry me, sweetheart. For the first time in my life I love a woman. You."

"You owe me nothing."

"I want to be with you. We would make a good team."

"Like horses?"

"No. Like a man and his mate. Pulling together. Sharing the good and the bad."

The pain behind her eyes caused her to close them for a long moment. When she opened them, his face was close, bending to hers. He placed a gentle kiss on her lips. The temptation to have someone share her troubles was too great. She leaned against him and felt once again his warm protecting arms around her. Her head pounded with pain. Her mind was awash with confusion. She was so tired.

T.C. reached for something to wipe her eyes. Her night-dress hung over the end of the bedstead. He used it to mop the tears from her face.

"Come on, honey. Let's go downstairs."

She let him lead her from the room and down the stairs. Herb was waiting in the hall and nodded toward the office.

"Get the others."

T.C. paused outside the office door and gently turned Jane toward him.

"I love you, Jane. You believe that, don't you?"

"I . . . guess so."

T.C. opened the door and greeted Reverend Davis.

"Sorry to call you out so early. Miss Love and I wish to be married. The reason for the haste is that she had an accident last night and is in pain."

The young minister looked at Jane's scratched and obviously tear-stained face.

"I'm sorry to hear . . . it. Perhaps you should postpone

the—" He stopped speaking when the others, including Stella, filed into the room.

"We want to be married today, Reverend. Please proceed."

"Miss Love?"

She nodded wordlessly, and the minister opened his Bible.

"Make it short. Jane needs to lie down." T.C. put his arm around Jane when the preacher moved to stand in front of them.

"Join hands, please."

The ceremony was indeed short.

Jane mumbled an answer to the minister's questions.

T.C.'s answer was firm.

Her new husband kissed her gently on the lips and then led her to the table, where she was handed the pen to sign her name to the wedding paper.

She looked up at him with tired, dull eyes. It had not yet registered with her that she had just made a lifetime commitment to this man.

Chapter 19

AFTER the ceremony Jane suffered the hugs from the women, the handshakes from the men, and the kiss on the cheek from T.C. She went along with the women back to the kitchen and sat down at the table. Maude poured her a cup of coffee. She felt as if she were out of her body, above, and looking down on what was going on. None of it was real. None of it was happening to her.

"I wish we had a doctor to look at that bump on her head." Maude was talking about her but not to her. Jane moved her tired eyes to Maude and noted the worried look on her face.

"It's all right."

"Do you want to go lie down, Jane?" Sunday asked.

"Oh, no. I've got too much to do."

"Like what?"

"Well, I've . . . got to clean and do the washing—"

"Oh, Lord." Maude turned away and put the back of her hand to her mouth.

"That'll get done. Come lie down."

Jane rose obediently from the chair. Sunday led her down the hall to T.C.'s room. Once inside, she closed the door.

"Take off yore dress. Yo're not wearin' a corset are ya? Jane shook her head carefully. She removed her dress and sat down on the side of the bed in her shift. Sunday took off her shoes.

"I'm . . . awfully tired."

"Just lie down. I'll put this cover over ya. Nobody will bother you and you can sleep."

When Sunday left the room she went back to the kitchen.

"She's sleepin'. She's just wore out."

"I wonder if she knows what she did," Maude said.

"She answered when the peacher asked her. I think she knows, but it hasn't sunk in yet."

"Where?" T.C. appeared in the doorway and spoke the one word.

"She went back to bed. She's not herself," Sunday said.

"I know that. Could the blow on her head have cracked her skull?"

"It bled a lot, but it wasn't that bad," Sunday said slowly. "She's worried herself sick is what she's done. Tryin' to go on like nothin' was wrong and then bein' shut up in the privy and that other—Her mind's just kinda shut down."

"Mr. Kilkenny, do you think she knows what she just did?" Maude asked hesitantly.

"Marrying me? She knows. I admit I hurried her into it, but I'll not take advantage of her. When she *really* becomes my wife, I promise you she'll know exactly what she's doing."

"I didn't mean—"

"I understand what you mean, and I thank you for your concern for my wife." T.C. felt good saying the word for the first time. "I wanted her before this happened and I said my vows sincerely. She'll be loved and respected. Whoever did this thing to her will answer to me."

"It's just a shame she can't enjoy her wedding day."

"I hope to make it up to her someday."

"Stella and I think a heap of her—"

"So do I." T.C.'s voice was firm. "I want everyone in town to know that we're married. The sooner the better. It'll either ferret out the one who hurt her, or they'll back off. Can you see to that, Sunday?"

"I always did like spreadin' good news."

The news that T.C. Kilkenny had married Jane Love was all over town by mid-morning, exactly as T.C. wanted. If whoever had attacked Jane was in town, that person knew now that it would mean dealing with him if anything further happened to her.

Paralee Jenkins, Bessie Miller and Minnie Perkins were

the only women left in the henhouse. Patrice Guzman Cabeza had moved into the best room at the hotel a few days earlier. Grace Schwab and Bertha Phillips had gone to share a room at the rooming house.

Sunday had been delighted to break the news to Paralee.

"He what? *Married* that old maid? She's twenty-five years old if she's a day."

"Yup, he married her, and they're as happy as a pair of bear cubs in a honey tree."

"He could'a had any woman in town without havin' to *marry her.*" Paralee's pouty face was creased in an expression of disbelief.

"Ya mean he could'a had any *whore* in town. There's a mite a difference 'tween a whore and a lady, Paralee. But guess you'd not be knowin' about that."

"And you would?"

"I know *yo're* no lady."

Paralee's mouth tightened and her eyes sparkled with anger. She would like nothing more than to jump on the blond bitch and scratch her eyes out. But there was no need for that. She had another weapon.

"Ya think yo're so all-fired smart! Ever'body in town knows ya've set yore sights on Colin Tallman. I'm here to tell ya that ya've got 'bout as much chance a gettin' *him* as ya've gota gettin' Abe Lincoln."

Sunday laughed. "Lincoln's dead! Ya dummy. Didn't ya know that?"

"He . . . is?"

Bessie laughed.

Minnie snickered.

Paralee's face reddened as her blood rose to the boiling point.

"Patrice's been pukin' her guts out ever' mornin' since she come here. Go ask her whose kid she's carryin'."

"Now why'd it matter to me whose kid Miss Snootypuss is carryin'?"

"Oh, it'd matter when she tells ya why she come lookin' for Colin Tallman and why she's so scared her husband's goin' to find her."

"Me and Miss Snooty-puss ain't been to no tea parties together . . . lately. And ain't had no chance to share confidences."

"Ain't ya sharin' the same man?"

"Are ya diggin' for dirt to spread?"

"I don't have to dig. Patrice come right out and told me. She's scared her *Ramon'll* fly off the handle and kill her when she tells him it . . . ain't . . . his . . . kid!" Paralee finished with a smirk on her face.

"So it ain't his kid. It's no business of mine, or yores, whose kid it is."

"It'll be Colin Tallman's business unless he's got 'em sprinkled about like raindrops and one more ain't going to make no never mind." Paralee waved her arms.

Sunday's desire to slap the girl was so strong that she clenched her fists and buried them in the pockets of her skirt. She would have died before she would let the jealous bitches know that just the hint that Patrice's child was Colin's had cut her to the quick. So she laughed . . . again.

"Got to hand it to ya. That tongue a yores is hooked in the middle so it can wag at both ends. But I didn't come to listen to yore gossip. Mr. Kilkenny sent me to tell ya three bright, upstanding *ladies* to pack up and get yore butts out of here." Sunday knew how to use her voice in an insulting way. She did that now.

"Why's he sendin' word by you? Why didn't he come hisself?" This came from Bessie, who usually let Paralee do the talking.

"He's busy . . . with his new wife."

"Doin' what? Cuddlin' up with that prissy old maid'd be like lovin' up to a sack a turnips that's been in the cellar all winter. And"—she cast a knowing glance at Paralee—"a man that's needin' lovin' ain't wantin' no sack a turnips. I can tell ya that." Both girls giggled.

"I ain't doubtin' that. Ya've hugged up to ever' horny lumberjack within a mile of ya. Now let me tell ya somethin'. If I hear of ya dirtyin' Jane's name, I'll find ya and I'll beat the tar out of both of ya!" By the time Sunday had finished she was shouting. Her patience was stretched almost to the limit.

The threat sobered both girls. Sunday continued in a calmer voice.

"Mr. Kilkenny said for you to move into the room behind the kitchen at the hotel today. You can work there, earnin' yore keep. He's goin' to turn this place into a bunkhouse for men who can't afford the hotel. Maybe he'll rent you the corner behind the curtain and ya can earn ya a nickel or two lyin' flat on yore back. It ain't smart to give it away even if it ain't worth much," she added the insults calmly.

Sunday was so hurt and angry that she hardly knew what she was saying. She glanced at the dark-haired Minnie, who had worked as a laundress at the army camp. Minnie never took part in Bessie's and Paralee's jealous attacks on Jane. She had lowered her head and appeared to be embarrassed.

"Minnie, I didn't mean any of that for you, but you keep trailin' with these two and ya'll be painted with the same brush they are."

"Ya want to explain that?" Paralee asked.

"Wouldn't do no good. The two of ya ain't got the sense God gave one of them turnips yo're so fond of."

Sunday left the henhouse feeling as if she had been kicked in the gut by a mule. Was Paralee trying to get her goat, or was what she said true? Last night she had been sure Colin liked her as much as she liked him.

Not one to dally around and stew over a bit of news tossed out by the likes of Paralee and Bessie, Sunday headed down the street, scarcely noticing the people she passed. If Colin Tallman was the kind of man to take another man's wife to bed, she had to know it now, and the only way to find out was straight from the horse's mouth.

She reached the hotel and walked quickly up the steps and onto the porch. The man sent to run the hotel was short, bald, and very businesslike. Sunday had met him the day he arrived. He was in the lobby rolling out a small piece of carpet when Sunday entered:

"What room is Mrs. Cabeza in?"

"Good morning," he said cheerfully. "That's easy. We only have four guests at the present time. She's in room three. Top of the stairs on the left."

"Thanks."

Sunday went up the stairs. Three weeks of work on the building had put it in good shape. The work was continuing. She'd heard Jeb say that eight of the ten rooms were ready for guests. It was grand, Sunday thought, what money could do, but she'd not heard of it fixin' broken dreams.

She rapped on the door of room three, rapped again and waited.

"Who is it?"

"Sunday Polinski. Open the door."

"What do you want?"

"Open it and find out."

Sunday heard the key in the lock and the door opened a crack. She pushed it open and came into the room. Patrice was wearing a dressing gown. Her hair was down about her shoulders. Her face was pale and she had dark circles under her eyes. The chamber pot was by the bed and the room smelled of vomit.

"What do you want?"

"You been pukin'?"

"I doubt you came to inquire about my health, so say what you came to say and get out." Patrice sank down on the edge of the bed.

"Who's kid ya carryin'?" Sunday demanded.

Startled, Patrice looked up. Her large dark eyes took in the misery on Sunday's usually cheerful face. She began to smile and brushed the heavy black hair back from her face.

"The little farm filly is not quite as stupid as I thought she was. But I guess the situation has to be made plain to her." Patrice stood and adjusted the belt on her dressing gown so that the folds fell open to partially reveal the globes of her swollen breasts.

"Why do you think I left a home where I was waited on hand and foot to come to this godforsaken place? Even *you* should have been able to figure it out. I came to find Colin Tallman, my one and only love."

"Is the kid his?"

"We were together a couple of months ago. Do you think he could have resisted the temptation?"

"Yore husband ain't carin' that ya get in another man's bed?"

"I've not slept with Ramon for months and months. Anyway, he's worthless as far as fatherhood is concerned or he'd have brats scattered all over New Mexico. He'll know it isn't his."

"Then why'er ya scared he'll find out?"

"Pride. He'll be duty-bound to try to kill Colin. I'm not in the least worried about that. Colin can take care of himself."

"Is Colin the pa?"

"Who else? Certainly not T.C. Kilkenny!" Patrice lifted her brows and smiled.

It was all Sunday needed to know. Her dreams died a sudden death. Her heart felt empty. It was as if she had lost some part of herself. Misery was eating her alive! She had to get out fast before she made more of a fool of herself. In her anxiety to leave, she never even noticed the satisfied smirk on Patrice's face.

When she left the room, she slammed the door and

walked quickly down the stairs and out onto the boardwalk. Her eyes were bright and dry. Singlemindedely heading for the rooming house and the privacy of her room, she never heard Colin call her name. He had come out of the store and was crossing the street to intercept her.

"Sunday . . . wait—"

She heard him when he called the second time, and she slammed to a halt and turned. At the sight of his smiling face, she took a deep breath. When she released it, anger boiled up.

"Where ya goin'? Mrs. Henderson's makin' a weddin' cake. I'm gettin' the stuff from the store."

"I'm surprised ya got time."

"I am in sort of a yank."

"In too big a yank to go get yore rocks hauled by that Mexican whore up at the hotel?"

At first Colin thought she was teasing, but these were pretty raw words. Then the look on her face told him that she was not teasing. She was angry, very angry. She glared at him with deep-rooted dislike on her face. It was a face he had not seen before. It was one without a smile.

"What put a bee in yore bonnet?"

Sunday took another deep breath to steady herself and spoke in a low, controlled voice, as she balled her fist and prepared to hit him if he came an inch closer.

"What put a bee in my bonnet, Mr. Colin Tallman, was you makin' up to me last night when ya been playin' around in Mrs. Cabeza's drawers."

"What?" Colin was stunned into silence for a second. "What in holy blazes are you talkin' about?" He reached for her arm, but she drew back and made another fist. He stepped back, sure she meant to strike him.

"Touch me and I'll . . . bust you in the mouth! Get the hell away from me and stay away, or I swear I'll shoot yore blamed head off and save her husband the trouble."

With head up, back ramrod-straight, Sunday marched on

down the street, leaving Colin shocked and perplexed. He stood for a moment, then went back across the street to the store.

Upstairs in the hotel, Patrice stood beside the window where she could look down on the street. She saw Colin come out of the store and cross the street to where Sunday waited. She watched them talk and saw Sunday, clearly angry, go down the boardwalk leaving Colin looking after her. Patrice wasn't sure, but she thought he glanced up at her hotel room.

With a satisfied smirk she began to pretty herself up in case a visitor might be on his way.

It was not the best day for some people in Timbertown. Both Colin and Sunday believed it was the worst day of their lives. Jane spent most of the day sleeping and was unaware of all that was going on. Maude and Polly tiptoed into the room now and then, worried that she was sleeping too much.

To the single women who had secretly hoped T.C. would notice them, his marriage to Jane was a disappointment. Much of the conversation centered on how she had landed the *prize*. Paralee and Bessie fabricated a version that took root since there was no other explanation. They claimed Jane had crawled into T.C.'s bed and that the two of them had been caught by Maude Henderson, who had shamed T.C. Kilkenny into marrying the strumpet.

To the women who had received nothing but kindness from Jane when they took their children to the surgery, however, the news meant that she would be staying on. They liked her and wished her happiness.

On this day of all days, T.C. had to deal with three more freight wagons that arrived. He posted Herb at the house and told him not to let anyone in who had not been there the night before. Colin checked in the freight, even though his mood was far from pleasant.

T.C. attempted to settle a squabble between the hotel cook and the hotel manager. The cook was not pleased with anything in the kitchen, nor was he pleased with the help that had been provided.

"It isn't Delmonico's, for God's sake!" T.C. shouted in frustration. By the time both parties had calmed down, T.C. was tempted to fork the cook on a horse and run him out of town.

On the other end of the scale, Mrs. Brackey had worked companionably alongside the men setting up the equipment in her tonsorial parlor, and her place of business was due to open the next day.

The courier returned from the train stop with the mail pouch, and in it was the news that the first stage would arrive in a week's time. Notices had been sent to be posted in all public places. A small building next to the hotel would serve as the station.

A letter from Garrick Rowe, sent from Laramie, said that within the next week or so the new doctor would make the trip to Timbertown on his new stage line. He was asking about the accommodations at the hotel.

At noon Tennihill rode in, dropped his horse off at the livery and, after stopping to chat a minute with a disgruntled Colin, went in search of T.C. He found him at a cluttered desk, cursing at the stack of bills of lading given him by the freighters.

"Howdy." Tennihill strolled in leisurely. T.C. wondered if the man was ever in a hurry.

"Have a seat, Tennihill."

"Heard ya got married this mornin'. Hell of a way to spend yore weddin' day." He took the makings of a cigarette from his pocket and rolled a smoke.

"I agree. What's on your mind?"

"Ya know, I been a watching the feller that calls hisself Milo Callahan."

"Calls himself? I thought you were sure who he was."

Tennihill grinned. "Feller ort never be *sure* of anythin' but dyin."

"I wondered why a man like you would be hanging around in a town like this."

"Ya'd be surprised at the places I've hung out in when somebody's payin' the tab. Back to Callahan. He got run out of the Bitterroot country over around Spencer a year ago. It was not proved but was believed he hired a couple a timber scum to kidnap a young girl and ruin her."

T.C.'s head came up. "Did they?"

"No, and they got a dose a lead for tryin'. Callahan had got hisself drunk and passed out in the bunkhouse so he'd not be blamed, but the ones that done it was his boot-lickers. He's not welcome in any timber camp in the Bitterroot." Tennihill struck a match on the bottom of his boot and lit his cigarette before he continued.

"To shorten the story, Callahan's got some money comin' from his step-pa. If this feller was the right one, I was to send him back to Coeur d'Alene."

"Is he the right one?"

"I ain't one hundred percent sure." Tennihill grinned again.

T.C. snorted an obscenity.

"I took notice a Bob Fresno right off," Tennihill said in his slow drawl. "Heard about him up around Great Falls. Heard a feller named Fresno took a widder woman for ever' cent she had, then beat the tar outta her. He's a mean one, but a smooth-type feller. I don't doubt there's a wanted poster out on him. I just don't happen to have one."

"I could send word to Laramie and find out."

"Might not be a bad idey. Got to thinkin' he'd be interested in the happenin' this mornin', knowin' he didn't take his eyes off Miss Jane, er . . . Mrs. Kilkenny, at the buryin' and got him a chance to rub up against her at the table. I saddled my horse and rode over to where they was workin' on that old shack him and Callahan was figurin' on winterin' in."

"I couldn't stop them from staying there," T.C. put in." "But Jeb and I already ruled them out of any work for Rowe Lumber Company. Fresno knows next to nothin' about logging, and Callahan's too reckless and too much of a hothead for dangerous work."

"Figured it. Makin' out as I was stoppin' to pass the day, I handed them the news of the weddin' kind a casual-like. Fresno didn't say nothin' right at the start. Just stood and stared at me. Then lightnin'-quick he threw the hammer right through the wall of that old shack."

"Callahan have nothin' to say?" T.C. asked.

"He kind a hee-hawed Fresno. Crowed, 'cause he's been diddlin' with the girl, Bessie, and Fresno don't have no woman. He'd been braggin' that he was gettin' Miss Jane."

"I'll see him in hell first!"

"Knowed ya'd feel that way. Callahan kept crowin' Fresno, and 'bout got hisself gut-shot. Man's a pretty fair hand with a gun. Drawed it, an' Callahan 'bout wet his drawers."

"Pity it wasn't the other way around."

"I moseyed on off but doubled back and stayed out of sight. They packed up all their gear and rode south. I followed for about ten miles. I ain't sure when they'll be back, but I got a feelin' ya've not seen the last of them."

"Where we goin', Fresno?"

"Place I know."

Aware that Bob was in a black mood, Milo had been riding alongside him for miles without asking the question.

"Never did know why ya wanted to sign on to work here," Milo grumbled. "Hell, they ain't got nothin' compared to Callahan Lumber."

"If they got so damn much, why aren't ya there?"

"I got my reasons."

"Yeah? Run ya off, didn't they?"

Milo bristled. "What'd ya mean by that?"

Bob didn't answer. He had too much on his mind to waste time explaining to a dumbhead. He and Milo had been at the stage station trying to decide if they wanted to sign up to work for Rowe Lumber when Jane had arrived.

One look at her, haughty and cold, and Bob's decision has been made. She was poor as Job's turkey. He had noticed the worn shawl and shoes. But she had class, and that was what he was interested in. If she was alone and down on her luck, and she'd had to be to come to a one-horse, rundown town, she'd appreciate what they could do together, once she got to know him.

He hadn't counted on being so smitten by her.

Why'd T.C. Kilkenny marry her? By holy damn, it made no never mind. He'd just have to kill the sonofabitch. It was better to get out of town, so he wouldn't be blamed when Kilkenny showed up back-shot. Fresno wanted no new wanted posters out on him when he took Jane and they headed west.

Bob began to plan. He doubted if many people in town knew the reputation of Herb Banks. Callahan didn't know or he'd never have fooled with him. Banks looked like a kid, acted like a kid, but he'd laid out a good number of men who had thought he *was* a kid. Raised on wolf milk, some said. He'd taken the woman Callahan wanted. Bob wondered how he could use *that* to his advantage.

Another thing was money. He was getting short. He glanced at Milo. If nothing else turned up . . . he'd take Milo's.

Chapter 20

JANE awoke in the late afternoon and sat up on the side of the bed for a long moment, allowing her head to clear before she went to the window. The sun had already gone behind the mountains to the west. She had spent the whole day in bed, something she had done only a few times in her life. What must everyone think of her—then like a bolt it hit her.

She had been married this morning to T.C. Kilkenny!

Jane put her palms to her cheeks as memory came roaring back. He had explained that she would be safe here as his wife. That he *wanted* to marry her. He had even said that he loved her. But she knew *that* to be a broad statement. He *liked* her. He was giving her his protection. Her mind could not come up with a logical reason why he married her to protect her. Under the same circumstances, would he have *married* Sunday or Paralee or Mrs. Brackey?

At the moment he suggested that they marry, her spirits had been so low that she would have done anything other than commit murder in order to stay within the safety of his arms, to lean against him, to believe that he cared for her. The feeling, however brief, of being loved, even cherished, had been undeniably sweet. She would remember it always.

T.C. had urged her to marry him, but had not insisted. It had been her decision. She'd had her chance to say no when the preacher asked her if she would take T.C. Kilkenny for her husband to love and to cherish until death parted them. She closed her eyes in an agony of humiliation at her weakness.

Oh, Lord! What had she done to him?

She would have to tell him now. It was the only *decent* thing to do. She could not, would not, see him ridiculed before the whole town. The preacher, after the situation was explained to him, would tear up the wedding paper because they had not become man and wife in the eyes of God.

Moving slowly, not sure if the pain in her head was completely gone, Jane put on her dress and her shoes. Her valise was on the floor beside the bureau and her shawl and bonnet hung on the pegs beside T.C.'s coat. For a moment she pressed her face to the soft leather and breathed in the scent of him. Then she took her mother's picture from her valise and moved the valise over beneath her shawl beside the door. She placed the picture face down on the valise.

At the small mirror over T.C.'s bureau, where a comb and brush were laid out, she brushed her hair, coiled it neatly and pinned it at the nape of her neck.

Leaning close to the mirror, she inspected the scratches on her cheeks and her forehead and the dark circles beneath her eyes. What a sight! She turned quickly from the mirror and straightened the bed so that there was not even a hint it had been occupied all day long.

She desperately needed to make a trip to the outhouse, but fear cut through her like a hot knife at the thought of going to that dreadful place. Instead, she labored up the stairs to the room she shared with Polly, hoping the chamber pot was there. It was, and it was empty. In the privacy of the room, she attended to her bodily needs, adjusted her clothing and gathered strength to go back downstairs. The sooner she faced the situation she had caused by coming here, the better for all concerned.

Jane paused in the doorway of the kitchen. Maude, Polly and Stella were there. The table was set with a white cloth. Looking more closely, Jane could see that it was a folded bedsheet. In the center of the table was a tall cake with a small candle in the center. Polly and Stella were giggling. Maude, her face flushed from the heat of the cookstove, laughingly scolded them.

"Jane!" Polly came to take her hand.

"Ya feelin' better?" "Much better. I feel like a sluggard spending so much time in bed while you two did the work."

"Ya sure ya feel better?" Maude asked, wiping her hands on her apron. "We were so worried."

"I must confess to being a little weak. I can't remember the last time I ate."

"Ma, give her the end of the bread. I'll get butter to go on it." Stella wrapped her arms around Jane's waist.

"That's your favorite part, Stella."

"I want ya to have it, Miss Jane." The little arms tightened about her.

"Thank you, puddin'. It'll fill the empty place until supper."

Jane's eyes followed the little girl, who danced away to help her mother. She was no longer the shy, scared child she has been when she arrived in Timbertown. The town had changed the lives of many who had come here. She now knew what it meant to love a man. Maude felt comfortable enough to reveal her warmth, and Polly's once-sad face was rosy and smiling.

"We're goin' to have the weddin' cake when Mr. Kilkenny gets home," Stella announced. "We have to eat supper first. Mamma made sugar-syrup icin'." She returned to lean against Jane's knee.

"It's very pretty."

Jane ate the hot bread, not because she was hungry, but because she needed strength to get through the next few hours, which she knew might be the worst in her life. She was unable to think beyond that.

"We haven't seen Sunday since right after the weddin'." Maude set a mug of hot tea on the table in front of Jane.

Jane tried not to flinch when they talked about the wedding. She hurriedly ate another slice of bread. She needed to be rid of that fluttery feeling in the pit of her stomach before T.C. came home. *Home*. The word held a world of meaning. She'd longed for one when she was young.

"She's working in the store, isn't she?" Jane forced herself to join the conversation.

"She wasn't at the store this afternoon. Stella and I looked for her."

"Colin hasn't been here either." Maude lifted a roasting pan from the oven. "Maybe they've gone off somewhere. Better light the new lamp, Polly."

"Herb says it's a Rochester harp lamp. He got it at the store today." Polly was proud of everything Herb did, no matter how small. "He hung it so it'd be right over the table. See? Ya can pull it down to light it, then push it up to where ya want it. They had 'em in a hotel where I worked in Laramie. It was a grand place." Polly lit the lamp. "Ain't it pretty, Jane? Herb says we'll get us one when we get our own house."

The yellow pool of light flooded the table and spread out into the kitchen. Jane looked at the happy faces smiling back at her. The two women, the child, and Sunday were the best friends she'd ever had. She would miss them.

Determined to maintain her composure, she blinked her eyes to keep them dry, and forced her lips to smile.

Darkness was falling when T.C. hurried down the street to his house. He had taken the first bath in Mrs. Brackey's not-yet-opened tonsorial parlor. She had insisted that he try out the new tub, and then she had shaved him in the new chair. He told himself that it was a well-deserved luxury.

He was eager to see Jane and spend some time with her. He had no intention of consummating his marriage this night, or any night, until she was completely well and wanted to be with him in the same way he wanted to be with her. He was not a rutting moose, he told himself. She would sleep in his bed; he would hold her in his arms even if he suffered the torture of the damned all night long. There would be no animal joining of his body to hers. It was important that they start this part of their union right.

He thought of crossing over to the cookhouse to see if Colin was there with Bill. His friend had made himself scarce for most of the day. He had merely grunted when told to get Sunday and bring her to supper because Mrs. Henderson was planning something special.

Evenings were getting downright cold, T.C. thought now, his mind forging ahead to winter. He hoped to have the surgery out of the house before too long. An addition to the hotel was being prepared for it. He expected to hear any day from the new doctor Rowe had located.

He would set up a small pot-bellied stove in his office and one in the bedroom he'd share with Jane. For as long as there were other people in the house, the bedroom would be their only private place. They would spend their evenings there as well as nights. He wanted to know what she thought about everything. She loved books as he did. He had no doubt that she would teach at the schoolhouse this winter. Then in the spring they would go to the ranch and build the home where they would raise tall, strong boys and small, sweet, courageous girls like their mother.

He could hardly wait to tell her about it.

Jane heard him coming down the hall and steeled herself for the meeting. She stood with the table between her and the kitchen door and was grateful that she was not alone when he appeared in the doorway, his hands, shoulder high, clutching each side of the frame. Although his dark face showed no expression, his silver eyes seemed to see only her, to pin her to the floor where she stood.

"Are you all right, Jane?"

"I'm . . . " Her first attempt to speak produced a croaking, gurgling sound. She tried again. "I'm fine. Just fine."

He smiled, and her heart leaped. He was breathtakingly handsome when he smiled.

"You look rested. Headache gone?"

"Most of it."

"Look at the new lamp Herb put up," Polly said breathlessly.

"It's a dandy," T.C. said, still looking at Jane.

An awkward silence followed. Jane seemed rooted to the spot. T.C. didn't come any farther into the room.

"Supper will be ready in just a little bit," Maude said. "Herb went to look for Colin." The door at the front of the house slammed shut as she finished speaking. "That's probably them."

T.C. moved out of the doorway and into the kitchen. Herb's eyes found Polly first, then Jane.

"Miss Jane! Ya feelin' better?"

"Much better, thank you."

"That Mrs. Miller at the rooming house said Sunday'd gone to bed. Said she wasn't feelin' good. I never found Colin. Wasn't in the saloon, or at the cookshack. His horse is in the livery so he's 'round somewhere."

"I just betcha Sunday ain't sick. I bet her and Colin had a spat," Polly said. "It's what I'd'a done if I didn't want to come face Herb in front of folks."

"You may be right." T.C. had moved over close to Jane. Stella was on her other side. "Colin has been like a bear with a sore tail all day."

"Ya smell good, Mr. Kilkenny."

"You like that, puddin'?" T.C. grinned and rubbed the top of Stella's head with his long fingers. "I had a shave at the new barber shop."

"Is it . . . toilet water?"

"It's Bay Rum." T.C. laughed and bent down so that Stella could press her nose to his cheek.

"I like it better'n rosewater."

"You may grow up to be a lady barber."

"I'm goin' to be a teacher, like Aunty Jane." Stella leaned against Jane, and Jane put her hand on the side of the child's head and hugged her close.

Maude turned back to the stove. She almost wept at the

kindness these people had shown to her and to Stella. The child would have a good life here—if she could stay.

They waited a half-hour for Colin, and when he failed to come, they sat down to roasted duck with rice stuffing, mashed potatoes and cream gravy. Maude was an excellent cook. She insisted on waiting on the table by herself, cutting the hot bread, pouring the tea, giving milk to Polly and Stella.

Jane did her best to do justice to the meal. Maude had worked all day, and not for the world did Jane want her friend to know that each bite stuck in her throat. T.C. knew how nervous she was and kept a string of chatter going to cover for her. One time, beneath the table, he reached into her lap and squeezed her hand. The thoughtful gesture made her want to weep.

The candle on the wedding cake was lit. Stella could hardly contain her excitement. Jane and T.C. were to blow it out together. Jane could muster up only a small breath of air, but T.C. let go with one powerful puff that extinguished the flame. Jane, urged by Maude, cut the first piece and placed it on T.C.'s plate.

"Kiss the bride! Kiss the bride!" Polly and Maude cried in unison.

T.C. turned to the red-faced woman by his side and placed a quick kiss on her lips.

By the time the meal was over, Jane, knowing what lay ahead, felt sick to her stomach. Her nerves were frayed, her hands shook, her eyes darted from the wall to the stove to the table but never to T.C. A hundred disjointed thoughts swirled through her mind. When Maude and Polly began to clear the table she got up to help.

"Not tonight, Mrs. Kilkenny," Maude said sternly. "This is your weddin' day."

"Oh, but you and Polly have worked all day, while I—"

"She's right, sweetheart. This is a special day. You can make it up to Maude and Polly later." T.C. took her hand and led her to the door.

Jane wished that he hadn't called her *that*. He would remember later and hate himself for it. She wanted to dig in her heels and refuse to leave the safety of the kitchen, but breathing deeply, to steady her nerves, she walked along beside him. In the near-darkness of the hall, he turned her to him with his hands on her shoulders.

"I don't want you to be afraid of me. I'm not going to demand that we consummate our marriage tonight. I can see that you think that. Don't be nervous, sweetheart. When we come together as man and wife it will be because we *both* want it to happen." Holding her chin firmly in his hand, he bent his head and placed a gentle kiss on her lips.

"I know nothing of men . . . or that," she said in a breathless whisper.

"I don't expect you to. Jane, I need to talk—"

"—I know."

"Come to the surgery. There are things in Doc's desk I want to show you."

"Wait." Pride stiffened her backbone and she pulled away. "I must talk to you first. But there's something I need to get from . . . your room." She went quickly to the bedroom and in the dark felt for her valise and her mother's picture she had placed on the top. Hugging it to her, she closed her eyes for a second or two, then backed out of the room.

T.C. had gone into the surgery and lit the lamp. Jane entered and closed the door behind her. He was standing beside the waist-high table.

"If this is going to be painful for you—"

"It is, but it must be done." She placed her mother's picture face up on the table. "This is my mother. I was born on her sixteenth birthday."

T.C. picked up the painting. It was of a young girl no older than Polly.

"She was pretty. You look a great deal like her. Do you remember her?"

"Faintly."

Head up. Shoulders back. Don't cower. Jane repeated the admonitions to herself as she had done a thousand times over the years since she had learned who she was.

She was about to reveal something she had never told before—to anyone. Even as a small child she had not shared her secret with the one or two girls that she considered friends. The stories that circulated throughout the school, the city of Denver, and, as she was told, the entire territory had made the revelation impossible.

She looked into T.C.'s face, recording every feature in her mind so she could call each one to memory again in the years ahead. She had the strength to tell him only because she loved him so much and wanted to spare him. He was so close she had to tilt her head to meet his eyes. And she must look him in the face when the testing was over. Seeing the hatred there would make it easier for her to leave.

"Please sit down."

He took the chair at Doc's desk and swiveled around to face her. She plunged into the story, determined to get it over.

"Your solicitor wrote, I'm sure, that I was raised in a Methodist orphanage. The trustees and the headmistress preferred to call it a boarding school, but in fact it was a home for children who had no other place to go."

T.C. nodded.

"My mother died when I was very young. I lived with my mother's friend, Alice Medlow, for a year or two before I was taken to the orphanage. This picture was the only thing I was allowed to keep. Aunt Alice brought it to me on the first of the only two visits she was allowed to make."

"Why didn't they allow her to visit?" T.C. thought questions would help Jane tell her story because at times her voice was almost breathless.

"I think, now, they wanted to tear me away from anything having to do with my mother." Jane walked around the table, clasping and unclasping her hands. "Most of the children knew about their parents and talked about them. Mrs. Gillis ran the school with an iron hand; each time I asked about my parents, she cut me off. I knew nothing of them until I was about ten years old."

T.C. wanted to break in but was afraid she would stop talking.

"Some children talked of the homes they once had had. A few had come to Denver in a wagon train. Others had been children of settlers . . . who had been burned out during Indian raids. All I had was a picture, and some wouldn't even believe it was my mother. I had one other memory that I never talked about. It was of a big man with black hair, a black beard and light eyes who came in the night, wrapped me in a blanket, took me to the orphanage and left me without ever speaking a word.

"One day I pried this wooden back off the picture frame." She turned the picture over. "I found two letters. One was written to my mother by . . . the man who fathered me, who was, I suspect, the one who took me from Aunt Alice. The other was to me from Aunt Alice, telling about my mother and how . . . I happened to be born . . . a bastard. She had put it there, hoping that someday I would read it."

"Jane, this isn't necessary—"

"I think it is. Please don't say anything." She turned from him, unable to bear the pity in his eyes now, and the hatred that would follow. She straightened her shoulders anew and continued.

"I took the letters to Mrs. Gillis and asked her to tell me what they meant. I was probably not even Stella's age at the time. She told me in no uncertain terms who and what I was. From that day on, I've lived in constant fear of being found out. When I was a child she threatened to tell the entire school if I misbehaved. For years I would cower in the corner afraid of being hated by the others. When I was older, I developed a backbone, of sorts, and stood up to Mrs. Gillis, telling her not to threaten me again.

"I was expected to stay at the orphanage and work for the rest of my life to atone for the blood that ran in my veins." She added the last bitterly. "I'm tired of the shadow that has hung over me. I read the letters again on my sixteenth birthday and have not read them since." She handed him the picture. "Take off the back and read them."

"No." He took the picture from her hand and placed it back on the table. "It doesn't matter to me who your parents were."

"It matters to me." She held out the picture. "Someone in this town knows. Someone plans to tell the story to humiliate me when the time is right, in the meanwhile tormenting me with the awareness that they know."

"I don't want to do this, Jane."

"You must." She was calm now. Her eyes pleaded with him. "I can't bear to go through this again."

Fear of what he would find made T.C.'s fingers tremble as he pried the wooden back off the frame with his pocketknife. Next to the back of the canvas he found two envelopes addressed with faded ink.

"Read the one addressed to Jenny Lou Love first."

Jane turned her back as soon as he picked up the letter and slipped the paper from the envelope. The silence in the room was deafening. Jane clenched her hands into fists and closed her eyes tightly as time stood still.

T.C. read the letter quickly. It was written in bold script, the words plainly visible. A few lines in the middle of the one-page letter stood out from the others.

It was the devil in you that caused you to seduce me. You flaunted your body when I was at my weakest. You used your soft naked flesh to lure me into fornicating with you. This child you bore is the spawn of the devil and you shall burn in everlasting hell for birthing her.

Do not attempt to contact me again. I care not if you or your bastard starve. It would be a fitting end.

The signature at the bottom of the letter caused T.C.'s mouth to go dry. He stared at it. The name was known by every man, woman and child throughout the Colorado and Wyoming territories.

He glanced at Jane's back, at her bowed head, and wanted to go to her, hold her and comfort her. Relief washed over him. He had feared her secret would be something he couldn't deal with. He held a tight rein on his exuberance and reached for the other letter. He read it quickly, then returned the two sheets of paper to the envelope.

Don't cower. Don't cower. Jane's head was up, her shoulders straight. She appeared to be staring at something on the wall ahead.

T.C. looked at her for an intense moment. Tall and slender, with that crown of glorious hair, she was like a wildflower, fragile, yet strong. She had been whipped viciously by the cruelties of life and had endured with her pride intact.

Warmth and beauty surrounded her like an aura.

He went to her and put his hands on her shoulders. She was as rigid as a board when he turned her around. The eyes that met his held so much pain that for a moment he couldn't speak. He could feel the tremors pass through her. He lowered his head to hers and pressed his lips to her trembling mouth.

"Jane, sweetheart. Did you think I wouldn't love you because of something your father did or didn't do?"

"I don't know. I honestly don't know."

"I'll always love you, Jane."

"Don't make a promise you can't keep," she cautioned, and met his questioning eyes directly. The pain of longing marked her face with sadness.

"It's been drilled into your head since you were a child that somehow *you* are disgraced because of what *he* did. It isn't true. Only you can disgrace yourself."

The look on his face was a look of love—for her. Oh, but later . . . when he came to understand, when it was known.

"I can't let you keep me with you. They'll hate me and pity you for having married me. I couldn't bear it. You must let me go."

The pain that pierced her heart whitened her face. She hurt so much that it seemed a flood of tears was trapped inside her body, yet she could not cry . . . not now. Pride had closed the valve on her tears so tightly that there was no way to release them.

"I'll never let you go. If you insist on leaving Timbertown, I'll come with you. We'll go to the ranch and to hell with everyone!"

"I couldn't let you leave after . . . all you've done here. The people depend on you."

"Then stay here, with me. I'm proud of the way you've handled the cards fate dealt you, and I'm more sure than ever that you're the woman I want by my side for the rest of my life. If it becomes known who your father was, we'll face it together."

"You . . . would do that?"

"I'd walk through hell barefoot for you. You're my love, my wife."

"You may be sure now . . . but later."

"Sweetheart, the idea that people would hate you was implanted in your mind when you were very young, and it has had an impact on your life far bigger than it should. Many people were affected by what your father did, not only at the time, but for years after. Still, it has nothing to do with you."

"After you think about it, you may change your mind."

"Don't say anything like that again." His voice was harsh in the quiet room.

"Some folks believe in bad blood."

"And they think Indians are stupid! An Indian would never think such a thing—would never hold a child responsible for its father's deeds."

"Someone here knows and plans to tell so that I, and now you, will be looked down on."

"I'll go out and tell the whole damn town tomorrow. And if one, just one—"

"—No! Oh, please—"

T.C.'s tone softened when he saw the pain on her face.

"Sweet, darlin' girl. I would never do that." She didn't resist when he put his arms around her and drew her to him. "I always hoped to find a woman like you to share my life. I think I knew right from the start that you were the one. I love everything about you, sweetheart. Your pride, your courage—"

He bent his head, hesitated for a moment, then kissed her lips. The emotional bruising of the past few days flowed away under the balm of his kiss. Her mouth clung in a moment of incredible sweetness.

Jane put her arms around his waist. She couldn't believe that the Indian part of him didn't blame her. After allowing herself a few minutes of closeness, she pulled away and looked up at him.

Very softly she said, "You're part . . . Indian—"

"My mother was English and Blackfoot. My father was Irish. Does my Indian blood bother you?"

"No! No! Oh, goodness no. But I thought that because of it you'd . . . never forgive me."

His hands moved up to her shoulders again. "You've done nothing that requires forgiveness. The day I told you that T.C. stood for Thunder Cloud you looked as if I'd hit you. Was it because I have Indian blood?"

"Partly, I guess. And partly because . . . I was liking you too much."

"You've not said that before." He was perfectly still, letting his eyes, soft with love, drink in her face.

"I couldn't . . . then."

"Can you now?"

Say it, her brain told her. Tell him you love him with all your heart and soul. The words had never been in her vocabulary. She knew about love but never in connection with herself.

"I care a great . . . deal for you."

"You care a great deal for Stella."

"But not the way I care for *you.*" Her palms caressed his cheeks.

"Do you *love* me?" There was an intense look on his face and his hands on her shoulders tightened.

"Oh, yes. Yes, I do!"

"Can't you say it, Jane? My pa used to say it to my mother every day. I grew up hearing it. He even said it to me. I love you, Timmie. When he was dressing me down for something I had done wrong, he'd say, 'Timothy Charles Kilkenny, 'tis no way fer a man to be actin'.' " He quoted his father in a heavy Irish brogue.

"Your name isn't Thunder Cloud?"

"No, darlin', I was teasing." He held her face between his palms. "Don't keep me waiting."

"I . . . love you, Timothy Charles Kilkenny."

"It wasn't so hard to say, was it?"

"I've said it before."

"The more you say it, the easier it'll be."

"I love you," she whispered.

He held her close, her head buried in his shoulder while he gently stroked her hair. He turned her face up to his and kissed her mouth fiercely, passionately, hungrily. Jane closed her eyes and moved her lips against his, loving the smell of his skin, his mouth that had turned demanding. He lifted his head and looked directly into her eyes, a faint smile softening that mouth.

"I wanted to marry you the second day you were here," he murmured. "You were spunky, willful, and bucked me at every turn. Even Doc said I'd be ten times a fool if I let you get away from me. You'll never be alone again, sweetheart. I'll find out who hurt you." He gently stroked the scratches on her cheeks. "No one will hurt you ever again. I swear it."

In a kind of fascination she watched his lips move. The soft light of the lamp shone on his face, on his hair. She felt the feathery touch of his lips against hers and sudden tears ached behind her eyes.

"Jane, love, you're mine now. We'll face whatever comes together."

Jane put her arms around his neck, moved her hand to the back of his head and gently stroked his hair. The very strange feeling of belonging washed over her.

And . . . the incredibly sweet feeling of coming home.

Chapter 21

COLIN knew that Herb was looking for him.

Earlier he had gone to the rooming house to see Sunday and had not been allowed past the front door. Mrs. Miller had told him that she was sick and had gone to bed. Sick, my hind leg, Colin thought. She had been madder than a stepped on snake and twice as dangerous when he had last seen her.

Keeping to the shadows, Colin watched Herb make the rounds: the cookhouse, the saloon, the store, the livery, and lastly the boarding house where he, too, had been turned away by Mrs. Miller.

Colin stayed out of Herb's sight until he saw him go back to the house. All day long he'd had it in the back of his mind that Sunday had talked to Patrice and that Patrice had told her some big yarn about the two of them that caused the remark about playing around in Mrs. Cabeza's drawers.

Hell! All the playing around with Patrice he'd done was six or eight years ago when he was a youth and as horny as a billy goat. At that, she'd only let him touch her with his hand. Even at a very young age, Patrice knew that her virginity was a valuable asset.

When the danger of running into Herb had passed, Colin stepped out onto the street and walked toward the hotel. Patrice was not going to give up something she wanted without using every dirty trick she knew to get it—and she apparently wanted his protection against Ramon. Something more was going on between her and Ramon than just her desire to leave him. Patrice Guzman Cabeza must have her sights set on something she thought to be higher and richer than Ramon Cabeza.

No one was at the desk when he walked into the hotel, and there was no bell to ring. When Colin slapped his hand down hard several times on the counter, a man came through a curtained door at the back.

"Evening, sir."

"What room is Mrs. Cabeza in?"

"Ah, yes. Lovely lady. Room three. Upstairs, first door on the left."

Colin took the stairs two at a time. He reached the landing and glanced back over his shoulder to see that the hotel man had come to the foot of the stairs to watch him. His boot heels sounded hollow on the wooden floor as he walked rapidly down the hall to room number three. He rapped on the door.

"Who is it?"

"Colin."

The door opened immediately. Patrice stood there in a soft, silky, white robe. Her black hair, parted in the middle, was loose and hung straight and shiny to her hips. The scent of rose petals wafted from the room and out into the hallway where Colin stood.

"Colin! Come in." Patrice reached out, took him by the hand and gently tugged.

He walked into the middle of the room and looked around. He heard the faint click of the door as it closed behind him. In the few days she had been there, Patrice had made the room her own.

With her unlimited funds Patrice had purchased from the store a china pitcher-and-bowl set to replace the tin sets hotels usually provided. On the chair beside the curtained window was a deep cushion. Soft blankets lay folded on the foot of the bed. Atop the bureau lay an ivory brush and mirror set and an array of small jars. A large bearskin rug covered the floor beside the bed.

Colin turned to Patrice, who was leaning back against the closed door. Her beautiful face was arranged in a smile of welcome.

"Take off your hat, Colin."

He had left it on deliberately. He knew and Patrice knew that no gentleman would leave his hat on while in the room with a *lady* if he respected her. He ignored the request and stared at her until she moved away from the door and toward him.

"I'm so glad you came—"

"What did you say to Sunday Polinski?" he asked, harshly shaking her hand from his arm.

"Who?" A questioning frown wrinkled her brow.

"You know damn good and well who I mean. What did you say to her?"

"Oh, you mean that woman who looks as if she's never used a hairbrush? The one with the vulgar laugh? Who walks as if she were a man? I wondered what her name was." She took his arm again, this time in her hands, and held it between her breasts.

"What did you say to her?" Colin shook off her hands again, grabbed her upper arms and held her away from him.

"Sit down if you want to have a conversation with me. It hurts my neck to be looking up at you."

Colin flung the cushion from the chair, turned it from the window and straddled it. His arms looped over the back. Patrice sat on the edge of the bed.

"She came here this mornin'—"

Patrice smiled. "You're jealous! You've been watching to see who comes calling on me."

"I have told you any number of times that any interest I had in you died when you married Ramon. Why don't you let it go at that?"

"I can't . . . now." She pulled a lace-trimmed handkerchief from the sleeve of her robe and sniffed.

"What do you mean?"

"Can't you guess?"

"Gawddammit! Stop dancing around. What the hell are you talkin' about?"

"Oh, Colin! You are terribly dense for a man your age. Remember when we were last together?"

"How can I forget? You came to my hotel room in Santa Fe and did your level best to get me shot."

"No, darling, no. I wanted to see you, had to see you."

"If Ramon had found you in my room, he'd have had a perfect right to come gunning for me."

"Not Ramon." She shrugged. "He'd have sent someone to do his dirty work for him."

"What's that got to do with now?"

"You made me pregnant that night. You're going to be a father, Colin."

For an instant Colin sat in stunned silence. Then his chair went over with a crash as he lunged to his feet.

"What . . . did you say?"

"You heard me. Isn't it wonderful, darling?"

"You . . . rotten—"

"—Bitch. Go ahead and say it." Patrice laughed. "You called me your hot little bitch . . . that night."

"It is not true and you know it," he shouted.

"Darling, keep your voice down. The hotel man will be up here with a shotgun."

"You're not any more pregnant than I am. You think Ramon will come looking for you, then come after me, and I'll kill him for you. Get another plan, Patrice. I'll not do it."

"You'd let Ramon kill you?"

"Of course not. I'll prove to him that you're a liar."

"Prove that you didn't make me pregnant? How are you going to do that?"

"We've never been together like that and you know it."

"Not because you didn't want to."

"I've not had a thought about you like that since you were sixteen."

"It's your baby," she said confidently. "Would you deny your own son . . . or daughter?"

"Why are you doin' this, Patrice?" Colin paced back and forth across the room.

"I want a father for my child."

"Your husband is the father of your child."

"Oh, pooh! Ramon will know it isn't his."

"You don't sleep with him?"

"You're hoping I don't!"

"I don't give a damn if you sleep with the whole Mexican army."

"Ramon would care. He's very possessive of his belongings."

"It's his right to expect loyalty from his wife."

"Loyalty? Ramon doesn't know the meaning of the word. You know as well as I that Ramon dips his wick in every little twat he lays eyes on. If he were *half* a man,"—her voice dripped sarcasm—"he'd have fathered his own Mexican army by now."

Colin stopped his pacing and stared at her. How could he, even when he was young and foolish, have thought he could care for this woman?

"You planned this."

"I didn't plan to get pregnant, but now that I am, I see that it was a good thing."

"I'm not going to kill him for you, Patrice. Get whoever you've been sleeping with to do your dirty work."

"Darling, I've been sleeping with *you*. Ramon knows I've always been fond of you. Now, sit down so that we can discuss our future."

Colin could only look at her and shake his head.

"This is what you told Sunday."

"I had no choice. And it was kinder than letting her go on thinking she had a chance with you."

Colin jerked open the door. For the first time in his life he wanted to strike a woman, and it was best for to get out while he still had control.

"Think about it, Colin. Once you get over the shock of being a papa, you'll see how right it is."

He went out and slammed the door so hard that the side of the building shook. Out on the street he was jostled by two men headed toward the saloon.

"Colin, Herb's lookin' for ya."

"Yeah? Thanks."

Colin walked rapidly away, turned into the darkness between two buildings, stopped and leaned against the side of one of them. Breathing deeply, he tried to think rationally, but his mind was clouded with rage. Years ago T.C. had told him Patrice was trouble. Colin suspected that before she married Ramon, she had wanted T.C. and he had not been interested.

He desperately wanted to talk to Sunday. He went down the street to the boarding house. Her room was at the side. It was dark. He turned away and crossed the street. A light shone from the kitchen window and from T.C.'s bedroom. Colin let himself in and went to the office where he had left his bedroll, rolled it out and lay down.

He had a lot of thinking to do.

"Did I hear Colin come in?"

Jane stood at the foot of the bed, happy but uncomfortable, not knowing how to act on this night of all nights when she would sleep in the arms of her husband.

"He'll not come in."

"He missed supper."

"He's got a lot on his mind." T.C. smiled down at her. "Are you nervous about being here with me, sweetheart?"

"A . . . little."

"I'm a little bit scared of you," he confessed. He took her hand and placed her palm over his heart. "Feel this. My heart is about to run away with me."

"I can't imagine your being scared of anything."

"That's where you're wrong, honey. I've been scared to death I was going to lose you. I took the first chance I had to bind you to me."

"I'm glad you did." She smiled up at him.

His eyes searched hers for a long moment before he bent his head and pressed a gentle kiss to her lips.

"I'll go out for a little while."

Jane watched him go out the door and wanted to run after him and beg him not to leave. This thing between them was too new, too fragile, for her to really believe that it was true. What had she done to deserve the love of a man like Timothy Charles Kilkenny? He was too honest, too decent, to say words he didn't mean. And there was no reason for him to do so.

It was almost beyond belief that this was her wedding night; that in a few minutes she would be in bed with her husband. She knew about what took place in the marriage bed, but she didn't know *how* to do it. *Lord, help her not to be a disappointment to him.*

Wondering if she had done everything she should have done, Jane lay in bed waiting for her husband. She had washed in the basin, used the chamber pot she found under the bed, and put on the nightdress she had worn only one time since it was washed. Trying not to look at her scratched face in the mirror when she stood before the bureau, she took the pins from her hair and turned away to brush it.

Jane listened for T.C.'s footsteps in the hallway. It still seemed to her that what had happened, was happening, was to someone else. She had never known a closeness with anyone, never shared her thoughts or her dreams with anyone but a dying man. She had talked endlessly to Doc late at night when it had seemed to her they were the only two people in the world. Though she had not been sure he was even listening, she had stopped short of revealing her terrible secret.

T.C. opened the door and came into the room. His eyes held hers as he came toward the bed, sat down beside her and studied her white face, her mane of thick dark-red hair gathered at the back of her neck and tied with a ribbon, her trembling mouth. He held out his hand. She placed her palm against his. He lifted it to his lips and kissed it gently and sweetly and with deep dedication.

It had been so long since anyone had loved her, almost a lifetime. She wondered if he could possibly know how he filled that vacant place in her heart. They sat quietly for a while just holding hands. The wonder of the love they had found kept them in an awed silence. Jane loved this man with the silver eyes. She loved the sound of his voice, the uncompromising line of his jaw, the curve of his mouth. Most of all she loved the strength of his character.

Jane made a silent vow to do everything in her power to be a good wife, a helpmate. But if fate tore them apart, if after all he found he couldn't bear the pressure of being married to the bastard daughter of one of the most hated men in the Colorado Territory, she would have a thousand sweet memories to call forth and cherish.

"Mrs. Kilkenny. Do you like the sound of that?"

"I like the sound of Mrs. T.C. Kilkenny."

"You're awful pretty, Mrs. Kilkenny." He bent over her. A soft, loving light shone from his silver eyes. Then his mouth was warm and sweet against hers.

"It's not true, but I like to hear it." Her arms slid up to encircle his neck. "You're pretty, too."

"It's not true, but I like to hear it." He laughed softly after repeating her words; then he whispered against her lips, "I love you." His words and the sound of his deep voice caused her heart to stumble, then to jump with joy. His eyes caressed her flushed face and moved to her hair, and with gentle fingers he brushed the strands at her temples. "I'll never, never force you . . . or hurt you."

Jane nodded and sighed deeply. She blocked out everything but this moment . . . this night. She heard his ragged breathing as if from far away.

"Can I call you Timmie when we're . . . together like this?"

"If you want to."

"Come to bed, Timmie," she whispered. *Oh, Lord! Did he think her brazen?*

He lifted his head and looked into her eyes, studying her with an ineffably tender expression.

"Yes, ma'am," he answered humbly, but his eyes shone with amusement, and she knew her invitation had pleased him.

Jane watched as he removed his shirt and hung it on a peg. His shoulders were broad and heavily muscled. She remembered Bill's telling her that T.C. was the one to beat in an exhibition of bare-knuckle fighting. His chest had a soft sprinkling of dark hair that tapered to his waist.

Could this magnificent man really be her husband?

His eyes caught hers. The tightness in her stomach intensified. He bent to blow out the lamp and the room went dark. She could still see him in her mind's eye: dark hair falling over his forehead, eyebrows that were as thick and straight as if put there by the stroke of a paintbrush, eyes that seemed to look into her very soul.

It seemed to her hours, but could only have been a minute or two until she felt the blanket being lifted and his weight on the bed.

T.C. stretched out beside her, raised his arm over her head and rolled her to him so that she lay alongside him, her cheek on his shoulder. Jane's body tensed as she tried to stop trembling. Her hand slid automatically over the warm hard flesh of his chest.

"You're trembling, honey." His voice was soft, urgent. He moved his hand caressingly up and down her back. "Don't be scared of me."

"I'm not. You . . . feel different without—"

"—My clothes on? I am different, sweetheart. I'm hard and rough, you're soft and sweet." He took her hand and placed it palm down on his chest and moved it up and down. "Do you like being here in my arms?"

"It's heavenly—"

"For me too."

He found her lips. Her mouth was as eager as his. While they kissed, his hand stroked her from her hip up her side to her breast and moved back and forth. Small and firm, yet incredibly soft, it filled his hand. No one had ever touched her there. Even through the cloth of her nightdress his fingers sent a message to the core of her femininity.

"Someday I'm going to love you with nothing between us at all." His voice was a ragged whisper.

"You can." Her whisper was a mere breath in the night.

Jane's fingers worked at the buttons on her nightdress. When it was open, she pressed her naked breast into his palm. His hand shaped itself over her tender offering.

"Sweetheart, I want to . . . touch you everywhere. I'm so hungry for you—"

His rough, calloused fingers found her nipple and stroked it to a hard peak. He ground his teeth and tightened his buttocks. His desire for her was a deep pain gnawing his vitals, but he was determined not to show any aggression.

"That feels good—" Her voice was urgent. She reached for his lips and kissed him with a hunger that surprised him. Her mouth was warm and sweet. She parted her lips, yielded and accepted the wanderings of his.

Her mound was pressed to his thigh. He could feel the heat through her nightdress. His hand, traveling from her back to the hem, slipped carefully under to flatten against her buttocks and hold her tighter to him.

The freedom to touch him made her almost giddy. Her palm slid down through the soft hair on his chest to his flat, quivering stomach. Her middle finger discovered his navel and lingered to feel it.

"I was going to wait," he said when her hand found the waist of his drawers. "You've been through so much—"

"You don't have to. I love you so much. I want to know all the wonder of being your wife."

Their lips met in joint seeking. Finally T.C. lifted his head for fear he would crush her soft mouth. She was every man's dream. He had not been sure her soft, feminine body would respond to the mating instincts of his. He had intended to let her get used to being in his bed.

"Sweetheart!" A great swell of elation washed over him. "My sweet, sweet wife." His voice trembled. Then with gentle firmness, he asked, "Are you sure you're all right?"

"I've never been better in all my life." Her fingers stroked his cheeks. "I'm just . . . scared this is a dream."

"Jane, my love. My sweet Jane. How could I have called you . . . Pickle." He had intended the words to be light, but they had come from his tight throat in a tormented whisper.

Jane's head was spinning. Reality began to slip farther and farther away, but before it was completely gone, the thought came to her that she was about to experience the mysterious mating between a man and a woman. Please God, she prayed, please let me give to him the joy that he is giving to me.

At that same moment, T.C. was vowing to be gentle with her and to show her that the mating of a man and a woman who loved each other could be beautiful. He thanked God for his Irish father who had taught him, his only son, that for every man there was a woman who would give meaning to his life. Together they would build something strong and enduring. When he found her, he would know her, and they would truly be one in every sense of the word.

He had found her.

And, miracle of miracles, she had found *him*. Jane's hand had moved down over his stomach, into his drawers and beneath his huge extended sex that jerked at her touch. He caught his breath sharply and waited for it to settle on the back of her hand. She had not been quite aware of what she was doing and waited, too, without breathing, for his reaction.

"Ah . . . love—" He jerked as if given a jolt, then his hand moved down and for an instant pressed his hardened sex against the back of her hand.

"May I . . . may I take off your nightdress?"

Seconds later she was back in his arms, her naked breast nestled in the soft hair on his chest. She heard a soft sound from his throat. Then his mouth fastened on her trembling lips, stealing her breath away. His kiss was filled with sweetness. Love for this gentle, understanding man swept over Jane like a warm summer wind.

He took her hand, moved it down between them, and closed her fingers around himself. She felt the tremor pass through him. Then he was still.

"I want you to know . . . me and not be afraid of it. I'll try not to hurt you, but I may, a little." She moved her hand over the full length of his hard flesh. It was torment for him to hold back and not push it against her hand, and he prayed he'd be able to control himself. After her wandering fingers ceased exploring, she placed little kisses on his chest. Relief flooded through him.

"I wondered what it would be like."

"Thank God I don't go around like this all the time." He sounded as if he were in pain.

"Does it hurt?"

"The sweetest pain you can imagine."

"Did you like for me to touch you there?"

"Lord, yes! Turn over, sweetheart."

He turned her on her back. She continued to hold him even as they turned and his mouth sought her breast and licked her nipple with his rough tongue. He felt the quiver that passed through her. When he caught it with his teeth and worried it, she exhaled sharply. He moved his mouth up to hers as his seeking fingers moved down to the sweet haven between her thighs and slipped into the warm wetness.

Something powerful throbbed in the area below her stomach. She moved restlessly, held him tighter, then began to squirm and arch toward his hand, to whimper as his fingers continued to work their magic.

"Do you feel what I feel? Tell me."

"Yes! Oh, yes!"

"The sweet pain?"

"Yes! Please—" Her arms clutched him, her hips moved in invitation. Blood swam in her head, pounded in her veins; and through it all, she heard his murmured endearments.

There was no room for fear as her desire for him consumed her. He lifted himself above her and, using all his strength of will to hold back, he slipped into her. She was warm, moist. He was so filled with love and desire that he forgot about the barrier that was sure to be there and rammed through it at the first thrust.

Jane jerked and gasped. He pulled out immediately.

"Sweetheart!"

"Don't go!" She pressed on his buttocks.

"Sure?"

"Please!"

She called his name as he entered her again, and he called hers. With muttered words of love, he moved within her in a careful rhythm that increased in speed and intensity as her body adjusted to his invasion. She was swept along with him in the turbulence of their desire. It was like flying, drowning, sinking, floating.

She heard the thunderous beating of his heart against her naked breast and heard his hoarse, murmured cries in her ear. A stunning, beautiful bloom of glorious rapture made her respond with a fierce ardor matching his. Through the crescendo of emotions, a sudden joy erupted within her and burst over her like a great splashing wave.

The climax of their joining left them gasping. Hands that had guided her hips now moved to either side of her and relieved her limp body of part of his crushing weight. He eased himself from between her thighs and shifted to lie beside her. His face to hers, he smoothed her rumpled hair and moved his mouth tenderly ever her throbbing lips. She gave quick answer, returned his kisses, then pressed her cheek on the smooth hardness of his shoulder.

Jane moved her hand down to his firm buttock and kept it there in a silent claim of possession. A tear pooled in her eye as she curled up in his arms, feeling the peace of being loved and cherished.

"Did I hurt you, honey?"

"It was beautiful, wonderful—"

"My Indian ancestors say it's a gift from the gods, and each time we give each other a little part of ourselves."

"I wanted to give you all of myself. I could feel you all through me. I keep thinking . . . is this real?"

"It's real, sweetheart. Did you ever think you'd be like this with a conniving, sneaky, stony-hearted horse's ass?"

"Mercy me! Did I call you all . . . that?"

"You sure did. Do you want to take it back?"

"I'll take back the conniving, sneaky, stony-hearted part." She laughed happily, nibbling at his chin. He hugged her, marveling at his luck in finding her and the miracle that she loved him.

T.C. held his breath as her fingers began to trace the line of downy hair from the light furring on his chest to his navel and beyond to the aroused flesh that refused to lie quietly.

She was a treasure a man would die for.

Later, she lay on his chest, her face nestled in the curve of his neck. They were silent and awed by the bliss they had found together. They lay in the warm cocoon of each other's arms. His fingers caressed the hair around her ears.

A long contented sigh escaped her.

"You've had a busy day, Mrs. Kilkenny."

"I don't want to sleep and waste a minute of this."

"You can't stay awake for the next forty years, my love."

He tilted her face so that her lips might meet his, and their mouths played with tender warmth. Incapable of further speech, they kissed each other tenderly again and again.

Chapter 22

IT was a day like no other in Jane's life.

Several times during the night she had been dreamily aware that her husband's arms were wrapped around her. Her back was pressed to his chest, her buttocks nestled in his lap, his knees were bent behind hers. Each time she awoke, his warm strong hand was cupped about her naked breast; and, feeling loved, cherished, and protected, she would drift back to sleep.

This morning he had kissed her gently, urging her awake. The scent of him filled her brain. She lay trustingly against him, a soft thigh snug between his, and moaned sleepily, her hand moving up from his chest to his cheek while she nuzzled her face against his neck.

"Wake up, sweetheart."

She tilted her head and gazed at him lovingly.

"You grew whiskers in the night." Her fingers stroked his cheek.

"I'll shave so I won't scratch your soft skin."

"I'm glad the lady barber isn't Theda Cruise."

"You don't like the idea of that Theda shaving me?"

"I'd shave you myself first!" She giggled happily.

Content to lie quietly and look at each other, they didn't speak for a long while. Finally T.C. stirred.

"I've been waiting for you to wake up so we can talk."

What did he mean? Had he reconsidered? The stab of fear that shot through her almost took her breath. She went very still as if her blood were draining from her body. She held onto him with all her strength, fearing her happiness was slipping away.

"But I'd much rather kiss you." His lips played over her face before reaching hers. "I didn't tell you this last night. For some crazy reason"—he kissed her on the nose—"it went right out of my mind, but sometime today we must go over some of Doc's papers and put them in order so that I can send them to his solicitor."

Relief brought a moistness to her eyes.

"Do you think he knows how happy I am?"

"I think he does."

"At first, he tried hard not to let me know how scared he was. Then after a while he seemed to get used to the idea of dying, and later, when the pain was bad, I think he prayed for it."

"He may have fallen a little bit in love with you, sweetheart."

"No! He liked me and I liked him. I wish I could have known him longer."

"You'll be very surprised when we go through his papers."

"I'll help if you want me to. And I'll help you with your books, if you like."

"Why do you think I married you?" he teased.

"For this?" Her lips traveled over his face and she moved her lower body close against his. She was giddy with the freedom to touch him, tease him.

"That too. Behave, Mrs. Jane *Lovely* Kilkenny. I've got more to say."

"Can't it wait?"

"No, sweetheart. I want to be sure you understand that I don't want you worrying about what you told me last night. You've got me now to do your worrying."

Her palm cupped his cheek. The smile left her face as her serious blue eyes looked into his.

"I got a bargain; you got a load of trouble."

"A trouble shared is only half a trouble. We'll get to the bottom of this, I promise you. We put the letters back behind your mother's picture. The notes are in safekeeping should we need them to compare handwriting—although I doubt the bastard will be able to write when I get through with him."

"I'm going to burn the letters."

"I don't want you to leave the house, honey, not even to go to the privy, unless someone is with you. I'll see to it that Colin or Herb will be close by if I can't be. And I don't want you in the house alone. Understand? I'll tell Mrs. Henderson that, if she must leave, to be sure that one of us or Sunday is here."

"I'm so much trouble to everyone."

"Shhh . . . You're the sweetest trouble I ever had. I just hope the son of a bitch makes another move. If I don't beat him to death, he'll wish I had."

"Bill said you were a bare-knuckle champion."

He grinned. "Did he tell you that my uncle, Moose Kilkenny, taught me? He lost his championship to Pack Gallagher over at Laramie. I was there that day. Folks are still talking about that fight."

"I couldn't bear to see someone hit you. I'd get a buggy whip and wade right in," she said staunchly.

"You would, huh?" He rolled her on her back and leaned over her. "As Doc would say, you're a pistol. I wish we could stay here all day, but I've got to get up."

"I'll cook your breakfast."

He gave her a quick kiss. "Someone has beaten you to it. I heard noises in the kitchen."

"Morning."

"Mornin', Mrs. T.C. Kilkenny." Colin sprang up from the table, grabbed her and planted a quick kiss on her cheek. He sat back down and grinned at T.C.

"Keep your hands off my wife!" T.C. pretended to be angry, but his eyes shone with pride. "Go get your own woman."

"Don't get all riled up and go on the warpath, Chief Thunder Cloud," Colin said good-naturedly. "I didn't get to kiss her yesterday."

To hide her confusion, Jane took a square cloth, folded it

to make three corners and tied it about her waist.

"What's to be done, Maude?" she asked.

"It's done." Maude put a platter of eggs on the table. "Sit down by your man and eat."

Colin didn't speak again. He ate his breakfast, excused himself and left.

"He's not hisself," Maude said sadly. "He was this way yesterday . . . the little I saw of him."

Herb came in to breakfast and then Polly. The people who shared this house as much family as Jane had ever had. Each one of them was concerned for her. She wondered if they would feel the same if they knew who she was. She reached under the table and placed her hand on her husband's thigh. As if he knew what she was thinking, his hard hand covered hers, giving silent assurance.

By mid-morning Jane's meager belongings had been put away in the room she would share with T.C., and she was busy at the cluttered table that served as his desk. He had already made three trips back to the house to make sure she was all right. Each time she looked at him her heart did strange things that made her dizzy with happiness.

She stopped her work and listened to the singing coming from the kitchen. Maude and Stella were singing together. Their voices blended in a sad ballad Jane had never heard before, which was no surprise to her because only hymns had been allowed at the school.

In the world's mighty gallery of pictures,
hang the scenes that are painted from life.
Pictures of youth and of passion. Pictures of
grief and of strife.
A picture of love and of beauty, old age and a
blushing young bride,
All hang on the wall, but the saddest of all,
is the picture of life's other side.

The mother and daughter sang several verses of the song: one about a gambler, another about the mother who waited for her son to come home. Jane hated for the singing to end. She waited, but heard Maude telling Stella to do her sums.

Not once had Maude mentioned where she and Stella had lived before. They never mentioned a husband or father. It was as if they had been dropped out of the sky. Maude had been pretty at one time. Jane couldn't help but wonder what had caused the scars on her face and why both she and Stella had acted so skittish when they first arrived.

Whatever had happened to them was over now. Maude sang as she worked or helped her daughter with her schooling. She was also helping Polly to read.

Jane returned to her ledger and was making an entry in the book when she heard the front door open. She looked up, expecting to see T.C. again, but it was Sunday who stood in the doorway.

"Ya don't look no different."

"Come in, Sunday. Why would I look different?" Pleased to see her friend, Jane rose to go to her, then hesitated. It was rare to see an unsmiling Sunday. "Herb said you were sick. Are you feeling better?"

"I'm *not* sick." Sunday came into the room and flopped down in the chair in front of the table. Jane sat down again. "I told Mrs. Miller to tell him that. I didn't want to come over here last night and see *him* I was 'fraid I'd poke his damned eyes out."

"Him? If you mean Colin, he wasn't here either."

"I can guess where he was." Sunday rolled her eyes. "The only reason I'm here now is 'cause I saw him on that big horse headin' out of town. And I wanted to see if yo're doin' all right."

"I'm all right. Thank you for what you did for me. You found me, didn't you?"

"Me and Maude. Is Maude mad 'cause I didn't show up for the big to-do?"

"I doubt that she is, but you'll have to ask her."

"Yo're lookin' chipper. Ya ain't sorry ya married that big, ugly, ramroddin' mick?"

Jane smiled. This was the Sunday she knew.

"Sorry? Oh, my no! Yesterday was the best day of my life. And he isn't ugly! He's beautiful."

"Lord help me! Ya've thrown away yore brains."

"Sunday . . . I've never had friends like you and Maude . . . and Polly. I can't imagine what you thought when . . . you saw me."

"Well . . . the first thing I thought was . . . phew! Then, after I got a look at you, I thought, if I could get a hold of the one who done it, I'd cut his damn throat with a dull knife."

"I was so scared that I think I went out of my head. I don't remember much after you found me. I was in a fog. I couldn't think and didn't want to."

"I never saw anybody in such a lather as that Irishman you wed. He was red-hot, do-do-stompin' mad."

"T.C. said that no one knows what happened but those of us who were here."

"Maude and I read the notes ya had in the pocket of yore dress. Somebody 'round here don't like ya much. I suppose ya told Kilkenny who it is."

"I don't know who it is. But I told him why. Someday, maybe, I can tell you."

Sunday got abruptly to her feet and went to the window.

"If ya was still wantin' to leave here, I was goin' to go with ya."

"What's happened, Sunday? Did something happen between you and Colin?"

Sunday spun around. "Nothin' happened atween *me* and Colin. Plenty happened atween *him* and Mrs. Patrice Guzman Cabeza," she said bitterly.

"My goodness! Don't tell me that Colin would . . . that he . . . She's married!"

"Shore she is, but she's havin' *his* babe!" Sunday blurted the words and then burst into tears. She placed her bent arm against the wall and hid her face against it.

"Oh, no!" Jane went to her and put her hand on her back. "Who told you that?"

"She did."

"And you believe her?"

"Why not? She's a snooty bitch, but she ort to know who's been atween her legs."

"Why would she run away from her husband? Won't he think the baby's his?"

"She says he ain't got nothin' in his balls to make a babe and he'd know it ain't his."

"Land o' livin'. Why did she tell you *that*?"

"Paralee and Bessie is spreadin' the story all over town. So I asked her. She said Colin's the papa."

"You like him a lot, don't you?"

"I did! Now I hate his rotten guts." Sunday ended her words with a wail. "It makes me so damn mad that I was fooled by a bird-turd like him!"

"I was sure that he was smitten with you. He couldn't keep his eyes off you the day we buried Doc."

"He honeyed up to me. And me bein' dumb as a stump I got all starry-eyed. But he ain't the only man in this town. There's others been givin' me the once-over. I'll go find me one and marry him."

"Don't do something hasty you'll regret," Jane warned. "From what I've seen of Colin, I'm sure he's an honorable man. I can't believe he'd carry on with another man's wife."

"Ha! All men is pretty proud a what they got in their britches. The other night he hinted for me to invite him to my bed, and I told him plain out that without his name tacked onto the end of mine, he'd not sleep with me."

Sunday bent over and wiped her eyes on the hem of her dress. "At the time I thought he was funnin', but I guess he wasn't."

"Why don't you wait and see what Colin has to say. I don't think I'd take Mrs. Cabeza's word."

"I sure ain't goin' to ask him!"

"Ask who what?"

Jane and Sunday turned to see T.C. in the doorway.

"You're so quiet. I didn't hear you." Jane's eyes shone as she watched him walk toward her.

"It's my Indian blood, honey. It helps me sneak up on helpless females." He put his hand possessively on her shoulder. "Hello, Sunday. I saw you come in. We missed you last night at the wedding supper."

"Well, I was busy sewin' ruffles on my ball gown gettin' it ready for the big hoopla." She tossed her blond head and stared at him defiantly as if daring him to contradict her.

"Do you think you could squeeze out the time to help dress up the town?"

"What for? It ain't the Fourth of July."

"The first stage coach will arrive in a few days"

"—That's good. When does it leave? I'll be on it."

"Oh, Sunday—" Jane murmured sadly.

T.C. ignored Sunday's remark about leaving.

"I was thinking we could get a bolt of red cloth and stretch it across the street in front of the hotel where the stage will stop. Honey," he said to Jane, "do you think you could make us some welcome signs?"

"If I had boards and paint."

"I want a sign to put over the door of the stage office that says: ROWE STAGE LINE. Herb will bring over what you need, and you can do it right out there on the porch. Will you stay with her, Sunday?"

"I ain't stickin' around here all day."

"Colin won't be back for one, maybe two weeks."

"I ain't carin' if he *ever* comes back." Sunday's face

turned a fiery red. She turned and started for the door.

"Sunday, it can be explained. I know it can." Jane turned pleading eyes to T.C.

"A woman either trusts her man or she don't, honey."

"That's askin' for a lot of trust," Jane said staunchly.

"I don't think so. Sunday, Colin said Patrice told you the baby she's carrying is his. Why didn't you ask him?"

"It ain't none a my business if he diddles with ever' woman in town! I ain't married to him," Sunday said angrily.

"Exactly."

Jane looked at T.C. as if disbelieving what he said. Sunday was her friend and she was hurting.

"We're getting the stage office ready and Jeb wants me to look at the school building. Thank God, the preacher has taken over the building of the church. I'll be back in a few hours." He dropped a kiss on Jane's lips. "I'm glad you're here with her, Sunday. Don't let her out of your sight and keep your eyes open," he said as he went out the door.

Sunday stayed, and as the day wore on, she became less angry and more melancholy. Herb brought the supplies for the signs. Jane, wearing an old wool coat of Doc's, painted on the board Herb had nailed temporarily between two porch posts. On the smaller boards she outlined the letters with a pencil and Sunday filled in with the paint.

In the middle of the afternoon Paralee and Bessie came strolling by and stopped.

"What ya doin'?" Paralee asked.

"We're suckin' eggs." Sunday resisted the urge to fling paint from the brush in their direction. "Stand back or ya'll get splattered."

Bessie giggled, then spoke to Jane.

"We heared Mr. Kilkenny married ya."

"It's true," Jane said, and smiled at both women. "And I married Mr. Kilkenny."

"How'd ya get him to do it?" Paralee asked, her eyes

wide with pretended innocence.

"It was easy. I threatened to pull out his toenails . . . one at a time. You should try it. It'll work every time."

Sunday whooped with laughter.

"Why is your face all scratched? Did ya chase him through a briar patch?" Paralee sniped, angered by Sunday's laughter.

"That's exactly what I did. I wasn't letting him get away."

"A friend of yours ain't too happy 'bout you getting married," Bessie said smugly.

"I can see that, but you two were not my friends anyway."

"I ain't meanin' us. Bob Fresno. Milo come to see me last night. He said Bob was like a bear with a sore tail."

Sunday looked at Bessie as if she'd suddenly sprouted horns.

"If yo're keepin' company with Milo Callahan, ya ain't got the brains God gave a crab apple. He's as crazy as a steer on locoweed."

"Ya say that 'cause he's courtin' me and not you."

Sunday lifted her eyes to the sky. "God bless all dungheads."

"Where'd Colin Tallman ride off to this mornin'?" Paralee asked.

"To the stage station for T.C." Jane answered quickly.

"Well, we got to be goin'. We're goin' to the hotel and call on Patrice. She's kinda . . . under the weather." Paralee waited to see what that announcement brought forth. What she got was more than she expected.

Sunday had dipped her brush in the paint and now she waved it to flick off the excess. The wind was just right to carry the drips of black paint toward Paralee and Bessie. One landed on Paralee's nose, a larger drop on the bosom of her low-necked dress, and yet another still larger one on her skirt. Bessie was also sprinkled with the drops of paint.

"Oops. I told ya to stand back."

"Looky . . . at what ya did!" Paralee gasped. "Ya . . . ruined my dress! Ya . . . ruined it!"

"Mine, too," Bessie wailed. "Its' my . . . good one!"

With the brush held in front of her, her wild blond curls blowing in the breeze, Sunday advanced on the pair, her face creased in sorrowful lines.

"Oh, gosh! I'm sorry, *dear friends*. Let me fix it. I'll put a black dab on yore other tittie and folks'll think they're yore nipples."

"Stay away—" Paralee screeched and ran a distance before she turned and shouted. "You'll be sorry!"

"I'm only sorry I didn't paint yore flappin' mouth shut!" Sunday shouted back.

Jane doubled over with laughter. "Oh, Sunday. That was rich! How did you manage for the wind to be just right?"

"God helped me." Sunday smiled broadly. "I hear he hates thieves, liars and bitchy females. Maybe he'll send a bolt a lightning into the Bismark Hotel. Wouldn't that be grand?"

"I'm so glad I met you, Sunday. I've got a feeling that we are going to be friends for many, many years."

Sunday stayed for supper. Tennihill and Bill Wassall came too. The men talked in T.C.'s office while the women fussed in the kitchen over the meal.

As they were taking their places around the table, Jane whispered to T.C. and he nodded. After they were all seated, she stood. All eyes turned to her. With T.C.'s hand held tightly in hers, she bowed her head.

"Thank Thee, dear Lord, for bringing me to this place and giving me Timothy Charles Kilkenny to be my husband. I will love him and be faithful to him until the end of my days. I thank Thee, too, for these wonderful friends who have become the family I never had. Please keep them safe and well, and may they be as happy as I am at this moment. Amen."

Jane looked at each of the faces at the table and her eyes misted.

"This is about as near to heaven as I ever expect to be." She sat down and turned her face against her husband's arm for an instant, then smiled. "You should all thank the Lord for Maude. She's a much better cook than I."

"Them biscuits ain't bad fer bein' made by a woman," Bill declared later as he used one to sop gravy from his plate. "But yore peach cobbler don't hold a candle to mine."

"How do you know that? You've not eaten my peach cobbler," Maude retorted.

Bill's blue eyes twinkled. "'Course I ain't. Ya ain't made none. If ya was good at it, ya'da made it."

"Oh . . . fiddle-faddle—"

"Mama makes good cherry cobbler. We had—" Stella stopped abruptly after a warning look from her mother.

"Pay him no mind, Mrs. Henderson. Bill is missing Mrs. Winters," T.C. said and reached for another biscuit.

"Harrumpt! Does a dog miss a flea?"

After the meal and after the supper dishes were cleared away, they all sat around the table and discussed the celebration they would have the day the stage arrived. Herb and Polly were as excited as two kids, which they were.

"If the weather holds, we can have a street dance in front of the hotel. But then we'll need to do something about lighting." T.C. looked over at Herb. "Do you think we could round up enough lanterns to hang? It'd be a hell of a note if we burned down the town trying to have a celebration."

"Store's got a bunch. Mr. Jenson'd let us use them."

"Lighting will be your job, Herb."

"What about music?" Jane asked.

"We got two fiddlers in town—Walter Jenson at the store and Theda Cruise." T.C. reached for Jane's hand under the table.

"That red-headed woman at the saloon?" Herb's boyish face broke into a smile. "I never knowed of a woman fiddler."

"What's so strange 'bout that?" Sunday raised her brows. "A woman can play a fiddle as well as any man. I'd show ya if I had one."

"You play?" At least three spoke at the same time.

"Been playin' all my life. Don't have a fiddle, though. Papa loved his fiddle better'n he loved me. Do ya have someone to do the callin'?

T.C.'s eyes went to Tennihill. "Didn't I hear you bragging about something?"

"Well, now. I don't know when that'd be. I ain't one to be shootin' my mouth off 'bout what I'm best at."

"We got a caller." T.C. said flatly and grinned at the lanky Tennihill, then down at Jane. "And signs. You're good, honey. I'm glad I married you. Got me a free sign-maker."

Sunday pushed back her chair and stood.

"Jane can work for free. I can't. I need a job if I stay here, Kilkenny. That soap-makin' job ya give me ain't lastin'. The lye and grease they gave me made soap only good for washin' clothes. The laundry's got enough to last till Christmas."

"There's work for you here. I'd like for you to be here in the house with Jane during the day. In a week or two we'll move the surgery out, but as long as it's here folks will come and I don't want her in there alone with *anyone*." His dark face was dead serious. "As soon as we ferret out the bas . . . person, there'll be other work. Meanwhile, I'll be more at ease knowing that three of you are here." His glance included Maude and Polly.

"All right, Kilkenny. As long as ya put it that way, I'll be here in the morning. 'Night, ever'body."

"Hold on, little gal." Tennihill unfolded his long length from the table. "I'll walk ya back to the roomin' house.

Ain't no tellin' what kind a varmints is pokin' round out there."

"Thank ya. I'd a brought my gun, but didn't think I'd be here after dark."

"Them was larrapin' vittles, Miz Henderson." Tennihill bowed with Old-World charm. "Thanky kindly."

"You're welcome, Mr. Tennihill." Maude's face had turned a rosy pink. It was clear to all that she was not used to compliments.

"I'll add my thanks on top of his and be leavin'. Herb's givin' me dirty looks. He's waitin' for me to get out so he can spark his girl." Bill rolled to his feet.

"I'm doin' no such thin' Bill."

"If you're not goin' to spark her, boy, I will. I've done a mite of it in my day, and this'n is pretty as a speckled pup."

"I know she's pretty, and I'm goin' to spark her as soon as you go, but ya don't . . . have to go . . . now." Herb stumbled around for the right words.

Bill clapped him on the shoulder and went along as Jane and T.C. followed Tennihill and Sunday to the door.

"Careful of the paint," Jane called as they crossed the porch. "It should be dry by morning."

Chapter 23

BOB Fresno sat before a fire at the mouth of a cave carved into the side of a mountain. The night was cold. Snow covered the peaks of the mountains around him. The geese had gone south for the winter and the squirrels were storing food. Time was running short for what he had to do before hard winter set in.

The fire was small because Bob wanted no glow to attract attention to his hideout. He had been brought to the cave a year or so earlier when he and an outlaw friend had wanted to make themselves scarce for a while. The outlaw who had shown it to him had proved to be no friend and no longer needed a place to hide out. As far as Bob knew, he was the only one that knew about it. Callahan knew now, but later . . .

Timbertown was ten or twelve miles to the north. The nearest cabin was eight or ten miles due east. He had stopped there in the summer and visited awhile with the two old trappers who lived there. They had not been very friendly. It hadn't mattered at the time. But the layout of the place, the supplies, had all been recorded in Fresno's mind. He would take Jane there to spend the winter. The cabin was good and tight and would be full of provisions. Best of all, the two old men would be easy to get rid of.

The night was still, with almost no wind. There was the smell of cedar smoke in the air and of crushed juniper. The coffeepot, blackened from many fires, stood in the coals on a flat rock. Bob leaned back on his saddle, clasped his hands behind his head and looked at the sky spangled with a million stars.

When he left Timbertown, he hadn't wanted Milo with him, but now he was glad he was along. Milo was useful to send to town for information. Fresno would use him again when he went in to get Jane. Just thinking her name made his pulse race. He'd not been so coldly rejected by a woman since he wore knee pants back in Kansas City. He fully intended to have her. Some women needed to be broken like a wild filly. After she'd been taught to take the bit, she'd eat out of his hand.

Fresno indulged himself in his favorite pastime: thinking of how he was going to snatch Jane out of Kilkenny's hands. The fact that he had married her, and been sleeping with her, irritated Bob, but it didn't make him want her any less. In fact, he wanted her more. Hell! All the women he'd had so far, but for one, had belonged to someone else first. It was part of the fun to make them give up something for him, be it money or a man.

Bob Fresno was a man with a plan. He would use Callahan to create a commotion to draw off Kilkenny and that kid who was so deadly with a gun. He had heard of Herb Banks but hadn't realized he was so young. Most of the gunmen he knew were older, hard-riding, hard-bitten men. This kid was still wet behind the ears. Still, he'd made a name for himself. Five men had tried him; five men were six feet under. He'd crippled a few, too. One had ambushed him, shot him in the leg, and gotten killed for the trouble. After that, it was said around campfires all through the mountains: face Herb Banks head-on and he'll shoot you right between the eyes.

Kilkenny, he knew, was tough as nails, meaner than a wild longhorn when he was riled. He'd been over the mountain, down the river and around the bend. Folks said he'd been across the ocean to one of them foreign places and had been to some fancy school. Bob knew for a fact Kilkenny had been responsible for cleaning up the town of Bannock a few years back. Lumberjack, ex-lawman, drover, freighter, and now town-builder.

T.C. Kilkenny was a difficult man to put into a niche. But never mind about that. If he were lucky, Kilkenny or Banks would kill Callahan, and he wouldn't have to. If he were *very* lucky, Callahan would get one of *them* before they got him. Then he'd only have to wait for the other one along a shadowy trail.

It was past midnight when Callahan rode in. He would have left his horse standing and helped himself to coffee if not for harsh advice from Bob.

"Take care a yore horse, ya damned fool. He's yore only way outta here if ya ain't figurin' to walk."

"A minute or two wouldn't a mattered," Milo grumbled. "Guess ya ain't so hot to know what I found out."

Later, after the horse had been unsaddled and rubbed down, Milo squatted on his heels beside the fire and picked up his tin cup.

"Well . . . spit it out," Bob growled.

"Stage is comin' in day after tomorrow. Town's plannin' a celebration."

"All day?"

"No. After the stage gets there."

"What time is that?"

"Sundown."

Milo was getting tired of being treated like a hired hand and now delighted in making Bob pull every tidbit of information out of him.

"Where's the celebration gonna be?"

"In the street, I guess."

"Where?"

"In the street."

"Gawddammit! Where, in the street?"

"In front of the hotel. They're havin' a dance."

"Why'n hell didn't ya say so?"

"Ya didn't ask!" Milo shouted, jumped up and dashed the last of his coffee into the fire.

"Sit down and cool off."

"Ya ain't had a good word to say since we left Timbertown."

"I've got a lot on my mind. This dance may be what

we've been waiting for. If we work it right, we can sneak in there, grab the women and head for a snug cabin I know of. We'll spend the winter eatin' good cookin' and humpin' our women. How does that sound?"

Milo grinned, showing his broken tooth.

"Mighty good. I ain't had none fer so long my balls is full as a tick and my pecker's so tight it skins back when I grin."

"Ain't that Bessie puttin' out?"

"She lets me feel her up, is all."

"Shit!" Bob snorted.

"Well, hell! Ya can't do much on the porch of a roomin' house, and that's as far as she'll go."

"That Banks kid scare ya away from that other young'un ya had yore eye on?

"Didn't scare me. I jist give it more thought. Why get in a briar patch to get a berry when ya can pick one up along the road? Bessie's jist as young, jist as pretty, and she's got bigger tits and a bigger ass."

"I like my women skinny. The closer to the bone the better the meat."

Milo shrugged.

"Tell me again everythin' ya heard about this dance. They got a fiddler? Is there goin' to be a steer roast like at the buryin'?"

Milo loved to talk when he had an interested listener. He refilled his cup, and he and Bob talked far into the night.

"Sonofabitch!"

T.C. had stepped off the porch and turned back to look at the sign Jane had painted the day before. In the early morning light, he saw black smears of paint going from one end of the sign to the other—smears put there by dipping a rag in the paint bucket that sat on the porch. The rag lay on the ground beside the steps.

At first he didn't notice the paper stuck between the sign

and the porch post. When he did, he jerked it out and read the short message:

HA HA HA

Anger washed over him in a hot torrent. His eyes glistened with the light of battle. He took a long, slow breath to steady himself and turned to view the street where scarcely a person was about this time of the morning. Who was this demented creature so warped with hate that he would torment Jane for something she had had nothing to do with? It occurred to him that both Jeb Hobart and Walter Jenson at the store had suffered great losses. And most folks in town had a relative or friend . . .

Herb came across the street from the bunkhouse where he had been sleeping. The sight of the smeared sign brought him up short.

"Hellfire! Who did that?"

"That's what I'd like to know. Take it down, Herb. We may have to post a guard at night until we find out who's doing this."

"I've been nosyin' around like ya said, T.C. I ain't heard a peep from nobody 'bout Miss Jane. Folks like her. Murphy, kiddin' like, acted like he was half put out when ya married her. Some of the fellers is braggin' 'bout how she helped their kids, but some of 'em think she's snooty 'cause she don't come out and mix with 'em."

"She's almost a prisoner here in the house." T.C. growled and stepped up onto the porch.

"Ya could take her to yore ranch."

"Then we'd never know who's behind this . . . unless they followed us. I'm not letting some sneaking coward who attacks women run us out of town."

"I ain't likin' towns much anyway. Always somebody wantin' to outdo ya."

"Somebody trying to crowd you into a gunfight, Herb?"

"There's a couple that'd like to try me. Bill told 'em I don't shoot to wing 'em anymore, that if they want a fight, it'll be right atween the eyes. They backed down a little. One of 'em's a back-shooter, or my name ain't Herb Banks. He won't face me. I'm thinkin' he ain't worth dog shit."

"Who's that?"

"Milo Callahan."

"I thought he'd left town."

"He was in the saloon last night nosin' 'round. Says he ain't lookin' for work, braggin' he's got money stashed away."

"He was *here* last night?"

"In the saloon. His biggest brag is that he ain't goin' to be shacked up all winter without a woman to warm him."

"Has he got one in mind?"

"He's been makin' eyes at that silly Bessie Miller, and she's been lappin' it up."

"If she's stupid enough to go with him, there's not much we can do about it. Birds of a feather flock together," he quoted.

"What's that mean?"

"It means that maybe he's her kind."

T.C. was a man accustomed to listening to his instincts. Several weeks ago he had sized up Fresno and Callahan as trouble; he should have refused them work at the time. Then they would have had no reason to hang around. He was getting tired of the itch he felt at times when there was nothing to show for it but an empty back trail. It was no comfort to remember he'd had this same feeling just before he was jumped by the Claibournes up near Bannock for turning their bank-robbing brother over to the federal marshal.

He watched Herb pull the nails from the sign and lay it face down on the porch.

"Been needin' to talk to you, Herb, since Doc passed on.

After you've had your breakfast, come to the office."

T.C. went back into the house. He had to tell Jane about the sign. He worried how she would take it.

She took it better than he thought she would. She insisted on seeing the damage.

"I'll paint another one. I saved the letters I cut out of paper. It'll take only half the time. This one will be much better. I wasn't too proud of that one anyway."

"Honey, you're a pistol."

They had gone back into the house. He put his arms around her and cuddled her to him. He loved this woman so much it scared him. Love had come on him so fast and so hard that it took some getting used to.

"Were you afraid I'd go all to pieces?"

"Not all to pieces, but I don't want you worrying."

"The more they do, the sooner they'll make a mistake, and we'll find out who it is. Then the test will be how folks feel about me. I'm not afraid as long as I've got you."

"You've got enough backbone here for a dozen women." He stroked her back, then kissed her gently. "You didn't get enough sleep last night."

"What we did was far better than sleep." Her cheeks turned rosy, and she hid her face against his chest.

"Do you like that part of being my wife?"

"What a thing to ask." She pounded his chest gently with her closed first. "I didn't think people talked about . . . that."

I want us to talk about anything and everything. Someday I'm going to ask you what you like best for me to do to you when we're in bed and I'm—"

"—Hush up, T.C.!"

He laughed happily and hugged her fiercely.

"I can't stop . . . loving you when I'm with you in that bed.

I'm afraid I'm wearing you out," he whispered the words in her ear, then looked into her flushed, happy face.

"Tonight I'll sleep on a pallet on the floor."

"Then you'd better make it big enough for two, my love."

"I love you, Mrs. Kilkenny. I'm going to keep you safe. You believe that, don't you?"

"I believe it. And I'm so grateful."

He put his fingers on her lips to cut off her words.

"That word doesn't exist between you and me." He put a little distance between them.

"Sometimes I feel sorry for that person who has so much hate—"

"I don't feel one bit sorry for him. I want to twist his head off! Herb took down the sign. There's no use letting the whole town see it."

"He's in the kitchen ragging Polly and Maude. Maude really likes him; so does Stella."

"What about Polly?"

"She thinks he's the greatest, smartest, most wonderful man in the world. Of course, she's wrong."

"You sure of that?" T.C.'s eyes caressed her face.

"Positive." In a quiet little corner of her heart Jane promised God that if he would let her spend the rest of her life with this man she would do the best that she could to make it a better world.

"I told Herb to come in here after breakfast. We'll tell him about Doc's will."

"Doc thought a lot of him. He'll know that now."

"He thought a lot of you too. Honey, are you sure you don't hold it against me for pushing you to marry me? You would have had the means to leave here and go anywhere you wanted."

Jane laughed lightly and kissed his chin.

"There is no place in the world I'd rather be than right here, and I think Doc knew that. Besides, I wouldn't have taken the money even if I had left after the burying."

"A thousand dollars is a fortune. Most folks don't see that much money in a lifetime."

"Doc knew that if things turned out between you and me as he hoped, I'd not take it. Knowing how conniving the rascal was, I think he was forcing you to make your move. But in case things didn't work out between us, he wanted to help me."

Jane's eyes became misty.

"I wanted you so much I played unfair."

"Shhh . . . Don't talk about it. I'd stay here and face a thousand people, an army of people, who hated me as long as I have you." She spoke quietly, sincerely, her eyes full of love for him.

"We'll face them together, sweetheart. Now we get to break the good news to Herb that he inherits Doc's entire estate."

Herb took the news of his sudden new wealth in stunned silence.

"When the stocks are sold and the money in the different banks tallied, you'll be a rich man, Herb." T.C. tried to explain the legal ramifications, then gave up and told him the things he would understand.

"I didn't know Doc was rich."

"He inherited some of his money from his family back in Carolina, then invested it. It doesn't appear that he felt the need to spend much."

"Why me? I ain't *blood* kin."

"He says here, 'To Herb Banks, my son in every way except through blood ties, I leave the bulk of my estate.' He told me the night he had me write this that he wished he had found you when you were a child. You gave Doc something to live for."

Tears flooded the eyes of the boy-man who had never had a family, never had a childhood. They rolled unashamedly down his cheeks.

"I wish he had, too. I never had nobody till Doc."

"He felt that he'd never had anyone to really care for him till he met you."

"I won't know what to do with . . . it."

"Don't worry about that now, Herb. Doc made arrangements for me and for Garrick Rowe to help you. Colin and I want you to come to the ranch next spring and work with us. You may find out that you like the cattle business; and, if so, you'll have the money to start your own ranch."

"I want to marry Polly before folks know the babe ain't mine."

"In that case, we'll fix up one of the cabins for you and Polly, or you can stay there through the winter. I expect we'll all be leaving here in the spring. I'm hoping you'll stay till then. I need you to help me patrol as you've been doing. We've not had much trouble yet, but with idle time coming, I expect some."

Jane had asked T.C. not to mention the thousand dollars of Herb's inheritance that Doc had willed to her should she decide to leave Timbertown. T.C. had agreed that it was something Herb needn't know. The boy was confused enough with the legalities of his new wealth.

"Congratulations, Herb. Go find Polly and tell her she's marrying a rich man."

"I can't do that, Miss Jane. It'd plumb scare her outta her wits." Herb began to smile, even though his eyes were still wet with tears. "T.C., can I go up to the store and buy her somethin'? She's not had ribbons or many doodads like that. I want to get her one a them pins with a face on it."

"Tell Jenson to put it on a tab."

"She'll want one of them pull-down lamps when we get our own place."

"You'll have the money to buy one."

At the door he turned and looked back. "Don't this beat all? I wish I could say thanky to Doc. T.C., I already decided to buy the biggest stone I could find fer his grave. I want one with a dove on top and lots of words about Little Doc and what he done in the war. Tennihill can tell me what to say."

"We'll write to a monument place in Laramie and find out how to go about it. We'll ask for a catalog and you can choose which one you want. I don't think we can get a stone cut and set before the snows, but we could get it here and set it up next spring."

"I'll tell Polly. I wish I could give her one of them fancy weddin's in the church, but we'd better not wait till the preacher gets the church house built. I'd just as soon get married up there on the hill where Doc is, but I don't know if Polly'd want to."

"T.C. and I were married right here. We feel just as married as if we had been married in the grandest cathedral in the world. Don't we?" Jane looked adoringly at her husband.

"You betcha!"

T.C. bent his head and kissed his wife. For a moment they forgot time and place. He kissed her lingeringly, gently and thoroughly. When he finally remembered Herb, he looked up to find him gone.

Chapter 24

EXCITEMENT was in the air.

In less than six hours the stage would arrive and the celebration would begin. It was a beautiful fall day; the sky was cloudless, and the sun was warm.

T.C. and Jeb stood back and admired the sign they had nailed above the door of the new addition to the hotel that would serve as the stage office: ROWE STAGE LINE.

"Looks as good as if it'd come from Denver. Miss Jane should go into business." Jeb wasn't one to pass out compliments, and T.C. was pleased.

"I'm not sure she wants to make it a business, but she's willing to do what she can until a real sign painter shows up."

A wagon came down the street with a load of firewood and T.C. walked out to speak to the driver.

"Pile it over there on the side of the street. Be sure to leave room for the stage to get through. We'll have two bonfires tonight a couple hundred feet apart, one here and the other one down in front of that vacant spot. They'll furnish light and heat. It'll be cold once the sun goes down."

"Hope we don't burn down the town," Jeb said as the wagon moved away.

"I thought of that. I'll have a man at each fire."

Red cloth had been stretched above the street. Strips of the red wound around the porch posts of the hotel. Streamers hung from the porches of some of the businesses. Signs in the windows said: WELCOME.

The mill had closed for the day, and lumberjacks from the cutting camps were coming into town by the wagonload as were settlers from around the area. People roamed up and down the street and into the stores. Children played, dogs barked, and men waited on the porch of the barbershop to take a bath or get a haircut. Mrs. Winters had pans of bear claws and fried pies set on the counter to be sold.

Jenson was doing a thriving business at the store. He had brought out two Roman candles to set off when the stage arrived. As it would not be dark enough at sundown to get the full effect, it was decided that he would fire them when the dance began.

At Kilkenny's house there was much discussion about what to wear. Maude insisted that it didn't matter in the least what she wore, but she wanted Polly and Stella to look pretty. Not only had she washed and ironed their best dresses but she had even run the iron over the yards and yards of ribbon Herb had bought at the store and proudly presented for them to wear in their hair.

Jane had not planned to go to the dance until Sunday declared that she would stay at home with her. Knowing that T.C. would have to be there and that he wouldn't allow her to stay at home alone, she decided that she would go so that Sunday would.

"Sweetheart, I'll be there. Herb will keep an eye on you and I'm sure Tennihill will too. Don't you want to hear Sunday play the fiddle?"

"I'd forgotten about that."

"I want to dance with my wife—"

"No! I've never danced in my life. I'd make a fool of myself before all those people."

"I'll teach you."

"Please don't make me."

"All right, honey. I'll never make you do anything you don't want to do."

"I want Sunday to have a good time. She's not mentioned Colin one time."

"He'll be back soon. They must solve their own problems without interference from us."

"I know that. It's just that I'm so happy and she's so sad."

A light rap sounded on the door, then it opened. Patrice, Paralee and Bessie walked into the house.

"Do come in," T.C. said sarcastically.

"It's an office, isn't it? I didn't know you had to be invited into a business office," Patrice said.

"It's my home for the time being. What do you want, Patrice?"

"No greeting? No how are you, Señora Guzman Cabeza?

"What do you want? I know this isn't a social call."

Patrice's eyes swept insolently over Jane.

"You've come down in the world, T.C. I can remember when your sights were set on a much . . . higher level."

"I remember, too, when I was offered . . . favors from the so-called higher level and recognized that that *level* was nothing but trash. Say what you've got to say and get out. Take these two cadgers with you."

Paralee bristled. "Cadgers? What's that?"

"Just what I said. I gave both of you jobs. You've not put in two days work. Yet the company is paying for your keep and feeding you. You're *cadging* off the company."

"I'm not working in the kitchen scrubbin' pots for that old cook at the hotel. Patrice says you're taking advantage of us."

"Then Patrice can pay for your keep."

"You owe me!" Bessie blurted and pointed a finger at Jane. "She splattered paint all over my new dress. If Patrice hadn't loaned me one, I couldn't go to the dance."

"*She* didn't splatter you. I did." Sunday spoke from the office doorway.

Patrice turned cold eyes on Sunday, then back to T.C.

"Where's Colin?"

"I wouldn't know."

"Is he at one of the timber camps?"

"I wouldn't know."

"It isn't like him to hide out. I suppose it was your idea."

"Think what you want."

"When is he coming back?"

"I don't know that either."

"I need to talk to him. We have to make plans. Ramon will show up here any time now, and we've got to be prepared. He told you I'm having his child? Of course, he did. He'd not be able to keep the good news to himself."

"He told me *you* were having one."

"He can't deny it's his. I was with him in his hotel room in Santa Fe. The desk clerk gave me a key. I can prove I was there."

"That's between you and Ramon and Colin."

Patrice's dark eyes turned back to Sunday, surveyed her with distaste, then moved to Jane.

"Your taste in women hasn't changed. You've always been attracted to the frowsy, loose types. But . . . you never *married* one before."

Sunday moved swiftly and silently. Her hand flew out and struck Patrice a solid smack on the cheek.

"*You're*" as loose as a goose in a berry patch—braggin' ya spread yore legs for a man not yore husband. What ya *think* 'bout me 'mounts to no more'n a chicken fart in a snow storm. What ya *say* about Jane could get yore ass up 'tween yore ears."

Patrice looked stunned. Her mouth opened to take in a gulp of air. Bessie and Paralee stepped back toward the door.

"What are . . . you standing there for" Patrice's angry eyes fastened on T.C. "Are you going to stand for this?"

T.C. shrugged. "If you're so outraged and you want something done, do it. Hit her back. But let me warn you: should you decide to do so, I'll not interfere, and she'll be all over you like a swarm of angry hornets." T.C. was unable to keep the grin off his face.

"It's just what I'd expect from you. I told Colin you'd revert to where you came from."

"And where was that?" T.C.'s voice had lost is amusement and was deathly quiet.

Realizing she was on dangerous ground, Patrice backed toward the door.

"Tell Colin I've had news from Ramon and need to see him immediately."

One of the three women slammed the door when they left.

"I'm tempted to hug you," T.C. said to Sunday and laughed.

"She's a bitch!"

"Always has been. But forget her. With luck she'll be gone soon." He turned to Jane. "I'm going to take five or six men and ride out to meet the stage. Herb will be here, and I'll tell Tennihill to keep his eye on the house. Stay in until I get back."

"Go on and do what you have to do. Don't worry. Sunday and I can handle most things." Jane looked at her friend and burst out laughing. "Sunday can, for sure. I don't know who was more surprised, Mrs. Cabeza or me."

An hour before the stage was due the four women and Stella put on shawls and went out to the porch to wait for the big event. Herb lounged against the wall of the cook-house across the street where he had a clear view of the house. Polly, wearing a new warm shawl and a blue ribbon in her hair, left the porch to stand beside him.

The narrow street was cleared of wagons. Horses were moved to hitching posts between and behind the buildings and horse dung was shoveled into wheelbarrows and taken away. People sat on porches or walked along the board-walk fronting the buildings.

When the signal shots were fired by the outriders, people scrambled off the street, and all eyes turned to the south end of town. It seemed forever until, after a second volley of shots sounded, they heard the steady sound of steel-rimmed wheels and iron-shod hooves. Minutes later the wildly racing team came into view and the booming voice of the driver reached them.

"H'yaw! H'yaw! Move, ya worthless, dang-busted, mangy buzzard bait! Hightail it on in thar, ya lazy sons-abitches! H'yaw! Get to foggin' it, ya draggletails!"

The whip sailed out over the backs of the steaming team. Insults continued to spew from the mouth of the driver in the box of the swaying coach as he whipped the horses into a full gallop and they raced toward the narrow street of the town. Two of the escorts rode in front of the stage. The two on the sides fell back as they entered the street.

The driver continued to express his displeasure with the team as it sped into town by issuing a stream of obscenities, even while he tramped on the brake as he neared the hotel. The coach rocked as the split reins curbed the horses to bring them to a standstill in front of the new stage station.

"Tim . . . ber . . . town!" the driver shouted.

A cheer went up.

The burly man swung easily down from his box, opened the door and waited to help two women and two small children take the long step to the ground. Two men followed them down. One stood looking around, slightly dazed. The other, a fashionably dressed portly man, reached up to get his satchel from the top of the coach and walked toward the hotel.

T.C. left his horse with one of the riders and, removing his hat, greeted the newcomers.

"Welcome to Timbertown. I'm T.C. Kilkenny."

The two women offered their hands.

"We're from Trinity. Mr. Rowe sent us."

"To run the eatery. It's ready for you. If the two of you can use the rooms in the back as your quarters for a day or two, we'll see about other arrangements if you wish." T.C. looked around in the crowd for Jeb, and, spotting him, called out, "Jeb, take the ladies down to the cookhouse."

From the top of the coach the driver handed down trunks and boxes.

"Welcome to Timbertown."

T.C. held out his hand to the passenger who waited beside the coach.

"Thank you, sir. Dr. Walter Bate."

"We've been expecting you."

"I didn't realize I would be making the first run. It was rather a wild ride."

"He made quite an entrance, didn't he?"

Dr. Bate's well-groomed beard was generously sprinkled with gray, as was the dark hair at his temples. He was thin and narrowly built. Garrick Rowe had written that he was a well-respected doctor in Chicago, but because of a tragedy in his family, he wished to move to a new location. He would purchase Doc Foote's equipment to furnish a new office.

"Your rooms above the store are ready, but they will be cold tonight, so I suggest you take a room at the hotel. Come to the dance tonight and meet the townsfolk."

"I'm not much for dancing."

"Tell you the truth, I'm not either. But what's a celebration without a dance?"

Timbertown would be a layover stop for the stage. The steaming team and the coach were led away, and willing hands brought out shovels to clean up fresh manure piles and rakes to smooth the earth where the dance was to be held.

It was almost dark and time for the dance when T.C. hurried down the street to his house. He had been to the saloon and had talked with Parker. Because quite a few rowdies were in town, Parker had hired Murphy and another man to help keep order. Tennihill was around, and T.C. was convinced that the man's sharp eyes missed nothing.

Supper was served earlier than usual. When it was over, all changed into their best clothes and made ready to go out onto the street. Jane walked between T.C. and Sunday. Maude and Stella walked behind them, followed by Polly and Herb.

Jane had never been more proud in all her life. She strolled beside her husband, her hand tucked firmly in the crook of his arm. Men tipped their hats; women smiled. Buddy Winters ran ahead of them, then turned and walked backward to show her the small flag in his hand.

"Is your mother coming to the dance?" Jane asked.

"She ain't. She's got to cook and get us some money. Mr. Jenson's got fireworks." He darted away.

Jane was almost as excited as Buddy. She felt gloriously alive and happy. It was a strange and wonderful feeling to know that she belonged to this tall man beside her and that he knew all there was to know about her and still loved her. Nothing could put a blight on her happiness, not even that unknown person who could be watching her, hating her.

Along the street, two large bonfires burned brightly, radiating both heat and light. A dozen or more lanterns hung on porches and on ropes stretched around the dance area.

As soon as Mr. Jenson thought it dark enough for full appreciation of the firework display, he came out of the store and set the rockets up in the middle of the street. When the first one went up with a loud ZZZBOOM, the crowd cheered. Bright sparks of light showered down from high in the sky. The second rocket went off even higher than the first one.

T.C. left Jane and Sunday standing beside the hotel porch and went inside. He returned a minute later with a fiddle and bow and handed them to Sunday.

"Play for us."

Sunday smiled. "I've never seen a fiddle this grand." She plucked the strings, then tucked the instrument under her chin and made a few strokes with the bow.

"Hold it, Jane, while I take off my coat."

Jane doubted that there was a bashful bone in Sunday's body. Totally at ease and delighted to be playing a fine violin, Sunday stepped out into the street and began to play "Beautiful Dreamer." The music had an unearthly quality like the wind. It settled into every crevice along the street, and folks stopped to listen. It was a song of love and pain, sorrow and joy. Some folks had never heard such music.

Standing alone in the street, Sunday played as if she were lost in the music. After the first tune she went into another, "Jeannie with the Light Brown Hair." Her mop of blond curls shone in the lamplight. She swayed as she stroked the strings with the long bow. There was a moment of utter stillness when the music came to an end. Then, sensing the crowd needed something livelier, she began to play "Camptown Races."

Murphy stepped out and began to sing in a surprisingly good voice. At one point he stopped singing and began to jig, much to the enjoyment of the audience, who clapped and yelled, spurring him on.

Sunday played another song, then stopped and looked around for the owner of the fiddle. Theda Cruise came forward.

"You play a heck of a lot better than I do."

"It's a grand fiddle."

Theda laughed. "My father would turn over in his grave if he heard his treasure called a fiddle."

"I meant no . . ."

"I know. Papa was a concert violinist. He insisted that I learn to play. Much to his dismay, I found that I'd rather play hoedown than classical. He died before I became a saloon keeper. Dear Papa didn't understand me at all."

"Thank you for lettin' me have a go at it. Guess I'd a been scared to touch it if I'd a known it was so fine."

"You've got a natural touch if I ever saw one, and I've seen plenty." Theda turned to survey the crowd. "Ready to dance?" she called to the couples waiting.

"Yeah, Theda. Let 'er go."

Theda played a slow tune and one brave couple started it off. Soon others joined them. A young man smelling as if he had just come from the barber shop asked Sunday to dance. She started to shake her head.

"Go ahead, Sunday," T.C. said. "I'll be here with Jane."

Standing close beside her husband, Jane watched her friend and wished with all her heart that she could be as free and uninhibited as Sunday. T.C.'s hand covered Jane's and she looked up.

"Someday we'll get Sunday to play the fiddle, and I'll teach you to dance."

Her eyes shone. "I never, ever dreamed I'd learn to dance."

He bent down again to whisper. "If that fellow comes up against the pistol in Sunday's dress pocket, it might go off and shoot him in the foot."

"I forgot about that."

As T.C. watched Jane's face in the flickering light, a smile softened the line of his mouth. Behind the smile he gave her, his mind raced. Fragile though she might appear, she had deep inner resources and strength, which constant use had intensified of late, allowing her to face the future as his wife without fear.

Jane. Little Jane, there's so much of the world I'd like to show you.

Sunday came back.

"He was a nice boy but still wet behind the ears."

"Have you seen Maude and Stella?"

"When I first started dancin', I saw them headin' back to the house. They was almost runnin'. Stella might a had to go to the privy."

"We'll watch for them to come back."

"I'm going to make the rounds and see how things are going. There are some rowdies in town. Will you two be all right?"

"Go on with ya," Sunday said. "I won't let 'er outta my sight." She patted her pocket.

Sunday and Jane stood together on the porch of the hotel and commented to each other on the dancers. Paralee danced with a logger who had a black beard and slicked-down-hair. He wore an obviously new checked shirt. He towered over her, handling her as if he expected her to break apart. She was bored. Her eyes searched the crowd for someone either more prosperous or more handsome.

In a dress much too tight for her, Bessie danced with Milo Callahan. He was holding her tightly so that her breasts rubbed against him. As they whirled around, Bessie saw Sunday and Jane watching her. She moved her hand up Milo's arm to his shoulder. Her fingers stroked his neck and she snuggled closer to him.

"She's goin' to get what she's askin' for if she ain't careful," Sunday remarked. "Let's walk a bit. It's cold just standin'."

They walked into the hotel lobby and looked around. So much had been accomplished in such a short time. They lingered a while, then strolled down the walk to the stage station. The stage driver was tacking a schedule to the wall. They stopped to read it.

"Day after tomorrow stage will come back through going south. I can remember when that would have been welcome news. But not anymore," Jane murmured.

"Yo're really happy, ain't ya?"

"Oh, yes. I hope things work out for you and—"

"Don't say it!"

"I won't! Let's walk down and look into Mrs. Winters' bake shop. I've not seen it."

They were strolling arm in arm along the walk in front of the buildings when they heard a woman's scream.

"What in the world? Somebody needs help!" Jane said.

Another shrill scream, then another and another, reached them, closely followed by several masculine shouts.

Jane and Sunday hurried down the walk to the space between the two buildings. They paused to peer down the narrow passage.

"Jane? What'er you doin' here?" The hoarse masculine

whisper came from the tall shadowy figure hurrying along the side of the building.

"What happened?"

The man reached them, and no sooner had both Sunday and Jane realized it wasn't T.C., than a fist landed on the side of Sunday's head and she dropped like a stone. Jane, shocked into immobility, had no time to open her mouth to yell when her head exploded, and she fell into a black pit.

Tennihill squatted on his heels, his back to the bonfire. The little twit dancing with Callahan was playing with fire. He had stood in the shadows and watched them on the porch of the rooming house a few nights earlier as he waited to see in which direction Milo headed out. She had let him feel under her skirt but that was all. It wasn't something a man like Callahan would be satisfied with for very long.

The lanky Tennesseean had been a little uneasy about his decision *not* to find Milo Callahan. He justified it by telling himself that he was not *positive* it was the same man he had been sent to hunt down and return to Coeur d' Alene. The bastard had hired camp scum to kill a young deaf girl to get back at her pa for giving him a beating after he'd beaten his own stepsister, Dory Callahan.

It seemed a damn shame, Tennihill thought, to take Milo back so he could collect a small inheritance that would be split between a stepbrother and sister, who were fine folk, if he wasn't found. Yet, he understood that the man who had hired him had been honor-bound to make an effort to find the other heir.

He stood, folded his pocketknife and put it in his pocket. Callahan and the girl were walking toward the area between the hotel and the new barber shop. Tennihill ambled along behind, watching them as they disappeared between the buildings.

The stupid little twit!

By the time Tennihill reached the back of the hotel,

Callahan and the girl were not in sight. He stayed close to the building, all his senses alert for sound. Several minutes passed before he heard what he thought was a whimper, then loud hurried whispers.

"I ain't goin' to let ya. Stop that!"

"Ya said ya would. Now be quiet. Ya want the whole town back here?" Callahan was impatient and angry. "I got a thin' to do in a little bit. Let me do it, and I'll let ya help me."

"What'er ya goin' to do?"

"I'm goin' back to the dance and raise a ruckus. I'm goin' to shoot out a couple of them lanterns and throw a couple shells in the bonfire. That'll stir 'em up."

"What 'er ya doin' it for?"

"I ain't tellin' ya that and I ain't waitin'. Here, feel it!"

"Let go my hand! I ain't touchin' it. Get yore hands off—"

"Damn ya for a teasing bitch! Ya said we'd do it all, and we're goin' to."

"Stop! I don't want ya to do that!"

"I ain't givin' a shit if ya want it or not, yo're gettin' it."

"Stop! Stop! Oh . . . " A minute later she screamed.

Tennihill launched himself away from the wall. Bessie screamed again. He saw the sheen on her white dress, and long, quick strides took him to where Callahan had her pinned to the ground. Her dress was up about her waist and he was rippin' off her drawers.

"Gawdamn ya. Ya've been rubbin' up against me, teasin' me with them tits—"

"Get off her, ya ruttin' hog."

Tennihill grabbed a handful of Milo's hair and jerked him off the sobbing girl and to his feet. Still holding him by the hair, he placed the tip of his knife beneath Milo's jaw.

"What . . . er . . . she was wantin' it."

"Not right now she warn't."

Several men, responding to the screams, had come into the area.

"What's goin' on?"

"Nothin' . . . yet. He was goin' to rape her"

"Rape her? Christamighty!"

"It ain't all his fault. She's been switchin' her tail at him for a while." The man who spoke was clearly disgusted with Bessie. "She's been actin' like a bitch in heat since she got here."

"Maybe," Tennihill said. "But she ain't much more'n a kid, and rape's a hard lesson."

"Tennihill?" T.C. was helping Bessie get to her feet. "Is this what I think it is?"

"Yeah. Better get 'er outta here."

"Callahan's yours then. You want to hang him?"

"Hang? Oh . . . my Gawd—"

"I'm studyin' on it." Tennihill turned Milo around so the men could get a good look at him. "Take a look, fellers. We can hang him, or run him outta the country."

"We ain't had no necktie party for a while." The man who spoke was the big logger who had danced with Paralee. "Might be kinda fun. Put some icin' on the celebration."

"Fun?" Milo choked.

"I ain't got no rope handy," Tennihill said. "Side a that, we'd have to bury 'im. Couldn't have 'im stinkin' up the town. Let's run 'im off like a mangy dog. Spread the word in towns, cuttin' camps, mills, and stations that Milo Callahan rapes women. And that he's a liar, a cheat and ain't fit fer dog meat."

"She . . . she . . . " When Milo tried to talk, the tip of the knife pierced the skin beneath his jaw.

"I'll fork him on his horse, T.C. I'm thinkin' Alaska would be a good place fer him . . . or Mexico."

"How about hell, Tennihill?" an angry man shouted.

"I thought of it. But I'm thinkin' not even the devil wants a peckerwood like him."

"Come on, Bessie. You've caused enough trouble for one

night." T.C. gripped her upper arm tightly and propelled her toward the street.

"I can't go with my dress tore," Bessie wailed and tried to dig in her heels.

"You can ask your friend Patrice Guzman Cabeza to give you another one."

Pushing the crying, disheveled girl ahead of him, T.C. marched her out onto the walk and down the street. People stopped to stare. He held onto her until he got her into the lobby of the hotel.

"I hate ya! Ya wanted ever'body to see me."

"You're damn lucky you're alive."

"I didn't do nothin'. It was *his* fault!"

"When the stage leaves day after tomorrow, be ready. You're to be on it."

Out on the porch T.C. paused to let his temper cool. The fool girl didn't have the brains of a flea. He looked up and down the street for Jane and Sunday, but they were nowhere in sight. He began to feel uneasy. She had said that she would stay by the hotel.

He saw Herb and Polly and had just started toward them when he heard the sound of gunfire. Two shots had been fired from a small-caliber pistol.

He froze in his tracks. *Sunday carried a small-caliber pistol in her pocket.*

He began to run toward the sound, dread making his feet feel like lead.

Chapter 25

SUNDAY saw the blow coming an instant before it landed and rolled her head to the side. Years of scuffling with siblings and cousins had honed her instincts for fighting or she would have been knocked out cold. Still, her eyes crossed and she saw a shower of stars as she hit the ground, but she did not completely lose consciousness.

Shaking her head to clear it, she sat up. Her hand went to the side of her head. Then memory came rushing back. Bob Fresno had hit her.

Jane! Where was Jane?

She scrambled to her feet too fast and fell back down on her knees. On her feet again, she staggered along the side of the building until she reached the back of the cookshack. She saw the shadowy form of a man with something slung over his shoulder moving along the cow fence attached to the barn.

The buzzard had taken Jane.

Keeping her eyes on him, she reached into the pocket of her skirt for the pistol, brought it out, cocked it and hurried after him. Silently she called him every derogatory thing she could think of, knowing that if she called out he would turn and shoot her. She couldn't use the gun with Jane slung over his shoulder, so she ignored her pounding head, gritted her teeth and followed him toward the line of trees behind what used to be called the henhouse.

Bob Fresno congratulated himself. It had been easier than he had imagined it would be. He had been watching Jane since she walked uptown with Kilkenny. He had watched her standing close to the son of a bitch while the blond played the fiddle. His fingers had itched to put a bullet right between Kilkenny's eyes.

Fresno had followed as Jane and the other woman strolled down the boardwalk. They had stopped at the new stage office and then had stood for a while watching the crowd. Finally they had continued down the walk past the tonsorial parlor toward the bake shop. He had hurried to get ahead of them and, with his hat pulled low, had crossed the street and concealed himself in the dark area between the two buildings they would pass.

The screaming woman, whoever she was, had served to draw Jane to the dark passageway between the buildings, and he had seen his chance to get her. This way was even better than waiting for Callahan to cause a ruckus.

His hand caressed Jane's rounded bottom as he hurried along the pole fence attached to the barn. She was his now. He was confident in his ability to woo her. He would teach her the delights of the flesh, and in a week or two she would not give Kilkenny another thought.

His horse was behind the privy. He would have Jane on it and be gone before Kilkenny knew she was missing. And when Kilkenny found out he'd not be able to track them in the dark. Callahan didn't know where the cabin was and couldn't lead him there. By daylight he and Jane would be at the trapper's cabin, well fortified should Kilkenny arrive.

Reaching his horse, Bob carefully laid the unconscious woman face down in front of the saddle. The animal shied a little, not understanding the unaccustomed weight on its neck. Bob spoke a few words to it until it calmed, then went to the tree limb to untie the reins.

When he turned to mount, a woman stepped out not three feet from behind the horse's rump. Surprise froze him in his tracks for a minute or two. He had not heard a sound. Her arms were extended out in front of her and she gripped the pistol with both hands.

"How'd you get here?"

"Ya ain't as smart as ya think ya are. Get away from her!"

"Or what?" he sneered. "You gonna shoot me with that pea shooter?"

"I'm gonna give it a damn good try."

"She . . . it! You couldn't hit the side of a barn with that thin'."

"Try me, you . . . horsecock!"

Fresno dropped the reins and reached for his gun all in the same motion. His gun had cleared the holster when Sunday's first bullet struck him just left of his coat button. Her second bullet struck where she thought his belly-button would be. He looked at her as if he couldn't believe what had happened. His gun hand dropped. He stumbled as if trying to get his balance.

"Ya . . . shot me—"

"Tol' ya I would, and I'm fixin' to do it again."

Bob sat down hard on the ground, then fell back. The horse shied a few steps and then stood still. Sunday advanced, holding her gun in front of her, and pointed down at him. She was afraid to take her eyes off him to see about Jane. She half-expected him to jump up, and she had to be ready to shoot again. She had been taught that if she had to shoot, shoot to kill, and that she'd done; but she wasn't sure yet if he was dead.

It seemed to Sunday she had stood there an hour waiting for him to move when she heard T.C. shouting first Jane's name and then hers.

"Here, T.C." she shouted, her eyes still on the man on the ground. "Hurry. See about Jane. She's on the horse. I got this sorry polecat covered. If he makes a move, I'll shoot his blasted head off."

T.C. ran up, looked down at Fresno, jerked the gun from his hand and tossed it aside, then went to where Jane lay across the horse's neck.

"What did he do to her?" He lifted his wife off the horse and gently lowered her to the ground. Kneeling beside her, he cradled her in his arms. "I'll kill the sonofabitch!"

"I think Sunday already did." Herb was not quite as fast as T.C. He pressed down on Sunday's hands until the gun she gripped was pointed to the ground. "Ya can put the gun down."

"Ya sure he's dead?" Sunday asked.

"I'm sure. He's not gettin' up. Turn loose the gun," Herb said patiently.

"I . . . he might get up—" Sunday's hands seemed to be frozen on the gun.

Herb took it from her, uncocked it and stuck it in his belt before he knelt down beside Fresno. The eyes were open and staring. There was a neat hole in his coat over his heart.

"He's dead. That little sucker works good at close range."

Sunday seemed to come out of her shock and went to where T.C. was holding Jane.

"Is she all right?"

"She hasn't come around yet. You?"

"He hit me on the side of the head. Knocked me cold for a minute or two. I'm just sorry as I can be for letting him get to her."

"You did well, Sunday. Herb, you sure he's dead?"

"Deader'n a doornail."

"That's Bob Fresno!" A man in the crowd that gathered around them swore.

"Godamighty! What'd she kill him for?"

"'Cause he was tryin' to carry Jane off, ya . . . dumbass!" Sunday turned and shouted. Her head hurt, her knees were scratched and bloody, and if not for the hairy faces looking at her she would have lain down and bawled.

"Sounds fishy to me! Why'd he want do that? Fresno was a good sort."

Herb's big hand settled on the back of the man's neck and propelled him to where T.C. knelt holding Jane.

"Take ya a good look at where he hit Miss Jane. Then open yore mouth again 'bout him bein' a *good sort* and ya'll be swallerin' teeth."

"I didn't mean . . . well . . . he *seemed* to be all right."

When Tennihill got there, he looked down at Fresno, then at the group of men gathered around.

"Make no mistake 'bout it. Fresno was a flimflammer and a killer. He's suspected of doin' away with more'n a few. He could charm a flea off a dog if he set his mind to it."

"I didn't know him or nothin'. I mean he was all right when he was here."

"That's why it was hard to pin him down. The women he bamboozled, for the most part, went with him 'cause they wanted to". Tennihill shook his head in amazement. "And when he was done with 'em he got rid of 'em one way or t'other."

"You a lawman, ain't ya?" someone asked.

"Why'd ya think that?" Tennihill asked in reply. "If I was, I'd a got him." He let out a dry chuckle. "He was laid out by a slip of a gal with a little old pop gun. Miss Sunday, yo're due a reward. A wanted poster came in on the stage for one Robert E. Lee Fresno, better known as Bob. Ya'll be collectin' ya a bounty."

"Hurrah for Miss Sunday!" Fielding, a logger from the north camp whose family lived in town, shouted, and the group of men took it up.

"I'd a shot him in the back and he'd not a got this far, but he had Jane over his shoulder."

Jane stirred and tried to push away from the arms holding her.

"You're all right, honey," T.C. murmured. "You're safe. Just lie still for a minute."

"T.C.? What—?" She groaned. "My head!"

"That head of yours has taken a beating lately."

"Why am I on the ground?"

"Bob Fresno was trying to carry you off. He hit you, knocked you out."

"I remember now. I saw him just before—Sunday! Where's Sunday?"

"I'm here, Jane. I'm all right."

"Where is . . . he?"

"Sunday shot him."

"Is he . . . dead?"

"Yes, honey. He's dead."

"Thank goodness Sunday wasn't hurt."

T.C. stood and lifted Jane to stand beside him. He put his arms around her for support, and she leaned against him.

Herb had gone through Fresno's pockets and put what he found in his hat. He had a roll of money, a pocketknife, chewing tobacco and a fancy cameo pin wrapped in a cloth. Herb took the saddlebags, rolled blankets and a food pack from the horse. All Fresno's belongings lay in a pile beside his body.

"He was ready to trail somewhere. What'll we do with this pile of bones, T.C.?"

"Roll him in his saddle blanket and leave him in the barn till morning. Fielding, will you give Herb a hand?"

"Shore will. Ya go and take care of the womenfolk. Miss Sunday, I'd sign on to ride the river with ya anyday. Air ya spoke fer, honey?"

"Fielding, you old flirt. I've a mind to tell yore wife what ya said," Sunday retorted sassily.

"Ya do and she'll clean my clock."

"It would serve ya right if she made you sleep on the floor for a week!" Sunday's voice was shrill and forced.

T.C.'s arms were still about Jane. He turned and looked at Sunday.

"Are you all right, Sunday?"

"'Course she ain't." Tennihill took Sunday's arm. "I'd be plumb proud to walk 'er to the house. She's got enough grit for a dozen gals her size, but she's used up a heap of it."

"I don't need no help."

"I aim to give it anyhow. If I was twenty years younger, no, make it ten—Hell, if I was five years younger I'd be after ya, gal, like ya was a swaller of fresh spring water when I ain't had no drink in a week."

"Well, now, ain't I got somethin' to crow about? I got two fellers wantin' to court—" Sunday's voice trailed away and she never finished what she was saying. She slumped in Tennihill's arms in a dead faint.

On arriving at the house, Maude and Stella had gone quickly to their room.

"What'll we do, Mamma?"

"Maybe he didn't see us."

"He did," Stella insisted. "He looked right at me. I moved behind Polly and peeked around. He was staring at you."

"There was so many people there, how did you happen to pick him out of the crowd?"

"I don't know. I just saw him there on the hotel porch. I hate him! I wish he'd die!"

"Oh, honey. I was so hoping he'd not find us. But he has, so he must know the name we're using."

"Will he come here?"

"Not tonight. He'll come in the morning as the successful man all broken up because his family left him after a very minor misunderstanding. Butter wouldn't melt in his mouth. He's practiced it for years. He could talk his way out of a jug with a cork in it."

Maude heaved a big sigh and sat down on the bed. Stella snuggled against her and began to cry.

"I don't want to go back there. I want to stay here."

"So do I."

"You won't let him take me?" Stella asked in alarm.

"We'll stay together. If you go, I'll go."

"What . . . if he don't let you come?"

"I promised, baby, that I'd stay with you and I will. Now don't worry."

Maude hugged the child who meant more to her than anything in the world. If she had to kill Eldon Cottington to keep Stella out of his hands, she would. It would mean she would forfeit her own life, but Stella would be safe.

Jane would take her to raise, or perhaps Polly and Herb. There was no family member to come forward to claim her.

Thinking about it now, Maude realized that she should have killed the man long ago.

Stella cried herself to sleep. Maude put her in the bed and covered her, then sat in the darkened room and tried to plan. There was no use running. She should have known that he had the ways and the means to find them. It had been a desperate on-the-spot decision that had caused her to sign on to work here. The last beating, when she thought he would kill her and Stella would be left alone with him, had given her the courage to steal the child out of the house and get on the train.

She had gambled and she had lost.

T.C. lay awake holding his wife in his arms. After bringing her and Sunday back to the house, Herb had gone to fetch Polly, then had stayed with the women while T.C. and Tennihill had patrolled the town, keeping an eye on the rowdies until about midnight when the fiddlers stopped playing, the lanterns were taken down and dirt was thrown on the bonfires. By then, the families had all gone home and only a few die-hards remained.

What more could happen to this sweet woman?

He was proud of the way she had accepted his assurance that her parentage was not important to him. She had given him her complete trust. She was not a woman who tried to hide her feelings and was surprisingly open about them for someone who had not had much love in her life. She hadn't wavered in her determination not to allow the threat from this unknown person to interfere with their future together.

Tennihill didn't think it possible that Fresno was the one who had sent the threatening notes and had attacked Jane out at the privy. Fresno had not had many women reject him as Jane had done, and Tennihill seemed to think

Fresno had wanted to prove to himself that he still was the lady's man he considered himself to be.

On the other hand, T.C. thought it possible the man had fallen desperately in love with Jane. He himself, certainly had.

By the time T.C. and Tennihill had walked back uptown, everyone had been buzzing with the news that Sunday had shot Bob Fresno. Not wanting any more gossip about Jane than necessary, T.C. had let it be known that the man was disgruntled about not getting the job he wanted and was trying to get back at T.C. by attacking his wife. Folks had seemed to accept the story.

Jane's soft thigh worked its way between his muscular ones. She snuggled closer and slept like a contented kitten.

T.C.'s arms tightened about his wife, and a low groan came from his throat when he considered what could have happened if not for Sunday and the pistol in her pocket. He had wanted to have the new doctor come and take a look at both Jane and Sunday, but neither one would allow it.

In the morning he would insist.

Morning came, bringing the first light snowfall and also trouble from an unexpected source.

T.C. awoke at dawn and looked down at his sleeping wife. He tried to ease out of bed, but she awoke as soon as his arms were no longer around her.

"You gettin' up now?"

"Yes, sweetheart, but you stay right here. I'll bring you some coffee in a little bit."

"I love you," she said sleepily.

"I love you, too." He kissed her on the nose.

He dressed and went to the kitchen, where Maude was preparing breakfast.

"Morning." He had washed his hands, splashed water on his face and dried himself with the towel before he realized he had received a mere grunt in reply to his greeting. "Polly said you and Stella came home early last night. Is Stella all right?"

"She was tired. Do you want eggs, Mr. Kilkenny? I'm cooking smoked meat and making gravy."

"No eggs for me, thanks. Jane and Sunday will sleep a little later after what happened last night."

"What happened?" She turned quickly, alarm on her face.

"That's right. You don't know. You were in bed when we came home last night. We had a hell of a night, Maude."

"What happened?" she asked again.

"Sunday killed Bob Fresno."

"Killed Bob Fresno! Forevermore! That girl's a rare one. She'd tackle the devil himself."

"If not for her, Fresno would have stolen Jane and been gone. I wouldn't have had a clue where to find her."

"I'm glad Sunday's been staying here nights. She's been mighty unhappy over what Mrs. Cabeza has been tellin' around about Mr. Tallman."

"That'll work itself out in time."

While Maude stirred the gravy, T.C. gave her details on the events of the night before.

"I thought there was something bad about that Fresno the day he came here."

"I didn't know he came here. When was that?"

"Before Doc died. Polly let him in 'cause he said he was sick. He followed Jane into the surgery and shut the door. I heard her telling him to open it. I was about to go up and get Herb when he came down. It was when Doc took the bad turn. Herb pounded on the door for Jane. Fresno let her out, but he was madder than a ruptured goose when he went out the front door."

"I never knew that was Fresno."

"Jane wasn't wantin' to worry anybody. Doc died right after that."

Maude was glad for the chance to visit. For a few minutes it kept her mind off what lay ahead. Sometime during the night she had wondered if she should tell T.C. about Judge Eldon Cottington, but had decided against it. The judge would come here, smooth as silk, and make her out a liar, a fallen woman he had tried to set on the straight and narrow path, a woman he had hired to work in his home and who had kidnapped his daughter!

There was one way and only one that Stella would ever be free of him.

Chapter 26

IT was mid-morning when the knock sounded on the door. Herb, walking down the hall from the kitchen where he and Polly had been talking with the others about the previous night's events, went to open it with a smile on his boyish face.

The man who stood there looked to Herb as if he had just stepped out of a mail-order catalog. He was big, robust, and wore a long, dark wool overcoat and a fashionable square-crowned hat. He carried a pair of fine kid gloves, and a large gold ring gleamed on the middle finger of his left hand. Snow had not dared to stick to his shiny black shoes.

"Good morning," he said pleasantly. "I'd like to see Mr. Kilkenny, please."

"Why shore. Come on in outta the snow. T.C.'s there in the office." Herb opened the door wide and stepped aside for him to enter.

The man removed his hat when he entered and smoothed his hair with the palm of his hand. A heavy mustache, fanned out and curled at the ends, gave him a look of solid respectability.

Herb pushed the office door open and yelled, "Somebody to see ya."

T.C. rose from his chair as the man entered. He recognized him immediately as the man who had come in on the stage and had gone directly into the hotel.

"I'm Kikenny."

"Judge Eldon Cottington, sir. I'm pleased to make your acquaintance. You've done a magnificent job here reviving this town."

"Thank you. Take off your coat and have a chair."

While this was being done, T.C. sat back down. *Cottington*. The name sing-songed through his mind.

Where had he heard it before?

Judge Cottington seated himself, then reached into the inside pocket of his coat and brought out two cigars.

"Would you care for one? I get them special from Cuba."

"No thanks. But here's a match for yours."

T.C. moved a match box across the desk toward him and waited for him to light the cigar. Something about the man's bearing and attitude, smooth as it was, put T.C. on the alert.

"What can I do for you?"

"Nothing, really. I came merely as a courtesy to tell you I'm taking my wife and child back to Laramie."

"I can't imagine that being important to me."

"She signed on to work for you. I've talked to one of your solicitors, J.E. Askland, in Laramie. He informed me that you have been put to some expense. You paid her fare to come here and for several days in a hotel. I'll reimburse you for those expenses."

T.C. didn't say anything for a long moment. He leaned back in the chair and studied the man. He was in his late forties. His hair was thin on top. He had sagging pouches under eyes that were as cold as sharpened steel. *Cottington.* Where had he heard that name?

"Who is your wife?" T.C. asked. He was sure that he knew yet could not believe that Maude would be married to this man.

"She's calling herself Mrs. Henderson. She has my daughter, Stella, with her."

The door that had been left ajar was pushed open. Maude stood there. Behind her were Herb, Jane, and Sunday. She had somehow found the courage to tell them who was in the office with Mr. Kilkenny and why.

"I am not your wife, not your *legal* wife that is."

"Come in and shut the door, my dear. You needn't make a spectacle of yourself. Where is Stella?"

"These folks are my friends, the only friends I've had for

ten long years. Stella is with another one of my good friends. She doesn't want to see you. She tried to hide when she heard you come in."

"We need to talk privately."

"No. I want my friends here as my witnesses."

"Witnesses to what, my dear? This is no court of law. I've come to take you and Stella home."

"Home? You call that house a home? It was a prison, a torture chamber. I'm not going back. I'll never go back and neither will Stella."

"Now, now, Maude. Don't excite yourself. You know what happens when you do. You're unable to think clearly and you make rash decisions."

The judge got up from the chair, pulled himself up to his full height and walked toward her with his hand outstretched. He stopped suddenly when Maude pulled a long, thin cutting knife from her pocket.

"Stay back or I'll cut you. I swear I will."

A look of complete surprise came over the judge's face.

"What has happened to you? Threatening me with a knife could get you into a lot of trouble. I couldn't have a woman raising my daughter who had been convicted of threatening a judge."

"She's *not* your daughter. I'm *not* your wife, although for years I endured your rutting in order to stay with Stella."

Maude had squared her shoulders and had not taken her eyes off the judge. Jane and Sunday, standing quietly on either side of her, were all the support she needed.

"That's enough!" Cottington said sternly. "I'll not have your insolence, and I'll not have you airing our family differences in public."

"We're not a family," Maude shouted back. "I was a whore working for a roof over my head and taking care of your brother's child so that you could spend the money he left her. This"—she waved her hand to include the others in the room—"is a family. And they have accepted me and Stella as a part of it."

"I'm warning you, Maude. You're about to push me too far, and you will suffer the consequences."

"What more can you do to me than you've already done, Judge Cottington? You've broken my nose, split my lip, knocked out my jaw teeth, and broken my arm. You've stomped me, screwed me, spit on me and humiliated me. You've—"

"Shut your lying mouth," he shouted. His control had snapped. His face was fiery red; his hands shook.

For the first time in ten years Maude was not one bit frightened by the outburst. The friends behind her, Sunday's hand on her back, gave her courage to look into the eyes of the man she had feared for so long.

"You'll not break Stella's spirit. She's got her father's guts and will stand up to you. You hated him because he'd not knuckle under to you. Stella is just a child, and you've cowed her by telling her that she's ugly and stupid and that her mother was a whore. You've slapped her face, beaten her little behind till it bled and made her go a full day without a bite to eat."

"Stop! Or, by God, you'll wish you had."

The judge was so angry that he forgot about the knife, and with a hand raised to slap her, he took two angry steps toward her. Before the judge knew what was happening, the barrel of Herb's gun was under his chin, tilting his head so that he had to look down his nose to see Herb's face.

"Touch her an' I'll blow yore head clear back to Laramie while the rest a ya stays here."

"Get . . . get away from me, you ruffian. Don't you know who I am?"

"'Pears to me ya ain't nothin' but a duded-up mule's ass. A man can't get much sorrier than one that'd hurt a little thin' like Stella. 'Sides, I ain't carin' if yo're Abe Lincoln come back to life. Ya ain't takin' Maude and Stella back if they don't want to go."

Herb backed the judge across the room until he was up against the wall. Jane and Sunday stared. They'd never seen the mild-mannered Herb so angry.

"I'll have a federal marshal here in a week."

Jane put her arm around Maude and whispered to her. "Don't worry. You're doing fine. T.C. and Herb will take care of him."

"Herb, let him sit down," T.C. said evenly. He had stood up quickly when the judge had started for Maude but had sat back down when he saw that Herb was handling the situation. "I've just remembered where I heard the name Judge Cottington."

Herb reluctantly removed the gun after giving the judge's chin another sharp jab with the end of the barrel.

"I certainly never expected to be assaulted here in your office, Kilkenny. I was under the impression that you were more civilized than that."

"Don't count on *me* being civilized, Judge. Some of my relatives are putting up their lodges right now out in the Bitterroot. It's rugged country. A man could disappear out there and never be heard from again." T.C.'s silver eyes looked pointedly at the judge, and the man's cheeks began to quiver under the intense stare.

"You . . . wouldn't—The stage driver knows who I am; he brought me here."

"You of all people should know what a little money can do. He'd swear he never set eyes on you. He likes driving the stage. The hotel man is indebted to the company. He won't say anything either if I tell him not to."

"That's called bribery!"

"It is. But none of that will be necessary because Maude is not your legal wife. Stella is not your daughter. And on top of that, you may very well be in the territorial prison over there in Laramie this time next month. They'll be better off here where we can look after them."

"Don't try and tell *me* about the law! No judge in the world would think twice about a man making his child mind, or slapping his ah . . . woman around a bit."

"I went to law school. I know how the law works. Damn shame isn't it? You can be jailed for beating your horse but not your wife and children." T.C. picked an ink pen up off the desk and studied it. "Do you know Dr. Nathan Foote?"

"Can't say that I do," the judge said belligerently.

"He knows you. I was talking to him yesterday or maybe it was the day before." T.C. sent a warning glance to the group standing inside the doorway. "He was telling me about a Judge Cottington who brought his sister-in-law to his office for treatment. The woman was sick with stomach trouble. Doc gave her some medicine and went to see her a few days later because it was in the back of his mind that the woman had been poisoned. She was in a deep sleep and died while he was there. Doc swore that after the judge left his office that day a bottle of laudanum had come up missing."

"What's that got to do with me? Is he saying I took it?" The judge jumped to his feet and began to pace back and forth.

"No, but it's been eating on him. He's sure you killed that woman. I suppose that was Stella's mother."

"You and that crackpot doctor can suppose anything you want to, but you can't prove anything."

"Doc knows that. He was thinking of going down to Laramie and talking to the fellow who runs the newspaper. What's his name? It escapes me at the moment. He's a good friend of Garrick Rowe, my partner here. No matter. I can find out later from Doc. Doc wants to put the story in the paper and see if anyone can come up with something to add to it. If they can, you're headed for prison. It nothing comes of it, you're still done in Laramie. Enough folks will believe it to cook your goose in that town."

"That's . . . blackmail!" He stopped and faced T.C., who got slowly to his feet.

"By damn! You're right. I never thought I'd be a party to blackmail. Damn your hide, Judge. You forced me to do it."

"You . . . you . . . backwoods—"

"Watch it. Don't get Herb riled up. You haven't shot anybody yet today have you, Herb?"

"It's only noon, T.C."

"He doesn't want to break his record. Tell you what, Judge Cottington. You get your sorry carcass back to the hotel and into your room. I'll post a man in the lobby to see that you stay there. Tomorrow when the stage leaves, you be on it. If I ever hear of you even trying to contact Maude or Stella, you'll disappear up there in the Bitterroot and not be heard from again until some hunter comes onto a pile of bones that's been picked clean by the buzzards."

Muscles twitched in the judge's cheeks and his nostrils quivered.

"The law—"

"Not much law here, Judge. Just me. Do you understand the situation you're in, or do I put it on paper and *in* the paper?"

Judge Cottington jerked on his coat. He fixed Maude with an insolent stare.

"You're back with your own kind at last. Trash is what you are, and trash is what you'll always be!"

Herb hit him square in the mouth. The judge staggered back against the wall, raising the sleeve of his fine wool coat to stop the blood that flowed from his lip. Then he took a handkerchief from his pocket and dabbed his mouth.

"Be careful, Herb, you might hurt him," T.C. cautioned.

"Ah, shoot, T.C., I didn't hit him very hard."

"Don't hit him again until you get him in his hotel room."

"Can I hit him then?"

T.C. shrugged. "It's up to you."

"Watch him while I get my coat."

When Herb turned away from the judge, he had a grin on his face and he winked at Maude.

Later, as they were leaving the house, Judge Cottington passed Maude without deigning to glance at her. He went out the door and didn't look back.

"Ya want me to break his nose for ya, Maude?" Herb asked cheerfully as he followed the man out.

Jane and Sunday began to laugh.

Maude burst into tears.

"Is it over? Will he leave now?"

"Ah . . . Maude." Jane put her arms around the woman. "You've had to endure so much. You and Stella will never have to go back to him. Isn't my husband wonderful? Didn't I tell you that he'd know what to do?"

"How did Mr. Kilkenny know about Stella's mother? The judge hired me right after she died, but a woman came one day who knew her and said she got sick all of a sudden after her husband got run over by a carriage. It didn't occur to me that the judge could have poisoned her, although I found out quick enough how mean he was."

"I didn't like his face when he came in the door," Sunday announced.

"He had one face for the public and one face at home. At times I thought of poisoning him myself. But then if he hadn't died, and I'd been caught, Stella would have been alone with him." Maude wiped her eyes on the end of her apron. "I just never knowed people good as you."

T.C. watched from the doorway with a grin on his face.

"Ya made that all up, didn't ya?" Sunday asked.

"Not all of it. Doc did tell me one time about the puffed-up judge and the sick woman, and he thought there was something fishy about how she died. But he had no proof. I made up the rest. Had to let him think Doc was still alive and able to go down there and talk to the newspaper man in Laramie."

"Mamma!" Stella came down the stairs followed by Polly. "We saw him goin' with Herb." She ran to Maude and wrapped her arms around her waist.

"He's gone, honey, and not comin' back. We're rid of him."

"Forever?"

"Yes, sweetheart. We don't have to worry about going back there. We'll stay here in Timbertown, and you can go to school and—" Sobs rose in Maude's throat and she could say no more.

Stella went to T.C. and wrapped her arms around his legs.

"Thank you. Me and Mamma were so scared when we saw him last night. I'll be good from now on. I promise."

T.C. reached down and picked her up. She wrapped her arms about his neck.

"Don't be too good, punkin, or I'll forget you're a little girl and think you're all grown up."

His eyes were on Jane as he hugged the child.

Tears rolled down Maude's scarred cheeks.

The new doctor came in the afternoon. After T.C. had introduced him he looked at the swollen bruise on the side of Jane's head and then at Sunday's. He looked at the pupils of their eyes to check for concussion. In his opinion, neither woman was seriously injured, but he expressed surprise that they were able to be up and about.

"Our women out here are pretty tough," T.C. said proudly.

Doctor Bate smiled. "It seems so. In Chicago most of my women patients would have stayed in bed for a week."

T.C., Herb and the doctor spent several hours in the surgery discussing Doc's equipment and taking note of the medical supplies on hand.

Doctor Bate stood silently, almost reverently, before the

framed medical school certificate that hung askew on the wall above Doc's scarred old desk.

"I've heard about Little Doc's heroic feats during the War. Everyone in the medical field is aware of his devotion to his work. Nathan Foote is held up to young medical students as an example of dedication. I am honored to be offered his practice here. A man is lucky if he meets a Nathan Foote sometime during his life."

Before supper a price had been agreed upon, and everything, with the exception of Doc's desk and his private papers, had been moved to the newly remodeled rooms above the store where the new doctor would live and practice. The stairway going up the outside of the building had also been repaired and a supply of firewood was stacked beneath it. A strong new door was hung at the top of the landing.

Dr. Bate's quarters would remain relatively bare until the furniture he was having shipped by train from Chicago arrived. The town, the living area and the surgery were far different from what he had experienced before, but he settled in quickly and was ready to receive patients by evening should an emergency arise.

It was painful for Herb to see Doc's possessions being taken over by someone else, but it was a necessary transfer. Herb would keep the desk, the certificate and the personal mementos to cherish and to pass down to his own children.

That night around the supper table the talk was of Herb's and Polly's wedding, which would take place in T.C.'s office. Polly's baby was due after the first of the year and they had decided to accept T.C.'s invitation to spend the winter here in the house rather than be in a cabin some distance away. The surgery would be made into their bedroom.

While these plans were being made, Jane looked with sympathy at Sunday. Everyone else in the "family" was doing so well: Maude and Stella were out from under the heavy blanket of fear that they would have to go back to Judge Cottington. Polly and Herb held hands and gazed into each other's eyes. Her own hand was clasped tightly in T.C.'s. Sunday tried to keep up the appearance of being bright and happy, but while her mouth smiled, her eyes did not. Jane realized she was hurting inside. Not only had she lost Colin, but she had killed a man, and it weighed heavily on her.

That night, after a wildly satisfying bout of lovemaking, Jane lay in her husband's arms and they talked about it.

"Killing a man isn't an easy thing to live with even though her life and yours depended on her doing it. It's going to take a while for her to come to terms with what she had to do."

"She looks so sad."

"We owe her a big debt." T.C.'s arms tightened about her as he nuzzled his face in her hair. "Honey, I thought my heart would burst when I couldn't find you."

"It was a danger I didn't expect. Not from *him*. What in the world was he thinking of he? It was insane of him."

"It was insane of him to think I'd ever give up looking for you. If he'd hurt you, I'd have hunted him down if it had taken me the rest of my life."

"Do you think he could have been the one sending the notes? I've thought about it. I started getting them at the station, and he was there."

"Tennihill doesn't think so, and he seems to know quite a bit about Fresno. I've looked into the face of everyone who came to town at that time and I don't have a clue as to whom it could be. And until we find out, I don't want you to be alone."

"Sunday is getting restless. She feels she must work to pay her way. I wish that Colin hadn't gone away. Even if . . . he did do what Mrs. Guzman Cabeza says he did, maybe Sunday could have forgiven him . . . in time."

"It will work itself out. I'd stake ten years of my life with you on it. The baby is *not* Colin's. How he's going to prove it, I don't know. But enough about all of them, Mrs. Kilkenny. Pay some attention to your husband."

Jane laughed softly, put her arms around him and brought his head to her shoulder. He sighed contentedly and caressed her soft breast. Her hand smoothed the hair at his temples. Her lips played along his forehead.

"You're getting spoiled, Timmie, my love. And I'm loving spoiling you. Have I told you today how much I love you? And how proud I was of you when you stood up to that horrid man, and kept him from taking Maude and Stella?"

"I don't remember. Maybe you'd better tell me again."

Chapter 27

AFTER the first light snowfall had melted away, a week of beautiful late fall weather followed. Work on the first group of store buildings was completed. When new merchants arrived and more space was needed, more building would be undertaken. Repairs were started on the funerary and an addition was being constructed for the hotel. The church and the schoolhouse were nearby ready for use. T.C. had sent to Laramie for school supplies, and a notice had been put up in the store asking parents to list names and ages of children who would attend classes.

Two things stood in the way of Jane's complete peace of mind: the fear of her unknown enemy and the threat of perhaps being an embarrassment to her beloved. She was always accompanied by either Sunday or T.C. when she went out on the street; she went to the privy only during daylight hours. Even then T.C. insisted that one of the women go with her.

Since there had been no untoward incident since the smearing of the sign, she was inclined to believe her tormentor might have been Bob Fresno. T.C. tried to tell her that the outlaw's attempt to kidnap her could have been a retaliation against *him* for refusing to give the man work. But she remembered that Fresno had singled her out for his attention that first day at the stage station. She hoped that he had been the note-writer, or maybe it had been Milo Callahan, who had disappeared from town the night of the dance after he'd tried to rape Bessie.

Jane trusted only the members of her "family" and looked into the face of every other person she met and asked herself: *Could it be you?*

Sunday's despair over loving Colin so desperately and being disappointed by him was also worrisome to Jane. Loving T.C. as she did, she could understand Sunday's pain.

Polly and Herb were married quietly with only the "family," Sweet William Wassall and Tennihill present. Polly was beautiful and weepy in a white dress she and Maude had hastily made on the sewing machine T.C. had brought down from the store. Theda Cruise generously lent her violin to Sunday, who played several selections before and after the ceremony.

The morning of the wedding Herb had visited the tonsorial parlor for a bath, shave, and haircut. After he had dressed in a white shirt, stiff collar, black string tie and new duck britches, he went into the office, where T.C. was making a list of out-of-pocket expenses to send to Garrick Rowe.

"Can I talk to ya a minute?" Herb asked, and closed the door.

T.C. put down his pen and leaned back in the chair.

"Getting cold feet, Herb?" he asked with a grin.

"Horse-hockey. Ya know I ain't. I want to marry Polly more'n anythin' in the world. It's just that I'm scared I won't . . . know what to do."

T.C. thought a minute, then asked, "What to do in bed?"

"I know *what* to do, but don't know if I ort to. I was with a woman . . . once. She was a whore. When I told Doc about it, he said I could get the French pox from messin' around with old whores and my pecker'd rot and fall off. Scared hell outta me. I never done it again."

"Good advice."

"The thin' that worries me is that feller that forced Polly hurt her. I don't want her to think I'm like him, and I didn't know if I ort to touch her . . . there, because she's already been caught."

"That's something I can't tell you. Jane or Maude would know."

"I couldn't ask *them*."

"I'll ask Jane and let you know. But I'm thinking that Polly may have to get used to being in bed with you.

Maybe if you just held her for a few nights even if you hurt so bad you think you'll die from it. Be gentle with her and when the time is right, she'll be more likely to accept you."

"I want her that way real bad, but I don't want to hurt her even if she says I can," Herb said worriedly. "She's just a little girl and hasn't had nobody to look after her."

"She's got you now."

"Yeah. And ya can bet yore boots nobody'll hurt her ever again."

Jane had to speak with Maude and Sunday before she had information for T.C. to relay to Herb.

It was the measure of her growing sense of freedom with him that she could engage in talk of this kind in the light of day. At first his half-teasing attacks on her modesty had wrought havoc with her ingrained inhibitions. When they whispered to each other in the dead of night, no word was unseemly, no act offensive. Now she was able to talk with her husband about the delicate subject wholly without embarrassment, and it proved to her just how completely their minds and bodies had merged.

"Both Sunday and Maude, who know more about this than I do, said that women usually can sleep and do other things with their husbands up until a month before the baby is due. Sunday, in her plain-talk way, said, 'that kid's in there tight as a pea in a pod and he ain't goin' to knock it out less Herb gets downright mean about it.'" "Jane's repeating of Sunday's words brought a smile to T.C.'s face. "Of course, Polly isn't very strongly built, although she's much stronger than when she first came here."

"Shall I tell him it's all right if he's careful?"

"Tell him it would be better to let Polly decide. She loves him. She'll want to give him all the pleasure she can."

"Like you give me?" T.C. kissed the side of her neck.

"And like you give me, love." She kissed him back.

The wedding supper was more joyous than the one following T.C.'s and Jane's wedding. Herb was as happy as a puppy. Polly glowed.

There was, however, a sadness, behind Sunday's jovial behavior. She had mentioned to Jane earlier in the day that she was considering taking the stage back to the rail station when it again went south, which would be in a few days.

"I've got no future here, Jane. I need to be rippin' and rearin'. It isn't my nature to sit in a room and sew all day long, or stand behind a stove and make bear claws or behind a counter and show ribbons and doodads to flitter-headed ninnies like Paralee. I don't know why I ever thought I could."

"Give it a little more time. Please, Sunday, I don't want to lose you."

On a cold but bright sunshiny day several weeks after Polly and Herb were married, Jane and Sunday washed clothes and hung them on the line behind the house. There would not be many more days when clothes would dry outside without freezing first. In the middle of the afternoon they took the laundry inside, where Maude was heating the flat irons on the cookstove.

Stella and Buddy Winters were playing on the swing Herb had hung from a limb of the big tree beside the house. Mrs. Winters had loosened her tight rein on the boy, and he was out and around town most of the day.

"She's lettin' that boy run wild," Maude exclaimed at one time. "And he's a bright child. His curiosity is what gets him in trouble."

"She works hard and does a good business." Jane dipped her hand into a pan of water, dampened a shirt and rolled it tightly. "Although, according to Bill, her bread and rolls are not as good as yours."

"Go on with you! Bill just doesn't like her very much." Maude scoffed, but blushed at the praise.

The door slammed and Stella came running to the kitchen where the women worked.

"Mamma! Aunt Jane! Come looky at what's comin'. C'mon, Aunt Sunday. It's a king in a coach."

"A king in Timbertown? Landsakes!" Maude exclaimed.

The women went to the door. Stella dashed out to hug the porch post and gawk. It was a rare sight in Timbertown or in any other small northern town to see a fancy carriage drawn by a matching pair of thoroughbred horses with plumes on their bridles. The carriage was escorted by six riders all dressed in bright, colorful uniforms. They rode with heads up, backs straight, as if they were in a parade. And indeed it was as near to a parade as Timbertown had ever had.

The driver sat on a high seat in front of the carriage. He wore the same kind of uniform as the escort riders. In the back, wrapped in furs, rode a man in a high-crowned hat. Lolling beside him, pointing this way and that, showing the visitor what had been accomplished during the town's renovation, was Colin Tallman.

Sunday spied him immediately.

"Why that . . . snake! He's got the guts of a mule to come crawlin' back here!"

"Who is that man? He does look kinda . . . like a king." Jane began to giggle. "Could he be the dreaded Ramon Guzman Cabeza?"

"He don't look like much," Sunday admitted. "But them fellows ridin' shotgun look tough enough to tackle a bear with a willow switch. That last one's leadin' Del Norte."

As the procession passed the house, Colin looked toward it, smiled broadly, and lifted his hat in a greeting. Jane and Maude waved, but Sunday turned up her nose and looked away.

"If I'm lucky that little king's bringin' the skunk back here to hang him," Sunday muttered.

"Seems awful cheerful to be goin' to his hangin'," Maude remarked, but his face wore a worried frown.

"He'd make a show of it," Sunday replied scornfully.

Watching her friend, Jane noticed the high color in her cheeks and the clenching of her hands.

"I wonder where T.C. is."

T.C. had been told by the mail rider an hour earlier that he had overtaken Colin Tallman riding with a high-born Mexican who was escorted by a half-dozen men. Because T.C. had realized immediately who it was, he had gone to the hotel to tell the manager to fire up the round Acme heaters in a group of rooms for Señor Ramon Guzman-Cabeza and his men. At first sighting, T.C. went out onto the hotel porch to await their arrival.

The carriage stopped in front of the hotel, and one of the riders went ahead to hold the bridles of the nervous team while the señor and his guest stepped down. Colin alighted and went to take the reins of his horse. Ramon threw off the furs and stepped down to shake hands with T.C.

"Welcome to Timbertown, Ramon. I never thought to see you in this cold country."

"As you know, T.C., I am not fond of the cold and stayed at our home in the mountains only when I had no other choice."

Señor Guzman-Cabeza was small. Without the hat, his head would have come level with T.C.'s chin; but his erect carriage created the impression that he was taller. His carefully shaped black goatee and the sideburns that curved down to his jaws brought an air dignity to his small stature. He had sharp dark eyes and a full-lipped red mouth.

"It's good that you came now. In a few weeks the south pass could very well be filled with snow."

"Yi, yi, yi," Ramon muttered and shook his head. "Why do you live here, T.C., when you could live where it is warm?"

T.C. grinned. "Every man has his preferences, Ramon."

Ramon's eyes went past T.C. to the door of the hotel when Patrice came running out. A thin colorful shawl was draped around her and her shiny black hair flowed to her waist.

"Ramon! Ramon! I've missed you—"

Patrice raced down the steps, threw herself against the small man, and wrapped her arms about his neck, being careful not to disturb the tall hat on his head. They were almost equal in height, Patrice perhaps an inch or two taller.

"Control yourself, Señora," Ramon said coolly. "You know I hate such displays in public."

"I know, Ramon, but I am so glad to see you. Come to my room. It's nice and warm there."

"Presently. I must see about my men first."

"Can't Francisco do it?"

"Francisco Perez is no longer a member of my household, Señora. You saw to that when you persuaded him to escort you to this place. Go along." He made a shooing motion with one of his gloved hands. "You will have my full attention presently. I promise you."

Patrice fled back into the hotel, hoping the rebuff by her husband had gone unnoticed by the gawkers who had come out of the stores to watch.

Colin waited until the baggage was unloaded and piled on the hotel porch, then mounted his horse to lead the way to the livery and to the barn where the carriage could be kept.

After Ramon spoke at length in Spanish to his men, he allowed T.C. to lead him into the hotel lobby. He took dainty steps in boots with two-inch heels. When he threw off his thick wool cape, it was apparent that Ramon was no longer slim and wiry. He had put on weight, and his small body was as round as a barrel.

"Colin tells me that you have taken a wife." Ramon carefully removed his tall hat. His black hair was still thick and brushed up to give him maximum height.

T.C. had forgotten that Ramon did everything carefully.

"I came down with a bad case of lovesickness. She's everything I ever wanted in a wife." T.C.'s expression showed his pleasure while speaking about his lady love.

Ramon felt a small flash of envy.

"Love! Bah! Did she bring money to your coffers? Can she arouse you again and again to new heights of passion? Is she so young and beautiful that men envy you? What is love if she does none of these things?"

T.C. knew that Ramon expected no response, and he offered none.

"I'll take my leave, Ramon. I know you're eager to speak to Patrice."

"Eager is not the word I would use, but, yes, I have matters to discuss with my wife. We shall leave in the morning to catch the eastbound train in the late afternoon. I have reserved a private car for myself and my wife and another for my men, the carriage, and the horses."

Colin came in and clapped T.C. on the shoulder.

"How's the wife?"

"Fine. You took off in such hurry she thinks you don't like her."

"I had things to do. Fellow in the livery said Sunday had killed Bob Fresno. Is she all right?"

"She did, and she is, It's quite a story, and she is quite a woman."

"I'd like to meet this woman who's got Colin so crazy that he talked of nothing but her for ten miles at a time, Ramon said.

"She's not your type, Ramon," T.C. said with a wide grin.

"She's a crack shot; she's no slouch with a hammer and nail, and she claims to be the best shingle-maker in the territory."

"Shingle-maker? Shingles that are put on a roof? Yi, yi, yi. You'll not have any competition from me, Colin. I like my women dainty and compliant."

"I'm going to marry her if she'll have me. I'm hoping to take her to New Mexico to meet my folks. You'll meet her then."

"It will be my pleasure."

"If you need anything, tell the man at the desk." T.C. was aware that Colin was eager to break away. "I'll be here to see you before you leave in the morning. By the way, our hotel cook is quite good. Meals will be served in your room if you wish."

"Good-bye, Ramon." Colin stuck out his hand and Ramon shook it. "I enjoyed our visit. It reminded me of when we were kids, and Grandpa Rain took us on a turkey hunt."

"I never told you how I hated the hunting part, but loved being with Senor Rain."

Colin's smile broadened. "You didn't have to tell me. I knew it and so did Grandpa."

Ramon glanced behind him to see his men carrying his trunks up the stairs. With a hand lifted in farewell, and with a great deal of dignity, he followed them.

On the porch Colin gave T.C. a sheepish grin.

"I always did kind of like the arrogant little bastard."

T.C. chuckled. "Not many folks in town have seen the likes of him. Did you convince him you had not cuckolded him?"

"Didn't have to. He knew that I hadn't. He was on his way here. I wired my pa, and he wired me back that Ramon was in Denver. I waited for him in Laramie. Came right out and told him what Patrice was up to. He said not to worry. I'll tell you all about it later, but right now I want to see my girl."

"Your girl?" T.C. gave his friend a long thoughtful look, then chuckled. "Christ on a horse, Colin. You went away and left that girl without a word. Sunday and everyone else in town thinks you've been blanket-rasslin' with Patrice. Sunday hates your guts!"

"Then I'm just going to have to change her mind."

Patrice hurried back to her room and began to prepare to meet Ramon. What had gone wrong? She had planned so carefully. When Colin disappeared, she was sure he had gone back to his ranch rather than face Ramon and have to kill him. Ramon's pride would have forced him to seek satisfaction on the one who had shamed him by making his wife pregnant.

Colin had come riding into town in Ramon's carriage. The two seemed to be thick as thieves. Had she misjudged Ramon once again? Didn't he care that she was carrying another man's child? He didn't know about it! That must be the answer; Colin hadn't told him, and there was still hope.

Patrice slumped on the edge of the bed in relief for only an instant before she jumped up to pull off her dress and slip into a flimsy gown and robe. She brushed her hair and sprinkled herself generously with rosewater, then hurriedly tidied the room. Ramon hated disorder.

Patrice had arranged herself in the chair, her hair loose and the neckline of her gown pulled to show a goodly amount of her plump breast, when the door was flung open. Ramon stood there and, without even looking into the room, spoke to one of his men in Spanish.

"Prepare my bath and see that I'm not disturbed while I renew my acquaintance with my wife." He came in and closed the door.

Patrice stood. Her face was calm; her large dark eyes held an expression of deep sorrow.

"I'm glad you're here, Ramon," she said in a small timid voice. "I've been so frightened."

He had given her a casual glance and was now looking around the bleak room.

"I did not realize your preference for a monk's lifestyle, my *poco puta*. I could have arranged for you to have such a room as this at the *hacienda*."

He had called her a whore!

"Ramon, please. I didn't want to come here."

"No? Another thing I did not know about my wife is that

she does things she does *not* want to do. Yi, yi, yi. How many more surprises are in store for me?"

Small as he was, his presence filled the room. Patrice sat down. Her husband liked to look down on a woman rather than up or at eye level. He moved toward her, his gaze fixed hard on her face. He was making a thin humming sound in his throat. Patrice hated that sound. It meant that he was very angry.

Ramon stood for a long moment looking down at the top of her head. Then suddenly he moved his hands so that the palms rested nakedly against her neck. His thumbs came together to form a V in the hollow at the base of her throat where the pulse beat swiftly. For an endless moment she looked up at him while he exerted a steady pressure. His nostrils flared and his red mouth thinned. His eyes speared into her like points of steel.

Suddenly and viciously, he slapped her and turned away.

"In most countries of the world a wife can be put to death for adultery." His voice was quiet, his manner cool. Patrice's face went ashen when she realized he was in the mood to kill her.

"You know?" Her question was barely audible.

"I know that you are about to present me with a son and heir."

"And you . . . let Colin go when you knew that he had . . . violated me?"

Ramon's laugh was humorless.

"My dear *esposa*. You haven't been *violated* since I took your maidenhead. You love every minute of the time a man spends between your legs."

"I don't understand you. I'm your wife and I'm carrying another man's child. Have you no pride?"

"I have plenty of pride, but I am not so foolish as to be led into a trap by a *puta*."

"You're afraid that Colin will kill you if you face him with the fact he has cuckolded you."

"Why would I do that? I like Colin and I think Colin likes me. I did him a favor when I married you. He had not had my experience with women, and he *thought* you were still an innocent."

"I was. You know I was a virgin. *You* took my maidenhead."

"There were many ways to satisfy a man's passion . . . and a woman's, without the breaking of the maidenhead. You were no innocent," he said emphatically, turning to regard her. The anger that had blazed in his eyes when he slapped her had changed to hard, icy contempt.

Patrice jumped up. Anger overriding her fear.

"The child is Colin's!"

"How did that come about? Tell me, Patrice. How do you happen to be carrying Colin's child?"

"I was with him in his hotel room in Sante Fe four months ago. What will your precious mother and uncles say when your wife gives birth to a blue-eyed, fair-haired child?"

"It will be a dark-haired, dark-eyed child. No one will doubt that it's mine."

Patrice gasped. "I was with Colin. Only Colin."

"This past year you have been with Señor Gabriel Valencia, Señor Domingo Santos, a homesteader by the name of Walt Winston, Señor Juan Trevino, and your latest lover, General Anastasio Pasqual, who impregnated you. And you may be interested to know that he has moved with his family back to Guadalajara to take a position of no consequence." Ramon listed her recent lovers with carefree indifference.

Fear made Patrice speechless.

"I have Señor Pasqual to thank for my heir." Ramon walked back and forth across the narrow room. His demeanor was cool, his smile mocking. "After he is born, I shall have no further use for you. You can go to Mexico to be with your lover. Although you may not be received graciously by

General Anastasio Pasqual, it is his *esposa*'s papa who holds the purse strings."

"You've . . . had me followed," Patrice said, when she found her voice.

"Of course. A man who has a straying wife wants to know with whom he is sharing her." He paused. A grin twisted his mouth as he insolently looked her over. "The homesteader? Yi, yi, yi. He smelled like a wet goat. Did he take off his boots, little *puta*? Or did he lean you up against a tree and pull up your skirt? Is that how you like it, eh?"

"You don't have to be insulting! You have your women." She avoided looking at him.

"Si, Señora. But what is a man to do when his wife is no longer a pleasure to him?"

"I *chose* Colin to be the father of my child," she said spitefully.

His face was stony, his eyes contemptuous and cold. He stood studying her for a moment before he spoke.

"You have seen Colin Tallman alone one time in the last two years. You went to his room at the hotel in Sante Fe. You were there for less than five minutes when he threw you out. I doubt that even the most potent man could impregnate you in five minutes. It would take that long to get your corset off."

"You're a bast—"

"Careful what you call me, Señora. I am a practical man. I've not fathered a child, but I'm expected to produce an heir. You've taken care of that for me very nicely. Why do you think I did not kill you when I learned of your first dalliance with another man less than a year after you exchanged vows with me?"

Now that his cards were on the table, Patrice began to feel a sense of power. *She had something he wanted*. The fog of fear lifted from her mind and she began to think. If he *wanted* the little bastard she carried in her belly, he would pay dearly to get it.

"All right, Señor Guzman Cabeza, little *big* man of Rancho Cabezas." She put emphasis on the insult. "If you want this *heir* there are going to be some changes. I'm—"

She never had a chance to finish what she was saying. Ramon exploded in a hot, jagged slash of fury. He swung his arm and hit her with his open palm so hard that she was flung back onto the bed.

"I will have respect from you, *puta*. You will obey me." His snarl was ground through with impotent rage. "Get on the bed and spread your legs. You've been playing the whore for other men, now you'll play the whore for me."

Chapter 28

"UNCLE Colin!"

Stella jumped out of the swing and went running toward him, Buddy close behind.

"Hello, punkin." Colin swung the child up in his arms, then set her on her feet and took her hand.

"Me'n Mamma don't have to go back to Laramie. Uncle T.C. told the old judge not to come back, and Uncle Herb hit him. I didn't get to see it. They made me and Aunt Polly stay upstairs."

"It seems a lot has been going on while I was gone."

"Aunt Polly and Uncle Herb sleep together now."

"That's exciting news, punkin." Colin looked at T.C. and lifted his brows in question.

T.C. shrugged. "You'll know it all by the time we get to the house. Our little Stella has turned into a regular chatterbox."

Stella giggled. "You say that all the time. Aunt Sunday sleeps in Polly's bed," she announced, hardly taking a breath.

Buddy, wanting to be included, shyly wiggled his fingers into Colin's other hand. Colin looked down at the small freckled face looking up at him.

"Mr. Banks made a swing."

"You don't say? Would it hold me?"

"It holds Mr. Banks. Did ya go to fight Indians?"

"Naw." Colin pulled a penny from his pocket and gave it to Buddy. "You and Stella run up to the store and tell Mr. Jenson to give you a penny's worth of candy."

"Gee-whillikers!"

"Say thank you," Stella reminded him sternly, when Buddy started to run away. "And wait for me."

"Thanks, Mr. Tallman. C'mon, Stella—"

Colin watched them run toward the store.

"I was about Buddy's age when my sister and I went to live with Addie Hyde. Until then we had been passed around like a couple of unwanted pups."

"The new teacher came in yesterday. School starts next week. Buddy swears he isn't going, but he'll go because Stella's going."

"Lettin' a woman lead him around by the nose already." Colin chuckled. "What's the teacher like?"

"He's a dressed-up little dandy—about this high." T.C. held his hand up to his shoulder. "If some of the rowdy boys get the upper hand, he'll fizzle out."

"You goin' to let Jane help him?"

"Hell, no. He'll sink or swim on his own. If he sinks, I'll send for another. Rowe pays well. There shouldn't be any trouble finding one."

They were almost to the house when Colin asked the question T.C. had been waiting for.

"Sunday moved to your place?"

"I asked her to help me keep an eye on Jane. She kept Bob Fresno from carrying Jane off. Shot him with that little pistol she carries in her pocket. I owe her a big debt. Treat her right, or you'll have not only me on your tail but all the women in the house and nearly every man in town." T.C. grinned.

"I meant it when I said I was goin' to marry her. This has been the longest month of my life. I've cursed a hundred times the day I met Patrice."

T.C. grinned. "Ramon probably has, too."

"Well, thank God, he's the one stuck with her."

They stepped up onto the porch. The door was flung open and Jane rushed out to welcome him.

From the upstairs window Sunday had watched the two tall men as they came down the street. She saw Stella and Buddy run toward them and Colin toss the child in the air. She lost sight of them when they stepped up onto the porch but heard their voices in the downstairs hall and opened the door so that she could hear what was being said.

"Mrs. Kilkenny, you're prettier than I remembered."

"Get your hands off my wife." This was T.C.'s mockingly harsh voice.

"After I kiss her. Don't be so stingy."

"Stingy? You're lucky I don't shoot you."

It'd save me the trouble. Sunday opened the door wider.

"There ya are, ya big galoot! Soon as I turn my back, ya up and get yoreself a wife. Pretty one too. Do I get to kiss the bride, Herb?"

Sunday let loose a snort of disgust. *Do I get to kiss the bride? Kissin' wives is all ya been doin', ya horny toad!*

"Get ya a woman a yore own to kiss, Tallman. This 'n' s mine." Herb's voice overrode the laughter from Jane and T.C. and Maude.

"*You* didn't get married while I was gone, did ya, Mrs. Henderson?"

"No. I was waitin' for ya to come home to see if ya'd been asked for."

"Not yet, but I will be. Want me to ask Bill for ya?"

"You do, and I'll put croton oil in your gravy."

I'd give him a load of buckshot in his rear!

"Where's Sunday? Is she hidin' from me?"

Sunday stepped back from the door. *Hiding? From a fornicating, wife-stealing mule's ass? That'd be a cold day in hell!*

"She's upstairs."

Maude, you traitor!

"Do I have your permission, Mrs. Kilkenny, to go up to my girl's room if I leave the door open?"

My girl! Sunday's breath came from between her teeth in an angry hiss.

"I trust you'll act the gentleman?"

"I won't promise not to kiss her."

Just try it, ya suck-egg mule!

Sunday heard a step on the stairs, then T.C.'s voice.

"Check her pocket to see if she has the pistol."

"She won't shoot me. She loves me."

The pig-ugly, wife-stealing, conceited ass!

Sunday stepped back and slammed the door so hard that the house shook. She looked for something to push in front of the door. The only thing was the washstand. She groaned when she picked it up because it was so light. The first rap on the door came as she was putting it in place.

"Sunday, open the door."

Silence. *She'd not answer if the blasted house was on fire.*

"I want to talk to ya, Sunday."

Go talk to Patrice Guzman Cabeza.

"I know what Patrice told you. I can explain."

I bet you can. You've had a month to make up a story.

"Patrice will be going back to New Mexico with her husband."

That's too bad. You'll have to find another whore, you rutting moose!

"I don't want to break down this door, but by God, I will. Now open the damn door. There's things I want to say to you in private."

"Ya just try to break in that door. I'll shoot you," she yelled.

"At least ya haven't forgot how to talk."

"I've not *forgot* a dad-blasted thing, you . . . you chicken shit!"

"If you think a little old door will keep me away from you, you don't know me very well."

"I don't know you a'tall. Now get the hell away from my door."

BANG! The door flew open. The washstand tipped over, the tin basin went rolling, the pitcher hit the floor and bounced. Water splashed on Sunday's feet.

Colin stood looking at her. His blue eyes burned into hers.

"See what you made me do?"

"Oh, sure! I forced ya to break the door!" Her voice was tight and strained.

"Hello, Sunday," he said pleasantly, as if they had just met.

"What do you want?" She eyed him with a peevish glare.

"You."

"Ha!" she snorted, her lip curled in contempt.

"I'm not the father of Patrice's child. I've *never* been with her that way."

"Ha!" Sunday snorted again, this time with disbelief. "Ever' time ya open yore mouth, Tallman, I get a earache."

He crossed the room in two long steps. He caught her in his arms and held her in a tight grip. She strugged like a wild thing caught in a trap.

"I've thought of you every minute for more than a month that seemed like a year! Now, if I have to throw you down on the bed and sit on you to make you listen to me, I will." Catching her flailing hands in his as she swung to hit him, he forced them behind her. She was strong, but he was stronger. "Why are you fighting me, for chrissake? You're as glad to see me as I am to see you."

"Damn you! Let go of me."

"Kiss me first."

"I'd . . . sooner kiss a warthog!"

He laughed. "I'm crazy about you."

"Horse-hockey!"

"I want everyone of our kids to be just like you."

"Yo're not gettin' in my drawers if that's what's on your mind."

"It *is*, and I *will*. But it'll be after my name is tacked to the end of yours."

"I'd sooner wed a . . . crazy three-legged buzzard."

"I'm crazy about you," he said again. "It's been a hell of a month. I couldn't wait to get back here to see you again." His voice lowered to a husky whisper. "Put your arms around my neck so I can kiss you."

Joy began romping up and down her insides. The misery of the past few weeks began to fade.

"Tallman, yo're—"

"Colin, Sunday. Sunday and Colin. That's how I want it to be. Say you forgive me for leaving without a word. But you were in no mood then to believe me, and I had to find Ramon and convince him I'd not slept with his wife." "How'd ya do that?"

"I didn't have to. He'd been having her followed. He knows, I imagine, who fathered her child, and he knows it wasn't me. Sweetheart, you're all I want. The first time I saw you, I fell in love with you."

Sunday looked searchingly at him, not yet believing, and then believing.

"Ya'll have to turn loose my hands." Her voice smiled. "If ya want me to kiss ya."

When she was free, her arms moved up and around his neck. She felt a deep singing joy. Did he feel it too? Then she knew. His hungry kisses covered her mouth and she returned each and every one. They went on and on in a rapturous union of eager mouths and tongues. When she could catch her breath, she laughed at the urgency of his lips.

"Did you miss me? Tell me," he whispered insistently, but she could not speak with his mouth tight against hers. His hands moved through her hair, down and over her back in soft rhythmic caresses.

Her hands stroked his cheeks; she nuzzled her face into his neck, inhaling the masculine scent of him.

"Did you miss me, sweetheart?" he repeated.

"Yes, damn you! Yes, yes, yes. I missed you," she declared with shameless intensity.

A grin lifted the corner of his mouth at her response; his eyes were soft with love for her.

"I love you. Does it shock you to hear me say it?"

"I ain't easy shocked, Tallman. I been a waitin' for ya to say it again."

He held her so tight, she could feel every hard line in his body. He rubbed his face in her mop of blond curls. She was so pretty, so sweet . . . so damned exciting. He was sure she could feel the hardness of his arousal against her, yet she hadn't shied away from it.

Sunday put her palms against his cheeks and looked into his eyes. "I love you, Tallman. Welcome home."

The following weeks passed quickly. A stout warm cabin for Sunday and Colin was built in a week's time. They were married in the new church on a Sunday afternoon. Jane thought it fitting for Sunday to be married on a Sunday. The church was full of well-wishers because Sunday was so well liked. Theda Cruise played the violin. No one seemed to think it strange that the saloon keeper—she had become partners with Mr. Parker—was in the church playing sacred music.

After the elaborate wedding dinner prepared by Maude and Polly and a send-off from the family, Bill, and Tennihill, the couple left for their cabin.

That night Jane was introduced to another custom that was even more foreign to her than the picnic that had been held after Doc's funeral.

The night was cold, the air crisp. Jane was bundled up in one of T.C.'s sheepskin coats. They stood with the group of townsfolk that surrounded Colin's and Sunday's cabin to beat on tin pans and ring cowbells.

Some of the men shouted advice to Colin.

"Hey, Colin. Air ya needin' help?"

"Did ya take a bath, Colin? Yo're sure to stink like a hog."

"Don't forget to take off yore britches—"

"—And yore boots!"

"Want me to show ya how, Colin?"

The noisy serenade continued with hoots and whistles.

"It's called a shivaree," T.C. explained to Jane. "I put out the word you were not well so that they'd not do this when we were married. Herb was sure such a racket would scare Polly to death. He put the kibosh on it by paying them off ahead of time. He left money with Theda at the saloon to buy drinks."

"They do it to get free drinks?"

"It's a good-natured form of blackmail."

"How long do we keep this up? My ears hurt."

The lamp inside the cabin had gone out shortly after the racket began.

"It won't be long now. Colin will come out and pay us to go away."

"Why, that's terrible!" Jane giggled and clung to T.C.'s arm.

He looked down into her smiling face, then dipped his head and kissed her warm lips. She had not had much pleasure in her life, and so small things were joys to her.

"Let's go home." He put his lips to her ear so that she could hear him. "I know of more interesting things to do."

"Like what?" Her eyes teased him.

"Get you in bed, take off your nightdress—"

"Sir!"

"Kiss your soft breasts—"

"How you talk!"

"Go into that warm, sweet place that's known only to me."

"Stop that talk right now!"

"Want me to show you how much I want to go into that special place?" He took her hand and pulled it under his coat. She jerked it away.

"Don't you . . . dare! T.C., someone will see you. I swear to goodness. You're as randy as a two-peckered goat!" Her hand went to her mouth. "I can't believe I said that! I'm picking up Sunday's expressions."

His mouth went to her ear again. "You're . . . adorable." He bit her ear lobe. "I'm waiting to hear you say you want me to"—he pressed his lips closer to her ear and whispered a word.

She gasped. "T.C. Kilkenny! I'll never say . . . *that*!"

They were laughing into each other's eyes, completely oblivious to everyone else, when the shot sounded.

BOOM! Colin came to the door with his double-barreled shotgun and fired into the air. The racket stopped.

"Ya done already, Colin?" Murphy yelled.

"What's the hurry? Ya got the next twenty years."

"—If'n ya don't wear it out."

"That you, Murphy? I'm not forgettin' this!"

"Well, I hope not. Wouldn't be sayin' much for yore bride if ya forgot yore weddin' night."

A roar of laughter went up from the crowd. Jane could see Sunday peeking from behind Colin and knew that she was enjoying this.

Colin took a few steps away from the door and set a cup on the ground. He sprang back to the safety of the cabin when two lumberjacks made a grab for him. If they were able to separate the bride and groom for an hour or two they would consider the shivaree highly successful.

"Theda, you out there?"

"I'm here, Colin. Does Sunday need me to tell her what to do?"

"Thanks," Sunday called. "I think I can figure it out."

"Theda, take these brayin' jackasses to the saloon and buy 'em a drink."

"It's about time, Tallman. I was thinkin' I'd have to stand out here all night while ya decided if ya'd rather bed your bride or part with a coin or two," Murphy yelled.

Colin and Sunday went back into the cabin and closed the door. Theda picked up the cup of money and the laughing, rowdy men followed her up the street to the saloon.

Jane and T.C. walked arm in arm back toward their house. "Are you happy, Mrs. Kilkenny?"

"Happier beyond anything I ever imagined." She looked up at him. "Sometimes I worry that it can't last."

"It will, sweetheart. You're not still concerned about that threat, are you?"

"I think about it. If it was just the notes, I wouldn't worry so much. But the other. The person who did *that* to me hates me very much. Yet if they had wanted to kill me, they had the chance."

"Sweetheart, it tears me up that I've not been able to take that load off your mind. It's been a month and a half since the last note. Whoever it is may have given up and left town."

"I hope so. Oh, I hope so."

They reached the porch and stopped to look up at the star-filled sky. He pulled her back against his chest and wrapped his arms around her.

"You'll love the sky out at the ranch. The stars are so close you can almost reach out and pluck them out of the sky."

She turned in his arms. "Do you ever pinch yourself to see if you're dreaming?"

"Sometimes." He dropped a kiss on her nose.

"I know somewhere I'd rather be . . . right now."

"Why, Mrs. Kilkenny, ma'am. You mean you want to take me to bed?"

"That's exactly what I mean, Mr. Kilkenny, sir."

Chapter 29

By Thanksgiving two feet of snow covered the ground. The branches of the pines and spruce sagged low under the weight of the snow and ice piled on them. The sharp odor of woodsmoke was strong in the cold, still air that hung over the town.

With Jane seated in front of him on his horse, T.C. took her with him when he visited the cutting camps to the north and to the south. The men were working thirteen hours a day and would do so as long as the ground was frozen. Swampers had prepared the roads by using tank sprinklers to ensure a heavy coat of ice in the ruts made by the sleds that carried great loads of lodgepole pines to the mill.

The men in the camps lived in a forty-foot-long building with side walls scarcely two feet above the ground. The walls were built of logs, the roof of shakes covered with evergreen boughs. Rowe Lumber Company provided the men in these camps with the best food that could be had in order to keep up their energy for the hard work.

On the way back through the quiet forest, T.C. explained the workings of the camps.

"The camp is divided into squads. One group, the teamsters, hauls the logs; another, the choppers, fells the giant trees; a third, the sawyers, saws the trees into logs; a fourth, the swampers, prepares the roads. It's dangerous work. Rowe Lumber Company makes sure a doctor is available."

"Bill says you've done all those jobs and were the best."

"I've put in more than one winter at a cutting camp. More than one summer at a sawmill."

"But you want to ranch."

"Yes, sweetheart, I do."

Jane cherished every minute of the time she spent with her husband in the vast forests that covered the mountainsides. She learned that he could mimic to perfection the song of any bird. He told her about every cloven-hoofed creature, every predator, rodent or reptile that lived there. When she asked him where he had obtained this vast storehouse of knowledge, he replied that it had been a part of him for so long he was no longer conscious of when or where he had learned his woodland lore.

She told him of her love of music and history. Her world had been books. Having been confined most of her life to one place on a ten-acre plot of ground, she had spread her wings through the writings of authors such as James Fenimore Cooper, Daniel Defoe and Sir Walter Scott.

T.C. came to realize during these shared times that his wife was as bright as she was strong, and he marveled that a person so sensitive could have endured so tragic a childhood.

Two weeks before Christmas Jane became aware of having missed her monthy flow and knew that it was possible she was pregnant. She held the precious secret close to her heart, not wanting to tell T.C. until she was sure. Her dream of having a loving husband and a family was coming true.

Jane genuinely liked Mr. Culbertson, the effeminate schoolmaster. He had surprised everyone with his skill at handling the rowdy boys who tried to disrupt his class.

When he first arrived and laid down the rules that no male would wear his hat inside the schoolhouse, he was challenged by a twelve-year-old whose height was equal to his own. After twice asking the boy to remove his hat and receiving only an insolent grin in return, the schoolmaster whirled, lifted his leg and kicked the hat off the youngster's head. It happened so fast that the class sat in stunned silence.

"I could have just as easily broken your nose, your neck, or your arm. Don't challenge my authority again."

None did.

On hearing the story, T.C. was convinced the schoolmaster would be well able to protect Jane should the need arise; and since no further attempts had been made to frighten or threaten her, he thought it safe for her to spend time at the school helping with the program to be presented at the church on Christmas Eve. Either he or Herb came to walk her home after school, or at times the teacher accompanied her.

A play about Joseph and Mary in the stable in Bethlehem would include most of the children in school. Jane insisted that none be left out. She assigned the older boys the task of building the manger and handling the scenery the night of the event rather than reciting a poem or singing. Stella would be an angel and Buddy a shepherd in the play. Both had speaking parts. In the evenings Jane rehearsed the pair until they knew their lines and their gestures perfectly.

Buddy was excited. He loved trying on the costume Maude had made for him to wear in the play and the praise he received for his acting ability. Herb found a branch and whittled it down to resemble a staff like one Jane has seen illustrated in an book. The boy soaked up information like a sponge and was enthralled by the story of the baby Jesus being born in a manger.

Theda Cruise ordered Mr. Jenson at the store to prepare a sack of candy and an orange to be given to every child in town after the program—her Christmas gift to them. It was one more thing about the flame-haired saloon keeper that surprised Jane.

The day before Christmas Eve, school was let out at noon to allow for one last practice. Mr. Culbertson had a fine voice and rehearsed the children who would sing. In the teacher's room behind the classroom, Jane listened and advised the ones who were giving recitations. Play practice followed. At dusk when rehearsal was over and the children were bundled up to go home, Jane put on her heavy shearling coat and fur cap and prepared to walk home with Stella and Buddy.

"You don't need to come with us, Mr. Culbertson. I know my husband told you not to let me walk home alone, but I'm not alone. I have Buddy and Stella. We'll be home in less than ten minutes. Wrap that scarf around your neck, Buddy. We don't want you getting a sore throat and being so hoarse you can't be heard tomorrow night."

Holding the mittened hand of each child, Jane stepped out into air so cold that it almost took her breath away. The warm air that came from their lungs made puffs of vapor as soon as it left their mouths. They walked out to the road and headed toward town, where lamps were already being lit. During the afternoon another light snow had fallen, and they followed the tracks made by the children who had gone ahead of them. The snow was soft beneath their feet and pristine white. For Jane it was truly a dream Christmas of peace on earth, goodwill to men.

"Let's sing, Aunt Jane." Stella skipped along beside her. Buddy stopped to kick snow; soon his britches were powdered with white to his knees.

"It's too cold to sing, punkin."

"Next year I'm goin' to sing," Buddy announced.

"I thought you liked being in the play."

"I like it, but I want to sing and recite a poem."

"It's wonderful that you like to perform. Maybe you'll be an orator or an actor when you grow up."

"I ain't goin' to be like that man that killed old Abe."

"Now aren't you the smart little boy to remember that?"

Talking with the children, Jane was unaware that a woman had approached them from the side until she called out.

"Buddy! Go home!"

Jane looked around. Mrs. Winters, with only a thin shawl over her shoulders and her head bare, came hurrying toward them.

"Maw? I ain't done nothin'."

Jane looked at the stricken little face, then back at his mother. Buddy was terrified!

"Go home!" she shouted again angrily.

Jane stopped. "We were practicing the play, Mrs. Winters. I didn't realize it was so late."

The woman reached them and yanked Buddy away, sending him sprawling in the snow. Jane had never seen her in such a state or Buddy so frightened.

"Ya ain't takin' my boy!" she screeched. Her eyes were wild; her hair stuck out around her head as if she had been pulling on it.

Suddenly her hand, gripping a knife, came out from under her shawl. She lashed out and only Jane's heavy coat kept the blade from piercing her skin.

"Mrs. Winters!" Jane backed away, her eyes round with horror.

"Maw!" Buddy cried. "What ya doin', Maw?"

"Bitch! Spawn of the devil! Ya ain't gettin' *him*! I'm aimin' to cut out yore black heart."

Jane backed up again, keeping her eyes on the woman's distorted face. The insane gleam of hatred that shone in her eyes terrified Jane.

"Run! Run!" Jane yelled, remembering the children. "Run! Run! Go on! Go!" She continued to back away from the advancing knife.

"Maw! Don't hurt Miss Jane . . . please—"

Mrs. Winters showed no sign of hearing her son pleading with her. Her hot fevered eyes were fastened on Jane.

"Ya killed my ma and baby sister. I was there when ya rode by and as if she was nothin' ya made a swipe with yore sword and took her head off. My man killed hisself 'cause he couldn't live with what ya made him do. Yo're the spawn of the devil and yo're goin' back to hell, but ya ain't takin' my Buddy."

"I never hurt anyone!" Jane's eyes flicked to the children, who had frozen in their tracks, then back to the knife. "Run!" she shouted, and held up her arm to protect her face from the slashing blade.

As soon as Stella turned to flee, Jane turned to run back toward the school. Her foot bogged down in the soft, deep snow and she fell. Before she could get to her feet, Mrs. Winters was upon her. Jane managed to roll to her knees, but she couldn't get up. The deranged woman had the strength of a man. She grabbed Jane's hair when her cap came off and, straddling her, she lifted the knife and stabbed it into Jane's back again and again.

Through her fear and pain, Jane was aware that young Buddy was on his mother's back, trying to pull her off. He was crying and screaming.

"Stop, Maw! Please stop!"

Jane's strength began to leave her. *I'm going to die here in the snow. I love you, T.C. Thank you for the happiest days of my life.*

Working at his desk, T.C. was nettled that he couldn't concentrate on the letter he was writing to the banker in Laramie. He found himself looking out the side window toward the road leading to the schoolhouse. The teacher was walking Jane home and she was late. He dipped the pen in the inkwell again and stubbornly wrote another line before he put the pen down.

He sensed that something was wrong about the late afternoon. It was in the very air he breathed. His awareness of danger was as acute and as instinctive as it was when he was stalking a cougar and he felt the animal circling around and attempting to come upon him from the rear.

He put on his coat and his hat and left the house.

I love you, T.C.

The words stopped him. He had heard them as clearly as if Jane had just said them. He stood for an instant on the porch, then stepped out into the street and looked down the road.

Coming around the bend from the schoolhouse, he saw a small figure running. From the red knit cap on her head, he knew it was Stella, and his heart began a painful rise to his throat.

Something had happened to Jane!

T.C. ran as fast as he had ever run in his life. When he reached the child, she was crying hysterically.

"She's hurtin' Jane!"

T.C. shook her shoulders. "Go home!"

Halfway between the last house in town and the schoolhouse, T.C. saw two people fighting while another stood beside the form lying in the snow. T.C. shouted his wife's name as he ran. One of the struggling figures broke away and ran off into the woods.

T.C. was gasping for breath when he reached the scene and threw himself down beside Jane. The teacher was trying to lift her head. Her dark-red hair fanned out ever the snow. She had lost her mitten and her hand was covered with blood. She looked into T.C.'s face.

"I was afraid . . . I'd not see you . . . again—"

"You'll be all right, sweetheart." He turned on the teacher. "God damn you! I told you not to let her—"

"I'm sorry—"

"It's not his fault. How could he know? How . . . could any of us know . . . she was the one?" Her eyes went to Buddy, who was sobbing wildly. "Poor little . . . boy."

Jane's eyes began to drift shut.

"I heard the screams and came running," the teacher said. "The woman was stabbing Mrs. Kilkenny. The boy was on his mother's back, trying to pull her away."

"Who?"

"Mrs. Winters. The boy's mother. I pulled her off . . . and she ran off into the woods."

"God help her when I catch her! Run get the doctor. Get him to the house by the time I get there," T.C. ordered harshly, as he lifted Jane in his arms. He seemed not to know or care that the teacher was without a coat in the below-zero temperature. The small, wiry young man took off down the road, his arms and his legs pumping.

"You're going to be all right, honey. Hold on until I can get you to the doctor."

T.C. staggered along in the snow with his precious burden.

"I love you so much—" He kissed her hair, her face.

Jane's head moved. She tried to look at him, trying to smile.

"Everything's all right now, sweetheart." His voice was strained and light, his face blurred.

Buddy, walking along beside him, looked over his shoulder toward the woods. Attracted by the shouts of the teacher, people came out onto the porches of the stores and some came hurrying to meet them.

Colin was first.

"What the hell happened?"

"Jane's been stabbed."

"Good Lord!"

"See about Buddy." T.C. never broke stride.

The child had lagged behind, unable to keep up with T.C.'s long steps. Colin picked him up. The boy wrapped his arms around Colin's neck, his legs about his waist. Sobs racked the small body.

T.C. didn't remember reaching the house or that Maude was waiting anxiously at the door. She held it open, then stepped aside for them to enter. T.C. carried Jane into their room and stopped beside the bed.

"Help me get her coat off—"

"Oh, my God! The blood!" As gently as she could, Maude pulled the coat and a thick sweater from Jane's blood-soaked back.

Jane was floating in and out of consciousness.

"Timmie, Timmie," she murmured. "We'll name him Timmie—"

While T.C. and Maude took off Jane's clothes, Colin took Buddy out to the kitchen and turned him over to Polly, who sat with Stella on her lap. He returned to open the door for the doctor and showed him into the room where T.C.

was easing Jane down on her stomach onto the bed.

Jane had been stabbed not only in the back, but in the buttocks and thighs. The doctor counted sixteen cuts. Some had scarcely broken the skin; others were deeper. Had Jane not been wearing the heavy shearling coat, and had the knife been sharper, she would have died at the scene. The madwoman who had stabbed her had been in a frenzy to kill her.

Maude stood by to assist the doctor. Nearly in shock torn by fear and anger, T.C. listened to what the teacher had to tell about what had happened. Then he met with Colin, Herb and Tennihill in his office. They were getting ready to organize a search for Mrs. Winters. It was snowing again. The large fluffy flakes would soon cover her tracks.

All the men knew that the woman would freeze to death if she were not found soon, not that any of them cared after what she had done to Jane. Those who knew of the attack on Jane at the privy had not even suspected it had been done by a woman.

Now the question was *why*.

After the doctor finished doing all he could, Maude and Sunday, who had arrived in a panic when she heard the news, carried out the blood-soaked clothes and bloody water. Dr. Bate motioned T.C. away from the bed.

"No doubt the coat saved her life. I don't believe the knife reached into any vital organs, but she has lost a lot of blood. That, and the miscarriage will weaken her."

"Miscarriage?"

"She has been carrying for more than two months."

"A baby?" T.C. asked stupidly.

The doctor smiled. Fathers are usually the last to know. She may have just realized it herself."

"Will she be all right?"

"It depends on how strong she is and if her body can get along on what blood she has left until it can make more. I'm going to stay here until I see whether or not she goes into shock. I've given her something to make her sleep. It's what she needs the most now."

"The woman was mad. I never suspected it."

"It happens that way sometimes. People can appear to be perfectly sane, then"—he threw up his hands—"they are suddenly out of control. I understand Mrs. Winters has a boy."

"He'll be taken care of."

"Small communities have their advantages. In Chicago, he'd more than likely be left to the streets if a relative didn't come forward."

"That won't happen to Buddy," T.C. said firmly. "Mrs. Henderson has supper ready in the kitchen, Doctor."

Sunday hovered near the door. "How is she?"

"We won't know for a while. Will you take the doctor to the kitchen and see that he gets some supper? I'll be with Jane."

T.C. put a stick of wood in the pot-bellied stove in the corner of the room, then pulled up a chair and sat down beside the bed. Jane lay on her stomach, her arms outstretched, so still, so white, so quiet. Even the dark-red hair tumbling over the pillow was curiously devoid of life. Not a deeply religious man, T.C. wondered for a long agonizing moment what he had done that would cause God to take her away from him.

He leaned over the quiet figure and kissed her cheek. Her flesh was cool and dry to his lips. He felt suspended, unable to accept this situation. It was unreal—how could it be real? He had promised he would let no harm come to her if she stayed, and now trusting him could cost her her life.

"Jane," he said, kissing her cheek again. "Jane, darling, can you hear me?"

His words echoed ridiculously in the eerie silence of the room. He took her hand. Her fingers curled around his, or so he imagined. He stroked the limp hand that lay in his.

"You're not going to leave me, sweetheart. You're not. I

was so sure I could take care of you. I never suspected her at all. I even wondered if it could be Theda, or Murphy, or Parker. I hoped it was Fresno or Callahan. Never did I even guess that it could be Mrs. Winters. Will you ever forgive me?"

We'll call him Timmie. These had been her last coherent words. Was she trying to tell him about the baby?

"We'll make other babies, my love," he said in a thick whisper.

He smoothed her hair and continued to talk to her in a low hoarse voice.

"Poor sweet little woman. You've had enough trouble to last two lifetimes. Besides that crazy woman, you had Fresno to contend with. I can't blame him for wanting you. I blame myself for being so wrapped up in building this town that I failed to see what was going on. If Sunday hadn't killed him, I would have.

"I've never told you how much it means to me to have you for my wife. Can you hear me, sweetheart? I never thought a woman lived who would capture my heart so completely. You did, darlin'. I love you!"

T.C. had not wept since he was a boy, but now tears filled his silver eyes.

Chapter 30

THE searching party returned at midnight, cold and weary, having found no trace of Mrs. Winters.

Colin, who headed the party, feared that some of their group would be lost in the blinding snowstorm and recommended that they give up for the night. Tennihill and Herb came to the house with nearly frozen faces. Colin talked while they tried to thaw out.

"The teacher said she wore only a light shawl and nothin' on her head. I know of no shelter in the direction she took. If she didn't find one, she'll be frozen to death by now. We'll go out again in the morning."

After taking Jane's pulse, the doctor decided it was safe for him to go home.

"Should she begin to shake, give her whiskey and sugar and send someone for me immediately."

T.C. walked with him to the door to make sure the snow had let up enough that he wouldn't get lost on his way back to his rooms.

"Thank you, Dr. Bate."

"I'll be back in the morning."

T.C. had appreciated the lack of questions from those who had helped look for Jane the night she was attacked in the privy. Colin and Sunday, Herb and Polly, Tennihill and Bill Wassall and Maude, the "family," as Jane liked to refer to them, were here keeping vigil now that she had been attacked again. T.C. felt certain that Jane would want them to know the reason behind the attacks.

Polly was sitting with Jane when T.C. sat down at the kitchen table with the others.

"I know you've all wondered about Jane and why someone would be sending her threatening notes, then doing what they did to her that night and again today. For Jane's sake, no word of what I'm going to tell you should leave this house. I don't want her to be embarrassed, humiliated, or put in the position of having to answer questions."

"We've all wondered who'd hate her enough to do what they done at the privy," Maude said, as she poured mugs of steaming coffee.

"You've all heard of Colonel John Chivington, who commanded the troops that wiped out the village at Sand Creek."

"Who hasn't heard of that murderin' sonofabitch?" Colin asked harshly.

"His troops were a collection of thieves, scoundrels, street toughs, claim jumpers and riffraff and were easily led by a Bible-spouting ex-preacher and Methodist missionary turned avenger who had a hatred for all Indians." T.C. said all of this without taking a breath. "They slaughtered four hundred women, children and old men. Chivington reported that he had met the enemy and had given them a sound whipping. For a month or two he was a hero.

"After his men began talking and an investigation was conducted, he became the most hated man in the territory. Because of what he had done, Indians all over Colorado went on the warpath in retaliation and killed hundreds, if not thousands, of settlers. Almost every person in the territory was touched in one way or another by what Chivington had done."

"What's he got to do with Jane?" Colin asked.

"She's his born out of wedlock daughter." The news fell into the quiet like the pop of a rifle.

"Ah . . . laws!" Bill exclaimed. "Poor little lass!"

"Well, so what?" Sunday was first to recover from the shock. "Lots a folks are born on the wrong side of the blanket."

"Her mother died when Jane was very young, and she thinks it was Chivington who came in the dark of the night, carried her off and put her in the Methodist orphanage. She has a letter he wrote to her mother admitting that he fathered her, but refusing to claim her. Since she was Stella's age it has been pounded into her head that because she was the daughter of such a man, she was a disgrace not only to the school, but to all the people of Colorado. The headmistress, a Mrs. Gillis, would threaten to tell her secret and shame her in front of the other children if she misbehaved. She had already told them that Jane was a . . . a bastard. Jane's childhood was hell."

"Why that mean old . . . bitch!" Sunday sputtered.

"Jane hasn't had too good a time of it since she came to Timbertown." Colin pulled his wife over to sit on his lap.

"She came here," T.C. continued, "thinking to leave all that behind her. She got the first note the day she arrived at the stage station."

"It ain't no wonder she wanted to leave," Herb said. "How'd she stand up to all that?"

T.C. continued determinedly.

"It was in her mind that if it became known that she had the same blood as Chivington she would be shunned, treated like a leper, and no parent would want her teaching their children. She couldn't bear to face that."

"It's hard to understand why Mrs. Winters wanted to *kill her*." Maude clicked her tongue. "My, my. Ain't it a shame to make her suffer for what *he* did? I just wish I'd a knowed what was ridin' her so hard. I could a told her that folk'd not hold her to account for what he did."

"Mrs. Winters must have lost her mind. I still don't know how *she* knew who Jane was or why her hatred was so unreasonable." T.C. stood. He wanted to get back to Jane.

"Mrs. Winters' mind warn't so steady when she come here," Bill said stoutly. "She'd go along quiet-like, than turn downright mean. It'd come on sudden-like. Times was I wasn't wantin' to be 'round her and a tub a hot grease at the same time. She warn't nice none a'tall to that little boy either when folks wasn't around."

"I been knowin' that for a while," Maude said. "Buddy let it slip that he didn't want me tellin' her that I was makin' his shepherd costume for the play."

"Good Lord!" T.C. sat back down "Now that I think of it, Jenson at the store was complaining that she didn't pay her bill. Just kept charging her supplies when he knew that she was taking in money to pay for them. When he asked her about the bill, she said that she had to hurry home and take care of her little sister. Jenson said it was strange because he knew she didn't have a sister here. He questioned her about it, and she became very angry." T.C. grimaced as if in pain. "I should have followed up on what he told me."

"Buddy's such a smart little boy. He may know some of the answers. Poor little tad," Maude said. "He's too tore up now to know much about anythin'."

"He was lookin' forward to the Christmas doin's. Now I guess there won't be none." Sunday pressed her fingers over Colin's mouth after he spoke.

"'Course there'll be a program. Jane'd want it to go on. All them little young'uns'd be put out if it didn't."

"You're goin' to see that it does, aren't you?" Colin loved every expression that flitted across her face.

"Ya can bet yore britches on that, Mr. Tallman."

He pulled her head toward him and whispered in her ear. "I'd rather be in yours, Mrs. Tallman."

Because of the raging snowstorm, Colin and Sunday spent the night in the room she had used before. Tennihill and Bill bedded down beside the cookstove, and Buddy snuggled on one side of Maude and Stella on the other.

T.C. left the lamp burning on the table beside the bed. After putting more wood in the stove, he lay down beside his wife, took her hand in his and lifted it to his lips. He pondered over and over again how it had happened that a madwoman had almost killed her right under his very nose.

He had jumped to the conclusion that the person threatening her was a man. He'd not had the slightest suspicion that it was a woman. Mrs. Winters had been so pleased, he'd thought, at having her own bake shop.

It was all over now. He vowed that from this day on he would do everything in his power to keep Jane safe and happy.

Once during the night she stirred, and he was instantly awake. She felt warm, but not feverish. She mumbled and went back to sleep.

Morning came and the doctor returned. Jane was awake and, although she was weak and in pain, he found nothing to keep her from a full recovery. He questioned her about her average monthly flow and was pleased when she said it usually lasted not over three days.

"That is good. You need to build your blood, not lose it."

"There will be other . . . babies?" she asked quietly, her eyes going to her husband, who hovered nearby.

"Absolutely. I see no reason why not."

The doctor's eyes went from the relieved face of the big woodsman to the woman on the bed. Love radiated between them. For a moment he remembered having such a love, but as fast as the memory came he shoved it back into the corner of his mind. Life had to go on.

"Doctor," T.C. said as the physician prepared to leave, "we would be pleased if you would join us for Christmas dinner. Mrs. Henderson has been cooking for three days. I'm sure you won't be disappointed."

"Thank you. If her dinners are anything like the supper she served me last night, I might not be able to push myself away from the table."

After the doctor left, T.C. returned to sit with Jane. He had hardly left her bedside. He brushed her hair and braided it in one long plait to keep it from tangling. Then he left the room for a moment and returned grinning like a schoolboy. He placed a box on the bed beside her.

"One of your Christmas presents. Open it now, sweetheart."

"What in the world?" She looked at it, then at him, and her eyes filled with sparkling tears. "I've never opened a present. I've read about it, but never—"

He leaned over and shut off her words with a kiss.

"Don't look back. Look ahead. Open it."

She lifted the lid to find a beautiful white lawn nightdress with lace at the neck and the cuffs. A tiny row of buttons went from the neckline to the waist.

"It's . . . beautiful—"

"You're beautiful," he said softly. "I'll never forget the picture you made standing beside Doc's bed in your nightdress, your feet bare, your cheeks rosy with embarrassment. I couldn't get you out of my mind after that."

"It's so . . . soft." Jane's fingers stroked the material. "Oh, thank you!"

"I don't know about the buttons," he said with a stern expression. "My fingers will have a time with them."

"Mine won't. All you've got to do is ask, my love."

She was fearful that what had happened would put a blight on the Christmas program until Theda, swathed in furs, arrived, bringing with her fresh cold air. Her red hair flamed around her shoulders and she wore a white fur hat perched jauntily on her head.

"Merry Christmas! Glory be! That's a pretty nightdress. You expecting visitors in your bed?" Jane laughed along with the flamboyant redhead.

"It's a present from T.C."

"Lucky girl. I don't know why I like you. I really shouldn't. You snatched up the best-looking man in town. But . . . I didn't come to complain. I've been to the schoolhouse and talked to that sissy-britches teacher. You know, he isn't so bad once you get to know him. The program will go on. It'll take both Sunday and me to fill your shoes, but we think we can pull it off."

"Theda! Thank you. The children have worked so hard. This is the first program they've ever had. But I'm worried about Buddy. This is a terrible time for him."

Theda went to the door and closed it.

"Mrs. Winters was found and brought in a little while ago. A lumberjack coming down from the cutting camp to spend Christmas with his family found her. She was frozen so stiff he had a time getting her on his horse. Her madness had carried her miles up the mountainside."

"Oh, goodness. The poor woman—"

"Poor woman, my foot! After what she did to you?"

"She was out of her mind, and we must make sure that Buddy realizes that she was sick in the head. He's a little boy, Theda, and he must not be made to feel guilty for what his mother has done."

The empty, sickening years of Jane's childhood rushed back to haunt her. The pleading tone in her voice registered with Theda.

"No one will hold it against *him*. We thought . . . if you agree, that we'll not tell him she's dead until tonight after the program. The teacher said that he has worked harder than anyone on his part. It'll be a double shame if he can't be in the play."

"You really are a nice woman, Theda. And you try hard not to let anyone know about it!"

"Horse-hockey! I'm a saloon gal. Men come to stare at my big tits." She laughed. "As long as they buy drinks, they can stare all they want."

All day visitors had streamed to the house bringing dishes of food and asking about Jane. The house was quiet now. Everyone had gone to the church for the Christmas program. Sitting beside his wife, who looked like an angel in her new nightdress, T.C. realized that she didn't know how deeply she had endeared herself to the people of Timbertown.

"I wonder how the program is going," she said, breaking into his thoughts.

"Worrier! They'll miss you, but it will go fine."

"Is Buddy all right? Has he asked about his mother?"

"He's attached himself to Colin, and it seems Colin is attached to him. He asked Colin about his mother. Colin told him that she was sick and that she didn't know what she was doing when she stabbed you. Colin kind of hinted that she wouldn't be back, but didn't come right out and say so."

"Buddy probably knows—deep down."

"Honey, I've something else to tell you." He paused and worked his fingers between Jane's. "Buddy asked if he would *have* to go live with his Aunt Ethel if his mother didn't come back."

"He doesn't want to?"

"He's scared to death he'll be forced to. Colin asked him who his Aunt Ethel was and where she lived. Sweetheart, his Aunt Ethel is Mrs. Gillis, the headmistress at the orphanage."

"Forevermore!" Jane was silent as she absorbed the news. "I remember when her brother-in-law died. She was terribly upset and blamed it on what had happened at Sand Creek. *She* told Mrs. Winters that I was coming here."

"It seems that way."

"Poor little boy. We can't let him go live *there*!"

"He won't go there, sweetheart. Colin asked me what I thought about his living with him and Sunday."

"Oh, would they take him?" Jane grasped T.C.'s hand tighter. "And if not, could we?"

"They want him, sweetheart, and I see nothing that stands in the way."

"Thank goodness! He'll have a good home."

"We're going to have plenty of boys of our own, my love. I'm planning on it." He kissed her lingeringly.

"We can't get one started for a little while," she said regretfully.

"I know. I can wait. Indians, especially Irish-Blackfoot Indians, are the most patient people in the world when it comes to the one they love. Did you know that?"

"I'm beginning to, Thunder Cloud, darlin'."

The program was a huge success. Before Stella and Buddy went to bed, they went in to tell Jane about it and to show her the sack of candy and the orange Theda had given each of them. Maude scuttled into the kitchen to continue preparations for the Christmas dinner. Sunday and Colin went home, promising to return bright and early Christmas morning.

After closing the bedroom door, T.C. stoked the fire in the heater and added more wood.

"I want my wife all to myself. I've had to share you all day," he added peevishly.

Lying on her side because of the wounds on her back and buttocks, Jane watched him undress. He was magnificent. She adored his great, strong body and the dark face below his thatch of blue-black hair, familiar to her now as her very breath and still as heart-quickening as if she were seeing him for the first time.

This, she thought, is magic given to only a few—this drumbeat of pulses when her beloved was near. For more than four months of days and nights she had looked into that face, heard the deep, growling strength of that voice; come into his arms, kissed that mouth and found heaven. Yet each time it was new to her—each time more moving and more dear than the last.

He lay down beside her, then gently, so as not to hurt her back and buttocks, turned her to lie half on top of him. She burrowed into the hollow of his arm and snuggled her face in the crook of his neck. Her breasts and soft belly were pressed tightly to him.

They lay contentedly for a long while. Her heart was filled with love for this man. He had given her so much and had asked for nothing in return. She moved her hand over his chest and her lips trailed kisses up his neck to his chin as she tried to convey to him all that was in her heart.

"Have I told you how glad I am that you refused to let me leave Timbertown? I'd have missed having the most wonderful man in the world for my husband."

Laughter rumbled in his chest.

"My dear Miss Pickle. Do you remember calling this wonderful man you married a conniving, sneaky, stony-hearted jackass who brought you here to marry you off to a horny lumberjack?"

Riding the crest of this new happiness, Jane rubbed her head against his chest, then lifted her face up to his.

"I remember," she sighed deeply. "I still think that's why you brought me here, but a couple dozen kisses might make me change my mind."

Epilogue

Timbertown, Wyoming—June 1898

The church was decorated with mountain fern and lily of the valley and crowded with well-wishers. The bride walked down the aisle on the arm of her stepfather, Marshal Tennihill, one of the most respected lawmen in the state. He would give her away to the groom, who waited at the front of the church. Maude's eyes were flooded with tears. The groom's eyes were riveted on the vision moving toward him.

Stella saw only the tall, sandy-haired man who stood beside the preacher. Buddy Tallman, adopted son of Colin and Sunday Tallman, was the youngest member of the Wyoming State House of Representives. This was their wedding day. Proud parents and friends had come to the church in Timbertown to witness the ceremony.

Every room in the hotel was full. T.C. Kilkenny, his wife Jane, and their three sons came from their ranch on the slopes of the Rocky Mountains. The Tallmans, with two girls and one son, came to see their boy wed his childhood sweetheart. Herb and Polly Banks were there. Their beautiful sixteen-year-old daughter was eyeing Tim Kilkenny. Her brother, Nathan, had teased her about him until their papa put a stop to it—after he had cornered his younger son, who thought it great fun to make faces at April Tallman.

Theda Cruise came from her hotel in Jackson Hole by automobile, the first many in Timbertown had ever seen. She had never married, but it was rumored that she had numerous lovers. Still flamboyant with her dyed-red hair, she was a striking figure even though she had put on weight. Thanks to her thriving business, Theda was a very wealthy woman.

Doctor Bate had stayed on in Timbertown. He had lost his family in the Chicago Fire back in '71 and, after years of grieving, had married a widow who had been among the group that had arrived in town with Jane, Polly and Sunday.

After the wedding, Colin and one of his sons helped Bill Wassall, called Sweet Grandpa by the Tallman children, climb the steps to the hotel where the reception was to be held. The old man was terribly crippled, but he was as sassy as ever, and proud of his family. Maude, Marshal Tennihill and their two younger daughters, along with the bride and groom, formed a receiving line to greet the guests.

In the evening T.C. and Jane strolled around town. Residents stared openly at the man who had founded the town and the lady he escorted so proudly and who was the subject of many stories about "the olden days." Slim and elegant, she was fashionably dressed in a gray silk suit decorated with navy braid. Her soft leather shoes were the same shade of gray, as was the hat that sat atop her dark-red hair.

Timbertown had lost its bid to be the county seat. Instead of a courthouse, a bandstand, surrounded by benches and walkways, stood in the town square.

"Oh, dear. So much has changed in such a short time," Jane said almost wistfully. "The henhouse has been torn down. The stage station is a millinery store and Sweet William's cookhouse is The Pheasant Resturant. Oh, look, T.C. Our house has a picket fence around it. I don't remember that tree where Herb hung a swing for Stella and Buddy being so big."

"Sixteen years is not a short time, honey. After all that happened to you here, I'd think you'd hate the place." T.C. moved his arm to encircle her waist as they paused to look at the house.

"I adore this place! Everything that happened to me here led me to my husband, my children, my home on the ranch, where I can walk out and look at and talk to the sky if I want to."

T.C. chuckled. She was the joy of his life. His love for her had grown over the years from the almost frightening love of youth to the enduring love a man feels for his life's mate.

"Sweetheart, you're a pistol, as Doc used to say. Let's walk up to the cemetery. I saw Buddy go there this morning and put flowers on his mother's grave."

"He was a poor lost little boy back then. It's a miracle that he came through that terrible time."

"The miracle was Colin and Sunday."

They walked past the place in the road where, if not for the protection of T.C.'s heavy shearling coat, Jane would have died. They didn't speak of it. Houses lined the road now, and there were more on beyond the brightly painted red schoolhouse, to which a bell tower and extra rooms had been added. A Sunday-afternoon baseball game had ended, and couples were walking back toward town.

The Kilkennys reached the quiet knoll dotted with pines and monuments. They stopped to listen to the mourning doves, then strolled among the grave sites.

A bouquet of wildflowers lay beside the stone Buddy had put on his mother's grave. Jane stopped to read the inscription.

She sleeps in Jesus, cease thy grief;
Let this afford thee sweet relief.
Now freed from life's torturous reign;
In heaven she will live again.

"Mrs. Winters would have been proud of Buddy. He turned out to be a fine young man. Even after going to Denver and accomplishing so much, he came back for Stella."

True to his word, Herb had seen to it that Doc had the largest monument in the cemetery. A dove of carved granite was perched on top. The plot was surrounded by an ornamental iron fence.

Jane and T.C. stood silently and reverently beside the grave of their friend.

NATHAN FOOTE
LITTLE DOC
Born June 22, 1838 Died Sept. 20, 1882
Received the Congressional Medal of Honor for service to both sides during the Civil War.
No man could have done more.
Farewell, Little Doc. Because of you, hundreds lived.

"I always think of Doc being old." Jane turned and rested her face against her husband's chest. "But he wasn't old at all."

T.C. held her to him, knowing that each time they came here and she read the inscription she choked up.

Presently, she wiped her eyes and lifted her face to the sky.

"Doc," she called softly. "Are you listening? Everything turned out all right just like you said it would. I'm having a wonderful life."

Author's Note

ON November 29, 1864, Colonel John M. Chivington, leading a force of 1,200 troops made up of Colorado volunteers, attacked the camp at Sand Creek. The camp contained several hundred Cheyenne and a few Arapaho. Black Kettle, a Cheyenne chief, had been negotiating for peace and had camped near Fort Lyon with the consent of its commander.

When the attack began, Black Kettle raised the U.S. flag as well as a white flag. Chivington ignored the flags and urged his men on to massacre more than 400 Indians. He gave these final orders to his men: "I want you to kill and scalp all, big and little; nits make lice."

So began a day given over to blood-lust, orgiastic mutilation, rape, and destruction. Children were bayoneted while still in their mothers' arms. Women were violated, then disemboweled—with Chivington looking on and approving.

Chivington sent a battle report to Denver fresh from the bloody field:

> Attacked a Cheyenne village of from nine hundred to a thousand warriors. Killed between four and five hundred. My troops did nobly.

The returning troops were proclaimed conquering heroes—for a while—until Chivington's report was proved a downright lie.

Once the public recognized what had really happened, Sand Creek became the subject of an investigation by the Congress and the Army. The charges were that Chivington and his men had murdered Indians who had thought they were under Army protection; most of the dead were women and children, and their bodies had been mutilated.

This incident was a chief cause of the Arapaho-Cheyenne uprising that resulted in hundreds, perhaps thousands, of settlers losing their lives.

I have no knowledge that Colonel Chivington had a daughter out of wedlock. Jane Love is a fictional character I created for my story. Nor do I have knowledge that Colonel Chivington was despised to the degree I describe, although, according to historians, he was thoroughly hated throughout the territory and was blamed for the decade of Indian wars that followed the Sand Creek Massacre.

Dorothy Garlock
Clear Lake, Iowa